FINAL STRIKE

FINAL STRIKE

WILLIAM S. COHEN

A TOM DOHERTY ASSOCIATES BOOK · NEW YORK

FINAL STRIKE

Copyright © 2018 by William S. Cohen

All rights reserved.

A Forge Book
Published by Tom Doherty Associates
175 Fifth Avenue
New York, NY 10010

www.tor-forge.com

Forge® is a registered trademark of Macmillan Publishing Group, LLC.

The Library of Congress Cataloging-in-Publication Data is available upon request.

ISBN 978-0-7653-8163-7 (hardcover)
ISBN 978-1-4668-8296-6 (ebook)

Our books may be purchased in bulk for promotional, educational, or business use. Please contact your local bookseller or the Macmillan Corporate and Premium Sales Department at 1-800-221-7945, extension 5442, or by email at MacmillanSpecialMarkets@macmillan.com.

First Edition: February 2018

Printed in the United States of America

0 9 8 7 6 5 4 3 2 1

To my friend John Glenn,
who touched the stars and now is among them,
and to his beloved, Annie, his hero and ours

PART ONE

Out in the darkness before all time began,
clouds of cosmic gas, dust and debris,
a hot cauldron of dark energy
floated in a fathomless sea.
Until a sudden crash, a blinding flash of light
cracked open the night, and a formless
dream burst into a silent scream.
Then came the cold, the long cooling of fire
That pressed matter into stars,
Planets, and galaxies.
It was the blinding birth of the Universe,
the work of God's hidden hand, some say.
True or false, yea or nay?
I have no way to know as others of renown
claim there's no beginning or end;
that time's not linear but round,
the answer to be found in the calculus
of physics and cosmology.
You decide if science is sound or apostasy.
But what of me? I came much later,
just four billion years or so ago,
the child of collapsing gas,
dark matter and mist.

I have no name or parents
to claim me as their own.
Who can I blame for giving me
two heads, a body half metal, half stone?
And once abandoned,
what choice did I have but to run
to escape the pull of the sun,
to take flight and live
in cold exile in a corner
of the night with other
orphans and poor refugees?
I'm destined to wander
among the stars endlessly.
It's not a life I'd choose
were choice mine to make.
To be awake in mind
but dead in limb.
What Demiurge would be so cruel
or cold towards its kin?
Still, if you think of me,
understand my world is wild.
A paradox where Chaos and Order
exist in strange harmony.
Take care to stay away.
I need no pity or sympathy.
I'm happy to be free.

From his suite in the Hotel Baltschug Kempinski, Robert Wentworth Hamilton had a panoramic view of the Kremlin, Red Square, and St. Basil's Cathedral—a skyline of fortress towers and religious spires that proclaimed Russia's long history of war and peace. Hamilton, a man of great wealth and few disappointments, turned away from the window and tried to focus his thoughts on what to do next.

His secretive business partner, Kuri Basayev, one of Russia's richest oligarchs, had summoned—*Yes,* Hamilton bitterly thought, *that is the proper word: summoned*—Hamilton to Moscow. Basayev told Hamilton he was to await word for a private jet that would take him from Moscow to Turkey, where a helicopter would fly him out to Basayev's yacht in the Black Sea. There, Hamilton expected, Basayev would try to force him to give up the company he had founded—SpaceMine. The name defined its purpose: mining in space, extracting riches from asteroids. Basayev wanted those riches, and he would do anything to get them.

On Hamilton's first day in Moscow, he ventured out of the hotel to cross the nearby bridge across the Moskva River, bending into the chill wind. Once in Red Square, he ignored Lenin's mausoleum and the huge GUM department store. He was drawn as if by a magnet to St. Basil's. Within the cathedral's cluster of colorful domes he wandered through a maze of galleries and narrow stairways, stopping at each chapel, praying to what he reverently saw as another manifestation of his own fundamental Christianity.

On his second day, he returned to the cathedral. While standing at the silver casket of St. Basil the Blessed, he was greeted by a white-bearded man in a long black cassock and a tall black headpiece; hanging around his neck was a pectoral cross on a golden chain. The man raised his right hand in blessing, and, speaking in lightly accented English, identified himself as Bishop Nikoli Vosnesenski. "We believe that here our ancestors built a place unlike any other," he told Hamilton. "It is a place that makes us think of the Heavenly City."

Hamilton introduced himself as a Christian and said, "Perhaps, after the Final Days, we will meet again in that Heaven."

"As you may know," the bishop said, "the original colors of the cathedral followed the depiction of the Heavenly City in the Book of Revelation. God's throne was of precious stones and there was 'a rainbow round about the throne, in sight like unto an emerald.'"

"No. I did not know that, Your Holiness. But I have great interest in the Book of Revelation and The End Time."

During Hamilton's visit to the cathedral the next day, the bishop invited him to join him and his driver on a trip to Krasnogorsk, a town about fifteen miles northwest of central Moscow. There, they visited a small brick church that could have been found on a country road in America. They stood together and gazed at an icon of Jesus. Hamilton told of his belief in the Last Days, the end of time, when God would punish Earth with war, famine, and plague. Then, finally, Jesus would return.

When Hamilton finished his screed, the bishop touched his arm and said, "Look at the eyes of Jesus. They are eyes of compassion. But your eyes are hard and troubled. Why?"

"I am a very rich man," Hamilton had said. "I should be able to do what I want to do. I am very angry."

They returned to Moscow in silence. When the bishop dropped Hamilton off, he gave him his card and a Russian bible. "I will remember the eyes of Jesus. Thank you," Hamilton had said. "And I will have one part of this Bible translated."

"What part?" the bishop asked.

"The part that tells of the Final Days," Hamilton had replied. "To me, that is the most important part of the Bible."

He had hoped that there would be a message from Basayev when he returned to his room. There was no message, and that night he had learned why. On the evening English-language GNN *News Hour*, the anchor-woman reported that Basayev's yacht had sunk in the Black Sea. There were no survivors.

Meeting canceled, Hamilton pragmatically thought. He could not mourn for Basayev. Mourning, it seemed to him, questioned God's plan; life comes and goes by His plan. Those thoughts were crowded out of his mind by a practical realization: He should return to America, but, at the moment, that would not be a prudent idea.

Now, after a good night's sleep and his usual ten laps in the hotel pool, he showered and dressed, donning a pair of gray slacks and a white shirt, and shuffled, sockless, into a pair of loafers. He was, at fifty-three, one of the wealthiest men in the world—and one of the healthiest. He prided himself on looking ten years younger, though he was graying, and new furrows appeared when he frowned, which was often. He looked forward to some days of solitude, dedicated to visiting St. Basil's, perhaps talking with the bishop, and playing out possibilities about his next moves. He believed that he was a smart, decisive businessman whose principal skill was analytical, long-term thinking. He could do that anywhere.

He responded to a soft tapping on his door with the command "Enter!" A maid wheeled in his breakfast of tea and toast and silently withdrew. Propped up next to the gilded teapot was a copy of the *Moscow Times*, an English-language newspaper. In America, he usually got his news from his iPad or, on occasion, GNN. So a morning newspaper was a novelty to him. On the front page was a story about the sinking of Basayev's yacht, which, he read, was caused by "a boiler explosion." Basayev was described as wealthy and secretive, which, Hamilton thought, summed him up rather well.

Hamilton firmly believed that God's Plan had kept him from Basayev's yacht and that he was destined to stay alive for some divine purpose. He found himself standing at a window and mingling his thoughts with his recollection of St. Basil's labyrinth. The cathedral's spires caught the morning sun and looked to him like the flames of a great fire reaching to the heavens.

Hearing faint sounds of sirens, he lowered his gaze to the streets below. Something was going on. Police in helmets and bulky gear were piling out of vans and stopping traffic at intersections and at both ends of the Moskva River bridge. Cars, trucks, buses, motorcycles, and bicycles pulled over to the curbs. Then, suddenly, three vehicles, blue rooftop lights flashing, sped across the bridge, turned and stopped at the entrance of the hotel.

A few minutes later, Hamilton heard a pounding on his door. Annoyed at being disturbed, he threw open the door and was about to yell at somebody when he saw two large men in black suits. The younger of the two said, in stilted English, "Come. See President Lebed." He pointed to the bedroom and pantomimed putting on a coat.

When Hamilton hesitated, the man brushed past him to the bedroom, took a blue windbreaker from the closet, held it up for Hamilton to put on, and nudged him forward toward the elevator, where a third man in a black suit waited. The four men entered, one of them fitted a key card into a slot, and the elevator descended. The lobby was empty, except for police officers and nervous-looking hotel employees. The three men in black escorted Hamilton to the hotel marquee. The doorman had disappeared. Hamilton shivered, reacting to the cold and not to fear, he told himself. One of the men opened a passenger door to an armored SUV, and Hamilton quickly entered.

Lebed echoed in Hamilton's head like a mantra that kept him from an angry, panicky reaction to what seemed to be an arrest. He knew little about Boris Lebed, the president of the Russian Federation, who had succeeded Vladimir Putin. He left politics, both domestic and foreign, to people who, as he put it, were paid to keep him from being surprised. This morning he was very surprised.

The three-SUV motorcade raced off and headed to a highway bare of traffic that paralleled the Moskva River. Two miles up the river, the SUVs turned at an exit marked by a large red sign with white letters—СТОП. *Stop,* Hamilton guessed. A guard stepped out of a squat brick structure, saluted the first SUV, and opened a massive gate. The motorcade continued a short distance to a wharf where a long, sleek white yacht was waiting. The 176-foot craft had been built at Sevmash, Russia's largest shipyard, best known as the place where nuclear submarines were built. Her features included an indoor pool that could be converted to a dance floor.

Hamilton stopped at the bottom of the gangway, his heart racing. *A yacht? Go aboard a yacht?*

One of his escorts shoved him forward. He tripped and fell. The man pulled him up and kept pushing him until he reached the end of the gangway. Hamilton was pointed to a stairway. He reached out both hands to grab the two railings and started down. At the lower deck a young man in a Russian Navy uniform took him aft to a suite that encompassed the stern. A brass sign over a door said something in Cyrillic. "President Boris Lebed," the sailor said, smiling and pointing to the sign. He opened a door and, pointing to the high threshold, helped Hamilton into a large room carpeted in red.

A man rose from a swiveling leather chair, stuck out his right hand, and said in English, "I am President Lebed. Welcome to the *Catherine.*"

Hamilton shook hands and asked, "Catherine the Great?"

"Yes, and it is my wife's name," Lebed replied. "I welcome you as Catherine the Great welcomed your John Paul Jones, a great American naval officer and great friend of Russia."

Lebed gestured toward another leather chair and Hamilton sat down. He felt the vibrations and motion of the ship as she left the dock and headed north on the Moskva River. Small boats armed with machine guns preceded and followed the *Catherine.*

The sailor went into another room and returned with a tray bearing an array of bottles and glasses, along with small sandwiches and a blue bowl containing caviar. "I will have a sparkling water," Hamilton said. "With a slice of lime."

Lebed plucked a glass full of vodka from the tray. The sailor served Hamilton, slipped out of the room, and closed the metal door with a soft clang.

"I love this boat. It's my only indulgence in luxury. One permitted by the people as a symbol of Russia's pride. I'm putting her up for the winter tomorrow. We've been blessed by unusually warm weather until now. Global warming perhaps?"

"I don't think so," Hamilton replied. "Weather, like the stock markets, goes up and goes down."

"Yes," Lebed parried, a smile breaking across his face, "but markets are man-made, are they not?"

Hamilton, not eager to indulge in further repartee, said curtly, "I assume you didn't bring me here to discuss the weather."

"Quite right," Lebed conceded, exhaling a soft sigh. "I am extremely saddened by the unfortunate death of Kuri Basayev, a good man, a good friend. A terrible, terrible accident."

Lebed paused to sip his vodka. "I . . . I know how close the two of you were," he said, leaning forward and touching Hamilton's shoulder. "And I—"

"You are quite wrong, President Lebed. Basayev and I were not close," Hamilton said emphatically, letting his anger finally show. "I have no idea why your . . . your minions . . . snatched me the way they did. And to a *yacht*! Real thoughtful and sensitive! Just think of how that affects me. I was to have been a passenger on Basayev's yacht."

"I am sorry, Mr. Hamilton. I didn't know that. As for 'minions,' they are security men, and polite behavior is not in their DNA."

Hamilton believed Lebed *did* know that he had been invited to board Basayev's yacht and was using this yacht meeting to rattle him. *Interesting psychological move,* Hamilton thought.

"I am sorry, Mr. Hamilton, that our meeting began on a sour note," Lebed continued. "I am interested in learning more about Kuri's role as a business partner in the asteroid project. He told me a bit about your venture. I found the economics quite daunting. The up-front costs are significant and the rewards are—"

". . . Even more significant," Hamilton replied enthusiastically. "One estimate has put the potential value of asteroid metals at one hundred trillion dollars. One hundred *trillion* dollars."

"Oh, I saw that number, Mr. Hamilton," said Lebed. "Pulled out of a hat, wasn't it? Statistically absurd. It would exceed the current GDP of all the nations on the planet. And the supply of minerals would far exceed the demand, undermining the market itself. As you can see, my years at the London School of Economics were not a total waste."

"But suppose SpaceMine had an absolute monopoly of the supply and could set whatever price we chose?" Hamilton asked.

"So, for your 'absolute monopoly,' you would continue to organize the violent miners' protests in Africa?" Lebed asked in reply.

Hamilton shot forward, gripping the arms of his chair and said, "That was Basayev's idea. Not mine."

"But you saw the advantage, did you not? Let us not quibble over a trillion here or there. To my thinking, an asteroid would be valuable in many ways. But it is my understanding that Kuri was providing substantial financing for your upcoming IPO," Lebed said, looking at Hamilton eye-to-eye.

Hamilton did not respond.

"That financing can be continued, Mr. Hamilton. I will find you another partner. On the same terms that Kuri Basayev had, of course."

"That's an interesting proposition," Hamilton said cautiously. "Some of my other investors are getting nervous about the initial public offering. I'll need to get back to reassure them that everything is on track."

"Why don't you stay and enjoy Russian hospitality a little longer? It's not often that we have such a prominent American visiting us these days."

"That's very kind of you, Mr. President, but I feel I must soon leave. I—"

"You were not in a hurry enough to call off a visit to Krasnogorsk," Lebed said, his voice touched by anger. "And a meeting with Nikoli Vosnesenski, an American spy."

"He is a bishop . . . a man of faith. And I resent that—"

Lebed stood and looked down at Hamilton. "*Resent?* Meeting with an enemy of the state?"

"I . . . I didn't know. I—"

"I believe the phrase, Mr. Hamilton, is 'ignorance of the law is no excuse.' Will that also be your defense in an American court? My sources tell me that the FBI is waiting to arrest you as a co-conspirator in the murder of four people, along with obstructing justice."

"You have better sources than I do," Hamilton said.

"I know everything about you, Mr. Hamilton, including the bill for those beautiful dental implants that you received at the hands of Dr. Larry Rosenthal in New York. . . . Seems that nothing in America can be kept secret. And might there be another secret about the sinking of Basayev's yacht? Interesting, isn't it? You were to be on the yacht and, by some twist of fate, you were not on board when the yacht sank. . . . Perhaps—"

"This is shocking, President Lebed. That you would even think—"

"Have no fear, Mr. Hamilton. I can assure you that there will not be an investigation about the yacht. But, as for the four murders—"

"I'm confident my lawyers will handle any issues that Basayev was responsible for," Hamilton said.

"Perhaps so," Lebed replied. "But in the meantime, you can enjoy the generosity of the Russian people. I'll personally see to it that all of your needs are met."

Lebed pressed a button built into his chair, the door swung open, and the sailor reappeared. Lebed snapped a few words to him, and in a moment the *Catherine* began slowly turning around.

"Excuse me, Mr. Hamilton," Lebed said, looking at his watch. "I must go to what I call my floating office. Boatswain Ovechkin will see that you safely depart."

Hamilton rose, and they shook hands. Lebed hurried to an elevator that took him directly to the bridge. At a door to a small compartment off the bridge, two sailors snapped rifle salutes and one opened the door. Without sitting at the small desk, he made a call on a secure phone. "I want a tap on Hamilton's phone," he ordered. "I expect that he will be making a phone call. Tap his phone."

"His phone has been tapped since he checked in, sir."

"On whose authority?"

"Mine."

"You have exceeded your authority again, Komov," Lebed said. "As soon as you get a transcript of today's calls, bring it to my office."

When the yacht returned to her berth, Hamilton was taken to the SUV that he had entered less than an hour before and returned to the hotel. He had the feeling of being in a movie that had suddenly begun playing backward.

The moment he entered his suite he went to the phone in the drawing room and went through the instructions necessary to make a call to the United States. He gave a hotel operator the number for the private land-line of Sandra Vanderlang, chief operations officer of the SpaceMine Corporation in Palo Alto, California.

Hamilton did not trust telephones. He privately admired the Al Qaeda model of secure communications: avoidance of electronic devices and a strict reliance on well-vetted couriers. But that system was impossible in the totally wired commercial world that he inhabited as one of the world's richest men. He was angry with himself for having left on the plane his encrypted cell phone that had been developed by Dark Circle, a firm in which he had been an angel investor. He'd requested that the airline return the phone to him immediately, but assumed it was now in the hands of Russia's spymasters.

And so here he was in a luxurious Moscow hotel, speaking into a dainty, creamy white telephone that was tethered to a wall outlet behind silken drapes. And he realized that his words were almost certainly being monitored by the Russian equivalent of the National Security Agency—and by the NSA, too.

But his vanity trumped caution.

"Hamilton here, Dr. Vanderlang," said Hamilton, who never used *hello* or *goodbye*.

"Mr. Hamilton," she said. "Where are you? We've been worried."

"I'm in Moscow. I had hoped to meet Kuri Basayev . . ."

"My God, Basayev! You heard what happened . . ."

"Please do not take God's name in vain."

"Sorry," Vanderlang said, angry with herself for forgetting Hamilton's fundamental Christianity, which ruled his life, including his vocabulary. As founder and CEO of SpaceMine, he insisted that his employees and contractors honor God's name. He even frowned on responding to a sneeze with "God bless you."

Vanderlang tried again: "When we didn't hear anything from you—"

"You thought I might be feeding the fish somewhere in the Black Sea?"

When she did not respond, Hamilton continued, "No. I am very much alive. Bored but alive. I never got to meet Basayev. I sincerely believe it was providential. I was to fly out to his ship . . . his yacht. . . . But it blew up and sank."

"I saw reports about the sinking on GNN," Vanderlang said. "No survivors. They believed a boiler exploded."

"Whatever. As I said, I'm still alive. And I have some interesting news. I have just come from a meeting with President Lebed himself. He made an interesting proposition, a deal, that I think will take care of all financial matters and give me some leverage in getting a deal with Oxley."

Suddenly, Hamilton heard a loud click, and his phone went dead.

Hamilton tried to call Sandra Vanderlang again from the telephone he was still holding. A woman's voice said, "I am sorry, Mr. Hamilton. Your phone is out of order."

"Well, fix it!" he shouted.

"I am sorry, Mr. Hamilton," the robotic voice repeated. "Your phone is out of order."

He hung up, waited a minute, and tried again.

Again, "I am sorry, Mr. Hamilton. Your phone is—"

He slammed down the phone, grabbed his key card and stormed out of the suite. He slipped it into a slot by the elevator and descended to the lobby, muttering to himself what he was going to say to the manager. But, after calming down enough to realize there were other ways to make a phone call, he strode to a niche, flanked by tall bamboo shoots in blue-and-gold planters. Behind them, seated at his faux Louis XVIII desk, was Sergey Algov, the concierge. When Hamilton asked to use his cell phone, Algov hesitated and Hamilton realized that he had rushed out without his wallet.

"I will put it on my bill," he said. "I have no rubles."

Algov bowed, smiled, and pointed to a nearby ATM.

Hamilton, fuming, pulled out the credit card he had placed in with the small embossed keyholder the hotel had given him upon his arrival. He slipped it into the ATM and punched in his pin number. A line in Cyrillic appeared on the screen. "It does not accept your card," the concierge said with a quick frown.

Hamilton now had a sense that something was going very wrong. "I will be right back," he said, rushing to the elevator for a fast round-trip to his suite.

Hamilton returned, handed Algov a fistful of rubles, and, standing behind one of the planters, dialed Sandra Vanderlang's cell phone.

"Mr. Hamilton, we need you back here to . . . ," she began. "Our investors are—"

"Divine providence put me here in Moscow, and I'm not coming home unless the FBI Gestapo drops all phony charges against me. I've done nothing wrong. . . . Listen, Sandra, you need to call the Greek."

"Who?"

"Akis Chris . . . Christakos. C-h-r-i-s-t-a-k-o-s. The Greek lawyer that went with me to see the FBI. Tell him I want immunity from—"

"I don't understand what you're talking about," she said. "Immunity from what?"

"Just call the Greek. He'll handle it."

"Handle what? I don't understand. Why can't you just—"

"Here's the situation, Sandra. I don't have my passport. They have my credit card number, and so they can keep adding to my hotel bill. But my credit card is being otherwise disallowed for some unexplained reason."

"Does this have anything to do with Basayev's death?"

"You know me and telephones," he said, lowering his voice. "We'll talk about that when I get home. I'm trapped in this hotel. I eat here, sleep here, go crazy here. But I'm staying here until I can enter America without worrying."

"Worrying about what?"

"Never mind about *what*. Just call the Greek."

"And tell the Greek what?"

"Tell him I want a grant of complete immunity. It has to be signed by Oxley himself. Nothing less."

"But. . . ."

"Sandra, just call the Greek. Tell him I am staying at the Hotel Baltschug Kempinski." He ended the call.

Vanderlang immediately checked SpaceMine's legal files but failed to find any reference to Akis Christakos. She vaguely remembered that some months before Hamilton had mentioned making a trip to Washington in the corporate jet. That must have been when he hired the Greek, apparently out of his own funds. As usual, he had not discussed the trip with her before he left or after he returned.

Through Google, she found the Washington website of Super Lawyers, a rating service. And there was the address and phone number of Akis Christakos, described as one of the capital's leading criminal defense lawyers. The Greek.

Colonel Nikita Komov was at home when Lebed called him. Komov some-times sought the solitude of his one-bedroom apartment when he was organizing an important action plan—or preparing a report for President Lebed. Komov had spent most of the night going over what information the FSB (the English initials for *Federal'naya Sluzhba Bezopasnosti,* Rus-sia's Federal Security Service) had about Robert Wentworth Hamilton. Knowing what was in that dossier and knowing the corrupt practices of the Lebed administration, Komov assumed that the conversation aboard the presidential yacht would be about a deal in which a Lebed-picked oli-garch replaced Basayev.

Komov accepted corruption, even when it tainted the FSB, as the way power and wealth interlocked in the running of the Russian government. But Hamilton's asteroid contained the potential for a defense of the Mother-land against the United States and its NATO cronies. To Komov, needs of the Motherland transcended the needs of politicians and their rich par-asites. He once again had to risk his career—and perhaps his life—to tell truth to power.

Komov lived in an apartment house that once belonged to the elite of the KGB. After the KGB was dissolved, all the officers had been pensioned off and evicted—except Colonel Komov. The spacious, high-ceilinged apartments had been modernized for the new tenants, bright young gov-ernment officials on their way up the ladder of privilege and corruption.

Komov walked to his sixth-floor balcony to watch for the car sent from the Kremlin. He saw it stop briefly at the unmanned guard gate, which opened automatically to the driver's signal. There was a time, Komov remembered, when he would have seen a guard station manned by sentinels who belonged to the same elite KGB regiment that guarded Lenin's tomb on Red Square. *Now, robots.*

He left the balcony, strode across his sparsely furnished living room, and locked his apartment door with the key he had demanded after having been given a key card. Walking down the corridor to the elevator, he turned his mind from remembrance to the real now. At ninety-two years, he still walked like a man who had urgent business to do, and he still had the steely eyes of command.

As Komov stepped out of the lobby, the driver at the open door of the black ZIL limousine saluted solemnly, acknowledging Komov's special status as a living relic of the old KGB. The driver was in civilian clothes because the FSB no longer had the military trappings of the KGB. Draped over Komov's broad shoulders, however, was a khaki greatcoat bearing the epaulets of a colonel. Beneath was the formal uniform of a KGB officer—blue tunic with aiguillette, blue trousers tucked into thigh-high black boots, and a gold-banded, high-crowned hat.

Komov could look back as far as Stalin, as far back as the Great Patriotic War. On his tunic, next to the Order of Lenin, was the medal for the Defense of Stalingrad. He had served the Motherland every day and every night since he enlisted in the Red Army on his eighteenth birthday.

Unlike other former KGB officers, Komov survived the demise of the KGB. The agency was dissolved in 1991 after its chief was involved in an attempted coup to overthrow Mikhail Gorbachev. He and subsequent Russian leaders broke up the KGB, converting one of its pieces into the the SVR (*Sluzhba Vneshney Razvedki*, Foreign Intelligence Service), an eavesdropping agency analogous to America's NSA.

Komov, called Comrade X-ray for his ability to see traitorous hearts, had used his seemingly mystic talent to ferret out the coup plotters. And so he stayed on, hailed as a counterintelligence genius. Four years later, after the fall of the Soviet Union, the FSB became Russia's prime counter-intelligence agency. In 1998 Boris Yeltsin, first president of the Russian Federation, appointed Vladimir Putin director of the FSB with orders that Komov not be retired. In 2006 the FSB was given the legal power to define, target, and kill "terrorism suspects" under presidential orders.

The FSB was touted as a modern intelligence agency that would reflect the principles of a democracy. But, as a candid FSB spokesman said, "We have been gradually given other tasks, such as fighting organized crime and gangs, contraband and corruption-fascist elements." A new law gave the FSB the right to operate its own prison system, infiltrate criminal gangs, create commercial enterprises, and obtain information from private firms without warrants. Komov realized that deep within the new agency the old KGB still managed to exist, especially after Putin succeeded Yeltsin as prime minister.

The span of Komov's career included Vladimir Putin's formative years as a KGB officer. Komov had first met Putin at the KGB counterintelligence school, which Komov presided over. Pupil and professor became mutual admirers. And Putin, as head of the KGB, ordered that Komov not be retired. After becoming prime minister and then president of the Federation, Putin put many of his supporters in high-level FSB posts. One of them was Komov, who was made a special presidential adviser. Komov's official title was Director Emeritus of the Archive of the President of the Russian Federation, meaning that he had access to any top-secret document that he wanted to see.

At Pushkin Square, Komov tapped on the glass divider behind the driver and ordered him to stop. He pulled to the curb, serenaded by a chorus of angry horns. Komov stepped from the car and slipped into his greatcoat. The first flakes of the first snow were dancing in the November air and disappearing as they touched the ground.

Komov gazed up at the statue of Pushkin, who looked as if he had stopped for a moment on a Moscow street, a line for a poem forming in his mind. Now Komov stood before the statue and thought of the glory of the Moscow winter, whose white curtain was rising this morning. The weather had changed suddenly, the warmth of autumn disappearing overnight. Soon would come the cold, the snow, the whiteness everywhere. Pushkin and winter entered Komov's mind:

The storm covers skies with darkness,
Spinning snowy whirlwinds tight . . .

Komov looked at his watch, calculated the timing of a two-kilometer walk, and determined that he would be on time for his meeting in the Kremlin. The car crawled alongside him until he waved it away. Snow-flakes swirling around him, details of his report taking form in his mind, he quickened his step. A tall man stepped out of the park and caught up with Komov, who turned and stopped, looking up at the man and frowning.

"I do not need to be followed, Lieutenant," Komov said. "I am going to the Kremlin and do not believe I will be attacked."

Lieutenant Pavel Shumeyko, a former champion hockey center and Honored Master of Sports, looked down and, smiling, said, "I will grant you twenty meters." He was six feet three inches tall and had the sport's iconic missing-one-tooth smile. He served as Komov's bodyguard, a duty unacknowledged by Komov but imposed by Lebed himself, citing Komov's age and host of enemies.

"Very well," Komov grumbled. He paced off twenty meters and Shumeyko resumed walking.

4

The Kremlin office of Boris Lebed, the president of the Russian Federation, could have belonged to a minor official. The walls were oak-paneled and unadorned, the carpeting was gray. His barren desk was the size of a restaurant table for four. The nearest wall had a two-shelf bookcase containing books that had the pristine appearance of being displayed rather than read. In front of the desk were two chairs with spindly legs and thin golden cushions. Behind his similar chair was the tricolor flag of the Federation, its bands of white, blue, and red adding the room's only touch of color.

The office was a stage set for Lebed, who projected an image that was at once confident but humble, and often reminded Russians that power had not changed him and that he governed in the same plain way that he had during his four years as the earnest young mayor of Volgograd. After Vladimir Putin died of what was officially described as "a rare blood disease," Russian kingmakers had found Putin's potential successor in the telegenic Lebed. He had run a tumultuous election campaign, promising voters that he could lead Russia out of the doldrums and into a prosperous economy worthy of a great nation. And he had convinced most of the outside world that he was not another Putin.

When he and Komov first met, Lebed recognized Komov's Defense of Stalingrad medal and noted a link between them. As mayor of Volgograd, Lebed had proclaimed that each year the city would revert to its previous name, Stalingrad, on six commemorative days, including February 2, the day that the Nazi invaders of the city surrendered to the Red

Army. The Stalingrad proclamation was well known because Lebed had frequently mentioned it during his election campaign, reminding voters how he venerated the supreme victory of the Great Patriotic War.

Komov had infuriated Lebed by presenting him with the fact that Basayev, Lebed's trusted moneyman, was running a Russian-American criminal gang—and was a homosexual, the worst accusation that could be made about a Lebed associate. Then came the Komov report that Basayev was aiding billionaire Robert Hamilton in his plan to mine asteroids, which have great concentrations of such precious metals as platinum and palladium. Basayev was a powerful enough oligarch to arrange for SpaceMine to secretly launch an asteroid-bound spacecraft from Russia's Plesetsk Cosmodrome. A massive publicity campaign orchestrated by Hamilton extolled the potential value of "Asteroid USA," drawing investors.

Lebed knew more about that asteroid than Komov did. Several months ago, President Blake Oxley of the United States had learned that the asteroid SpaceMine chose for mining was on a collision orbit and would strike the Earth in 2037. Oxley had informed Lebed and Chinese President Zhang Xing. The three leaders had agreed to keep the probable collision secret until three selected scientists, working together in secrecy, could devise a way to defend the Earth. Hamilton, a believer in what he called God's Plan, chose to ignore the collision prediction, apparently because he believed it might be divinely ordained.

After the formal protocol of saluting the President and standing at iron-spine attention until told to sit down, Komov took a red folder from a blotched brown briefcase that had served him almost as long as he had served the Motherland.

"Proceed," Lebed said solemnly, entertained, as usual, by Komov's antiquated manners.

"Eighteen minutes after arriving in his suite at the hotel," Komov began, "subject Hamilton made a telephone call to his subordinate, a woman, at his office in California. We are going through the American identification files that the FSB has obtained to see what we have on her.

But, as you know, the procured Office of Personnel Management digital files are extensive—about twenty-one million files on federal workers, military personnel, and contractor employees. And so—"

"Yes. Yes," Lebed said irritably. "You have frequently told me about the great FSB coup of hacking into American government files. However, the director of the SVR tells me that the credit for that belongs to his agency. And Americans say the Chinese did it. Please come to the point of the conversation."

"Yes, sir. After an exchange with the subordinate, he boasted that you, sir, want to place a substitute for Basayev into secret partnership of Space-Mine. But he also said"—Komov read from a document to find the exact words—"We can use the deal with Lebed as 'leverage.' "

Komov looked up and said, "Our American translators say that this is an analogue of a lever, pivoting so as to influence people and thus—"

"My God, Komov! I *know that*. Give me the essentials."

Komov, accustomed to dealing with an impatient, irritated superior, went on as if he had not been interrupted, looked down at the document and repeated, "We can use the deal with Lebed as 'leverage' to gain a deal with Oxley. Then—"

"One moment, Colonel. What is the 'deal with Oxley'?"

"As you know, sir, from many sources, sir, we have learned that Hamilton is being investigated for possible criminal activity. Basayev . . ."

"Why must I hear anything more about Kuri Basayev?" Lebed demanded. "He's dead."

"I am well aware of his death, sir. A terrible accident . . . but there is unfinished business about Basayev."

"Unfinished? Meaning what?"

"It is imperative, sir. As you know from our daily Presidential Intelligence Summaries we had the traitor Basayev under total surveillance and learned that he had become a CIA spy. As spillover, we also learned much about Hamilton."

"Continue," Lebed said, putting down the paper he was supposedly reading. He had a sixth sense about Komov, tuning into him when he spoke with a certain assertive cadence.

"A SpaceMine engineer threatened to reveal that the SpaceMine asteroid might be on a collision course with Earth. To protect Hamilton and SpaceMine, Basayev ordered his gunmen to kill the engineer. As so often happens in badly planned assassinations, things went wrong. They killed four other people. The gunmen themselves were killed by American police."

"And?"

"Oxley's lawyers—in his department that prosecutes criminals— believe that Hamilton is complicit in the murders ordered by Basayev. Hamilton said he will return to America—or attempt to return, I should say—when all legal matters are resolved."

"So Hamilton is using another form of 'leverage' as you noted?" Lebed asked, arching his eyebrows.

"Clearing his record would be very attractive to Hamilton. And there may be good reason for the Americans to make a deal with Hamilton so that he leaves Russia."

"What are you suggesting, Colonel?"

"It is imperative, sir. Hamilton must remain in Russia."

"And why do you dare to say 'must' to me, Komov?"

"You perhaps have heard of Ivan's Hammer, sir?"

"Yes, yes. I heard my father mention it. Some scientist of your era having a crazy dream."

"With respect, sir. Not a dream."

"You have perhaps become a space scientist?"

"Hamilton controls an asteroid," Komov said. "It can become a weapon. He cannot be allowed to return to America. Not until we know where the asteroid is located. You cannot allow the Americans to take control of that asteroid and allow them to use it as a weapon—as Ivan's Hammer. We need to send our cosmonauts to that asteroid so that it becomes a Russian weapon, not an American one."

"Don't be ridiculous, Colonel. Even if the Americans wanted to threaten us, how credible would it be to threaten the entire planet with extinction? Oxley tells me to get out of Georgia, the Ukraine, Syria or what? That he will destroy Mother Earth? Ridiculous."

"You make light of the circumstances, sir. We don't know what asteroid Hamilton has moved. Now that Basayev is dead, Hamilton is the only person who has information about the asteroid. He could be exaggerating its size to increase its value to investors. It might be a much smaller asteroid than Hamilton expected. One that could be manipulated to hit us. They could—"

"Only if one of the lunatics that keep running for President of America was ever elected. And what do you think we would do in response to such a threat? Surrender? Did we fight the Great War to surrender to idle threats? We would send our own threats that our nuclear weapons would be released well in advance of any giant rock. We would make a mutual suicide pact," Lebed said.

"But, sir, they have a defensive shield against our missiles."

"Colonel, you have been a valuable asset to our country. But you are overly paranoid. You are looking for bombs under every bed."

"It is my duty to be paranoid, sir. At least let me see if I can persuade Hamilton to divulge the technical information that our scientists can use to—"

"No, Colonel. It is too early for your techniques. We have time enough for that should it become necessary. For the time being he has no interest in returning to America. He is our partner. We will treat him as a guest. Continue to make sure that Hamilton remains in the Hotel Baltschug Kempinski. It is a fine place to be. Meanwhile, just to ease your fears, I'll explore whether we should prepare our cosmonauts to take control of Hamilton's asteroid." Lebed's clipped tone signaled that he had tired of the briefing. The time had come for Komov to leave.

"Anything else, Colonel?" Lebed asked.

Komov looked up from the transcript and said, "Nothing significant, sir."

"Did Hamilton make any more calls?"

"I listened to the electronic version—even before I got a transcript. I have ordered that he not be allowed to make or receive any phone calls."

"As usual, Komov, you have exceeded your authority. But I reluctantly agree . . . for now. That will be all," Lebed said, picking up a paper from his desk.

5

Akis Christakos finished eating his usual breakfast—pineapple juice, eggs Benedict, black coffee—at the usual place, the restaurant at The Hay-Adams, a landmark hotel on Lafayette Square. From the hotel's rooftop terrace and through the windows of many of its rooms, there was a clear view of the White House, a fact well known to the window-watching Secret Service marksmen on the White House roof.

As he left, Christakos nodded to someone he recognized but did not wish to chitchat with. At the pillared street entrance, he and the doorman greeted each other in Greek. Then he turned left and began walking several blocks to his office on L Street. A chill was in the air today, and Christakos was glad he remembered to bring the monogrammed scarf he had purchased earlier in the week in London's fashionable men's store, Turnbull & Asser.

Christakos was something of an oddity in Washington's legal community. He was a "sole practitioner," unheard of in a city where lawyers congregated by the hundreds in the high-rise office buildings that bore the names of their firms' founding fathers.

"Eagles don't flock," he would say, teasing those who needed the company and competency of others. He didn't begrudge any who chose the grinding, decade-long climb from associate to partner status in the mega-firms that had metastasized in the nation's capital. But the thought of measuring out his life in coffee spoons or six-minute billable segments was something he simply couldn't do. And he didn't have to.

Christakos, son of immigrant Greeks, was called "Christo" by his friends, who had trouble pronouncing "Akis." Was it "A Kiss"? "A Kees"? They were never quite sure. Christo was so much easier, and conveyed a sense of flair that captured the man, the "Anointed One."

He had one of the best legal minds in town. And he was the lawyer to call when the FBI or the U.S. Attorney's office or publicity-hound politicians were trying to drag you to an interrogation or a televised congressional hearing.

Tall, thin, as telegenic as a movie star, and dressed as well as any Washington diplomat, Christakos would sit calmly beside his client until he sensed that a threshold was about to be crossed. At that point, his demeanor changed quickly from a gentle golden retriever to an attacking Rottweiler. And it was not just a matter of bluster. The charm or menace, depending upon the circumstance, masked a tough legal mind, which seemed to anticipate every misstep by an adversary before it was made. He would then move to exploit the error with the swiftness of a samurai warrior.

Rarely was a Christakos client convicted, and the few who were would get only a token jail sentence. His success was the product of his obsession for preparation. No aspect of a case escaped scrutiny. No rumor or whisper was discounted. No investigator's or prosecutor's life, however private, went unexamined. And Christakos' many media friends made sure that no victory in the courtroom or in the halls of Congress went unheralded.

As he made his way along L Street, he glanced at his antique Patek Philippe watch—worth more, he often mused, than his father had ever earned during his life as a plumber in every borough of New York City. Sometimes he wondered if his remembrance of his father and his tools was the reason he had vowed to eschew every convenience that modern technology had to offer.

He rebuffed the allure of a smartphone and refused to connect to the Internet except on the computer in his office. Email and texting were not part of his vocabulary. Anyone searching for his office website, Facebook, or Twitter account would come up empty-handed. But those who really needed his services—and could afford them—knew how to find him.

He was running behind schedule this morning, having dallied too long over breakfast. Being late for a meeting was unacceptable. His personal mantra was, "If you're on time, you're already late."

His day was launched by a call from a member of Congress who was being investigated for misuse of campaign funds.

"Christo, I called to say I've decided to resign my seat," the Congressman said. "I do this with a heavy heart, and I—"

"Don't be crazy, Ted. And don't give me any more bullshit about a heavy heart. All that's involved here is a tangle of irregularities in your congressional spending accounts and a prosecutor who's looking for a couple of headlines to propel him out of the U.S. Attorney's Office and into a law firm. This is a media circus over a *Post* story about so-called lavish spending and flights on a constituent's private jet. All the *Post* has is a vengeful staffer who handed a reporter some spreadsheets full of simple arithmetic errors."

"But I've made up my mind."

"No you haven't. I'll be damned to let you and your heavy heart make that mistake. Let's get together Tuesday in my office—ten a.m. Okay? You bring your accountant and press secretary and I'll bring my consultant, who used to work for the Office of Congressional Ethics. We'll draft a statement of innocence and betrayal that will bring tears to the eyes of that half-assed prosecutor."

"Okay, Christo. You know best."

"You bet I do, Ted. See you Tuesday."

Christakos called his office manager, Vicki Butera, into his private office, gave her the details of his Tuesday meeting with the Congressman, and began going through the day's upcoming appointments. "No calls for the next two hours, Vicki," he said, picking up a thick file folder from a neat pile on his desk.

As he worked over the briefs and other documents, his curt and bristling manner gave way to calm and concentration. He was working, and he enjoyed working more than anything else in his life, mostly because that work took place in the sanctum of his private office, which exuded old-world luxury. Persian carpets covered chocolate-dark hardwood floors. Rosewood paneled walls with built-in bookcases. The shelves contained a couple dozen books and many framed photographs of celebrity clients. Several shelves held museum-quality ancient artifacts that he had collected during his numerous visits to Greece over the years. Daily newspapers neatly rested on a deep-seated leather couch next to a coffee table. On it were stacked law books whose pages bristled with yellow page markers.

Less than an hour into Christakos' two-hour phone-call embargo, Butera entered his office. He looked up frowning. Before he could remind her about the embargo, she said, "It's the COO of SpaceMine. About Hamilton. She says she has to speak to you urgently. She said 'urgently' twice."

Still frowning, Christakos put down the file folder and picked up his phone. As usual, Butera had judged right; anything about such an important client as SpaceMine's CEO warranted an immediate response.

"I am Sandra Vanderlang," the caller said. "Chief operating officer of SpaceMine. Our CEO, Robert Wentworth Hamilton, is in Moscow and says he will stay there until you get . . . 'a grant of complete immunity.' " Her voice had a slight echo, which Christakos recognized as the product of a scrambler phone.

"Did you just read those words from notes you took during a telephone conversation you had with Mr. Hamilton?"

"Yes," she replied, sounding surprised. "I—"

"Destroy those notes immediately. I will wait."

After hearing the sound of a shredder, Christakos said, "Good. Now, tell me about that conversation."

"But . . . why—"

"All conversations with me are covered by client-attorney privilege," Christakos replied. "I assume you are calling as a client? Mr. Hamilton, as you know, is already a client."

"Well, I didn't exactly know he was your client. He told me to call . . . to call 'the Greek' and spelled your name. Yes, I see the point. I am a client."

"Thanks for the clarity," Christakos said, laughing. "Yes, I am 'the Greek.' Now let's go over the conversation you had with Mr. Hamilton."

As she recounted what Hamilton had said, Christakos asked a few questions and then said, "So you assume that Mr. Hamilton made this secretive meeting with Mr. Basayev to arrange for further investment funds for SpaceMine. Is that correct?"

"Correct."

"But did he say that he was staying in Moscow because he feared some kind of criminal indictment, not because he was searching for a source of further funding?"

"I have told you all he said. He told me to call you. He gave me the name of the hotel. I looked it up on Google." She spelled out *Baltschug Kempinski*. "He said he wanted you to call him."

"I'll do so immediately," Christakos said.

"Fine, and I will see you immediately," Vanderlang said.

"Is that necessary?" Christakos asked.

"Yes. Obviously, his decision to stay in Moscow is somehow connected with the matter you helped him with. I think it's best for me to talk to you about this in person. I'll be in your office tomorrow morning."

As soon as the call ended, Butera, slim and quick-moving, entered Christakos' office and handed him a thick folder. It contained a neatly tabbed collection of information about Robert Wentworth Hamilton. "Nothing new here since the FBI session," she said. "Except a gossip note in the *Star* saying Philip Dake is on leave from the *Post* and is rumored to be writing a book about Hamilton. And there's this."

She opened the folder and pointed to a clipping of a *New York Times* business section piece headlined BANKING ON AN ASTEROID, illustrated by a NASA photograph of an asteroid that looked like a gray potato.

"And it says?" Christakos asked. He relied on her not only to find important haystacks but also to reach in and find the needle.

"Basically, the mining of asteroids has run into some legal problems because of questions rising about who owns what in space. There's a UN outer space treaty that raises legal questions about ownership and something called 'protection from interference.' Three companies are specifically mentioned. One of them is SpaceMine."

"No mention of Hamilton or the FBI visit?"

"No. Looks like you convinced Patterson to keep the lid on." She was referring to J. B. Patterson, Director of the FBI.

Christakos shrugged. "Luckily, J.B. doesn't have much love for publicity."

"Especially publicity about a case going nowhere."

"Exactly. So why is Hamilton saying he wants a grant of immunity?

Now *that* would produce publicity." He hefted the folder. "You found all that was findable. What do you think of this guy?"

"Brilliant. Very rich. And a little queer."

"Queer? Meaning . . . ?"

"Nothing like *that*. . . . Strange. Driven. Aloof. A real loner . . ."

"Nothing so strange in that," Christakos said, dipping his chin to his chest. "Mmm?"

"And the religious stuff," she said, shaking her head. "Like that award for 'Christian Science.' "

"Yes," Christakos said, smiling. "The Christian Scientist who proved— what was it? That God had created the universe less than ten thousand years ago? Not so strange to others. Ever talk to our cleaning lady? She believes Steve Jobs is the Antichrist and points to the Apple-with-a-bite symbol as proof. Lot of odd believers out there, walking around, holding down jobs . . . and voting."

He gave her the phone number of the Hotel Baltschug Kempinski and asked her to put through a call. "It's evening there, right?"

She nodded, and as she turned to leave, Christakos said, "And get me whatever you can find about the sinking of that yacht and the guy who owned it, a Russian named Basayev."

Hamilton **is a** *bit strange,* Christakos thought, recalling where and how they had first met three weeks before: the J. Edgar Hoover Building, on Pennsylvania Avenue, headquarters of the FBI. Looking back on that day, Christakos remembered when Butera answered the phone and heard the name Robert Wentworth Hamilton. She had not hesitated to put Christakos on the line. Hamilton was not on Christakos' retainer client list. But he was one of the richest men in the world.

Hamilton had not said, "Hello," like an ordinary mortal. He began by saying, "I called you because I read somewhere that you are one of the best defense lawyers in Washington." Hamilton had sounded indignant, like a man who had just been handed an unexpected parking ticket.

"I'm flattered, Mr. Hamilton," Christakos said. "What is—"

"I find I suddenly need a lawyer," Hamilton had interrupted. "I've been summoned to meet tomorrow at ten with an FBI agent who is working on a shooting at my lawyer's office. He said I am 'a person of interest.' "

Christakos instantly knew that Hamilton was referring to the murder of a partner, a secretary, and two clients at Sullivan & Ford, a major Washington law firm.

"So Harold Davidson was your lawyer?" Christakos asked, naming the partner who was slain.

"No," Hamilton replied irritably. "Never met Davidson. My lawyer was someone else. Now my *ex*-lawyer. Not worth going into. I'm flying to Washington tonight. I will meet you tomorrow at the FBI."

"I suggest that we meet at my office first," Christakos said. "We need to go over what brought on that 'person of interest' label. And see what—"

"Not possible," Hamilton interrupted. "I'm on a tight schedule. I will see you tomorrow." *Click.*

Christakos remembered hearing that Paul Sprague, managing partner of Sullivan & Ford, had just resigned from the firm, and he assumed that Sprague had been Hamilton's lawyer. Like every lawyer in Washington, Christakos had heard dozens of rumors about the shootings at Sullivan & Ford. He wondered if the FBI's interest in Hamilton had to do with the shootings or SpaceMine.

After a spectacular public relations campaign, SpaceMine had sent a spacecraft to an asteroid that had been selected as a site for mining platinum and other valuable minerals. Hamilton was about to turn SpaceMine into a publicly traded corporation. But traders and hedge-fund managers, after looking into the technical challenges and literally astronomical costs, were losing enthusiasm for such an out-of-this-world venture. All this went through Christakos' mind as he waited for the call to Hamilton.

Now, closing the file folder, he realized that his most finely etched memory of Hamilton was of his body language, not his staccato delivery of words during the short FBI interrogation. Christakos drilled into the heads of his clients that it was against the law to lie to a federal officer. Many times he had explained that FBI agents were trained to gain the confidence of a potential suspect and then ask questions. If the person asked immediately for a lawyer, the questioning usually stopped. But, if the person answered a question with a lie, the federal law could be invoked.

Hamilton, perhaps already schooled by Sprague, had not needed any instructions. He remained calm, almost impassive, as an FBI agent listed the litany of charges the Bureau was prepared to bring against him as an accessory to the murders. Hamilton never flinched. Never. Behind the cool exterior, Christakos saw a diamond-hard toughness and an arrogance that was different . . . somehow strange.

Typically, someone questioned by an FBI agent shows some nervousness, some opening that the agent could exploit. Not Hamilton.

Christakos quickly realized that the FBI agent lacked enough of a case for a U.S. attorney to present to a grand jury. So the agent had hoped to lead Hamilton into a trap by getting him angry enough to blurt out an incriminating statement or a careless remark. The agent failed. Christakos had little more to do than look stern and keep corralling the agent.

Just about all the FBI seemed to have on Hamilton was a dubious claim that he had tampered with evidence, namely a laptop that had been taken from the Sullivan & Ford offices by the shooters. The FBI claimed that a SpaceMine engineer's memo had been erased from the laptop. Christakos had mocked the memo as invisible evidence. The engineer—Cole Perenchio—had later also been murdered, apparently by the same two gunmen who had shot up the law office.

Police had tracked and killed the gunmen when they chose to shoot it out. So, as far as Christakos could see, from a legal standpoint, the murder cases were closed and Hamilton's handling of the laptop was more moot than indictable. The short interview ended with Christakos convinced that Hamilton's person-of-interest label was realistically nothing more than the pipedream of an overly zealous FBI agent.

As they'd walked out of the Hoover Building together, Christakos said, laughing, "You didn't need me. You seem to have an instinct for warding off trouble. Did you ever think of being a lawyer?"

"Never!" Hamilton had exclaimed indignantly. He made a call on his cell phone and in moments a black limousine pulled up. Without saying goodbye or offering a ride, Hamilton sped off to Dulles Airport to board his private aircraft and return to Silicon Valley. That was the last Christakos saw or heard of Hamilton until Sandra Vanderlang's call.

"The hotel operator—her English is fine—says she cannot get through to Hamilton," Butera said. "I asked why and she just repeated, 'can't get through.'"

"Any explanation?"

"No. I looked up the Baltschug Kempinski online. It's a five-star, very expensive, very posh. I asked for the concierge and did get through. His English was poor, but he just said that Hamilton was 'not available.'"

"Interesting. 'Not available' is not the same as 'can't get through.' Try again in an hour. That won't be too late, will it?"

"No. And maybe we'll luck into another operator."

"I want to talk to him before Ms. Vanderlang shows up tomorrow."

"Right. And here's a rundown on that yacht sinking. Also, a little background on Basayev. Interesting stuff," she said, handing him two printouts.

Basayev's *Aglaya*—"Splendor" in Russian—was 532 feet long, had four topside decks, and was second in size only to the 590-foot yacht owned by the Emir of Abu Dhabi. *Aglaya* had two helicopter pads, two swimming pools, and accommodations for a couple of dozen guests.

Christakos remembered the couple days of newspaper and television coverage of the sinking of the *Aglaya* in the Black Sea, off the Turkey coast. According to a spokesman for the Turkish Navy, the first report of the sinking came from a fisherman who heard an explosion and saw flames. A Turkish destroyer sent to the area at first light found wreckage identified as the *Aglaya* but no survivors. The *Times* quoted an unidentified U.S. official as saying that the cause of the sinking was a boiler explosion. According to the official, Basayev went down with the yacht, along with an unknown number of crew members and guests.

A *Times* obituary called Basayev "a shadowy oligarch whose fabulous wealth had been grounded in the favor he found with Vladimir Putin and his successor, Boris Lebed." The obituary also said that "some law-enforcement officials linked him to a criminal group rooted in Russia and branching out to the so-called Russian Mafia in the United States."

Christakos went back to the description of the *Aglaya* sinking, underlined "boiler explosion," and had Butera put in a call to a cousin in Greece who owned a shipyard. After the usual round of family news and promises of visits to each other, the cousin, Dimitri, switched to English and said, "Okay, Akis. I believe your fee is a thousand dollars an hour. Mine's much less. What exactly do you want for one of your cases?"

"A simple question, Dimitri," Christakos replied in English. "Does any modern yacht have a steam engine?"

"Oh, you're nosing around the *Aglaya*. I should have guessed. First, the answer is no. The *Aglaya* had two diesel engines, and they had been routinely inspected two weeks before she was sunk. It's the most suspicious loss in years. Everybody at first said it was an insurance dodge. But no one has come up with an explanation. She was a Monaco-flagged ship, famous for her odd sailing courses, which looked like they were designed to outwit satellites' orbits. The International Maritime Organization is looking into it and so is Turkey's Maritime Casualties Investigation Council. As you know, things are not going so well with the Turks and Russians these days. But the word is they are getting nowhere. Not a trace of her, Akis. Not a trace."

"And the insurance dodge?"

"The owner—I guess you know, Kuri Basayev—did not have any insurance on her! I have to wonder what her flag-registration papers look like."

"So what is the rumor of what sunk her?"

Dimitri shifted to Greek to say he did not want to talk any more about the *Aglaya*. Christakos said goodbye with a solemn promise of a spring visit.

As the day wore on, Butera reported three more unsuccessful attempts to reach Hamilton.

"That's enough, Vicki," Christakos said. "I'm afraid our client has become incommunicado."

7

Sandra Vanderlang swept into the reception room. Before Butera could offer her a seat or coffee, Vanderlang said, "Coffee, please. Black." She pointed to the door to Christakos' office. "In there?"

Butera stood and nodded. She felt the slight breeze of Sandra Vanderlang's black cape as, continuing nonstop, she opened the door to Christakos' private office and strode to the high-backed chair in front of Christakos' desk. He had hardly managed to stand before Vanderlang sat down, opened the clasp on her cape, gracefully shook it off her shoulders, and tossed it over an arm of the chair. She wore a black skirt that ended below her knees and a sharply tailored jacket over a blouse the color of cranberries.

"Welcome, Ms. Vanderlang," Christakos said, coming around the table, extending his right hand and turning on his charm. A serious fan of old movies, he often classified women by their resemblance to his favorite stars. Sandra Vanderlang—he judged her to be in her mid-thirties—was definitely in the Joan Crawford category.

"For the record," she said, "it's *Doctor* Vanderlang."

"Excuse me, Doctor," Christakos said with a slight bow. "I wasn't able to find anything about you—nothing on Facebook, no LinkedIn profile."

"I can say the same for you, Mr. Christakos," she said with a quick smile.

"Oh, yes. That social media business. Like you, I have my own understanding of what 'social' and 'media' should be. Now, Dr. Vanderlang, please tell me why you are here."

At this moment, Butera came through the open door carrying a tray. She gave Christakos a raise of her eyebrows as a comment on a tough client. Then, after placing the tray on his desk, she disappeared behind the closing door.

Vanderlang reached for a gilt-edged porcelain cup and saucer. She took a sip before answering, "I'm very, very worried about Mr. Hamilton."

Christakos closed the Hamilton folder and turned to a yellow pad. With a monogrammed silver pen he wrote the date and *Sandra Vanderlang* on the upper left corner.

"First, should I assume you want me to continue to represent *you*, Dr. Vanderlang?" he asked.

Vanderlang simply nodded.

"Assuming there is no conflict in my representing Mr. Hamilton, then at this moment, we are entering into a lawyer-client relationship. If a conflict should emerge, then you'll have to secure the services of another attorney. But from now on, everything either one of us says to the other is inside that relationship and absolutely confidential."

"I understand," Vanderlang replied.

Christakos changed his tone from professional to friendly. "First of all, I have not been able to communicate with Mr. Hamilton."

"I . . . I don't understand," she said, looking stunned.

"I have tried repeatedly to ring his room, and I have been repeatedly told that he is 'not available.' When I made my first attempt, right after your call to me, the hotel operator said she 'can't get through.' Then the message changed: He was 'not available.' That very much sounds to me like an official description. I believe he is being held incommunicado."

"You mean the Russians have . . . arrested him?"

"Probably not officially. They may be confining him to the hotel."

"But if he . . . he's an impatient man. I'm afraid that he'll try to . . . escape."

"From what I've heard about him, he's also a smart man, and won't try anything reckless. Look. He's been there—what, more than a week? I'm betting he's waiting for another meeting with Lebed or one of Lebed's cronies. From Mr. Hamilton's viewpoint, there's a deal cooking, and he knows that deals take time."

"But I don't like the feel of this. He knows he's needed at SpaceMine. I think the deal he's most interested in is this immunity deal. What can we do, Mr. Christakos?"

"Call me Christo," he said, smiling. "As to what we can do, I can call the U.S. Embassy in Moscow and ask the ambassador to invoke the right to consular visits, which are guaranteed under a treaty signed by over one hundred countries, including the United States and Russia." After a short pause he continued, "Now, an important question: Are you absolutely certain that he will leave Moscow *only* if he is granted immunity?"

"Yes. He was quite adamant. And he wanted it on the authority of President Oxley."

"I'm sure that the signature of the attorney general will be sufficient and should be easy enough to arrange. But, first, some background. When was the last time you saw him?"

"I see him every day—a usual morning meeting—where we go over various SpaceMine matters. The last time I saw him was ten days ago, the day after he came back from Washington. I guess that's when he met with you."

"And with the FBI," Christakos added. "What did he tell you about that?"

"Absolutely nothing. But that wasn't unusual. He did not confide in anyone, including me."

"Aren't you on the verge of an initial public offering?" Christakos asked. "As I recall, Mr. Hamilton had said on one of those GNN SpaceMine shows that the company's IPO was imminent."

"That's right. Some Wall Street people are asking questions about the delay."

"What do you tell Wall Street?"

"Well, of course we blame the delay on our lawyers," she answered with another smile.

Christakos smiled but quickly regained his serious mien. "Of course. Standard excuse. Now, why exactly did he tell you to come to me?"

"I got the impression that Mr. Hamilton believes he needs a criminal defense lawyer because of whatever it was that led him to want you to go with him to that meeting with the FBI before he left for Moscow."

Christakos nodded and said, "Let's go back to the last time you saw

Mr. Hamilton." He held his Montblanc pen poised as if he were a student eager to take notes.

"We always meet in his office."

"Which is where?"

"At SpaceMine's headquarters in Palo Alto."

"So you had your regular meeting. He had been here, with me, the day before. And he said nothing to you about the FBI interview?"

"Right."

"And he gave no hint that he was going somewhere?"

"No. No hint." Vanderlang shrugged, pursing her lips.

"When did you become concerned?"

"Next morning I went to his office. He always is there before I arrive. But he was not there. I called his personal assistant. He acts as a kind of errand boy and has nothing to do with day-to-day SpaceMine operations. He told me that Mr. Hamilton was not in his residence—a suite on the top floor of the headquarters building. I called him there a couple of times during the day. No answer."

"Did you go to the residence, as you called it?"

"No. I have never been in the residence," Vanderlang said, the tenor of her voice and Joan Crawford–like stare warding off any notion that her relationship with Hamilton was anything less than professional. She might wear gold, but she made it clear that she was not one to dig for it.

"So he apparently went off somewhere without notifying you?"

"He's often mysterious," Vanderlang responded. She finished the coffee and placed the cup and saucer back on the desk. "It's in his DNA to simply disappear once in a while, sometimes for two or three days. But he has always given me advance notice about his absences—telling me he would be gone, but usually not telling me where or why."

"Interesting," Christakos said. "So he keeps you only partially informed? Even though you are a close business associate? Chief Operations Officer. That makes you second-in-command, right?"

"Corporately, yes, more or less. I have to monitor what is going on, keeping things on track. He's clearly running SpaceMine. One of my real jobs is to keep him in touch with the world beyond SpaceMine. He lives alone. Spartan apartment *from what I'm told.*"

"Point made and taken," Christakos acknowledged.

"Security cameras. Few visitors. Employees with special clearance do the maintenance and cleaning. For food deliveries—he's very particular about what he eats—he has his personal assistant call in his order to the same caterer that supplies the cafeteria."

"Looking back, do you have any clues about why he wound up in Moscow? Did he, for instance, get any odd phone calls?"

"He's not very communicative. He has an unlisted landline with a scrambler device. I also usually use a scrambler, but I don't have access to his line. And his cell phone is rigged so that he can press a button and send to my cell phone numbers that he judges pertinent to SpaceMine. The numbers are usually accompanied by cryptic instructions that I take care of."

"Such as?"

"Right now, with a spacecraft attached to Asteroid USA, we're focused on the future—the nuts-and-bolts of robotic mining. So I am developing potential customers, working on a business plan, analyzing operational costs."

"From what I know from following Wall Street news, some of your potential competitors have lost interest in space mining."

"It's a high-risk industry. Long lead times. You need to be tough," Vanderlang said. She had waited a beat before responding and had moved slightly in her chair. Christakos swiftly appraised her behavior and asked quietly, "SpaceMine is in financial trouble, isn't it?"

"Yes. . . ."

"Is it possible that he panicked and absconded?"

"Oh, no! He would never panic. And . . . well, I am confident that no . . . funds . . . no irregularities . . ."

"All right, let's eliminate absconding," Christakos continued. "Does he have a phone log? Or a visitor log?"

"No way," she replied. "He essentially doesn't want to tell anybody anything."

"I'm beginning to see the picture," Christakos said, shaking his head and making a note. "So, do you have *any* clues about his mysterious trip?"

"The day after I last saw him, my assistant received a call from our travel office. It was someone at Lufthansa in San Francisco who said she was in passenger security. She said that Mr. Hamilton had bought a one-way ticket to Moscow. For cash. She said that it was necessary to report such travel arrangements to Homeland Security, and she wanted to assure SpaceMine that such reports were routine."

"Moscow! One way?" Christakos exclaimed. "Didn't *that* get you curious?"

"He traveled to Russia frequently in the months before we launched the spacecraft. As you may know—it came out in a congressional hearing—the launching was from a facility in Russia."

Christakos flipped through the Hamilton folder and scanned one of the pages. "So Asteroid USA, as he named it, did not lift off from U.S. soil. But the launch was some time ago. Why would Mr. Hamilton go to Russia now? Are you planning another launch?"

"As far as I know, no."

"Dr. Vanderlang, do you mean to say that, as COO—second in command—you wouldn't know whether SpaceMine was going to send up another spacecraft? Forgive me. I don't know much about corporate organization. But this sounds very strange."

"I agree," Vanderlang said, shifting in the chair. "There are many ways to be a COO."

"How did you become one?"

"My field is computer science. I enjoy finding interesting problems and feeding them to a computer. I was teaching at Stanford when about a year ago I was approached by an employment counselor hired by Mr. Hamilton. I didn't know exactly what the job would be. But the pay sounded very good, and I agreed to an interview.

"Mr. Hamilton had my doctoral thesis on his desk. 'Principles of knowledge engineering,' he said, reading from a copy of my doctoral thesis. He looked up and asked me if I thought an engineering-based knowledge system could be installed at SpaceMine. I told him that knowledge engineering was mostly just a concept, a model. 'So,' he said, 'not practical in the real world?'"

She did her signature shrug and continued: "Well, this went on for about half an hour—a discussion of my thesis that took me back to when

I had defended it. I didn't know where he was going until he said, 'I need a chief operating officer—a COO. Never had one. Didn't think I needed one. Now I think you're the one. You'll keep an eye on knowledge here and report directly to me.' And that's the job he gave me."

"Strange world out there where commerce meets science," Christakos said. "So it's perfectly possible that he might just decide one day to fly off to Moscow without letting you into his plans."

"For him, that's very possible. But this trip was odd, very odd. He never flies commercial. He always uses the company jet. And he always travels with a security team. And paying cash? It's as if he didn't want to leave a trail."

"Or maybe someone else didn't want him to leave a trail," Christakos said, leaning forward and tapping his pen on a page in the Hamilton folder. "Isn't it possible that the one-way ticket for cash was the idea of Kuri Basayev?"

"Why would he do that?" Vanderlang exclaimed.

"What do you know about him?" Christakos asked, a noticeable edge in his voice. He suspected that his new client suffered from a convenient lack of curiosity.

"Not much."

"Well, you do know he is presumed dead. Right?" Again Christakos' tone changed, this time to staccato. "You know Basayev's yacht sank—presumably with him on board. And you know it sank when Mr. Hamilton was in Russia. Come now, Dr. Vanderlang. You had to know all this. And yet you sit there and keep that information from me. Why?"

"I . . . I thought . . . I thought that if I brought up Basayev, you might think I was paranoid. I held back because I wanted to hear it first from you."

"Hear *what*, Dr. Vanderlang?" Christakos said, deliberately sounding exasperated.

"Hear whether you saw a connection between Basayev and Mr. Hamilton's decision to stay in Moscow."

Christakos stood, theatrically took a deep breath and said, "There certainly could be a connection. But what was Basayev's association with SpaceMine?"

"He owned forty percent of SpaceMine. I suspect that he wanted control and he wanted SpaceMine to be a Russian corporation. He did not want there to be an IPO. Mr. Hamilton did."

Christakos looked down at Vanderlang. "So," he said, "there were fundamental disagreements between them."

"Yes," she said, looking up at Christakos. She started to fidget in her chair, her composure suddenly less authoritative.

"You knew Basayev was a bad character," Christakos continued. "So did you fear that he might . . . do away with Mr. Hamilton?"

"Yes."

"Who is Mr. Hamilton's next of kin?"

"To my knowledge, he doesn't have any. No siblings. Both parents dead."

"If Mr. Hamilton died, what would happen to SpaceMine?"

"Basayev would probably be able to leverage a buyout," Vanderlang said.

"So SpaceMine and Asteroid USA would wind up being Russian. And if Basayev died?"

"My guess is that SpaceMine will wind up in the hands of one of Lebed's pals."

"So Lebed would be able to turn Asteroid USA into Asteroid Russia," Christakos said. There was a long silence. Then he tapped his pen on his yellow pad. "Are you familiar with the name Cole Perenchio?"

Vanderlang looked startled and did not immediately respond. "I . . . I knew . . . He was an engineer. He . . . left the company."

"Yes. And then he was murdered, as I am sure you know and did not feel the need to mention." Christakos was tempted to terminate the meeting and send his new client on her way back to Silicon Valley. "Look, Doctor. If I'm going to represent you, you need to put everything on the table. Pretty as your teeth are, I'm not interested in pulling them out."

"I'm sorry. . . . I just don't know what I should say . . ."

"I think you're right to be worried about Mr. Hamilton. You need to trust me. I'm going to get him back to America."

Sandra Vanderlang did not devote much time to social graces. As she left Christakos' office, he followed her and invited her to lunch. "No thanks. Must fly back," she said. She took her phone from her bag and called her pilot at Dulles. With a nod to Butera, Vanderlang said, "Thanks for the coffee," then breezed out the door as swiftly as she had entered.

"Well, then, take me to lunch," Butera said to Christakos. "I hear the Metropolitan Club's crab cakes are divine."

"No way. It's downstairs to the food truck for you."

"And yogurt at your desk for you."

"Correct," Christakos said. "But first I need to make a couple of calls."

He returned to his office, sat at his desk, and scrawled a page full of notes. A case was taking shape in his mind. As he saw, there were two issues that he had to keep compartmentalized: One was Hamilton's desire for a grant of immunity; the other was the possibility that he was being held against his will. The immunity request was real and had to be pursued; the status of his stay in Moscow was unknown and had to be confirmed.

Christakos unlocked a desk drawer and took out a small notebook that contained his most confidential numbers. Using his landline phone, he punched the digits of the private number of J. B. Patterson, the director of the FBI.

Christakos pictured Patterson's twelfth-floor suite and imagined a computer recording the origin, time, and duration of the call, but not their conversation. Patterson was not the NSA. He played by the rules.

"Christo!" Patterson exclaimed. "I've got to get this phone number changed."

"Before you do, J.B., please remember that I rarely call."

"True. You may be a lawyer, but you're not a pest. What's up?"

"Robert Wentworth Hamilton," Christo said.

There was a moment of silence, which Christo translated as *Say nothing.*

"What about him?" Patterson asked.

"He's a client . . . in Moscow . . . and I'm not able to communicate with him."

Again Patterson paused before saying, "I don't know what I can do about that. Thanks for calling. Keep in touch."

"Please hold on for a minute, J.B. Is Robert Hamilton still a person of interest?"

"Absolutely."

"On what basis?" Christakos asked.

"I assume you'd know that. Possible accessory to murder and obstruction of justice. In fact we need to see him again."

"I'm afraid that's not going to happen."

"And why is that?" Patterson asked, his voice tightening.

"Because, as I just told you, he happens to be in Moscow."

"Seems to be a popular vacation spot for lawbreakers these days."

"My client's broken no laws."

"Maybe the Department of Justice will just spell it out in an indictment."

"And what?" Christakos asked. "Seek to extradite him from Russia? Good luck."

"Well, if he likes Russia so much, I hope he enjoys the Bolshoi—or maybe there's a Russian prosecutor who'll put him in a cell in Siberia. Gotta go, Christo."

"Please hold on for a minute, J.B. I have reason to believe that Mr. Hamilton is being held incommunicado. If the Oxley administration doesn't want to do something about it, I think I have to put up a kind of Amber Alert."

"Meaning?"

"Meaning the media," Christakos replied.

"I'm not part of the Oxley administration, Christo. I'm an employee of the Department of Justice. And if you want to tell the media something, that's your privilege. Sorry. Gotta go."

Patterson's remark about "not being part of the Oxley administration" convinced Christakos that Patterson's first reaction would be to contact the White House and warn them.

Christakos looked up the confidential cell phone number of Ray Quinlan, President Oxley's chief of staff. Then Christakos went to an antique lowboy chest that held a miniature refrigerator and a tray of white plastic spoons. He returned to his desk to consume his regular lunch of plain yogurt, giving Patterson time to alert the White House.

For his next call, Christakos again used his landline. He didn't trust cell phones, although he was compelled to have one because he had clients who did not like landlines. He pictured a great cloud full of words that rained down on the NSA Data Center, code named Bumblehive, in Bluffdale, Utah. A lawyer involved in a privacy case, knowing Christakos' obsession about the NSA, had sent Christakos a snapshot—by cell phone, of course—showing the sign outside Bumblehive's front door: WELCOME TO THE UTAH DATA CENTER. IF YOU HAVE NOTHING TO HIDE, YOU HAVE NOTHING TO FEAR.

Quinlan was notoriously snappish, especially to the media. But, seeing Christakos' ID on his phone, he answered with a rapid-fire of goodwill: "Christo! Long time no see. What can I do for you?"

"Thanks for taking my call, Ray. What you can do for me is help me get my client, Robert Wentworth Hamilton, out of Moscow. Mr. Hamilton plans to stay there unless all charges are dropped and he receives a presidential grant of immunity."

"I have no idea what you're talking about. In fact, I don't know who your client is," Quinlan said.

"Then you've been living on some other planet. He's the billionaire who is going to bring an asteroid into a close orbit so it can be mined."

"What's this got to do with immunity?" Quinlan asked, his usual cantankerous tone suddenly returning.

"The FBI has been harassing him about the murders that took place at Sean Falcone's law firm. They say Mr. Hamilton is a person of interest and may be charged as an accessory to murder and obstructing justice. They are defaming my client and I'm going to sue the government for millions and—"

"You're sucking wind, Christo. I'm no lawyer, but I know the king can do no wrong and there's a thing called governmental immunity. That's the only immunity that you should be talking about."

"I think you'd better check with White House counsel on that. Better yet, check with your boss."

"Your client's got a problem with the law," Quinlan snarled. "You work it out with the FBI or Justice. The President doesn't get involved with that shit."

"Well, maybe I'll just call Philip Dake. He's writing a book about my client. He might be interested to know why another American citizen has to seek asylum in Russia."

Christakos knew that just saying the word *Dake* instilled panic and inspired fear or murderous thoughts. For many years, people in the White House, the Pentagon, and the intelligence community had opened the day's edition of the *Post* and found Dake's byline over a story that exposed government secrets, officials' shoddy behavior, or fraud and theft involving millions of government or political funds.

"Yeah. Well, be my guest with that prick, Dake," Quinlan yelled, calming slightly to add, "Maybe the American people will be sympathetic with a billionaire who wants to have a bunk bed with Edward Snowden. Make a real nice story."

Quinlan, as usual, ended the call without a goodbye.

A dark-windowed SUV roared through the southwest gates of the White House and pulled to a rough stop at the lower-level entrance to the West Wing. Frank Carlton, a retired four-star Air Force general, stepped from the vehicle's rear seat, and, accompanied by two burly security agents, walked under the canopy-covered entrance located directly across from the old Eisenhower Executive Office Building.

Carlton, a short and compact onetime military man, maintained the erect bearing of that profession. He wore black-rimmed glasses that added a stern look to his chiseled face. His close-cropped dark hair was just starting to gray. He rarely smiled.

Carlton was President Blake Oxley's national security adviser. It was his job to oversee the entire galaxy of all that the American government did to protect the nation and all it did to advance its interests around the world. This was a task that would short out the circuits of almost anyone.

Carlton's predecessor, Sean Falcone, had managed to stick it out for six years. In his farewell advice to Oxley, Falcone had urged that Oxley appoint Carlton, who was the director of National Intelligence when Oxley made him national security adviser. Falcone especially admired Carlton's skillful handling of the endless cacophony of the seventeen agencies made up of what was hopefully called the intelligence community.

On paper, as national security adviser, Carlton was just a West Wing aide to the President. He had no direct power over the Department of State, the Department of Defense, or the intelligence community. His power came from two indisputable facts: He occupied a corner office in the White House; and Blake Oxley trusted him.

Oxley knew that Carlton could withstand the thunderous assault of Washington's bureaucracies, and he knew that his advice would be objective and independent. Lately, Carlton had focused on the National Security Agency, whose massive surveillance apparatus was penetrating the phones and computers of ordinary citizens—and foreign leaders.

Carlton had to advise the President on how best to make sure that the homeland was protected against all enemies, foreign and domestic. Included in that advice was Carlton's assessment on how the NSA and counterintelligence officials were gathering all the information they needed—while not trampling on citizens' rights or stepping on the toes of egotistical members of Congress. When he was serving as director of National Intelligence, Carlton had cracked that the American people demanded the "immaculate selection" of intelligence.

Well, the crack did not make Carlton smile today.

Out of long habit, Carlton snapped a quick salute to the two guards as he passed through a set of doors and entered a small vestibule and second set of doors. He skipped stopping at his office upstairs, turned right and quickly descended a short set of stairs. At the base of the stairs, he turned right again and dropped his cell phone into the hands of a Navy lieutenant commander who motioned for the Marine guard to open the door to the Situation Room.

If there was a room that was completely protected against any form of electronic penetration, it was this. To the unknowing public, the room was perceived to be as large as a football field filled with giant LED monitors that gave the President and his national security team a window into any place on the planet, day and night. From here they could monitor SEAL teams taking down Islamist leaders or send a Hellfire missile into the lair of a jihadist before he could lop off the head of an American soldier.

In truth, the room was only big enough to accommodate a dozen or more people. Most corporate boardrooms would dwarf the President's security quarters, but then, of course, virtually everything said in the corporate rooms of splendor could be monitored by cyber spies among competitors or in other countries. Size doesn't always have its privileges.

Carlton had made it a practice to arrive a few minutes before scheduled briefings with President Oxley, who was a stickler for punctuality. In those stolen minutes alone with the President, Carlton could make a direct report unheard by the other officials who would soon be sitting around the table.

Today they would be briefing the President on things that were going to hell fast. The North Koreans were acting up again. China and Japan were in a face-off over the Senkaku or Diaoyu Islands, the name depending on which nation you believed actually owned them. With winter just a few weeks away, the Russians were threatening to cut gas supplies to Europe. A new Islamist group had surfaced in Pakistan, and the Centers for Disease Control had failed to come up with an antidote to the mysterious new viruses spreading across Southeastern Europe.

But there was something that weighed more heavily on Carlton's mind. He needed more than ever to have a private moment with Oxley. He had to explain to the President why he had decided to resign from office. He couldn't wait any longer. . . .

10

President Blake Oxley checked the world clocks arrayed on a wall to his right, then impatiently turned back to Frank Carlton. Oxley recognized the look on Carlton's face. *Crisis. Trouble. Well, what else is new?* Although Oxley maintained a cool exterior, his mind operated at an aerobic tempo. He displayed little patience in dealing with slow-talking staff members, however high their rank. And here was Carlton looking as if he didn't know what to say.

"What's going on, Frank? I don't have much time. Why the private session?"

"Mr. President, I have some bad news, and I'm afraid that I need to tender my resignation effective immediately."

"Jesus, Frank! What now? Pardon my French, but the fucking world's coming unglued!"

Oxley was not given to vulgar speech, but the edges of his famed cool personality were starting to fray and unravel. "What can make things any worse?"

"Mr. President, in the wake of the Snowden scandal and the problems he caused us with our European friends and others, you gave a very specific directive. No more electronic monitoring of foreign leaders. No exceptions."

"And I damn well meant it. So?"

"Well, some of the guys at NSA thought you went too far."

"Too far? They're questioning my decision?" Oxley said with a flare of anger, which until recently, was rarely close to the surface. Lebed had become president of the Russian Federation around the same time that Oxley had begun his second term. Oxley had let it be known that, after tense times with Putin, he wanted a new start with Lebed.

"Sir, they know that you were trying to strike up a new friendship with Lebed. But they didn't want—"

"Not a new friendship, Frank. A new start. I know that Boris Lebed's looking more like the new Putin. But I don't want the Cold War to start up again. Well, anyway, what is the new problem?"

"One of the NSA guys decided to keep on bugging Lebed. We've got most of the conversations he's had in his Kremlin office in the past two months."

"I get the picture, Frank," Oxley said impatiently. "That's exactly what I wanted stopped."

"Yes, sir. But . . ."

"Okay. I may have gone too far with that order," Oxley said. "But that's *my* decision to make, not some anonymous Peeping Tom working for us out at NSA. I'm not a leftwing bumpkin, for Christ's sake! I put a hold on those activities until we can figure whether we're getting disinformation from Lebed and others. I'm not convinced they're not feeding us horseshit and we're thinking it's filet mignon. I—"

"Mr. President, I understand," Carlton said, seeming unaware he was interrupting. "You're right. You gave me a specific order to shut down NSA's eavesdropping on heads of state. NSA did obey—except for Lebed. After what happened in Syria, Iraq, and . . . they thought you should know what . . . I let it go, thinking maybe they were right given everything that's going on. *I'm* responsible, not anybody else. I decided that someone has to be accountable, and it should be me. Maybe everyone will get the message that the ax will come down on them in the future."

Carlton paused for an instant. But, before the stunned Oxley could speak, Carlton took a stapled sheaf of papers from his suit coat pocket and lowered his voice. "I was just at NSA. Read the riot act to them. The Lebed intercepts absolutely stopped. But the NSA admits that the shutdown was at the other end."

"The Russians found the tap?"

"That's what it looks like," Carlton said. "It was a pretty elaborate setup involving the CIA and the NSA. An analyst at NSA put together a package of what she thought were the most important conversations—a sort of highlights reel. I think you need to see what they picked up a couple of days ago, just before the shutdown."

He handed the papers to Oxley, saying, "This is from a long transcript. I have extracted what I consider the most significant . . . most important . . . dialogue."

Scanning them quickly, Oxley saw that it was a translation of a conversation between Lebed and someone identified as Nikita Komov, a name that seemed familiar.

Komov: It is imperative, sir. Hamilton must remain in Russia.

Lebed: And why do you dare to say 'must' to me, Komov?

K: You perhaps have heard of Ivan's Hammer, sir?

L: Yes, yes. I heard my father mention it. Some scientist of your era having a crazy dream.

K: With respect, sir. Not a dream.

L: You have perhaps become a space scientist?

K: Hamilton controls an asteroid. It can become a weapon. He cannot be allowed to return to America. Not until we know where the asteroid is located. You cannot allow the Americans to take control of that asteroid and allow them to use it as a weapon—as Ivan's Hammer. . . .

Oxley kept reading. "There are some mentions of Basayev," he said. "Do we know anything new about Basayev?"

"Nothing since I briefed you on the sinking of Basayev's yacht, sir. As you know, Basayev was a CIA asset. I've looked into his reports. He was not much of an agent. Spent most of his time becoming a billionaire through his connections with Putin and Lebed."

"And the yacht?" Oxley asked.

Carlton shrugged and did not speak. The shrug was enough. The yacht had disappeared without a trace in a world where objects as large as airliners can similarly vanish. The verdict on the sinking—"a boiler explosion"—had come from Turkey. One of its warships had sped to the scene of the sinking after a fisherman reported hearing an explosion and seeing a plume of smoke. When pressed by GNN, a U.S. official had confirmed, on background, that "a boiler exploded."

"Komov. I've heard that name before," Oxley said. One CIA briefing officer had called him Putin's Rasputin; another one had compared Komov to James Jesus Angleton, chief of CIA counterintelligence during the height of the Cold War.

"He's an old KGB officer whose specialty is counterintelligence," Carlton answered. "And he's very good at his job. He's called Comrade X-ray for his ability to see traitorous hearts. Too bad the transcript doesn't give you the tone of their voices when they mentioned Basayev's yacht. Lebed ordered the missile that sank it, and Komov knows it."

"How sure of this are you?" Oxley asked, pointing to the transcript pages.

"Authentic, sir. We have multiple assets in Russia, and we've known about Komov for a long time. He's been a confidential adviser to Soviet presidents going back to the seventies. Putin loved him. Lebed knew his value and kept him on."

Oxley went back to reading the transcript.

"So Hamilton was to be on Basayev's yacht? Close shave. And I assume this is true about that SpaceMine engineer?"

"Never heard about that, sir."

"And Ivan's Hammer? Ever hear of it, Frank?"

"Hear of it? No, sir. I plan to have that transcript combed by our best Russian analysis team. I'll especially task them to dig into it, and whether it would ever be possible for Russian cosmonauts to take control of an asteroid."

"Hold up on that, Frank," Oxley said, turning his gaze again to the clocks. "I don't want 'Ivan's Hammer' to get any circulation. It must be tightly held." He paused and added, "How long have we had this . . . capability? I mean right into his office."

"About two months, sir."

"I assume that you drew on some of the conversations for use in your daily brief," Oxley said.

"Yes, sir. NSA, as usual, kept everything in their data mountains but sent me, by special courier, translated, non-verbatim digests. It sometimes was golden stuff."

"So good, it was worth defying my order to stop the Lebed eavesdropping?"

"In fact, sir, most of the conversations were tedious, even mind-numbing."

"Sounds like the conversations in this office," Oxley said, laughing.

Carlton did not respond, but went on as if he had not heard; he never believed that anything about his job was amusing.

"And then came this one," Oxley continued.

"Yes, sir. It was so jarring I felt I had to show you portions of the ver-batim transcript."

"What was so jarring?"

"Hamilton, sir. The idea that the Russians are holding an—"

"And not 'Ivan's Hammer'?"

"No, sir. That could be more fiction than science. I'm not convinced. But Hamilton is a Silicon Valley icon, and if word . . ."

"You trust those sources? Absolutely trust them?" Oxley asked, speeding up the pace of his questioning.

"Yes, sir. The source is a fine asset."

"I know spy talk a bit, Frank. This kind of 'asset' usually is someone we recruited."

Oxley turned, sitting face-to-face with Carlton, who answered by nodding.

"Okay, Frank. Don't turn your analysts onto this yet. I want this nar-rowly known. Keep it in your pocket for a while." He handed the tran-script back to Carlton. "You can forget about that resignation. And tell those eavesdroppers to keep on eavesdropping."

"Sir? I thought—"

"There's more here—much more—than you know, Frank."

Carlton, looking puzzled, went to his regular seat next to Oxley in preparation for the daily intelligence briefing.

"Better get started. Can't keep the others waiting," Oxley said. Standing outside were Secretary of Defense George Winthrop and other members of the national security team, including the secretary of state, the CIA director, and the chairman of the joint chiefs of staff.

"Little chilly in here," Oxley said, nodding to the Army major who sat at a small desk near the entrance to the Situation Room. Here it was December and there still was the feeling of filtered air stirred by air conditioning. Oxley never liked the place. No windows. A lot of faces of people who never took their eyes off him. Grim news, carefully parsed talk, nods of approval. *How I miss Sean Falcone,* Oxley thought. *Once in a while, at least, he'd crack a joke in here.*

Oxley turned to Carlton and said, "Okay, Frank, what's the situation?" That was how Oxley always opened the meeting, ever since the first time he sat at the head of the long table six long years ago. He now remembered that at one particularly tortuous session, Falcone had answered, "SNAFU, sir, as we used to say in the army."

"Meaning?" Oxley asked.

"Situation normal, all fucked up," Falcone had said, smiling at the trace of embarrassment that passed over the President's face.

"The situation is . . . complicated, sir," Carlton answered, puzzled by the quick smile the President flashed.

"In other words, Frank, SNAFU'd."

Carlton looked startled. Then he glanced at the red folder before him and delivered the situation: "North Korea has started taking advantage of the unrest caused by China's occupation of Uotsuri-shima in the Diaoyu or Senkaku Islands," he began. "The Korean People's Army has begun methodical shelling—a clockwork twelve artillery shells an hour, eight hours a day—with most of the shells landing on the Yellow Sea island of Daeyeonpyeongdo—"

"Where?" Oxley asked. As usual, he was taking notes on a yellow lined pad.

"Daeyeonpyeongdo," Carlton repeated. "It's—"

"How do you spell it?" Oxley interrupted. Carlton smiled, as did others around the table.

Carlton spelled it out and continued, "It's the main island of a group of islands. A familiar target for North Korea when Kim Jong-un decides to stir things up. There was a shelling like this in 2010. South Korea returned fire, shell for shell, but most of them landed in the sea."

Oxley leaned forward, as if to interrupt again. But instead he slumped back, thinking of the folded transcript in his pocket. *If only those bastards knew. If only they knew,* he thought.

"China," Carlton continued, "has named the occupied island 'People's Liberation Army Island' and has begun what appears to be a steady resupply operation, following up its initial landing of about forty People's Liberation Army marines. Analysis of satellite photographs shows no increase in that force or their weaponry. The largest weapons are 120-millimeter mortars. But the amounts and items of resupply—food, water, cooking fuel—is consistent with long-term occupation."

"But still only forty men?"

"Yes, sir. But, to Japan, occupation by even that small a force is highly provocative. And President Zhang Xing himself, rather than a spokesperson, announced a few hours ago that quote 'China affirms its right to control its own territory and warns that violations of its Air Defense Identification Zone will be dealt with severely and without remorse' unquote."

" 'Without remorse,' " Oxley repeated. "What's the meaning of that? As ominous as it sounds?"

"Yes, sir. It's another provocative step. Like hacking into our databases. Like building artificial islands . . . sorry, artificial edifices, on atolls and reefs in the South China Sea, raising alarm in the Philippines, Malaysia, Vietnam, and Brunei."

"What's the military significance?"

Before Secretary of Defense George Winthrop could answer, Carlton did: "One of the edifices, by our analysis, has a runway long enough for Chinese military aircraft, bombers as well as fighters. And the Chinese are also creating a harbor deep enough to dock their growing fleet of warships."

But Zhang Xing knows. He knows. How can he be doing this? Oxley thought, almost saying the words aloud. He nodded for Carlton to go on.

"Taiwan, which might have been expected to protest, has kept quiet—probably because it takes the Chinese moves seriously. We know from communications intercepts that Taiwan has already secretly notified China that it's going along with the occupation. Japan is treating 'without remorse' as a serious threat and we believe it is about to declare SIASJ."

That sounds like a drunk trying to say size-ass, Oxley thought, memories of Falcone again flitting through his mind. He had to keep a straight face while he remembered the acronym stood for Situations in Areas Surrounding Japan. SIASJ, Oxley thought, was like a smoke alarm: you hear it and you wonder if it's a false alarm. Under the U.S.-Japan Mutual Defense Assistance Agreement, a SIASJ declaration called for a stepping up of American defense activities in Japan. The treaty, Oxley knew, included the tiny bits of rock under Japan's administrative control. If China decided to militarily take the island away from Japan, the United States would have to come to Japan's aid.

"And there's also some economic activity," Carlton continued. "I briefed Rita on what we know, and her folks got some intelligence on their own." Carlton leaned back and Oxley raised his right hand toward Rita Oliphant, Secretary of the Treasury, who rarely found herself in the Situation Room. She was a tall, patrician woman wearing a green jacket over a white silk blouse.

She put on black-framed glasses and spoke in a voice still touched by her British birth and childhood: "Thank you, Frank. Starting five weeks ago, Mr. President, China started selling U.S. debt, as secretly as its brokers could, and my China watchers started to see trend lines begin to change. We thought at first it was a short-term move to build up a sudden increase in liquidity, maybe for a sudden need to finance its rapid development of urban centers. But Frank tipped me off that NSA is picking up Chinese requests for bids going to Russian and French armaments companies."

Secretary of State Benjamin Hale was on his way to China to protest the territorial claims and the building of islands. And Oxley was holding off further reaction until Hale returned. There was no point in bringing up the sell-off of debt or the arms purchases, Oxley decided. The stock market was not so bullish these days about Chinese investments. *No need to upset the stock market any further,* he thought. And then he thought of the asteroid. *And what will Wall Street do when the world finds out about that?*

Oxley looked down the table at Winthrop, a former senator from Oklahoma. He was in his mid-sixties, rotund and balding. He looked soft, but he was as tough as he was on the day when, as a deputy sheriff, he had faced a gunman who had just killed two shoppers in a Walmart. Winthrop took a 38 round in the shoulder and, still standing, shot the man twice in the forehead. A few months later he began his political career and was often introduced as 2-shot Winthrop.

"With the concurrence of the Chairman of the Joint Chiefs of Staff and the Commander of the Pacific Command, sir," Winthrop solemnly said, "I recommend a DEFCON 3 level, restricted to that command."

"I agree," Oxley said, just as solemnly. "Please notify Admiral Gerhan."

Winthrop and Oxley, after a conference call with Gerhan, had already agreed on the restricted rise to a Pacific Command DEFCON 3, knowing that it would become public knowledge, alerting China to how serious the United States viewed Chinese actions. A rise from DEFCON 4, a fairly mild increase in readiness, to DEFCON 3 indicated a tense military and geopolitical situation. Aircraft carriers and Air Force units in the region would be kept ready to launch within fifteen minutes of orders, and all military communications went to a high level of encryption.

When Oxley declared the meeting over, he asked Carlton to stay—a move he often did when Falcone had been the National Security Adviser. He could depend on Falcone to size up the meeting and point Oxley toward decisions that had not yet been made. Carlton had not filled

Falcone's shoes, but Carlton, over the past two years, had developed his own style. Oxley sometimes called Falcone out of the blue to get a quick second opinion. But Oxley had come to accept Carlton's no-nonsense, stay-the-course manner of steering through rough waters.

"I got a man-to-man call from Lebed," Oxley told Carlton. "He offered to help mediate the China-Japan crisis, along with the crisis between the North and South Koreans."

"And?" Carlton asked, trying hard to hide his annoyance over not being on the call.

"And I politely thanked him for the offer. It's just like the Russians to offer to play a role as a big global player while taking pleasure that the U.S. is in a lose-lose position. If I side with the Japanese, we could end up in a shooting war with the Chinese in the Pacific. If I back away from Japan, I'll be faced with a humiliating loss of credibility with Japan, China, and just about the rest of the world."

"Well played, Mr. President," Carlton said. "No way Russia can be a player and a mediator. Lebed's been playing footsie with China. But he's also enjoying seeing China squirm over Little Kim's mischief with South Korea. China will have to put several hundred thousand troops on the border to prevent a flood of North Koreans from crossing over into China, seeking refuge from what looks like an imminent war."

"Serves the Chinese right for failing to rein in that man-child dictator," Oxley said.

Both men stood, and Oxley preceded Carlton out of the room.

"You're right, Frank. It's complicated."

Damn complicated, Oxley thought as he headed for the Oval Office. *Lebed and Zhang Xing and I are playing around with war when we all know about an asteroid that may hit the Earth in 2037.*

12

As President Oxley's Chief of Staff, Ray Quinlan often accompanied him to Situation Room meetings. When he was not invited, Quinlan would fume and start to weave groundless West Wing conspiracies aimed at getting him exiled from power. Sitting now in the anteroom of the Oval Office, he awaited Oxley's return from the meeting on Pacific strategy, and a tantrum was rising within him. He had just about gotten over not having been invited to the Situation Room when Christakos called and he was presented with a new grievance. *Why,* he asked himself, *didn't I know that Lebed was holding Hamilton?*

Quinlan had a full head of curly red hair, which topped a pale face tending toward roundness. His blue-and-white striped tie was yanked down from the open collar of a blue shirt. A veteran of Yale's heavyweight rowing crew, he had the sturdy body of a former athlete who kept fit.

A Secret Service agent told Quinlan that Oxley had returned from the Situation Room. Trained to spot signs of rage, the agent took the precaution of walking in front of Quinlan as he hurried to the Oval Office door. A young woman at a desk said into a console, "Ray Quinlan on the way, Mr. President!"

Oxley was standing by one of the windows, his back turned to the opening door. Without turning around, he said, "Take a seat, Ray. Be cool."

In a sudden quiet, they sat opposite each other on pale-yellow sofas flanking a low table topped with a bowl of apples. "Now, Ray, what's causing you to be a pain in the ass this time?"

"What the hell is going on about Robert Hamilton . . . sir?"

"It's been tightly held," Oxley said, reaching for an apple.

"His lawyer—Akis Christakos—called me," Quinlan said. "Says Hamilton wants a grant of immunity—from *you*—and threatens to go to the media—to that son of a bitch Dake—if he doesn't get it."

"It's not a White House matter, Ray."

"Well, then, what is it . . . sir? Surely one of America's richest men being holed up in Moscow—a la Snowden—*is* a White House matter. It seems to me . . . sir."

"Well, Ray, here's what the White House is working on right now: The Chinese have taken over one of the Senkaku or Diaoyu—whatever the hell they're called—Islands. They're making artificial islands for bases in the South China Sea, and Japan is pounding war drums. Crazy Kim Jong-un is suffering from a global attention deficit about his nuclear power. North Korea and South Korea are mobilizing and preparing to shoot at each other, and China is pouring troops to the North Korea border to hold off refugees. I just put the Pacific Command on DEFCON 3. And you want me to spend time worrying about a missing billionaire?"

Quinlan forced himself to stand silent. He could feel words and shouts welling up. He knew he was probably one outburst away from being fired.

Oxley went back to the window, stared at the brilliant day beyond, then turned around and said, "Okay, Ray. There *is* something going on. I've kept it close. But now I think it's time for you to know about it." He held up his hand when Quinlan stood, his face twisted in anger. "Hear me out."

Quinlan nodded, still not daring to open his mouth.

"There's a complex issue that calls for absolute secrecy," Oxley continued. "I want you to know about it so you can keep an eye on it while I wrestle with the Pacific crisis," Oxley said. "You remember Dr. Benjamin Taylor?"

Quinlan thought for a moment. Taylor, a former NASA scientist, was Assistant Director of the Smithsonian's Air and Space Museum, a well-known author, and host of the popular television show *Your Universe*.

"Yes, sir," Quinlan said. "I remember that he was lined up to be your science adviser. And he turned it down. I never could—"

"Right. Well, I did give him a job. Its highly classified label is 'Defense of Earth.' He's working with scientists from Russia and China."

"On *what*?" Quinlan asked sullenly.

"You'll find out soon enough. I am going to call him and tell him to come over here and brief you—and Frank. He's not in this loop either, by the way."

"Carlton? Why is he involved? And Taylor? I don't get it."

"You'll get it, Ray. I can promise you that."

13

Dr. Benjamin Franklin Taylor was in the Air and Space Museum, having coffee with his assistant, Molly, in her cubicle when her desk phone rang. He reached toward it, but she beat him to it, lifting the phone to hear, "This is the White House for Dr. Taylor. Please bring him to the phone."

"Another tinfoil hatter," she said, moving to hang up the phone. Molly Tobias, a widow in her sixties, had given herself the mission of shielding him from deranged or time-wasting fans of his monthly PBS show, *Your Universe.* Taylor, who had heard the words "White House," intercepted the phone and said, "Taylor here."

"Please stand by for President Oxley," the voice said.

A moment later Oxley, speaking rapidly, said, "Ben. Please do me a favor."

A surprised Taylor nodded, then, feeling foolish, stammered when he said, "Whatever you want, Mr. President."

"Just this, Ben: As soon as you can, I want you to brief Ray Quinlan, my Chief of Staff, and Frank Carlton, my National Security Adviser, on . . . on what you have been working on for me. Planning to be in town for a while?"

"Yes, sir. Whenever you want."

"Okay. I'll tell Ray to set it up as soon as possible."

"Mr. President?"

"Yes?"

"Has something happened?"

"Nothing special," Oxley replied. "Except . . . I'm sure you remember that guy Ivan with the Hammer."

"Yes, sir!"

"Frank Carlton . . . heard about that. He's particularly interested in that, Ben. But don't get him all hopped up about it."

"Yes, sir."

"And, of course, still keep everything under your hat unless you hear otherwise from me. And I mean directly from me. Thanks, Ben. Good-bye."

Taylor leaned back for a moment, and then looked sternly at Molly. "You didn't hear anything. Right?"

"Right," she said.

They touched coffee containers in a silent toast and Taylor walked into his office.

Molly, he thought, *is handling this well.* She didn't ask questions about his absences or about cryptic calls from people with odd accents.

Taylor—well over six feet, short-cropped salt-and-pepper hair, broad shoulders, seemingly always in motion—did not look like a pensive man. But a life of science had made him into a man who looked for reasons, for patterns, for answers.

Sometimes he looked back and saw that his life had been on a track with a lot of switches. Growing up in Detroit, he switched from a black kid heading toward a gang to a son who was being pushed to advance placement courses—and simultaneously toward a football scholarship at the University of Michigan. Then came the Heisman Trophy and another switch: Go pro or go for a Ph.D. He chose the Massachusetts Institute of Technology and a doctorate in astrophysics. Then, MIT professor-scholar or NASA scientist. Next switch: NASA's Jet Propulsion Lab in Pasadena or NASA's Goddard Space Flight Center near Washington. Then Assistant Director at Goddard or assistant director of one of the most visited museums in the world. The next switch, labeled "potential" presidential science adviser, almost sent him hurtling into oblivion. But here he was, back on track.

When Quinlan called to set up the briefing, Taylor recognized the Boston twang. The first time they talked, Taylor remembered, was when Quinlan called to say that he was under consideration for the post of Adviser to the President and Director of the White House Office of Science and Technology Policy.

But at that switch, Taylor was derailed. He had said very publicly that Robert Hamilton's venture into asteroid mining was threatening to destabilize an asteroid and put the Earth at risk. Taylor's warning had taken the form of a PBS NOVA show called *An Asteroid Closely Watched*. Two Senators, acting as Hamilton's vassals, saw to it that PBS "indefinitely postponed" the show. He nearly lost his post at the Air and Space Museum. And, at Quinlan's urging, Oxley quietly withdrew the science adviser offer.

But Taylor and his friend Sean Falcone managed to prove that Hamilton's company, SpaceMine, had a secret partner: corrupt Russian billionaire Kuri Basayev. Taylor and Falcone discovered that a Space-Mine engineer, Cole Perenchio, had been murdered after learning that the asteroid selected for mining was on a highly probable collision course with Earth.

Things sure have changed, Taylor thought after Quinlan politely ended the call. *I'm the whole Earth's science adviser.*

14

The briefing the next day was preceded by a quick visit to the Oval Office. Oxley shook hands all around and said to Carlton and Quinlan, "I'm going to set the same rule we have for briefing leaders of congressional committees on extraordinarily sensitive intelligence: 'No notes. Just keep it in your heads.'"

Then Quinlan led Carlton and Taylor down a corridor to the large room known as the White House Library. A fire was crackling in a fireplace beneath a portrait of George Washington by Gilbert Stuart. "When John Adams lived here," Quinlan said, "this place was a laundry. Jackie Kennedy turned it into this room. She wanted an early eighteenth-century look." He pointed to a gilded-wood chandelier with a red band and said, "Belonged to the family of James Fenimore Cooper, keeping the theme that the books on the shelves reflect American ideas. I come here sometimes just to get out of the twenty-first century for a few minutes."

"I work in a museum all day," Taylor said, looking around. "And here I am in another one."

In the center of the room, under the chandelier, were three spindly-legged chairs and a small round table. "If you don't mind," Taylor said, nodding to each man, "I'm used to talking to an audience while standing. So you can just sit down, and I'll tell you what I know." Quinlan and Carlton sat, flanking the empty chair and facing Taylor, who stood to the right of the fireplace.

"First, a little background," Taylor said, standing silently for a moment and getting into his familiar role as a lecturer. "I'm sure you remember the event in Chelyabinsk, Russia, in 2013, when an asteroid zoomed over the city and burst into a fireball. The shockwave damaged buildings and broke thousands of windows, causing a glass blizzard that wounded about twelve hundred stunned people. If the explosion had occurred over India or Pakistan, each nation probably would have blamed the other for dropping a nuclear bomb, setting off a panic and triggering a nuclear war.

"The reports that started coming included videos of a fiery object speeding across the sky. Cole Perenchio, an old NASA friend of mine, immediately went to his superiors at Goddard Space Flight Center and said he wanted to drop the work he was doing on Earth-Moon gravitational variations. He proposed setting up a NASA task force to study the Russian event to see how it affected what we know about the probability of asteroids hitting the Earth.

"Cole's proposal was turned down, and Cole, who always was an obstinate guy, left NASA and went to work for Robert Hamilton's company, SpaceMine. He was welcomed with open arms because he was a world-renowned expert on gravity in space, and that knowledge would be valuable for dealing with asteroids.

"Cole believed that once he showed Hamilton the potential perils of mining asteroids, Hamilton would close shop. Besides being obstinate, Cole was naïve. SpaceMine was on the brink of launching an initial public offering. And neither Hamilton nor his Russian silent partner, Kuri Basayev, were about to give up their investment. So—"

"Basayev?" Carlton said. He often delivered PowerPoint briefings, and he added: "Russian oligarch close to Lebed. Killed when his yacht exploded in the Black Sea." He switched to normal language and said, "The Agency has a pile of intelligence on Basayev. But I never heard he was mixed up with Hamilton."

"Right," Taylor said, nodding. "A silent partner. And that's how he comes into the story. Hamilton fired Cole. But not before Cole managed to write a report about Hamilton's so-called Asteroid USA. It—"

"That's the one that GNN made such a big deal out of," Quinlan said. "Come to think of it, I thought it was supposed to be sending a signal. And—"

"Yes. We're supposed to hear a constant stream of 'USA' in Morse code," Taylor interrupted with a touch of impatience. "And we haven't heard it, have we? Well, that gets into the story, too. Cole's report says that Asteroid USA was actually a pretty big asteroid known to astronomers as Janus. Hamilton, with help from Basayev, had sent a spacecraft to Janus and was planning to change its orbit to make it easier to mine.

"Coincidentally, in my writings I had used Janus as an example of a big asteroid with an orbit that one day could be on a collision course with Earth. I mentioned Janus in a NOVA show that never got on the air because Hamilton started throwing his weight around.

"Cole was really concerned that SpaceMine was putting the Earth in danger by messing with Janus' orbit. He decided to act. He put his futile report to Hamilton in a SpaceMine laptop and hacked into confidential SpaceMine databases to get whatever he could find about Asteroid USA. Then he encrypted all this and headed for Washington."

"So far, Dr. Taylor, I don't see you giving us any big secrets," Quinlan said, conspicuously looking at his watch.

"Call me Ben," Taylor replied. "Sorry, but you have to hear this if you want to understand the secrets—and why they are secrets. But I'll try to speed this up. Cole gave the laptop to a friend, a Washington lawyer named Harold Davidson. He and three other people in his law office were killed. So was Cole."

"Holy shit!" Quinlan exclaimed. "The law firm shootings! Falcone's firm. And Falcone killed one of the gunmen."

Taylor nodded and said, "Yeah. I worked with Sean on this. We managed to get the information that Cole was trying to deliver. I guessed that he was using the code we had used in college—and I decrypted it. We— Sean and I—told President Oxley what was in it, and that's why I'm here today, doing this."

Taylor paused and added, "Any questions?"

15

"Let's start with Basayev," Carlton said. He had been squirming in his chair and tapping his fingers on the gleaming tabletop. He was much more used to giving briefings than receiving them. "I know he was a crook and a great pal of Lebed, like a lot of other Russian billionaires. But did he order the killings? And did Hamilton get him to do it?"

"That's beyond my briefing," Taylor replied. "But I do know that the FBI considered Hamilton 'a person of interest.' And, for that matter, they hung the same label on me and on Falcone for a time. To me, the point of the murders is this: Terrible as they were, they validated the basic warning in Cole's message: SpaceMine's Asteroid USA is on an orbit that is likely to collide with Earth in 2037. To be precise, on April 7, 2037."

After a long silence, Quinlan spoke up: "Well, that's twenty years away. We've got time to do something about it. Right?"

"Ivan's Hammer," Carlton said quietly. "My God! Twenty years under Ivan's Hammer."

"What?" Quinlan asked, scowling and turning to Carlton. "What the hell is that?"

"Now *I'll* have to do a secret briefing," Carlton said, rising from his chair and stepping back so that his gaze encompassed the other two men.

"A few days ago," he continued, "we learned that the term 'Ivan's Hammer' came up in a . . . a . . . briefing given to President Lebed. And—"

Quinlan lunged forward and said, "How the hell—"

Carlton held up his right hand in a traffic-cop gesture and, looking at Quinlan, said, "I can't say *how* we know. But I can tell you *what* we know."

He swung his head to resume directing his words at both men. "The term first came up in the 1980s when the United States and the then–Soviet Union were looking at space as a potential battlefield. It was an idea that didn't go anywhere with American strategists. But we learned—"

"Learned?" Quinlan asked. "Who's your goddamn professor—"

Carlton raised his hand again and said, "Sorry. Can't mention how we got it. The point is we knew that the Soviets kept working on the idea of taking control of a small asteroid and using it as a first-strike weapon by putting it on a course to hit the U.S. It was a crazy idea, but not to the Soviets. They called the project 'Ivan's Hammer.' Carl Sagan heard about it and publicly said he thought it was feasible. The CIA asked RAND to make a study of it, and RAND's experts also said it was feasible. Then the ideas just seemed to disappear—until we learned that Lebed had talked about 'Ivan's Hammer' a few days ago."

Carlton looked toward Taylor and, before sitting down, said, "As a scientist . . . Ben . . . What do you think about the possibility that it could actually work? Is it science . . . or just fiction?"

"It's crazy—but it could work if all you wanted to do was hit a random place from Maine to California. They could probably figure a way to move an asteroid in a general direction toward Earth, with somewhere in the United States as the target. But would it hit the target? Imagine a rodeo rider trying to control a steer and you get the picture: a skilled rider and a wild massive beast."

"How about threat control?" Carlton asked. "Let's say Lebed claims he has control of an asteroid and makes certain demands . . . or else."

Remembering Oxley's request, Taylor kept his expression unchanged. "That's more geopolitics than science. . . . Frank. I don't see how a threat like that would be . . . realistic."

"What do you know about the U.S. Air Force Space Command?" Carlton asked, using his grim national-security voice.

"Not much," Taylor replied, trying to not look irritated by the interruption.

"The U.S. Space Command has thousands of airmen in place all over the world. And when you talk to the commanding general about space, the first thing he usually says: 'We're not NASA.' "

"Meaning?" Taylor asked.

"Meaning there is a fairly big and expensive piece of DoD that takes warfare in space pretty seriously," Carlton said. " 'Ivan's Hammer' in Lebed's hands would be a very real threat to the Air Force space guys."

"And it sounds realistic to me," Quinlan said. "That son of a bitch Lebed is capable of anything. I'd advise the President to take a threat like that as real."

"Have you heard of the Magneto Hydrodynamic Explosive Munition or the X-37B, also known as the Orbital Test Vehicle?" Carlton asked Taylor.

"No, Frank," Taylor replied. "I would assume that that kind of information is classified."

"Well, as a former Air Force officer, I wish it was," Carlton said. "But a lot of Pentagon contractors like to advertise. The munition with the long name is an electromagnetic bomb and the X-37B can carry it. Due to our society's ridiculous belief that nothing should be secret, you can find all about it on the internet. An electromagnetic bomb eludes the agreement to keep nuclear weapons out of space, and—"

Taylor, who prided himself as a scientific showman, rarely felt he was losing his audience. But he realized he had to turn the dialogue—and issue a warning. "Please, Frank, and please, Ray," he said. "Remember this is a briefing about a real threat: an asteroid hitting the Earth. And remember that the President ordered strict secrecy. What I tell you has to stay in this room."

"My job," Carlton said, "is to watch over all events and possible events that threaten—or *seem* to threaten—the United States. If I decide that the Space Command needs to hear about Ivan's Hammer, I will—"

"You will clear any further revelations with the President," Taylor said, staring Carlton down. As he returned to his seat, Taylor added, "I need your word on that."

Carlton nodded but did not speak.

"Let's get back to asteroids," Taylor said. "Every week I get a report from a NASA office called 'Gnats,' but spelled 'N-H-A-T-S.' NASA likes acronyms. Maybe because it's an acronym itself. Anyway, Gnats is the 'Near-Earth Object Human Space Flight Accessible Targets Study.' You can see why everybody uses the acronym."

"You're plunging into the weeds," Quinlan muttered.

"Sort of," Taylor said, nodding with a smile. "This NASA agency looks for near-Earth objects that might be accessible for future human space flight missions. As a side benefit, Gnats gives us a handy catalogue of asteroids. I may get notice of more than a hundred in a week. In one week last summer, Gnats counted six hundred and eighty-one."

"Six hundred and eighty-one!" Quinlan exclaimed. "Why the hell aren't there more hits?"

"Most of them—the overwhelming majority—are in orbits that don't imperil the Earth," Taylor replied. "And a lot that could do damage are so small that they burn up when they hit our atmosphere."

"But so many? Why so many?" Carlton asked.

"We're seeing more because we're looking more. And what we're discovering is that there are more—considerably more—asteroids out there than we had thought. Thanks to Gnats, we have an ever-growing catalogue of asteroids. There are millions of NEOs—another acronym: near-Earth objects. In recent times we have discovered nearly twelve thousand new near-Earth objects. Some are as small as, say, a washing machine, and some probably big enough to have their own moons."

"You mean there are *new* asteroids?" Quinlan asked. "I thought that they were like little stars—up there, hard to see with the naked eye. But up there and known."

"Asteroids," Taylor said, "are the orphans of space. Stars, sun, planets, they all get a lot of attention from astronomers. But it's only recently that asteroids got much attention. Right now, I can tell you, there's a lot of work being done at a place close to here—in a building at the Goddard Space Flight Center. It's called the Cauldron. A lot of scientists and engineers are working on NASA's Asteroid Redirect Mission."

"Pardon my French, but what the fuck is that?" Quinlan asked.

Taylor shook his head at Quinlan's profanity. "Sorry, I never studied French . . ."

"It's pretty universal," Quinlan quipped.

"Okay," Taylor said, "then let's stop fucking around. . . . Essentially, they're working on how to build an asteroid lander, which could be programmed to head for an asteroid and change its course by using its thrusters to shove an asteroid that's heading for Earth. Or its own gravitational pull could make tiny changes to an asteroid's course. Or the lander could pick up a very small asteroid, or a piece of an asteroid, and bring it back."

"What for? The palladium?" Carlton asked.

"No," Taylor answered. "So we can examine it and find out how it's put together."

"How privy is NASA to Ivan's Hammer and Hamilton's asteroid?" Quinlan asked.

"NASA's not in the loop about the possible 2037 collision," Taylor replied. "And I don't think anyone there does much thinking about Asteroid USA. It's an all-but-forgotten news item. They're being scientists thinking about all asteroids. . . . I'm just interested in one of them."

"Hamilton's," Quinlan said. "The one he calls Asteroid USA? And Lebed calls Ivan's Hammer?"

"Yes," Taylor said, nodding. "What I'm doing is defending Earth. Another secret to deliver: I'm representing the United States in a tripartite science group that is working on ways to defend against that one asteroid, which is almost certainly on a course to hit the planet in 2037."

"Tripartite?" Carlton asked, his voice edgy. "What the hell are you talking about? The United States doesn't have any tripartite science agreements."

"We have ever since President Oxley signed up President Lebed and President Zhang Xing at the G20 Summit in Istanbul."

Quinlan sprang to his feet and said, "Istanbul! Goddamn! I knew he was up to something. He closed me out then, and he's been closing me out ever since."

"Fuck!" Carlton said. "We've got China kicking our balls in the Pacific, Russia scaring the shit out of NATO in Europe. And now—*now*—I find out we're all in some kind of tripartite scientific tea party. Jesus!"

Taylor gave up being a lecturer. He walked to the table and sat between Carlton and Quinlan.

Leaning back, Taylor said wearily, "That's right. Tripartite. The three major spacefaring nations are working on this. I'm leaving out the EU, Japan, and India. . . . Each of the three leaders appointed a space scientist.

The three of us have met five times so far. It's been working pretty well. Our common language is English—the Russian scientist got his Ph.D. from MIT, just like I did, but somewhat more recently. My Chinese colleague learned English in China—at Duke University's China campus near Shanghai. She then got her Ph.D. in theoretical astrophysics at Stanford. In China, her brilliance was recognized and she was assigned to asteroids, which the Chinese worry about much more than we do. It's a good team."

"What exactly are you doing?" Carlton asked. "And how are you managing to keep this secret?"

"We're talking, trading ideas, trying to dream up something that could be presented as an effective defense," Taylor explained. "Our cover is that we're working on possible changes in the United Nations Outer Space Treaty. It's been around since 1967, and no one knows anything about it or cares anything about it. It focused primarily on preventing the use of space for military purposes."

"Well then, what about Ivan's Hammer?" Carlton asked.

"It's never come up," Taylor replied. "That's military. Political bullshit. We don't deal with it."

"It's not bullshit to me, Ben," Carlton said. "You can bet your Russian colleague knows about it. What's his name?"

"No need for you to know, Frank," Taylor said.

The two men glared at each other for a moment. Then Carlton leaned closer and, lowering his voice, said, "I need to know because my job is to defend the United States, not the goddamn planet, I'm betting dollars to doughnuts that those fuckers are going to put cosmonauts on that asteroid and take control of it."

Taylor realized that sitting down had been a mistake. He lost his position as controller. Now he was flanked by two type As—ambitious, impatient strivers for making and holding rank. Carlton had reverted to being a General. Quinlan was seeing himself as a stand-in for the President of the United States. And here they were being fed information from a mere scientist, an *assistant* museum director.

"The President doesn't know the names of my *colleagues*, as you call them," Taylor told Carlton. "He trusts me."

Carlton looked away and began tapping the table again.

"We've met five times in a conference room at the UN campus in Geneva," Taylor resumed. "Just the three of us, no assistants. I take notes and after each meeting I put them in a safe to which only I know the combination. At the next meeting we go back over the notes and see if anyone has any new ideas. It's amazingly like other cooperative scientific projects I have worked on over the years. We kick around ideas. But we're working in secret, and we know we can't take the usual next step by circulating our ideas among peers and writing articles for journals."

"I can see that," Quinlan said. "I can imagine what would happen if that story got out." Then, remembering the call from Christakos, he added, "Jesus! We've got to figure a way to keep the lid on."

"We—my *colleagues* and I—know that the 2037 secret has to come out at some time. And, of course, we're worried about panic. The political leaders have to do more than *warn*. President Oxley told Sean and me—"

"Sean? Falcone's mixed up in this?" Quinlan asked.

"He's been with me on this since the beginning," Taylor said. Now it was his voice that was edgy. "Once he knows that you're being told about this, I am sure that if you ask, he'll answer that question."

Taylor waited a moment for Quinlan to cool down and then continued: "President Oxley told me that he and the other two leaders would be 'warners' and everyone else on Earth would be the 'warnees.' To prevent worldwide panic, the warners had to do more than warn. They had to tell the warnees that there was a *defense*, that our scientists had figured out a way to save Earth."

Carlton and Quinlan both looked as if they were both about to speak. Carlton spoke first. "Well, what *is* the defense?"

Taylor shook his head. "We don't have a defense."

"Jesus!" Quinlan said. "Nothing?"

"We have some good solid ideas, and we have some solid knowledge," Taylor replied.

"Such as what?" Quinlan asked.

"Well, we know that the Earth moves the size of its own diameter every six minutes," Taylor said. "So, to avoid a collision, all you have to do is change the arrival time of the asteroid by six minutes. And we know, Frank, there are policy questions on the horizon."

"Such as?"

"Such as," Taylor continued, "should the United States assume responsibility for defending the planet, or should this be a UN project? But the biggest question is: What's the best way to prevent a collision?"

"What have you come up with?" Quinlan asked.

"Basically, three notions," Taylor said. "One, a solar sail—capturing solar light and using it like wind to move the asteroid to a non-collision course. My Chinese colleague is specifically working on that. Two, blowing up the asteroid with a nuclear bomb, like in that old Bruce Willis movie. As a matter of fact, two government agencies are looking at a nuclear defense. NASA and the National Nuclear Security Administration—"

"The guys who manage the making and stockpiling of nukes?" Quinlan interrupted.

"Yes," Taylor responded. "They're talking to NASA about what would happen if you tried to nudge an asteroid by hitting it with a spacecraft whose nose was a nuclear bomb. The bomb the nuclear guys are mostly interested in is the B83, about seventy-five times as powerful as the bomb that was dropped on Hiroshima."

"Jesus," Quinlan said. "That's a big nuke!"

"And its use in space is technically in violation of international nuclear agreements," Taylor said. Glancing toward Carlton, he added, "And so is a spacecraft carrying an electromagnetic bomb."

"Is the Nuclear Security Administration involved in this defense of Earth business?" Carlton asked.

"No," Taylor said. "Neither they nor NASA know about the twenty-year warning. The President decided to keep them out of that. But they have done some research on the possible use of nuclear weapons to destroy asteroids."

"So they're for the nuclear bomb solution and you guys aren't. Is that it?" Quinlan asked.

"You could put it that way," Taylor said. "But in fact, I think the solution is our third idea: Using the SpaceMine spacecraft already attached to Asteroid USA to nudge it into a new course."

"That's the best?" Carlton asked. "Option Three?"

"Absolutely," Taylor answered. "Take control of the SpaceMine space-craft, which is attached to the asteroid, to precisely move it."

"So why not announce that as the defense?" Quinlan asked. "Sounds like good news for all us warnees."

"I told you there is one big problem," Taylor said. "We don't know where the hell Asteroid USA is."

Quinlan and Carlton looked at each other, as if waiting for the other to ask. After a moment, Carlton spoke: "But what about all that Gnats information you get?"

"When a new asteroid is discovered, the NASA watchers try to get as much information as they can before its orbit takes it out of the sky area being searched," Taylor explained. "Usually they can get orbital data and an idea of its probable structure. Their job is to focus on characteristics that may make it a potential target for future manned missions. A list of new asteroids is a by-product."

"Okay, okay," Quinlan said. "Cut to the chase. You've got this long list. Why in hell can't you just figure out which asteroid on the list is the one that's going to hit the planet in twenty years?"

"Because a lot of asteroids just sort of get lost," Taylor replied. "A lot of asteroids cannot be seen from the ground because they're in the glare of the sun. The asteroid that blew up over Chelyabinsk was one of them."

"Why can't you put a filter on a telescope?" Quinlan asked.

"Our telescopes on the ground can't look into the sun," Taylor said. "What we need is to put a telescope in space. NASA hasn't got the money to do it. And another problem: Asteroids have enormous orbits that take them far beyond optical telescopes, and even radio telescopes. NASA de-fines near-Earth objects as asteroids and comets whose orbits put them within twenty-eight million miles of Earth's orbit around the sun. The Gnats zone covers a lot of territory."

"But you said you think the SpaceMine asteroid is the one you picked for your show Janus, right?" Carlton asked. "So why don't you know where Janus is?"

"We know where Janus *was* when it was first spotted more than thirty years ago and then seen again ten years later. But we lost it. That happens quite often. Right now we simply don't know where it is—and we can't tell anybody who might help us find it. Like the Gnats team."

"Hamilton knows," Quinlan said. "That son of a bitch knows."

"Hamilton's in Moscow," Carlton said. "For us warnees, that's very bad news."

16

Taylor realized he had nothing more to tell. He knew that he had done more than reveal a secret; he had set something in motion. He thought of a pond he had played near as a kid and how fascinated he had been by the rings of water that radiated out from a tossed stone.

The session ended with handshakes all around. Quinlan whipped out his cell phone and arranged for the car that had delivered Taylor to take him back to the museum.

"And then Dulles," Taylor said. To Quinlan's puzzled look, Taylor added, "I'm booked to Geneva. May as well save cab fare."

Quinlan shrugged, added the Dulles drop-off and laughed. "Saving the world and saving cab fare," he said, patting Taylor on the back.

As soon as Carlton reached his office he called the President and said, "We need to talk immediately."

"Ray, too?" the President asked.

"No, sir, if you don't mind."

"Okay. Come on in."

Carlton walked into the Oval Office a moment later. The President pointed to the cushioned wooden chair next to the President's desk.

"How did it go?" he asked.

"Taylor did pretty well, Mr. President. He's good at translating science into regular words. But he has a rather innocent view of today's world. It'll be damn hard to keep this a secret."

"We—Lebed, Zhang Xing, and I—felt we have to contain this as long as we could," Oxley said. "We knew we had to get the scientists into the picture, and Ben Taylor looked like the ideal guy. Lebed and Zhang Xing also agreed that each of us could decide on when to tell our most trusted advisers. We also agreed—this was at the Istanbul meeting—that, when it was time, we would all three make a tripartite announcement under UN auspices."

"Yes, the Istanbul meeting," Carlton said. "And the secret session went well?"

"Yes," the President replied. "Lebed was playing his usual imitation of a responsible statesman. As for China, it turned out they were ahead of us—just like they are with hacking. Zhang Xing has had some scientists looking at asteroids as a potential danger for some time. I guess you heard about the solar sail?"

"Yes," said Carlton. "And about the 'warners' and the 'warnees.' Good frame for how to handle disclosure. Any idea when?"

"Oh, plenty of ideas, but no decision," Oxley responded. "I'd appreciate any suggestions from you. Toughest decision I've ever had to make."

"I must tell you, Mr. President," Carlton said, "I believe that this secret isn't going to keep much longer."

"You're right, as usual, Frank," said the President. "I just heard that Hamilton's lawyer—Akis Christakos—is trying to talk to him and threatening to go to Philip Dake and tell him Russia's kidnapped an American citizen. And the administration is doing nothing about it. I'll tell Ray to hold him off by saying we are dealing with the Hamilton issue and it's at a sensitive stage, but I don't know if that'll hold Christakos for very long." Oxley sighed and asked, "So what now?"

"We know from the transcript, sir, that Lebed isn't interested very much about defending the Earth," Carlton said. "He seems to be interested in using Hamilton and his asteroid as a weapons system. He's taking us right back to the Cold War."

"You may be right," Oxley said. "So, Frank, what options do you think we have?"

"We have to bring him back, Mr. President," Carlton replied. "And quickly."

"You want me to authorize a covert rendition operation?" Oxley asked, sounding surprised.

"No, sir," Carlton replied. "You surely cannot authorize any such operation."

Carlton practically knew the National Security Act of 1947 by heart. The law says that a covert action is legal as long as the President signs a Memorandum of Notification declaring that "such an action is necessary to support identifiable foreign policy objectives of the United States and is important to the national security. . . ."

The law requires the President to notify congressional intelligence committees of any covert actions that he had authorized. Carlton, well aware of how hostile Congress was to Oxley, knew there was no way that Oxley would get support for what the CIA calls "rendition" and the dictionary calls "abduction." The action would have to be described in a written "Finding." That Top Secret executive order, also called a Presidential Study Directive, would be issued by the President. Congressional intelligence oversight committees had to be notified as soon as possible after the Finding was approved.

If this mission was to be on the books, President Oxley would have to lay out the reasons that he had decided to kidnap one of the nation's wealthiest citizens. The law said that the Finding "may not authorize any action that would violate the Constitution or any statute of the United States."

If Hamilton was staying in Moscow voluntarily, a presidential abduction would be not only unconstitutional, but, quite likely, an impeachable offense. Both men knew this but did not mention it.

"What if we could prove that he was being held a virtual prisoner?" Oxley pressed.

"If the mission failed, and we lost men, it would be Jimmy Carter time for you," Carlton said, shaking his head with disapproval. He was referring to President Carter's failed mission in 1980 to rescue the fifty-two American hostages who had been imprisoned by the Iranians.

"You know the national security law better than I do," Oxley said wearily. "As for the politics and Congress, we could charge Hamilton with being an accessory to murder and demand that he be extradited. But if we tried that route, we'd have to take it into court and make the 2037 asteroid collision public. And even if a U.S. court takes our side, there's no way that Lebed will extradite him."

"Agreed, sir," Carlton said.

"And I certainly don't want *you* mixed up in this," the President said. "That's for sure. I need all your brain cells for what's going on right now."

Before Carlton could respond, Oxley spoke again, asking, "What about Ray?"

A thought formed in Carlton's West Wing brain: *Oxley thinks Quinlan's expendable.* "How much does he already know?" Carlton asked.

"Not much," Oxley replied. "We had a spat about the way he was acting like a junior president. He had even made it a firing offense if a White House staffer allowed someone to meet with me without him. Every time I thought of telling him, he would piss me off about something and I'd keep him in the dark."

"Why do you keep him?" Carlton asked.

"He's damn smart, Frank. And I guess I make him mad because when he gets mad he gets even smarter," Oxley said with a tight smile.

"I think Ray should be told all you know about this, sir," Carlton said.

"And about what is to be done with Hamilton?" Oxley asked.

Carlton hesitated, knowing that every word of this conversation was loaded with potential trouble—very big trouble—if what was said ever left the Oval Office. "Yes, sir," he said. "I will put him in charge of the Hamilton account."

Oxley stared at Carlton for a moment, knowing that Carlton was giving him deniability of what action was to take place and then said, "I think I know what you're not saying."

"And I think, sir, this conversation is over," Carlton said.

17

"Well, glad to see you back. Imagine! My goodness! Spending nearly a whole half a day in your office!" Molly Tobias said when Taylor knocked on her cubicle wall. She vaguely knew that he was doing something for the White House. Whatever it was, she knew that every once in a while he would, as she put it, "step out of the loop." He would close his office door and make a lot of calls on a cell phone she did not recognize. A few days later he would come in pulling a suitcase and tell her he would be away for four or five days.

"I . . . I have to pick up my bag," Taylor said, looking at his watch. "Anything going on?"

"What's going on is you are going into your disappearing act again and will reappear sometime like next Monday. And what else is going on is you've missed a deadline for getting an okayed script back to Lou."

"I'll work on it on the plane."

"And you'll miss Sam's birthday party. Darlene will be furious. Call her."

"She doesn't like to be called at work."

"Call her."

Taylor nodded and retreated to his office. On his desk was a pile of papers a couple of inches high. He went through them and made two piles, one for now, the other for later. He checked his email, deleting dozens of messages, and sent all surviving senders, including his television producer, Lou Goodman, his standard "Away from the Office" message.

Then he called Darlene, his twenty-three-year-old daughter, at the American University library.

"Don't tell me," she said. "No. *Do* tell me. You're off to somewhere again."

"I'm leaving very soon."

"And you can't say where."

"That's right, sweetie."

She did not respond for a moment, then icily said, "Thanks for telling me, Daddy dear." Another pause. "And, of course that means you will be missing the surprise party for Sam."

Taylor winced. He liked Sam Bancroft, an Air Force officer whom Darlene had met at the library of American University, where she was a graduate student in international affairs and he was taking an accelerated summer language course in international affairs. A veteran of combat in Afghanistan and Iraq, he was now stationed at the Pentagon.

"I'm very, very sorry, sweetie," Taylor said. "It can't be helped. Someday you'll understand. Please say happy birthday from me, and tell Sam I'll call him when I get back. He's military. He'll understand."

"Oh, I see. Unlike my boyfriend, I'm a mere civilian. Well, bon voyage."

Taylor picked up his laptop and rolling suitcase and stood staring at his office door, bracing before opening it and facing a glare from Molly.

"I'll call an Uber," she said, turning to her desk.

"No need, Molly. I . . . I've got a ride. See you Monday."

On the way to Dulles, Taylor wondered how his two associates managed the secret. If, as it appeared, neither of the two powerful men he had just briefed knew the secret, it would have been kept even better in the not very open societies of China and Russia. Still, he had to assume that intelligence services in all three nations at least knew that the three scientists were holding meetings in Geneva. Someone had arranged for their use of the UN room. And somewhere there would be records of the money being spent to cover their travel expenses.

He had volunteered to handle the scheduling of meetings. Getting three people to the same place at the same time was not as easy as he thought it was going to be, particularly the need to book flights and hotels through the United Nations travel office. He knew that the White House had arranged his funding through the U.S. Ambassador to the United Nations, as part of the Outer Space Treaty cover, and he assumed that his Russian and Chinese colleagues were similarly funded. He envisioned a small, secretive bureaucracy working behind the scenes to sustain the cover for a project without knowing what that project was.

He had just made the arrangements for the next meeting of the SwissTrio, as they called themselves, when he got the summons from Quinlan. He arranged to give his briefing on the same day that he was bound for Geneva on a 5:20 flight. Getting to Dulles in a White House car was an unexpected bonus.

During the flight, Taylor slept more than he worked on the script of his popular PBS show, *Your Universe*. He was feeling ready for work when he stepped out of the Geneva terminal and into a cab that dropped him off at his hotel. He checked in, had an eggs-and-bacon breakfast that would shock Darlene, and, after a third coffee, set out for a fifteen-minute walk to his new job, saving the world.

The massive United Nations office building spread across a hill overlooking Lake Geneva. The building dominated the 113 acres of Ariana Park, which had been bequeathed to Geneva on three conditions: that the donor be buried in the park, that it always be open to the public, and that peacocks forever roam freely on its grounds.

A peacock strolled past Taylor as he crossed the road and mounted the broad stairs of the building, once the home of the League of Nations. The building contained thirty-four conference rooms and twenty-eight hundred offices. Once it was thought that the fate of the world would be decided in this place, then grandly called the Palace of Nations. As he headed for one of those offices, he thought, *Well, fate of the world, here we go again.*

18

As usual, Ben Taylor was the first to arrive at Room 782, a standard, windowless office for middle-rank bureaucrats. The system that operated the Palace of Nations decreed that he was chairperson of his section, small as that might be. He was given two identical keys with instructions, in the six official languages of the United Nations, that he use one and keep the other in a safe place.

On a table near the door were three neat stacks of UN documents pertaining to the United Nations Treaty on Principles Governing the Activities of States in the Exploration and Use of Outer Space, Including the Moon and Other Celestial Bodies. On the wall above the table was Taylor's contribution to the sterile room: a sheet of plain paper bearing these words:

"Sooner or later human civilization must confront the asteroid/comet collision hazards or become extinct," Carl Sagan.

Next to the table was a wooden desk bearing a phone console, a reading lamp, and a pen and pencil desk set. In the center of the room was a larger table and three caned chairs. On the table before each chair was a white lined pad bearing the blue-and-white UN emblem and a yellow pencil freshly sharpened.

Taylor decided to wait for the others before opening the safe. All three knew the combination, but Taylor realized that if he opened the safe in the absence of either colleague, distrust would almost certainly enter Room 782, reflecting a world in which Russia, China, and the United States were not on the best of terms.

Taylor and his Russian and Chinese counterparts, as scientists, paid more attention to their work than they did to the political alignments of their homelands. But distrust hovered over them in this room, always threatening to strike. Without speaking about that threat, they were more cooperative than their competitive natures normally tolerated. And they shared a mission they all passionately believed in.

They had agreed at their first meeting that they would keep their work secret until their nations' leaders chose to reveal that an asteroid would probably smash into the Earth in twenty years. To ensure—and symbolize—the keeping of the secret, they had agreed that their sessions would be free of all electronic devices. There was a possibility, of course, that one, two, or all of them were secretly recording their discussions. They at least acted as if they trusted each other. Take away their nationalities and they were, at heart, scientists who had devoted their lives to space, which knew no boundaries.

Dimitri Shvernik entered next, flinging a black overcoat on the narrow table by the door. His body, clothed in a three-piece dark brown suit, was large and oblong. His hair was white and slightly wavy, neatly trimmed like his beard. He greeted Taylor with a bear hug and a loud "Good morning!"

Dimitri Shvernik was ten years old on October 4, 1957, when the Soviet Union launched Sputnik 1, the world's first artificial satellite, into low Earth orbit, stunning the world and spurring the laggard American space program. "I was determined on that day to go into space," he told Taylor when they met for the first time three years ago at a conference in Berlin. "I began studying very hard in school. Won prizes. Went to university. Became a scientist. And so forth, and so forth. But I remain on Earth."

Taylor was surprised and pleased that Shvernik had been chosen as Russia's representative. He was an acknowledged expert on satellite communications and had taken up the problem of the silent Asteroid USA. "I have a theory," he had said at the last meeting. "But I want to do a little bit more calculating before I put it on the table."

Communication with Asteroid USA would mean that the scientists could go ahead with their defense of Earth planning without getting any help from Hamilton. Taylor assumed that Hamilton was holding back information about the SpaceMine spacecraft until the Oxley administration allowed him to return to the United States without facing any criminal charges. But that was for the politicians of both countries to figure out. The three scientists were working independently of Hamilton and everyone else on the imperiled Earth.

There was a faint knock on the door. Taylor and Shvernik looked at each other and smiled. Shvernik, nearer the door, opened it and admitted Liang Mei, giving her a mild hug. She always knocked, ignoring the pleas of her colleagues. "In my country," she told them with a smile, "people always knock."

She wore black jeans and a pale green quilted coat, which she draped over one of the chairs, revealing a blue Duke sweatshirt. She was small and slim, with the quick, sure moves of a Qigong practitioner. During lulls in discussions, she often left the table and raised her arms in a slow sequence that began a Qi Gong session that ended with a hands-thrust martial pose.

"Good morning," Liang Mei said, bowing her head slightly to each man.

"*Dobroe utro,*" Shvernik said, laughing and bestowing a theatrical shrug.

"Good morning," Taylor said, impatiently adding, "Let's get started. When last we met, Dimitri had an idea hatching in his skull."

Taylor opened the safe, took out a thick black loose-leaf binder, sat down at the table, and said, "Okay, Dimitri. What've you got? Anything cosmic?"

Liang Mei always looked slightly puzzled at the start of a session, as if she had to reach into her brain for the cells that handled American speech instead of what had been known as English in her secondary school. Knowledge of the English language had been a requirement of the *Gaokao*, China's college entrance examination. It was at Duke's Kunshan University in Wuhan where she first learned how to speak the American language, a skill topped off by campus life at Stanford.

As for Shvernik, he had been formally introduced to English at Moscow State University and studied it himself, mostly from recordings, while attending the Moscow Institute of Physics and Technology. Many papers and textbooks there were studied in their original English because translations into Russian, usually supervised by security officers, were not reliable. At MIT, he learned American English. And he picked up Americanisms over the years from chatter at scientific meetings and movie DVDs. He was a fan of American crime films.

"Let's go back to the communications issue," he said. "First a little history. When our Sputnik was going around the planet like a little moon, some people didn't believe what the communists had done. But people could see it—and people could hear that *beep, beep, beep,* and—"

"Beep?" Mei asked.

"Like the sound of a bird, a little bird. Beep, beep," Shvernik said to Mei, sounding like a baritone bird. "But electronic."

"Yes. Thank you," Mei said, nodding.

"Sputnik carried two battery-powered transmitters that produced the beeps on twenty and forty megahertz. Amateur radio operators in many places heard it. It was propaganda, to prove to 'backward peasants'—as an American commentator called us then—that communists could put a satellite into orbit. Hamilton had the same idea for Asteroid USA. People all over the Earth would hear USA in Morse Code. I thought maybe that if we listened harder, we would hear that because it's so—"

"Specific?" Mei asked.

"Yes. Specific. So I asked my people to do a search for certain transmissions."

"Didn't they want to know why?" Taylor asked, fearing Shvernik's request for a test would reveal their mission.

"No. Many Russian people are not . . . curious."

"Did they come up with anything?" Taylor asked.

"I, of course, am aware, Ben, NASA is, what, do I say, 'civilian'? And not 'military.' But NASA sometimes does little missions for the boys in the Pentagon."

"I know of no such thing," Taylor said, bristling.

"Technician does hear something," Shvernik went on. "She works hard to find exact. She checks our register of American military signals. It is that. She checks to find where. Signals—military signals—were coming from what NASA says is 'space junk,' a dead communications satellite. It is a spy satellite, Ben. A spy in a junk mask. I get thanks from security officer," Shvernik said, laughing. "He thinks you told me about it."

"And did he tell you that two weeks ago Russia sent up a rocket that was supposed to carry three civilian communications satellites?"

Not waiting for Shvernik to answer, Taylor continued, "Your people did not mention a fourth object in the cargo. America calls the object 'military' and keeps it under surveillance."

"I believe," Liang Mei said quietly, "that we should discuss what we know about moving Asteroid USA. I would like to remind you of a solar sail's characteristics."

"I agree!" the men said, speaking almost in unison.

Taylor realized from Shvernik's quick response that he, too, had felt the chill of distrust. Liang Mei was right to intervene. "Thanks, Mei, for bringing us down to Earth," Taylor said, expecting smiles. Then he realized they didn't get his joke.

Both Taylor and Shvernik had doubts about solar sails, an idea that went back to Jules Verne. He realized that when photons—particles of light—strike a shiny surface, they carry energy that can act like wind pushing a ship's sail. NASA had developed a small solar sail that had spent months in low-Earth orbit. Working with data from that experiment and from her own experience, Liang Mei calculated that a solar sail could be used to move an asteroid. But the sail would have to be enormous—miles wide and miles long. And it would be difficult to control.

Mei was also looking at the possibility that a solar-sail reconnaissance craft could aid in assessing Asteroid USA once it was found. "I can see it in my mind," she said. "It could be—what is the word—a scout?"

"Right," Taylor said.

"A scout," Mei said enthusiastically. "It could get close to an asteroid and get data we aren't able to get from telescopes. Perhaps the scout would not be able to push an asteroid, but we could give it sensors and we would get a spin rate, mass, and perhaps what the asteroid is made of."

"The solar sail can't be ruled out, Mei," Taylor said. "Time is on our side. Earth has twenty years to mount a defense." *Twenty years is a long time,* Taylor thought. *But when will the politicians get started on defense of the Earth?*

19

Back in his office after Taylor's briefing, Carlton sat at his desk and stared at Frederic Remington's painting of a U.S. Cavalry trooper at the gallop on a wild-eyed horse. Sometimes he felt a kinship with this soldier, dashing to a place unknown, dispatched to his fate by duty and chance. Carlton had once been a fighter pilot, drawn to speed and sky. Then had come the desks, the Special Operations in Afghanistan, and the general stars, one by one.

He had just retired when a new President, looking beyond the CIA for a new face, had made him Director of National Intelligence, and then National Security Adviser. Now comes this mission, not as an adviser but as steward to the sovereign, hiding behind the drapes, arranging an unlawful deed.

What President Oxley had just asked for, in words unsaid, was deniability for himself and for Carlton—but not for Quinlan. If the Hamilton abduction leaked and Congress decided it was a White House operation, it would be Quinlan who would be tagged. A rogue Chief of Staff acting on his own. Oxley would take a big political hit, but it would be Quinlan who would be hauled before a congressional committee or maybe into a federal court. Oxley could be ruthless when he judged that he needed to be.

When Carlton was Director of National Intelligence, he had one customer, the President. And Carlton had lived by one maxim: It's not for me to reason why. His title had changed, but the customer and the maxim were unchanged. He decided that handing the Hamilton account to Quinlan was not enough. The account could not be managed out of the White House.

Carlton had no doubt about who should be the manager: a private citizen with a personal motive. And that would be Sean Falcone. If the operation became known, Carlton would leak a CIA report to one of his media contacts that Falcone had been obsessed by the belief that Hamilton was behind the law-firm shootings. As a private citizen, he had followed the example of Ross Perot, who in 1978 had recruited a commando team to rescue two executives from an Iranian prison.

When Carlton was Director of National Intelligence, his principal aide was a longtime CIA analyst who, as a rookie, had been asked to give her opinion about the likelihood that a KGB officer's defection was real. After poring through all that was known about the would-be defector, she had to say true or false. She had said true, and she turned out to be right: The KGB walk-in really was a defector, and he became a valuable CIA asset.

While congratulating himself for thinking of Falcone, Carlton remembered what that analyst had told him. "Luck's almost always involved in making the right call," she had said. "But make sure you're making the call for the right reasons. If you're wrong, bad luck is no excuse. But 'the right reasons' is always a good defense for a bad call."

Carlton spent an hour thinking of the steps he had to take. Usually he would have covered several sheets of a yellow pad with scrawls that evolved into an outline and timeline. For this op, there would be nothing on paper.

Carlton decided that he would have to claim "for the right reasons" if this operation exploded into what the media would unfailingly label "Moscowgate." He would obey the President and hand Quinlan the Hamilton account. But he would go beyond the presidential order for the right reason—trying to protect the President.

He picked up the phone and hit the button labeled DCI.

20

Because Frank Carlton had been the director of National Intelligence, he was one of the few people in the seventeen agencies that formed the U.S. intelligence community who knew where the DNI ended and the director of the Central Intelligence Agency began. He knew, for instance, that the DCI button on his console was inaccurate. The Intelligence Reform and Terrorism Prevention Act, signed into law by President George W. Bush in December 2004, created the DNI and abolished the position of DCI, ending the fifty-seven-year reign of the director of Central Intelligence as the nation's chief intelligence officer. (The official initial abbreviation was supposed to be D/CIA, meaning director *only* of the Central Intelligence Agency.)

In the handover briefing that Falcone had given Carlton, Falcone had told him that when he needed solid information and a dependable partner, he should turn to Sam Stone, director of the Central Intelligence Agency. Falcone had said that Stone had been his most valuable resource in the resolving of an unprecedented crisis. After a nuclear bomb had all but destroyed Savannah, powerful Washington foes of President Oxley blamed Iran and demanded war. Stone, undaunted by pseudo-facts, had rightfully insisted that Iran had not detonated the bomb. He had helped Falcone prove that the bombers were members of The Brethren, a fanatical American religious group seeking a way to bring about Armageddon.

While Carlton was DNI, he had trod carefully around Stone, even more the lone wolf after the suicide of his wife while he was in Afghanistan; childless, he had nothing in his life but the CIA. Dealing with what Oxley called "soft power" in various crises, Carlton had no need to call on Stone for special not-soft needs.

Now Carlton took Falcone's advice and called Sam Stone. "We need to meet, Sam," Carlton began. "Just you and me, no staff."

"Okay. Seven o'clock at my place," Stone said in his peculiar half-growl. "I'll grill a couple of steaks." After a moment's silence he added: "A driver will pick you up at the Old Ebbitt Grill at six thirty." Before Carlton could respond, Stone hung up.

Stone's abrupt style was well known among the relatively few people who directly dealt with him. He preferred to run the agency as if he were the foreman on a series of jobs rather than as a manager or a distant CEO. He had spent most of his career on the dark side, when the CIA's undercover missions were run by the deeply silent Directorate of Operations.

Stone was one of the first CIA officers into Afghanistan after the 9/11 attacks, the spearhead of the U.S. war on Al Qaeda and the search for Osama bin Laden. That small CIA team launched America's war against Islamic terrorists. But the daring episode was also the requiem of the Directorate of Operations, which was disbanded on the recommendation of the 9/11 Commission and replaced by the National Clandestine Service. The new unit's main purpose was to coordinate the CIA with the FBI and the other sixteen members of the intelligence community.

Largely because of the backstage work of Sam Stone and his closest associates, the dark side was retained in the form of SAD, the Special Activities Division. Sam essentially left the running of the CIA to various aides while he ran SAD. He knew that a call directly to him from Carlton was in reality a call from one veteran covert operator to another. As Stone well remembered, Carlton, then a two-star general in Air Force Special Operations, had gotten Stone and his team what they needed in the early days of what became the Afghanistan War.

The Old Ebbitt Grill called itself Washington's oldest saloon. Presidents from Andrew Johnson to Warren G. Harding had bellied up to the Ebbitt's long bar. And the jutting heads over the bar belonged to animals that reputedly had been slain by Teddy Roosevelt. The Old Ebbitt, a block from the White House and across from the Treasury building, was still a place where government workers met.

Carlton, followed by a lone Secret Service agent, left the White House grounds via an Eisenhower Executive Office Building gate and walked the length of the plaza in front of the Treasury building. They crossed Fifteenth Street to the Old Ebbitt Grill and passed through the revolving door. The antique clock over the door showed ten minutes after six. At the jammed and noisy main bar, Carlton ordered a Jameson for himself and a Coke for the agent. He rejected the offer and took up a watch near the door.

Fifteen minutes later, a man in a dark suit entered. He spotted Carlton and nodded to the Secret Service agent. Carlton gulped down the last of his drink, left money on the bar, and walked out behind his new guardian. The car entered traffic and made its way to the Fourteenth Street Bridge across the Potomac to the George Washington Memorial Parkway, then north to McLean, Virginia.

On a wall of the CIA's Visitor Control Center at the Agency's main entrance, there is a drawing of a small wooden building identified as a Union Army "Guard House Near Langley"—a reminder that Langley was the original name of this area and is still used as an insider's name for the CIA. Today Langley is an unincorporated community within McLean, Virginia, but Sam Stone says he and the CIA live in Langley. His small ranch-style home, inherited from his father, is surrounded by the mansions of McLean, the Washington area's richest community.

Sam Stone was at the door—balding, hard-eyed, fireplug physique, white shirt, sleeves rolled, tie gone, dark-blue slacks, black loafers, holding a glass—when the car swung up the driveway, deposited Carlton, reversed down the driveway, and drove off. The two men walked in silence to the kitchen, where steaks sizzled on a countertop gas grill.

"Perfect timing. Join me," Stone said, holding up his glass. "Jameson, right?"

Stone gestured to the kitchen table, where Carlton sat while Stone, glass in hand, flipped the steaks and judged them done. He put down his glass at the plate opposite Carlton's and in a series of quick motions, forked the steaks from the grill, two potatoes from the oven, and two wooden salad bowls and a bottle of ranch dressing from the refrigerator. He sat down, picked up his glass, and said, "What's on your mind?"

Carlton curbed his PowerPoint urge and simply answered, "Off the shelf."

Stone sliced off a piece of steak and said, "Okay."

Carlton, wondering if Stone's okay meant the steak or Carlton's words, continued. "I need plausible deniability and some good people."

"By good people, I assume you mean people as good as mine. But not mine."

"Right."

"Tell me about it."

Carlton plunged into a six-minute Hamilton briefing, starting with SpaceMine's silent partner Basayev, his order to murder four Americans, Hamilton's possible complicity, and Basayev's violent end aboard the *Aglaya*. He decided not to mention the 2037 asteroid arrival or the Lebed-Komov transcript about Ivan's Hammer.

Stone poured them a second drink and said, "So you want an unauthorized snatch for an American mucky-muck who you think was involved in a murder case? Pretty small fish for such a high-risk operation. You telling me everything, Frank?"

"Everything I can, Sam," Carlton said, his voice soft with acknowledged regret.

"I thought we were on the same team. Wasn't it you who used to say, 'One team, one fight'?"

"We're one team, Sam. But there are a lot of moving parts to this."

Stone thought for nearly a full minute. "Okay. I'll instruct our Moscow station chief to find out exactly where Hamilton is. And then—"

"I know where he is. Hotel Baltschug Kempinski."

Stone smiled the kind of smile that was supposed to mask anger and said, "Fucking NSA Special Collection Service. We're supposed to coordinate with those guys when they move into our space. They're like leeches, bringing their magic machines into our embassies, putting their antennas on the roof, getting diplo cover, operating all on their own. They pull down cellular signals, bug offices. And they risk our assets."

"We get good stuff sometimes from those special collectors," Carlton said defensively.

"I know. I know. And they claim they've got Lebed bugged. But everything we get from them is sanitized. Paraphrases instead of transcripts. They treat us like we're Chinese spies."

"Well, let's leave it at this: I've got the name of the hotel."

"Okay. That helps. It so happens . . . coincidentally . . . that we've got a small line on Hamilton."

"Nobody in this business believes in coincidences," Carlton said, smiling.

"Like you said, Frank. 'Lots of moving parts.' "

"Stove pipes inside of stove pipes, nothing has changed. . . . What have your boys got?"

"An Orthodox bishop—he hates Lebed—is one of our Moscow assets. He's spent a little time with Hamilton, who turns out to be an enthusiast of The End Time."

"I've heard that about him," Carlton said, tempted to add more about Hamilton's asteroid. He resisted the temptation.

"Our bishop also told his case officer that Hamilton had evil eyes."

"Sounds like my awful brother-in-law," Carlton said.

"No, really. The officer put it in her report. Evil eyes. The bishop said he had seen eyes like that only once before, when he was a young priest and he walked a serial killer to his execution."

"I wonder how many other American billionaires are psychopaths," Carlton remarked. "Well, I guess it's better to have him in our hands."

"I agree," Stone said. "But my instinct is to keep my station chief in Moscow out of this. So we also would get the deniability you're setting up. And I've got to tell you. Snatches never go off as planned. Never."

"Any ideas?"

"Global Special Services," Stone replied.

"There's no need my telling you what you already know," Carlton said. "Ever since I succeeded Sean Falcone, I've used them a couple of times. But Sean didn't like going into the dark world."

"I know that about Sean. He's a damn good man. Trustworthy. Smart. But he was sometimes too much the lawyer," Stone said.

"I could have gone to GSS myself," Carlton said. "But I thought I'd touch base with you to make sure you think they're still okay."

"GSS is still very quiet, very dark. Some powerful money behind them. And we slip enough dough to them to help keep them solvent. They'll give you deniability. I'll make a very careful call to General Drexler. From what I know, I can attest that he's clean and okay for use. Unless I hear otherwise from you, I'll get him working on it. Give it a couple of days. Drexler's outfit can move a helluva lot faster than our so-called intelligence community."

"Thanks, Sam. You're the man," Carlton said, raising his glass.

"Who's going to be running this?" Stone asked. "I assume not you."

"Right. I can't be sure who'll run it until I get his acceptance. Then I'll give you the name."

"Okay. I don't need the name to get this rolling. Give me three days. Now dig in. The potatoes are getting cold."

21

Carlton began the process of getting the right man by calling Quinlan. As usual, Quinlan did not answer. He treated his telephone console as a relic. At the age of thirty-six, he had brought to the West Wing his generation's disdain for the landline telephone. He saw the smartphone as a pocketed bearer of apps and an indicator of status, and incidentally as a device for communication.

Quinlan picked up for POTUS, of course, and for most Cabinet members. Depending upon his mood and his interest in what Congress was doing, he usually picked up for calls from the majority leader of the Senate and the Speaker of the House. He also was likely to pick up a call from his harried assistant, who risked a profanity-peppered outburst if she called him for any reason less than what he deemed important.

The President nearly always picked up a call from Carlton, but the national security adviser had not yet gained pickup status with Quinlan. Carlton, however, did rate a personal and fairly prompt callback. So two minutes after Carlton called, his phone rang and CHIEF OF STAFF appeared in the identifier slot.

"What's up?" Quinlan asked, in an undertone that carried a sense of interruption and an urgent need to get back to some vital task.

"It's about what we were briefed on," Carlton replied.

"When?" Quinlan asked, now sounding irritated.

"Immediately," Carlton said, hanging up to prevent any dickering over where to meet. Five minutes later, Quinlan appeared in Carlton's office.

"What the hell is this about?" Quinlan asked.

Carlton pointed to a chair in front of his desk. Quinlan, frowning, slumped into it.

"There has been one White House conversation on this matter," Carlton began, leaning back in his chair. "It was between the President and me. This is the second conversation. There will be no more."

Quinlan looked as if he were about to speak, but he remained silent.

"The President believes that Robert Wentworth Hamilton's presence in Russia is an existential threat to the United States," Carlton said. "Hamilton must be removed from Moscow."

Again, Quinlan looked as if he was about to speak. Carlton held up his hand, traffic-cop style.

"This conversation has two parts," Carlton continued in an even voice. "I've told you of the President's belief about Hamilton." Carlton stood, walked to the door, closed it, and returned to his chair. "Now we get to the second part. It's between you and me, Ray. The President has no knowledge of what I am going to say. I am going to tell you what you are to do, and—"

"Wait one fuckin' minute, Frank," Quinlan said, half-rising from his chair. "I work for the President, not the National Security Council."

"I am going to tell you what you are to do, Ray," Carlton repeated, lowering his voice. "That is all there is to it. I am in charge of making something happen and also making sure that the President is not involved. It's called deniability."

Quinlan frowned but nodded. He was beginning to see that this was not a routine West Wing conversation.

"Look, Frank," Quinlan said. "I'm just a guy the President found on Capitol Hill and decided to make his chief of staff. I've never been involved in black ops. I just—"

"Here it is, Ray. I am setting something in motion. The President wants you to play a role in it. If you do not do what I am going to tell you to do, your only alternative is resignation. It will be for reasons that will not be disclosed, but I assure you that you will be secretly smeared so that you'll not get any invitations for any jobs or even a publisher for your memoir. I hope you understand this, Ray."

Quinlan's mouth opened and shut, but he remained speechless, as if he could not summon the words for a response.

Carlton waited for a moment, then went on: "This is an off-the-grid operation. You are being made aware of it because that is what I want, and I represent the President. No one else will become aware of this except the man I am going to ask you to call. I am going to give you a telephone number. Do not write it down. Tell the man to call that number. Here is the number: eight zero zero five five five seven eight two zero."

Carlton repeated the number slowly and asked Quinlan to repeat it.

Quinlan recited the number the way a sullen high school student would recite the first line of Hamlet's soliloquy. Then he asked, "Do I have the right to know whose number is that?"

"No. All I can tell you is that I got this number from a person with whom I have had dealings over the years. I trust him and the man at this number. I trust you will do what I tell you to do. And I trust the man to whom you must give the number."

"Okay. Who is the man? Christ, I've got to at least know his name."

"Sean Falcone."

Quinlan sprang from his chair. "Falcone? Is this some kind of fuckin' joke?" he said loudly.

"He is the best man for the job."

"You're shitting me! Falcone?"

"What have you got against him? Jesus, after what he sacrificed for his country!"

"Frank, you've been drinking too much of Falcone's Kool-Aid. He's been trading off hero status for way too long."

"Didn't know there was a time-limit on patriotism."

"Gimme a break. The press has sucked up to him ever since he got out of a Vietnam jail."

"That was no jail. It was a goddamn torture chamber. But I still don't get it. What did he ever do to you?"

"Nothing. I just don't like him. He's not a team player. He never contributed to either one of Oxley's campaigns. Not a dime. And he didn't even endorse him for the presidency. And he gets to be national security adviser? How many of our guys did he screw out of a big-time job?"

"He was the best man . . . person . . . for the job. And you know it."

"There were better picks, Frank. Much better. And when things got too rough, what did he do? He bailed."

"He resigned after six years. How many advisers have stayed on that job for that long?"

"I'm still here. And he should be here."

"If you've got someone else in mind, give me the name. The clock is running."

"Maybe you're right," Quinlan said. "Falcone should be the go-to guy on this. If it works out, no one knows. If it goes south, he gets the blame. Okay. Bring your buddy in on this. But, Frank, if he fucks it up, you're going to go down with him. And President Oxley has no idea what you're up to. I believe—"

"I don't give a goddamn what you believe," Carlton cut in. "Let me make this as clear as I can, Ray. I am designing this op— . . . this matter . . . so that if Congress or the Department of Justice ever decides to inquire, they will find Falcone. He takes the fall. He'll realize that you were carrying a message from me, although you will not name me. He'll understand that what he is being asked to do is important to the President. And he'll know that deniability is essential."

"Message carrier," Quinlan sputtered. "I'm supposed to be a fuckin' message carrier."

"No, Ray," Carlton shot back "You are part of a plan to protect the President. You and me. Please repeat the number."

Quinlan did, in his now exaggerated surly tone.

"Fine. Take a walk to Lafayette Park," Carlton said, opening his desk drawer, and removed a clamshell cell phone. "Use this to call Falcone so that, if the shit ever hits the fan, we can honestly say the call did not come from the White House. When you meet, give him this phone and tell him to dispose of it after he makes the call to that number. And tell him exactly this: 'Remove the man from where he is.'"

22

When Carlton succeeded Falcone as national security adviser, Falcone had warned Carlton: "You have to politely inform the President that direct access is a condition of your taking the job, just as it was for me." Oxley readily gave Carlton what he wanted.

Quinlan was outraged that Falcone had passed the direct-access baton to Carlton. Quinlan had had little to do with Falcone in the White House. He marked Falcone's departure by putting him on the Quinlan enemies list, which even included some members of the Cabinet. Men and women in the West Wing may have served at the pleasure of the President. But they might not serve very long at the displeasure of Ray Quinlan.

Falcone was in his office on the top floor of a gleaming ten-story building of steel and glass at the foot of Capitol Hill. He was chief executive partner of one of the world's largest law firms, Sullivan & Ford, soon to be Sullivan, Ford & Falcone. The firm had more than four thousand lawyers in offices throughout the world. Clients included more than half of the names on the Fortune 100 list of the world's leading corporations.

When Falcone's executive assistant, Ursula Breitsprecher, did not answer by the third ring, Falcone knew that in her console phone's caller ID slot she had seen a name or number that he would want to answer personally. He saw no ID on his console, and he wondered if this was coming from what he knew as a disappearing phone. On the day he became national security adviser, a polite young man from the NSA had dropped by his office, given him five such phones, and told him they were untraceable. He remembered bequeathing three phones to Carlton.

Falcone picked up his console phone and said, "Falcone here."

"This is Ray Quinlan."

"Ray!" he said. "What a surprise."

"For me, too, Sean," Quinlan said from his bench in Lafayette Park. "I need to see you. Four o'clock in the bar at The Hay-Adams." He closed the phone and returned to the White House.

Falcone told Ursula he would be leaving shortly for the day and asked her to call a town car. She came into his office to report that the car would be out front in ten minutes. He knew that she could have told him that on the intercom. But he realized that she wanted a moment in his presence. There was a bond between him and her, a boss and his assistant, and it had always been business only. They knew a lot about each other from personnel files: birthdates; for both of them, blanks in the *next of kin* line; in his file *widower*, which he preferred over *unmarried;* for her the choice was *unmarried*, he thought now, glancing up, his eyes meeting hers.

She was as slim and elegant as she was when the Berlin Wall fell and she was a teenaged ballerina in the Leipzig Ballet. She had traveled alone to what had been West Germany and called an aunt who invited her to Philadelphia. She learned English, worked her way through the University of Pennsylvania by teaching dancing, and married a graduate student. They went to Washington, where both of them found jobs at the Environmental Protection Agency. In a couple of years they had drifted apart and agreed to divorce. He passed the Foreign Service examination and began a State Department career; she registered with a staffing agency that specialized in placing smart non-lawyers in law firms. All Falcone knew about her love life was the office rumor that she was having an affair with a South Carolina congressman. He found himself wondering if that was still going on.

They smiled at each other, each one wondering why, when in fact there was nothing to smile about.

Falcone closed the thick yellow folder on his large mahogany desk, embellished with lion's heads and knightly emblems. Ten minutes later he was emerging from the Sullivan & Ford Building and getting in his regular town car.

He decided to get to The Hay-Adams a little early to think about what the hell Ray Quinlan—presumably President Oxley—wanted. He knew that North Korea's little man had sunk another South Korean coastal patrol ship, and serious saber rattling was underway in Seoul. China was causing trouble again over the Senkaku Islands, the Japanese name that President Oxley preferred. But he knew little more about that issue than what he read in the *New York Times* and the *Washington Post*. And he didn't think this was a crisis beyond what Carlton and Oxley could handle. Carlton seemed to be a solid man, as Falcone's Irish mother used to sing: "As I walk the street, each friend I meet says, 'There goes Muldoon—he's a solid man.'"

When, as a kid, he asked her who she was singing about, she said, "A man like your father. His folks may come from Italy. But he's a solid man." And that became Falcone's standard for who to trust, who to help, who to be. A solid man.

Maybe there was a need to get another voice into the White House debate over how to handle the current crisis. But that would be a call to an old China hand or some former ambassador to Japan. That couldn't be why Quinlan called; a call like that would come from Carlton. *So what can this be about?* Falcone thought. *And on a disappearing phone.* A moment after that thought, *Hamilton?* flashed through his mind. But, as far as he knew, Quinlan had not been read into the Hamilton matter, as his lawyerly mind phrased it.

Quinlan's choice for the meeting was a bar beneath the elegant lobby of The Hay-Adams. The bar tried to live up to its name, Off the Record—a recognition of Washington geography: From the plush, low-lit bar to the White House was a brisk nine-minute walk across Lafayette Square. Although some journalists went there to hear politicians and agenda pushers hold forth off or on the record, the bar had a tradition of discretion, symbolized by its underground location.

Falcone decided to wait at the bar instead of in a booth. He ordered a Grey Goose vodka and remembered how he had met his predecessor here on his first day as national security adviser. And now he was having another drink with a guy who hated his guts. Well, that's Washington. Where Harry Truman said you could only trust your dog.

Quinlan came in and sat with his back to the red-velvet wall at the two-person table farthest from the door. Falcone picked up his glass, walked over, and took the seat opposite Quinlan. A red-vested waiter promptly appeared and Quinlan ordered a Yuengling draft.

As the waiter walked away, Quinlan said, "I've got something to give you. I can't tell you who got me into this. But he thinks you will guess who sent me. First, I guess I should thank you for meeting on short notice."

"You are more than welcome, Ray," Falcone said. Knowing there was no point in chatting, he added, "What's going on?"

Quinlan splayed his hands on the table, looked down at them, then raised his eyes to Falcone, and said, "I'm supposed to give you a phone number to call and you take it from there."

"A phone call to whom?" Falcone asked.

"The phone number comes from someone who figures that you will know," Quinlan replied. "He says . . . Christ, Sean. I'm not good at this cloak-and-dagger shit. The guy with the unmentionable name, the guy who said you would guess the identity of, told me to give you a phone number to call."

Falcone nodded. "Okay, Ray, I kind of understand. This is a setup that has little to do with you and a lot to do with me. When I was national security adviser, I had a couple of situations like this one."

Quinlan, looking relieved, said, "I know I've been a pain in the ass to you, Sean. But here we are. Somehow, Carlton—hell, you know it's Carlton, right?—Carlton says this is helping the President. But—"

"I've got an idea," Falcone interrupted. "Let me tell you. I assume that the word 'deniability' came up when you were told to give me a phone number. I also assume that if I take that number, I am taking the whole thing. Right?"

"I guess so, Sean. This is a new thing to me."

"Well, not to me, Ray. My guess is that it involves Hamilton."

"I think so," Quinlan said. "I just got briefed—by your buddy Taylor. And Carlton said Hamilton is in Moscow, and—"

"Hold it, Ray. Don't talk about it. I know the background."

Over Falcone's shoulder Quinlan saw the waiter coming back and said "Thank you" when the waiter placed the glass of beer on a coaster. It had a cartoon of a donkey and an elephant trying to wrest a gavel from each other.

Quinlan took a sip, put down his glass, and said, "Sean. I don't know what the hell I'm getting into. Carlton and I got the asteroid briefing together. Jesus! A killer asteroid! But there are secrets inside secrets. I'm sure Carlton knows more—much more—than I do."

"That's just as well, Ray. Just give me the phone number, finish your beer, and that will be it."

Quinlan took out a pen from his shirt pocket and wrote 800 555 7820 on the back of the coaster. "Oh," he said, "and I'm supposed to give you this"—he took the cell phone from his pocket—"and you're supposed to get rid of it. And I was to tell you exactly this: 'Remove the man from where he is.'"

"Okay. Thank you, Ray. I think you've done something damn important."

"What have I done?"

"When they write the history of this time, Ray, they'll say that President Oxley saved the world. And you helped."

23

Quinlan left first. Both men knew that there was no point in leaving together and perhaps inspiring chatter about mysterious doings in the notoriously secretive Oxley White House. Falcone lingered for a few minutes and then walked up the stairs, rapidly crossed the lobby, and got out the front door before the doorman reached it, relieved to see no one he recognized. He was in no mood for small talk.

He decided to walk to his Pennsylvania Avenue apartment, mulling over exactly what he was getting himself into—again.

As soon as he entered his penthouse suite, he loosened his tie, stripped off his suit jacket, and, carrying it over his right arm, went into the kitchen. He pulled a chilled martini glass from the refrigerator and headed for a well-stocked bar in the living room. He poured a double vodka, draped his suit jacket over the headrest of an Eames lounge chair, and sat down.

Once again Oxley was dragging him back into government service. This time, though, there'd be no one to protect him or back him up. Out on a limb in the dark. He'd been there many times before. But this was different.

Oxley. He was always an all-take-and-no-give man. He was the President and always the smartest guy in the room. Everybody owed him their absolute fealty and respect. He demanded it as an entitlement. Nothing ever bounced back. Nothing ever shook his self-confidence, a character trait that one pundit called his egotistical self-absorption. Others just considered him arrogant.

In politics, there's a price to be paid for hubris and conceit. Oxley's party had been pummeled in the most recent national elections. The losses were unprecedented. The public wanted to bring Oxley down to earth-bound levels. And while he wasn't on the ballot, those politically affiliated with him were. In voting against them, people were voting against him.

Most of Oxley's cabinet officials were bailing out of a sinking ship, to the surprise of Oxley, who expected everyone to go down with him. He insisted on loyalty, but he had shown none to others.

And now this, whatever it was.

Falcone assumed that the mission had something to do with Hamilton. A couple of days ago he had received a call from Akis Christakos, who asked for the Sullivan & Ford files on Hamilton.

"Christo, what's up?" he now remembered asking.

"This is just a routine change-of-counsel request, Sean," Christakos had said, his tone suggesting that he wanted to stay lawyer-to-lawyer within professional bounds.

"How about lunch?" Falcone asked.

"Not for a while, Sean. Lot to do."

"Okay," Falcone said, surprised by the turn-off from the usually ebullient Christakos. "As you might expect, Christo, some of the files are in FBI hands. Hamilton's original attorney was Paul Sprague, who resigned. He mostly handled SpaceMine matters. The FBI also took Harold Davidson's files. As you know, Hal was killed in the shootings here."

"I'm well aware of all that, Sean. Just send me whatever you have that refers to Mr. Hamilton as a Sullivan & Ford client."

"Sure thing, Christo. Hope to see you soon," Falcone said. He had been tempted to make a crack about the way Hamilton ran through lawyers. But he realized that Christakos was in no mood for levity.

A short time later, a messenger had arrived and Falcone signed off on the transfer of the Hamilton files.

Hamilton. **Falcone drank deeply** and felt an immediate sensation of heat filling his throat and moving up into his head. Picking up a remote control, he flipped on the sound system that was already keyed to his favorite iTunes album by Enigma. The band's name seemed particularly appropriate at this moment. Secretive. Shadowy. Mysterious. The allure of a hypnotic melody pulling him into the dark, into what was most likely to be an impossible and probably disastrous mission.

Hamilton. Last I heard he was in Moscow, Falcone thought, going back over what he knew and what he suspected about an operation that was supposed to give Oxley deniability. *What did Oxley hope to do once he got Hamilton back? Put him on trial for murder? Give him a full pardon? Tell the world that Hamilton had put a large asteroid on a collision course with Earth? Or maybe it would be on a course that would end with a big hole in the United States. Maybe Oxley was thinking about the end of the world—and how that would work out for him.*

The questions and the wicked thoughts about Oxley continued to drop into Falcone's mind like crows on fresh road kill. *"Remove the man from where he is."* Just like that. *"Remove the man from where he is."*

Falcone had been involved with some rendition operations in Nigeria and Somalia. Special Forces men and women worked with the CIA on some of the renditions. *By now a lot of them have retired,* he thought. *And the private security guys with that kind of ops experience are pretty much out of work since we've pulled almost everybody out of Iraq and Afghanistan.*

Finally, he decided he would call Quinlan and tell him, *"No dice. Get some other damn fool to carry out a mission impossible. . . ."*

Falcone finished off what was left of his drink and returned to the bar to replenish it. On his way back to the chair, he glanced at the photograph of Karen and Kyle and felt a familiar wave of darkness coming. He had abandoned them when he went off to Vietnam to satisfy what he claimed was his patriotic duty, knowing that he was just as much going to war to satisfy some primordial blood lust for combat. And they died and were buried while he was caged and beaten in a sweltering hellhole. A tragic accident. They became just another highway statistic.

While most Americans treated him and his fellow POWs as heroes, Karen's parents were cool, distant. They blamed him for not being there to protect their only child and grandson. It wasn't fair, but there was no way Falcone could lighten their grief and resentment. Besides, he shared their assessment of guilt.

Falcone rarely drank anything but strong black coffee before nightfall. In fact, his doctor warned him that his normal ten cups a day were the reason he couldn't sleep more than a few hours at night. He was overtaxing his heart, and one day, its thump would go silent.

But what was he to do? He needed the caffeine to keep a mental and physical edge. And the hour-long workouts—sometimes twice a day— gave him a clarity of mind and indefinable sense of well-being. So he was fit. But for what?

Or so he tried to rationalize. Falcone knew that a deeper reason than fitness compelled him to burn up calories and unwanted pounds. Activity, even if inefficient, prevented him from being alone with his thoughts, with himself.

Relaxing with vodka in his hand, he inevitably felt the fall of the barrier that warded off introspection. The years in Hanoi's prison had given him too much time alone, too much time to think about the choices he'd made, or those that had been made for him before he entered an unforgiving world.

In that world, he managed to live with his contradictions. Once he had been a public man living behind the facade of an engaging and empathetic leader, a man reflecting the very best of what Americans cherished and demanded. Ironic, he thought, how he and President Oxley each possessed this essential political ingredient. But there the similarity ended. Oxley was never given to self-doubt. He was never haunted by the ghosts of his past. Maybe those who lived charmed lives never had any ghosts. . . .

Behind Falcone's facade of optimism and confidence, which he frequently flashed for public consumption and reassurance, hid a man who carried a lifetime of concealed regrets in a pin-striped rucksack.

He knew that guilt can hide inside a man, lurking somewhere in the corners of consciousness, floating like smoke in the darkness, sometimes causing him to lose a line of thought, pulling him away from a momentary state, not of happiness, but of grace. Guilt was Falcone's inner companion that refused to leave. He had abandoned his wife and child in the call of service to his country.

Even in prison, his patriotism had trumped his survival. He had been part of a spy network—a fact that had been kept secret for forty years after the war. Sending intel back through microdots in letters. Admiral Jim Stockdale ran it right under the noses of the guards. Prisoners sent coded messages in their letters home, risking execution as spies. Information in the letters—such as recommended bombing targets and plans for escape—preserved the captives' sense of service to their country. Then one day he had no one to write to, no one to get letters from. . . .

What a waste it had all been: all the killing—the slaughter of innocents who had no role in the stratagems of those who had unleashed the dogs of war. For this Falcone had survived years of torture and solitary confinement. But what of the anguish, the cries from those families who would never see their sons again? All of them wiped away with a diplomatic eraser, as if they never existed, never bled in a land they never knew, in a war they never asked for.

Melancholia was the mood he tried to ward off with sheer motion. But it was back now, nagging him, taunting him with self-doubt. Just what was he getting into? Frank Carlton had to have set this up and used Quinlan as the messenger to signal that this was a presidential decision—unspoken, unrecorded. But a decision, nevertheless.

So he was being asked to serve President Blake Oxley once again—and, officially, the President would never know what Falcone had done. But how long were they going to keep asking him to do something for his country, anything for his country, everything for his country?

He went back to the kitchen, took the phone Quinlan had given him out of his jacket pocket, and started to punch in Quinlan's number. But he abruptly stopped and put the phone in his pocket. He stepped out onto his balcony and for a long time stared at the statue below of the Lone Sailor. Off on a new venture or just back from a long one? Falcone never could tell. No one could. He was just out there standing at the edge of the Earth that had been etched into the Navy Memorial's stone palazzo.

And me, Sailor. What exactly do I have to look forward to at this point in my life? Counseling well-heeled clients on some merger or acquisitions deal? Advise a corporate giant on how to secure an exemption from the latest Chinese effort to stifle competition?

He drained his glass and stepped back into the apartment. He knew what he had to do. He went to the kitchen and took the phone that Quinlan had given him, along with the coaster that had 800 555 7820 written on the back.

24

After one ring, a soft female voice answered: "You have reached 800 555 7820. You have been recognized and given the name 'Chamberlain.' We are prepared to meet you tomorrow. Please expect to stay overnight. If this is acceptable, you will be picked up at your residence at seven a.m. If this is not acceptable, hang up, dial the number again, and ask for another appointment in the name Chamberlain. Thank you." *Click.*

Falcone stood for a moment, the phone in his hand. *Chamberlain:* A clear sign that this outfit—whatever its name—knew him quite well. When he had traveled overseas during his time as national security adviser, he had picked Chamberlain as his code name. Falcone admired Joshua Chamberlain, whose decision to charge and rout the Confederate forces at Little Round Top led to the Union victory in Gettysburg.

He stomped on the phone, which shredded into a half-dozen shards, then picked up the pieces and extracted the subscriber identification module, the heart of the phone. He went to the sink, turned on the water, switched on the garbage disposal, and dropped in the postage-stamp-size SIM chip. Then he cracked the shards into smaller pieces, wrapped them in paper towels and walked around, dropping the packets into different wastepaper containers, which the housekeeper would empty.

He next went to the kitchen phone and called Ursula, who never was without her cell phone.

"Yes?" The word of greeting that she preferred over "Hello."

"Ursula, I'm going to compose a letter of resignation and email it to you on your private email tonight. It will have my regular email signature," he said. He knew there was no need to tell her to keep it secret; she routinely kept everything secret.

"Yes," she said, this time without the question mark.

She's in the I-not-to-reason-why club, too, he thought as he continued: "I want you to hold it. If you do not hear otherwise from me within ten days from tomorrow, please release it to the senior partners. They'll take it from there."

"I shall resign also," she said with an emotional tone that surprised Falcone.

Falcone was touched and said, "Please, Ursula. The firm will need you more than ever. You're the brains, the memory of the firm. Besides, I'm just being overly cautious. You'll be hearing from me. Don't worry."

"I will worry, sir. I will worry. . . . I assume this means you will not be in tomorrow."

"Right."

"I was about to call you," Ursula continued. "Akis Christakos called at seven fifteen on my cell phone. He said it was urgent."

"Christo says everything is urgent," Falcone said. "Tell him I'm tied up in a case and will get back to him as soon as I can. He'll be mad, but that can't be helped."

"Very well. And good luck."

"Thanks, Ursula. And don't worry."

"Sorry, Sean. But I must worry. Goodbye."

Never before had she called him Sean.

Next morning, precisely at seven, the concierge called Falcone to say that his driver from Global Special Services was in the foyer. Falcone emerged from the elevator a few minutes later. A large man in black jeans and a black leather jacket led him out the door. He did not offer to carry Falcone's overnight bag, showing he was an experienced bodyguard who always wanted his two hands free.

At the curb was a black SUV with Virginia plates, motor throbbing. *Global Special Services,* Falcone thought. *A private little army for the real dirty work.*

A second man, who could have been a twin of the driver, sat in the front passenger's seat. "This will be a drive of approximately two hours and twenty-five minutes, sir," the driver said. Neatly piled next to Falcone were the day's *Washington Post, New York Times,* and *Wall Street Journal.*

He picked up the *Journal,* scanned the headlines, then put it aside and leaned back, savoring liberation from the oppressive density of Washington, and the machinations and schemes of low-brow, ambitious power players. Washington was no longer a place for the elite, the cultural intelligentsia bearing degrees from Harvard, Yale, and other academic waterholes for the rich. After-dinner deals, brokered by cigar-chomping committee chairmen in the homes of media moguls, had been relegated to the ink of cartoonists long ago.

But change and progress aren't synonymous. Those who came riding into the city on white horses during the past decade were not sent to repair the city but to destroy and tear it down so that usurped power could be returned to states. The irony, lost on the champions of change, was that the problems plaguing us were global but the politics were all parochial, too small to do anything about the existential threats heading our way.

Falcone's gloom began to fade as the SUV left Washington suburbia behind and headed for a country highway. Winter was officially only a few weeks away, yet the weather continued to defy predicted drops in temperature. Many of the trees rippling by along the country highway displayed leaves that refused to bow to the calendar. There was a clarity, a freshness that lifted Falcone's spirit and caused him to forget thoughts that weighed on him like stones.

"Where are we heading?" Falcone asked.

"Southern Virginia, sir," the driver said.

"*Where* in Virginia?" Falcone asked.

"Near Williamsburg," the driver replied. Falcone recognized the two words as a kind of covert address. He began remembering a trip he took by White House helicopter while he was national security adviser. The travel log in his office would show that he had gone to Colonial Williamsburg, the living museum of patriotic life in eighteenth-century America. Actually, he had spent the day a few miles away, at the Armed Forces

Experimental Training Activity, commonly called Camp Peary but known to the CIA as The Farm. Operatives in the National Clandestine Service, the dark side of the agency, were among the CIA men and women trained at The Farm. It was also the remote, no-questions-asked site for highly secret rehearsals of missions involving Special Forces teams.

When Falcone had served as a United States senator and national security adviser, he had often been driven to The Farm. He particularly remembered a visit with Frank Carlton when he was commander of Air Force Special Operations, his stepping-stone to director of National Intelligence. Carlton had proudly shown him the high spots, including an obstacle course that reminded Falcone of the Army Ranger training he had gone through during the Vietnam War. A briefing officer had introduced Falcone to a hard-eyed SEAL who led a team heading for Somalia under a mission with "lethal findings," the delicate phrase for a killing authorized by the President.

Now Falcone was going to the headquarters of Global Special Services, which had chosen a location that was, in his mind, a little too close to Camp Peary for legal comfort. Proximity to an official federal site just about advertised GSS's closeness to the U.S. government. GSS was one of the private security firms that had sprung up in the wake of the Afghan and Iraq wars and recruited veterans of Army and Navy Special Forces.

But this one, he knew, had real connections, which was why Carlton had steered him to it. GSS specialized in off-the-shelf "special missions," the ones that needed no presidential authorization, no notice to Congress, no scrutiny by White House lawyers. And offered the gift of deniability.

The last time Falcone had been involved in such operations, he was a senator investigating how President Reagan could possibly have authorized one. It became known as the Iran-Contra scandal—the U.S. government's secret sale of arms to Iran, then at war with Iraq, with the payments from the sale going to the Contra rebels fighting Nicaragua's communist regime.

As far as Falcone and other congressional critics were concerned, motivations didn't matter and good intent wasn't an excuse for breaking the law. It was the law in which we trusted, not the declaration stamped on our currency. And yet, here he was on his way to carrying out a mission that was outside the law he had sworn to uphold. He'd be no better than the brigands he used to chastise.

The critic was about to become a conspirator.

25

After passing the exit for Williamsburg, the SUV traveled about ten miles along a farm road, then turned onto a secondary road leading east, toward the York River. The road narrowed like a sharpened pencil until two cars barely had enough room to pass each other.

At a gated checkpoint was a small building constructed of stone and what Falcone presumed was bulletproof glass. Two men with automatic weapons signaled the SUV to stop. They wore black visored caps bearing the GSS diamond logo, and what soldiers call BDUs—battle dress uniforms—over armored-vest bulges. But these BDUs were black rather than the U.S. Army camouflage pattern. While they lifted their weapons and aimed them at the SUV, a woman in a well-tailored BDU stepped out of the gatehouse carrying a mirror on a pole. She checked the underside of the vehicle, leaned the pole against a fender, and pressed a smartphone-size device against the laminated identifications handed to her by the driver and his partner.

The window next to Falcone lowered and she leaned in. She was blue-eyed and did not cover her short blond hair with a cap. She aimed her handheld device at Falcone's right eye, and, satisfied that his iris matched the image in her database, nodded to the driver. As soon as she entered the gatehouse and the two men stepped aside, the steel gate opened and the SUV rolled under a sign made with the words *Freedom Land* formed in twisted black metal. It reminded Falcone of those signs that greeted all who entered the Nazi concentration camps: *Arbeit macht frei,* Work Makes You Free. . . .

The vehicle bounded down a rutted dirt road, a warning to visitors that life beyond the gate was not intended to be gentle. They turned into a long, tree-lined drive that passed between the brick gate posts and ended at the pebbly circular driveway of a perfectly restored plantation mansion. On the columned veranda waiting to greet him was Harold William Drexler, ramrod-straight in a pair of neatly pressed chinos, white shirt, red-and-blue striped tie, and a blue blazer. Drexler still looked every bit the stone-jawed military officer he had once been.

Harold William Drexler was little known outside the world of secret deeds and undeclared little wars. He had risen to the rank of U.S. Army Lieutenant General in that world only to fall after a scandal that was, as he put it, little bigger that a pimple on a gnat's ass: A whistleblower claimed that Drexler had allowed his wife to travel with him aboard military aircraft when there was no official function that required her presence. A British prime minister once said, "A scandal may amount to a tempest in a teacup. But in politics, we sail in paper boats."

Drexler thought the charge was pure horseshit and was quoted as saying so (with four letters turned to dashes) in the *New York Times*. Recriminations followed, all petty in the scheme of things. This was a man who had gone toe-to-toe, mano a mano in a knife fight with Abu al Zakari, one of the most sadistic of terrorists in Western Africa, and had nearly cut him in half. But past heroics were irrelevant. His wife should not have been granted transportation on a military aircraft. Rules were rules, the hidebound Army declared.

Drexler had said, "Fuck it. Take the stars and shove them where the sun don't shine." He retired rather than accept a public reprimand.

On the day he retired he received several calls on his unlisted and encrypted cell phone from prominent officials of what President Eisenhower described as the military-industrial complex. The callers from the industrial axis of the complex did more than sympathize with Drexler. They put him on their boards, employed him as a consultant and an unregistered lobbyist, and finally financed his own entry into the complex via Global Special Services, a small private army.

Drexler's feats in special operations were legendary. While credited with a number of major combat operations against Al Qaeda, he operated in the shadows and back alleys of unconventional warfare. He was no moth drawn to the media's tantalizing flame. In fact, he forbade all attempts to interview him, and his photograph never appeared on the cover of popular magazines. Those who lived in the cruel and violent world of counter-terrorism treated celebrityhood like an Ebola virus.

Drexler had aged well since Falcone had first met him. His hair, always severely cut to reflect his military profession, had thinned, but not to the untrained eye. Although his waist was not as muscled as it once was, he looked every bit as menacing and in command as he did five years earlier when Falcone attended the ceremony marking his promotion to a three-star Army General.

And here he was now, still in charge, still in command of a cadre of skilled operatives who, Falcone surmised, could kill upon a whispered signal. Drexler and his comrades no longer had anything to lose.

Drexler hurriedly descended the stairs to greet Falcone. "Sean. Long time," he said, embracing Falcone with a chest bump.

"Five years at least, Drex," Falcone said, embarrassed that he had never called to offer support to Drexler or to condemn the miserable way the Army had treated him.

"You've been busy. A nuke in Savannah. And a mass murder at your law firm," Drexler said.

"Yeah. The gods seem to have it in for me."

"Gods?" Drexler said, pausing on the stairs, looking down at Falcone. "You think there's more than one?"

Falcone knew better than to trade barbs on religious matters with Drexler, a Christian fundamentalist. "I don't think a lot about things these days," Falcone said.

"Maybe if you did, you wouldn't have so many problems," Drexler said, opening the broad white front door and motioning Falcone inside.

"You're probably right," Falcone said, surprised when he instantly realized that his offhanded response veiled a deep feeling of discontent.

Drexler led Falcone through the entrance hall and up the curving staircase to a wide landing and through the open door of what was obviously

Drexler's office. A fire was burning in a stone fireplace that stood nearly seven feet high. Falcone walked over to the fireplace and held out his hands.

"Maybe not enough chill for a fire," Drexler said. "But I like the sound. Besides, these bones need a little warmth." It was Drexler's way of confessing that after a career of absorbing physical pain, he suffered from arthritis.

"Okay by me. And, by the way, I have a few more miles on you. So I understand what you're saying."

Drexler went to his desk and motioned Falcone toward a chair between the fireplace and Drexler's high-backed leather chair. On the wall behind his desk was a plaque bearing these words in the kind of pseudo–Old English lettering that Falcone connected with the Bible or outdoor church signs:

> The oath of office is an individual covenant with Almighty God, from which no man can be released by un-Constitutional actions, orders, or decisions.
>
> **—MAJOR GENERAL EDWIN WALKER**

"You know, Sean. I have often seen people 'looking askance' in novels," Drexler said, laughing. "I think that might be just what you're doing right now."

"You're damn right, Drex," Falcone said, pointing to the plaque. "It does make me wonder—"

"About me?" Drexler asked, still laughing. "Don't worry. Many of my conservative clients—and those are most of my clients these days—feel comfortable in front of General Walker's words. But I'd bet they really don't know who the hell he is."

"President Kennedy fired him for insubordination," Falcone said.

"No, Sean. Kennedy formally admonished him after he told his troops how to vote and called Franklin Roosevelt and Harry Truman pinkos. No, Walker resigned. Like me."

"As I remember," Falcone said, "Oswald took a shot at him once."

Drexler nodded and said, "Yeah. Sometimes even generals get shot at.

Keeps them on their toes." He leaned forward and abruptly changed the subject: "What's up, Sean? Why are you here?"

"Frank Carlton didn't call you?"

"Nope," Drexler replied.

"Well, what inspired him to give me your phone number?" Falcone asked. "And how did you get that code name 'Chamberlain'?"

"Sorry, Sean," Drexler said, laughing again. "You know I can't go into sources and methods."

So, Falcone thought, *no fingerprints. A number to call, a visit to make. The rest is up to me. I'm walking into the deniability zone.* He turned his eyes away from the plaque, looked out a window to a stand of trees silhouetted against a bright sky, and said, "I have not been given specific instructions, but I believe that I need your services to help me make an extraction."

Drexler put a finger to his lips and said, "We'll get to your business at a better place than this office. No details yet."

"Okay," Falcone said. "You're the General. Tell me what you can about GSS."

"It's a changing world out there, Sean," Drexler said, shaking his head. "In the heavy days—Iraq, Afghanistan—we were getting contracts in the millions. Like State's Bureau of Diplomatic Security. Instead of hiring their own security guys, they signed contracts and described us as 'crisis analysts.' Well, anyway, the U.S. started getting out of those nightmare places, and things started changing. Well, you know all that."

"I'm in what they call the private sector now, Drex," Falcone replied. "I don't know a hell of a lot of what's really going on anymore."

"Well, that's interesting, Sean. Very interesting. So you're here as a private citizen?"

"Yeah," Falcone said. "That's the deal."

Drexler looked uncomfortable as he handed Falcone a sheet of paper and said, "Sorry, Sean. But you have to sign this non-disclosure agreement. And I need your cell phone while you're here."

Falcone handed over his cell phone and read the agreement, getting to the point with a lawyer's eyes and translating two pages into a few words: Don't tell anyone of your visit here. No notes, in writing or electronic.

"That 'don't put the visit in your electronic calendar' is new to me," Falcone said.

"It's the damn Chinese hackers and the so-called cloud," Drexler said. "Nobody has any privacy protection. Everything goes into the cloud and can be seen by any son of bitch with software he can pick up on the street. The non-disclosure order comes from my backers. They tell me how to run things. . . . safely."

"Well, whatever they've ordered, you seem to have done all right," Falcone said with a broad sweep of his hands.

"This place is rent-free," Drexler said. "Owned by a conservationist who saved this plantation mansion from falling into ruin. He's GSS's biggest stakeholder, and he wanted the place occupied by a trustworthy tenant. I liked the mansion and its hundred acres even more. Privacy. And, when it was built in 1765 no one knew how to build mikes into brick walls."

"And you have an interesting neighbor if your boys need a workout. Where are your barracks?" Falcone asked.

"Don't need barracks. Most of my guys are temporary hires who sign mission-based contracts," Drexler said, pausing before adding, "We make a point of being in the private sector. We do not have any relationship with Langley or anyone in the intelligence community."

"Okay by me. That's what I want, too. Absolutely off-the-shelf."

"Right. Absolutely," Drexler said.

"But . . . it's . . . expensive," Falcone said. "And I'm not paying. Who is?"

"No need for you to know, Sean. Sometimes GSS is philanthropic. Don't worry. Okay?"

"Okay. No more unnecessary questions," Falcone said. He had learned long ago that sometimes there were situations with no questions and no answers, particularly about large amounts of money. He had to trust Drexler, just as Carlton had trusted him. And Drexler had his own need for deniability. *So from now on,* Falcone thought, *we talk as if this is happening but not happening.*

Drexler pressed a button on his desk console. The door opened and a young woman—in her mid-twenties, Falcone guessed—stepped into the room. The men stood. She was wearing tailored gray slacks and a pale-green long-sleeved blouse. *The young-but-professional look,* Falcone thought.

"My daughter, Annie," Drexler said. She was as tall as her father and resembled him in a softer, subdued way. "She'll take you to the library and find you a cup of coffee. Black, right?"

"Right."

"I'll join you in a little while, and we'll talk some more," Drexler said, leaving the room.

Annie Drexler lingered when she took Falcone to the library next to her father's office. Falcone felt as if he were stepping into the eighteenth century. "It's my favorite room," Annie said. "Book, books, books. Those sliding ladders. Floor-to-ceiling windows. That big old globe with all those blanks for unknown places." He recognized her voice from the Chamberlain instructions.

She pointed to a chair next to a table with a ceramic lamp that looked old but was topped by a modern shade and contained a gleaming bulb. "Make yourself at home," she said. "I'll be right back with coffee."

Falcone walked around the room, looking at titles. He recognized many of the gold-embossed names; the newest one was Kipling. Magazines were neatly spread on a table in the center of the room. He picked up a recent copy of *The Intelligencer: the Journal of U.S. Intelligence Studies,* and headed for the chosen chair just as Annie returned with an old-fashioned white coffee mug. "See you in a few minutes . . . Chamberlain," she said.

26

Thumbing through his second copy of *The Intelligencer,* Falcone had just come upon a John le Carré quote—the only real expression of a nation's subconscious is its secret service—when Drexler's daughter entered the library. The idea that he was part of America's subconscious brought a smile to Falcone's face.

"What are you smiling at?" Annie asked, smiling herself. "*The Intelligencer* usually doesn't have any funny things to say."

"Sometimes, Annie, laughing at the world is the only way to stay sane," Falcone said, standing.

"Dad says things like that sometimes," she said wistfully. "Well, he asked me to escort you to the briefing room. Please follow me."

Annie led him down a short corridor with doors along each wall. She opened one, revealing a metal door behind it. She tapped six numbers on a keypad where a doorknob would ordinarily be and the door swung open.

"A skiff," Falcone said, using the acronym for "Sensitive Compartmented Information Facility." She did not respond. The door swung closed behind them and recessed overhead lights came on as they entered. They were in what was basically a huge metal box.

Falcone knew that the Department of Defense and intelligence agencies required that certain contractors entrusted with sensitive matters be obliged to work in skiffs containing special computers whose key strokes and other electronic emanations were also shielded from the outside world. The contracts laid out skiff specifications in great detail; no approved skiff, no contract. *So*, Falcone thought, *Drexler is a government contractor. He's getting paid from a black covert fund. He's in the nation's subconscious, too.*

Drexler sat at a metal table. Falcone recognized the design: The table's legs were solid aluminum bars and its top was a solid aluminum slab. There was no place to accommodate eavesdropping bugs designed to slip into the recesses of conventional furniture. The chairs across the table from Drexler were similarly designed. Falcone sat directly in front of Drexler; Annie sat at Falcone's right.

"Welcome to my inner sanctum," Drexler said. "I hope you have a good memory. We don't take notes here. So, what brings you?"

"I need an extraction," Falcone replied.

"Where?"

"Moscow."

"A Russian?"

"No. American."

"Snowden?"

"No. I hope that bastard stays there forever."

"What do you need?"

"I was hoping you could tell me."

Drexler raised his head to the metal ceiling for a few moments as if it held the answer. "Minimum, I figure four or five men. A getaway vehicle. And a Gulfstream G-550 to get him back to the U.S."

"Does a G-550 have enough legs?" Falcone asked.

"Thirteen hours, maybe even fourteen, that should be enough," Drexler answered.

"And, I assume, you know how to get an untraceable G-550," Falcone said.

"Right," Drexler said. He looked at the ceiling again and in a moment added: "You'll need at least two guys who speak Russian. A top-notch driver. A technical guy—locks, turn off security cameras. That sort of thing. And two shooters—to create a diversion, if necessary."

"Shooters? In Russia? But—"

"Don't worry, Sean. They'll just have Tasers."

"Fine," Falcone said, looking relieved.

Drexler smiled faintly and said, "Now then, who's the extractee?"

"Robert Wentworth Hamilton."

Drexler tapped the keyboard and an image of Hamilton appeared on the monitor at the end of the table. "Here's our boy, right?"

"Right," Falcone said, hiding his amazement. He thought he recognized in the background a drab wall of the FBI conference room where Falcone had been questioned about his temporary possession of a Space-Mine laptop that the FBI had linked to the law-firm shootings. He knew that Hamilton also had been questioned, and the FBI must have interviewed him in the same room.

Falcone leaned forward and saw that Hamilton was at a highly polished table, which Falcone also remembered. And he could see another item dredged up from his memory: an aperture, presumably for a video camera, in the wall. At the corner of the image he could make out the edge of a yellow pad and a ruby pinky ring on someone's left hand. *Christo!* Falcone thought, the nickname for Akis Christakos. Falcone knew that Christakos had gone with Hamilton for the FBI interview. And he knew that Christakos wore a pinky ring.

"That's an FBI photo," Falcone said. "You got it from Carlton—maybe even from the FBI. This is a goddamn game. How much else do you know?"

"Not much, Sean. All I know is that he's there and wanted here. I honestly don't know why he has to be extracted."

"Please, Drex, how can you say 'honestly'? You're obviously very well connected—and you've been briefed. Private citizen, my ass."

"It's no game, Sean," Annie said quietly, with a touch of anger. "Three days ago we were told we'd probably be hearing from you. And, from a source I can't reveal, we received information that Hamilton is in the executive suite of the Hotel Baltschug Kempinski. I looked it up. The hotel is on the Moskva River, across from the Kremlin."

"That's about all we were given, Sean," Drexler said.

"And you code-named me 'Chamberlain' because you knew when I heard 'Chamberlain' I'd figure that you had a file on me, complete with an old code name. And I'd know something funny was going on."

Drexler shrugged, smiled, and said. "Let's get on with it, Sean. We can lay out a few things now, and tomorrow morning—"

"So I'm definitely here overnight?"

"Right," Drexler said. "You'll be sleeping in a bedroom that George Washington slept in."

"And a tin bathtub?"

"I believe you'll find our accommodations quite modern," Drexler said. "Now, down to business. You'll run the op from the scene. There will not be any backup."

"What about the Agency? Will the Moscow station chief know?"

"Not my call, Sean. But this is freelance, off the grid. Right?"

"Right," Falcone replied, suddenly seeing himself walking into darkness.

"You'll be registered in the hotel that Hamilton's in."

"Under my name?"

"You're too well known for a cover name."

"And why am I in Moscow?"

"You'll be attending a conference on behalf of your firm. And three associates are coming, too. But not with you. They'll be coming, from, say, Los Angeles, Chicago, and New York. They'll be in other hotels."

"And what conference am I attending—along with my associates?"

"Well, how do you get four American guys into Moscow without arousing suspicion? Annie came up with a brilliant answer. She checked out a Russian online page that lists—in English—conferences and trade shows at Moscow exhibition sites. I mean, there's even an international tattoo convention next week!"

"That wouldn't work, at least not for me," Falcone said.

"You'll be attending the International Conference on Cyber Defense. It's on next week. A thousand bucks a head. So it's serious. And—get this. They—"

"Hold on, Drex. You've got to be kidding. Cyber defense? In Russia? The country that has some of the best criminal hackers in the world, guys who drain bank accounts, sell credit card numbers, get into IRS data banks. I can't—"

"That's the point," Annie Drexler said, softly interrupting. "The guy who set up the conference is a British software developer. He thought he would get more publicity by, as he put it, 'going into the lion's den to find out what the lions are up to.'"

"Where did you get the information on this lion's den guy? A CIA suggestion?"

"We're never connected to—or beholden to—the CIA," Annie said. "I read about the conference on his blog. One of many that I faithfully read, believe me. And—"

"Annie's my research department," Drexler broke in to say.

"And, to continue," Annie said, sounding annoyed at the interruption, "when Dad gave me an idea this morning about what you needed, I . . . well, I thought of this."

"This morning?" Falcone exclaimed. "Come on, Drex. This has been in the works a while."

"Look, Sean. You're wise enough to know that there are a lot of things on the edges of ops like this. Lots of things that—let's face it—aren't worth going into. The deal is to get this guy out of Moscow. That's all we need to talk about. Now, getting back to that, you'll be working with four of my guys plus a guy in Moscow. His code name is Domino."

"He's not 'one of your boys'?"

"Basically, he's freelance. On a retainer."

"Retainer?" Falcone asked. "Who else does he work for? China? Russia?"

"Come on, Sean. He's been vetted. He's okay. Trust me."

"You know, Drex, the funny thing is that you say 'trust me' exactly at the point when that's all I can do. Sure. I trust you. Okay. Let's say that the conference works as a cover for me and my associates," Falcone said. "What about the op? How do we snatch Hamilton?"

"You run the op out of your room in the Hotel Baltschug Kempinski."

"How the hell do I do that?"

"Don't worry, Sean. We've had ops like this. We know how to get people out of places they shouldn't be in. Including Moscow. I just told you. I've got a fine asset there."

"Tell me about the rest of the team," Falcone said, rapidly growing suspicious about how much people in the official U.S. government knew about the abduction plans—while knowing that he had passed the point of no return.

27

Drexler leaned back, stretched his arms, wriggled his fingers, and twisted in the cold, unyielding chair. He was a man of action trapped at a keyboard in a skiff. He was a man who spent most of his life giving orders, risking lives, thinking fast. But he had also given numerous briefings to men in suits. And through the strength of his will he was a man determined to be as good at that job as he had been when he had stars on his shoulders.

"Before I tell you about your team, let me tell you about my force," Drexler said. "We have what I call a Prior Service Corps: battle-tested vets—Navy SEALs, Delta Force, Rangers, Air Force Special Ops. Funny, most of them are Southern boys—rednecks like me. We were taught by our elders—fathers and grandfathers and uncles who had worn the uniform. They taught us to be courteous, taught us how to be kind to strangers, polite to women. And, sure enough, that all comes in handy lots of times on deployment in the Middle East."

"I noticed that back in my combat days," Falcone said. "My best men were usually from the South."

Drexler smiled and continued, "A few of my people are on retainer contracts that guarantee a certain number of service days a year. Many have native-speaker language competence. The rest of them are men—and some women—who are willing to sign short-term contracts for planning and carrying out an op."

"What about those guys who picked me up?" Falcone asked.

"They—and the people at the gate, the perimeter security force, and logistics and clerical people—are full-time GSS employees. Most of them rotate through a standby group, ready twenty-four-seven to roll out for a contingency op," Drexler replied.

"But they opted out of the service and became contractors."

"Right. I guess basically they had enough of life in uniform."

"What did they want? Money?" Falcone asked.

"Each guy has his reason, Sean. We vet them closely, based on their service records, which are a helluva lot more reliable than civilian résumés. An honorable discharge is a must. But we're a little like the French Foreign Legion. We don't ask a lot of personal questions. There's one guy—ex-Delta—who is in the federal witness program. I don't know why. He has an honorable discharge. That's good enough for me."

Falcone nodded and asked, "And what about security clearance?"

"When it's needed for a mission, we find people whose clearance is up to date," Drexler said. "That covers a lot of my people. And I hire combat vets. They and the other members of the Prior Service Corps are *my* men and women. A client tells me what's wanted, we work out an ops plan, and I pick the team because I know what is needed and who can do it. Okay?"

"Okay," Falcone said. "I'm sure they're all good vets with fine service records and medals. But when you get down to it, Drex, they're mercenaries. That's what I've heard a SEAL call them. And they're unlawful combatants under the Geneva Convention."

"That's bullshit, Sean," Drexler said, his voice rising. "They're warriors, American warriors of a certain kind. They're risking their necks in ways worse than when they were in the service. A Special Ops soldier fucks up and accidentally kills a couple of Iraqis, the Army does the judging. A contractor soldier makes a mistake and he gets arrested and dragged into a civilian court. Look at what happened to those Blackwater guys. They shoot some Iraqis and are accused of murder. Thirty years to life! Thank God, the sentences were reversed. But you're off, Sean. Way off. Take my advice and don't say 'mercenaries' around my guys."

"Okay," Falcone conceded. "But I'm still concerned about who is financing this. I guess you know I'm a private citizen and there can't be any government funds involved in this . . . event."

A frown rippled across Drexler's brow. "I told you, Sean. Philanthropy.

Look it up." He hammered the keyboard and *philanthropy* appeared on the monitor, with a definition, compliments of dictionary.com: altruistic concern for human welfare and advancement, usually manifested by donations of money, property, or work.

"So this is all altruism," Falcone said. "Pure altruism."

"Let's get to who I picked," Drexler said.

"You're right, Drex. Let's get to the op," Falcone said. "Tell me about your guys."

Drexler did not look up from the keyboard. He struck a few keys. On the monitor *philanthropy* was replaced by the round, florid face of a man who looked to be in his forties.

"This is Gregor Ivanisov," Drexler said. "Code name Iceman. He's our house Russian. Speaks it with a Moscow accent. Plays the *domra,* an old Russian kind of guitar. So he can always cover as a musician."

"I thought you said we needed *two* Russian speakers."

"I did. The other one is Domino."

"Okay. Back to Iceman," Falcone said. "Where's he fit in the plan?"

"He's our driver. Knows the city. Can handle a van."

"What else do you know about him?" Falcone asked.

"This is not like you're picking a jury, Sean," Drexler said, sounding irritated. "*I* do the picking. I know these guys inside and out. I don't hand out résumés." He felt his irritation heading toward anger and, looking at Annie, said, "Maybe it would be better if we switched to talking about communications."

Drexler turned, spun a combination dial on a metal cabinet and opened the heavy door. He took out what looked like a standard black smartphone and handed it to Annie.

"Looks pretty much like my phone," Falcone said.

"Looks are deceiving," she said. "This is a special kind of phone, called a Blackphone 4. Each member of the ops team will have one. When you speak or text, every word is encrypted by a system that was developed specifically to stymie the NSA, meaning stymie everyone. NSA may be able to crack open iPhones, but not this baby," she said, holding the phone up like a trophy. "You can also press this All button and talk to everyone in a conference call. You will be in a very private network, using what's called peer-to-peer encryption, based on algorithms that constantly change."

She pointed to an app button incised with a white outline of a skull. "This will be only on your phone. The Remote Wipe button," she said. "If you press this twice, the phone deletes all its data and all the data in your peer-to-peer network. Then it powers down to zero. All phones die and cannot be brought back to life." She handed it back to Drexler, who returned it to the cabinet.

He then stood and stretched, ending the skiff session. "How about a walk?" he said. "Sometimes outdoors is a better skiff than a skiff is."

"Sounds good to me," Falcone replied.

The two men followed Annie, who locked the skiff behind them and headed for Drexler's office. He led Falcone into the front hallway, at the foot of a double staircase. "I'll show you to your room. You brought a heavy jacket, right?" Falcone nodded and followed Drexler.

"They call it a horseshoe staircase," Drexler said, stepping on the first red-carpeted stair and gesturing. The stairs ascended to the landing, which was graced by a multi-paned window that framed a landscape rolling toward the York River. The stairway here rose to the left and the right. Falcone followed Drexler to the left and to his room.

Someone had already taken Falcone's overnight bag to the room. He wondered if it had been opened and examined. The room was slope-ceilinged, its cream walls and narrow roof bathed in light from a lamp at the side of the bed. Falcone wondered if there was an outlet where he could charge his phone. Then he remembered that he had turned in his phone.

He put on a leather, fleece-lined jacket and joined Drexler at the bottom of the stairs. They walked down the central hall to a back door. "The idea," Drexler said, "was to air-condition the place by channeling the river breeze through the back door to the front. Smart guys back then."

A worn path wound down about a hundred yards to a gazebo that overlooked the river. Drexler and Falcone sat on a bench in a long silence, broken finally by Drexler. "As I'm sure you guessed," he said, "I've been briefed—well, I think, *partially* briefed. All I know is that the President wants Hamilton out of Russia for some good and sufficient reason. And I suppose you know the reason."

Falcone did not respond.

"Okay. Maybe this is a super-important op, Sean. But I don't like it," Drexler continued. "And I don't like that deniability bullshit. Somehow, this will come out. Kidnapping. It will drive Lebed nuts. We could be back in the Cold War in an instant."

Falcone nodded but again did not speak.

"What I want most of all," Drexler said, "is to keep Annie out of this. She loves all the electronic stuff, but she doesn't know how things get twisted, how a guy goes on a mission expecting to be a hero and winds up on a YouTube video pissing on a guy he just killed. And that's what gets remembered."

"The President thinks he's saving the world. But he's got to wonder whether it's worth it."

Drexler nodded, signaling the end of their conversation. "Let's go to work," he said.

28

Within sight of the main house was a former stable next to a white-fenced corral that two women and a man were using as a running track. They obviously saw Drexler and Falcone approach, but did not show any notice of them. Falcone sensed that invisibility was a requirement for anyone walking these grounds.

All of the stalls but one had been removed, creating enough space for a gym, showers, and a couple of motel-like rooms for anyone who stayed overnight. In the gym, a dozen or so men and women were in a grunting whirl of motion at rowing machines, stationary bikes, and treadmills. The remaining stall had been converted into an office, which the two men entered. There was a faint scent of horses.

Sitting on the edge of a table scarred with generations of initials was a man Falcone recognized as the house Russian, Gregor Ivanisov, arms folded across his massive chest.

"All here?" Drexler asked, taking an old wooden chair behind the table. He motioned Falcone to a folding chair against the wall. Falcone unfolded it and sat down.

"All here," Ivanisov echoed.

"Round 'em up," Drexler ordered. Ivanisov left, closing the door behind him. He had not acknowledged Falcone.

Ivanisov quickly returned with three men, all in black sweat suits and sneakers. Each one dipped his head as Drexler called his name—"Jack Beckley. . . . Harry Reilly. . . . Bobby Joe Pickens"—and then said, "Grab a chair."

They unfolded chairs similar to Falcone's and sat before him and Drexler.

"The op is an extraction," Drexler said. "The man who will be running it is Sean Falcone." Drexler nodded at Falcone. "I've known him for many years. Way back in Vietnam time, he was a Ranger. Wounded. Captured. And—you're too young to remember—three years in a Vietnam hellhole of a prison. That's right, North Vietnam, when there were two Vietnams. A lot of tourists go there now."

Drexler paused and added, "Falcone. He's one of us."

Falcone felt he had to say something. "Good morning," he began, not quite knowing where he was going next. "There's an American in Moscow. He needs to be in the United States for reasons I can't explain. I'll do my best to help you get him out."

Drexler clapped a hand on Falcone's back and said, "Good man!" His voice subtly changing to the cadence of command, he looked at his men and said, "The person being extracted is someone you may have heard of. Robert Wentworth Hamilton. The billionaire. He probably will resist and will need to be sedated and restrained. This op will necessitate the use of your real passports. And you'll have cover-story jobs."

"What kind of jobs, General?" Pickens asked. He had the build of a linebacker.

"Lawyers."

"Lawyers, General?" Reilly asked. "Can I keep my beard?" A thick black beard and curly black hair framed his face.

"Lots of lawyers these days have beards," Falcone said, then added, "well-kept beards."

"Get a trim," Drexler said. "And that goes for the rest of you. When you pack, remember: Lawyers. Suits. Ties. Shined shoes. Everyone okay with that wardrobe?"

They looked at each other, shrugged almost in unison, then mutely looked back at Drexler.

"Come on, guys," Drexler said. "Just think you're going to a buddy's wedding. Or a funeral. You think you need anything, let me know. Like a decent suitcase. No backpacks."

"Maybe Annie would . . . ," Reilly began.

"Annie's out of this. Absolutely out of this," Drexler said harshly. "Period."

"How long will we be in-country, sir?" Beckley asked. He was the shortest of the three, wiry with close-trimmed blond hair.

"Figure you leave from three airports three days from today," Drexler said. "A travel day. One day of acclimation in Moscow. Allow two days for the op and return."

"Where in Moscow, sir?" Ivanisov asked.

"The subject is in the Hotel Baltschug Kempinski," Drexler answered.

Ivanisov whistled softly and said, "Five-star. Lot of security cameras."

"They'll be taken care of," Drexler reassured him. "Remember that op at the Moscow Marriott? We'll be using Domino again."

"That's good news, General," Ivanisov said.

"There's a Marriott in Moscow? So that was a Moscow op?" Falcone asked.

"Just a friendly reminder, Sean," Drexler said, looking at Falcone face-to-face. "We don't talk about what we do."

Drexler turned back to the others and continued: "Okay. Let's reassemble at the skiff in an hour and go over details. We'll have walk-through rehearsals with Sean tomorrow, starting at o-eight-hundred. Any questions?"

"No, sir," Ivanisov said. "Sounds like a piece of cake."

That was the chronic GSS joke line. Everyone but Falcone laughed.

On the way back to the house, Falcone said to Drexler, "I'll need their passports to get the visas. Russian visas are very detailed. And what about the TSA? I assume that sometimes these guys travel under aliases."

"We don't talk about that," Drexler answered, slowing his pace. "All I can tell you is that usually—not always—they use their real passports. But information about destination, flights, and passport numbers don't show up in TSA databases."

"Why not?" Falcone asked.

"Because we don't trust the fuckin' Transportation Security Admin-istration and its whacky No-Fly List," Drexler answered. "We've had our people slowed down by bullshit at the gate, questioned by the FBI, threatened with arrest. And some of our people travel with weapons. They have to. So we managed to make some arrangements at a higher level."

"I just got another suspicion about your being a so-called private citizen," Falcone quipped.

Drexler smiled, but did not respond.

"Okay," Falcone said resignedly. "No sense going into that."

"You're right," Drexler said, stopping for a moment, looking as if he were about to speak. But he remained silent.

29

In the crowded skiff, Drexler spun the dial on the combination metal cabinet, took out a wooden box, opened it, and selected four passports. He returned the box to the cabinet, closed it, and spun the dial again.

Handing the passports to Falcone, he said, "The cover is they're your associates, from Sullivan and Ford offices in other places. We'll arrange for the team to fly to Moscow from different U.S. airports—Boston for Gregor, New York for Jack, Los Angeles for Bobby Joe, Chicago for Harry. You can use a stopover in Frankfurt to go over last-minute details of the snatch. You won't be able to have secure conversations once you hit Russian soil. Not that anyone checking passports here or in Moscow is going to be looking for job information. But it's better for your cover if you think of yourselves as lawyers, hard as that may be."

"A lot of personal information has to go on the visas," Falcone said. "I'll need that to get the visas."

"Right," Drexler said. "And Russian visas are damn tough visas."

"It's complicated. Even the best visa service takes a lot of time," Falcone said.

"You've got a lot of time," Drexler said, with a hint of a growl. "The conference opens in ten days."

"Ten days? For getting a Russian visa, that's practically overnight," Falcone said. "You know how complicated it is. Besides, certainly Gregor is known from previous jobs."

"Last time we had other names," Gregor said. "We didn't use our real

passports. I had a beard. And some money passed hands at Sheremetyevo."
He laughed and added, "Don't worry about us getting *into* Russia."

"Are these names real?" Falcone asked, holding up one of the passports. Gregor and the other three men all smiled.

"We all have lots of names," Drexler told Falcone. "These are real."

Drexler focused on the three other men. "Remember," he said. "We're
not just getting out a drunk CEO who roughed up a whore. We've never
done an extraction op this tough. Hamilton doesn't want to leave, and
it looks like Lebed wants to keep him, like Snowden. It's a real rendition. Also, real names mean these guys are blown for any future ops in
Russia."

Falcone looked up after closely examining the passports and said, "I
worry about the visas. I'm sure you've used fake visas before. Why do you
need new ones for this op?"

"All I can tell you, Sean, is that we cannot have any connection with
Langley."

"So I have to get *real* visas? With all those damn questions on the visa
applications? I'm chief executive partner at Sullivan and Ford. The firm's
name will go on those applications. There'll be a paper trail."

Drexler thought for a moment and said, "Let's table the visa issue for
a while."

He handed out floor plans of the Hotel Baltschug Kempinski's executive suite and said, "We just got these from Domino. As you can see, there
are four rooms, two really big, around nine hundred square feet. He could
be anywhere when we start the op. And there could be a Russian security goon nearby. Domino's working on that. We'll walk through the op
tomorrow. See you at the stable. O-eight-hundred."

As everyone began filing out of the skiff, Drexler tapped Falcone on
the shoulder and said, "Let's talk for a minute." He closed the door behind
the others and sat down next to Falcone.

"I can see why you're going to need deniability," Drexler said. "White
House deniability."

"It looks to me that Carlton gave you a pretty thorough briefing. To
say I'm surprised is putting it mildly."

"I can hear your resentment, Sean. In fact, he told me Hamilton had to get out as a matter of national security. And he did give me the distinct impression that if the extraction goes public, you'd be the fall guy."

"That's *not* a surprise. It's the way he set it up, and I bought it. That's the reason I'm here, talking to a retired general who is a 'private citizen' running an outfit that has amazing connections to the dark side of the U.S. government."

"GSS is as far as private can go on the black ops spectrum, Sean. After us comes the CIA. You know damn well that Sam Stone would love a chance to kick Lebed in the balls. But then goodbye deniability. And hello Iran-Contra."

"And hello impeachment, Drex. Reagan wasn't hit, but with this Congress Oxley doesn't stand a chance. They'd nail him."

"World of difference from Iran-Contra in this op," Drexler said. "You know that better than anybody. We're not diverting funds for a covert operation to destabilize another government. We're simply trying to extract an American citizen out of the claws of the Russian Bear."

"And if this goes south?"

"You know the drill, Sean. 'We had no knowledge. . . .'"

"Sure," Falcone said. "'President totally blindsided by a rogue operation conducted by an adviser he had to let go because he started getting wacky. A long-delayed PTSD case from his experience in combat and as a POW during the Vietnam War. Manchurian Candidate. . . .'"

"Not bad, Sean. You've got your own insanity plea. But seriously, why the hell is this going on? Why is this so damn important? What the hell *is* this? Snatching Snowden I can understand. But Hamilton? Why?"

"All I can tell you, Drex, is that it has to be done."

"Okay. So do it. Figure a way to get those visas."

30

Dinner for Drexler, Annie, and Falcone was in a restored eighteenth-century dining room, softly lit by bulbs shaped to look like candles in a chandelier and wall sconces. The wine was Madeira—"Washington's favorite," Drexler said, smiling proudly. And, just as proudly, he said "Williamsburg caterer" when a woman in black blouse and slacks appeared with platters of roast beef, hominy, and mashed potatoes. Plates of mince tarts followed. Drexler himself served what he called small beer brewed according to a George Washington recipe.

Pointing to the wallpaper painting of palm trees and peaceful Indians, Annie began talking about the restoration. "They really loved looking at scenic views while they ate," she said. "This wallpaper is copied from what Thomas Jefferson used in Monticello."

As soon as Annie concluded her architectural and décor lectures, Drexler began his view of the Battle of Williamsburg, the first firefight of the Peninsula campaign. Falcone looked intent but thoughts of Moscow crowded out the Civil War. . . .

". . . Longstreet threatened the Yankees' left flank until Kearny's division arrived and . . ." As soon as the battle ended, Annie slipped away.

Drexler poured glasses of whiskey "made and casked at Washington's restored distillery at Mount Vernon." Then he opened a leather-covered humidor bearing the winged-sword emblem of the Air Force Special Operations Command, and extracted two Cohiba Cuban cigars. After lighting them, Drexler raised his glass and said, "To success." Instead of a toast, Falcone, with Iran-Contra on his mind, asked Drexler, "Which U.S.

President toasted 'the people of Bolivia' at a White House dinner honoring the president of Brazil?"

"Carter," Drexler said.

"Nope. Reagan," Falcone said, raising his glass. "Here's to *secret* success." With those words he excused himself with a forced smile.

He had barely managed to get through the dinner because he'd understood immediately that any talk about the op was forbidden. *Jesus! Drexler has put me in a time machine!* All he had on his mind, and wanted to—*needed* to—talk about was getting Hamilton out of Moscow.

He went up to his room, got his jacket, and headed for the front door. Outside, he found himself drawn toward the stable. Glad to see a light, he hurried toward it.

He found Gregor Ivanisov at a speed bag, his fists a blur as he rhythmically and rapidly punched away. Falcone, who no longer worked out on a speed bag, admired Ivanisov's style but remained silent, realizing Ivanisov was on a roll. When he stopped, he looked toward Falcone and smiled. In swift, smooth motions he peeled off his weighted gloves, grabbed a towel, wiped off the sweat, and fished in a cooler for two water bottles. He tossed one to Falcone and nodded toward a bench.

"Nice rhythm," Falcone said. "And you always hit with your knuckles."

"Yeah. If you hit with the back or side of your hand, that's what your movement memory remembers. And that could mean that's what you subconsciously do when, all of a sudden, you want to throw a real punch."

"Ever in the ring?"

"Just in the Marines. Battalion middleweight champion."

"How'd you get from Marines to GSS?"

"I was a Marine sniper attached to SEAL Team Five. Four years of hairy times. I burned out. Then a couple years at Cornell. I was getting fat and lazy. I heard about GSS and signed up. They liked that I speak Russian. My father and mother left for America when I was five, part of the Jewish exodus. I've been to a few places. Got some action. Between you and me, this is my last job."

"And what's around the corner for you?"

"Back to Cornell. Marry my girlfriend. Get a job, maybe on Wall Street."

"Any particular reason for leaving GSS?"

"Not really. You know, in the SEALs there was always something behind the mission, something that your country wanted you to do."

"If it will make you feel any better about it, there is a good reason—a very important reason—to get Hamilton out of Russia. Some day you'll find out why. And you'll be glad you helped get that son of a bitch onto U.S. soil."

"You sure sound like you think it will work."

"I do. And you?"

"Probability. I give it fair probability."

"Probability? Doesn't sound like you really think the plan will work."

"I know Russia. I know Russians. They—at least the kind of Russian working in a fancy hotel—don't want trouble. But there is something else, something outside the plan."

"What's that?"

"Look. I know who you are, what your job was. This is big. Has to be."

"Okay. Suppose it is."

"The other Russians, the ones who get paid to get Lebed what he wants. If those guys nail us . . ." Ivanisov's voice trailed off.

"They won't," Falcone said as confidently as he could.

"If they *do*," Ivanisov continued, "we'll never see America again. Well, maybe *you* will, after a while. You have connections. But us? The smash-and-grab guys? We'll be lucky to be alive. And me? To those bastards, a Russian is always a Russian. They'll treat me like a traitor. A bullet to the back of the head."

"Maybe you should back out. Right now."

"Hell no, Sean! No. No. I can't do that. Never. Semper Fi! But when this op is wrapped up, I'll be out of this business."

"Call when you start back to the real world. I mean it."

"Yeah. Thanks. I will," Ivanisov said. "Good night."

He went off toward the overnight rooms, and Falcone, feeling lighter, decided to sprint back to the house.

Falcone stood by the window in the little room. The fog was rolling in from the river, blurring the moon and shutting the old house off from time.

His mind drifted from thoughts of Washington and Moscow . . . to Kipling. He had seen the name on the spines of those books in the library, but this was coming from deeper memories.

He went to bed, and as he struggled to find ever-evasive sleep, he was remembering his father's lined composition book, passed out to night school students learning English. His father was the son of an Italian immigrant who married the daughter of a second-generation Irish immigrant. In that night school class he wrote down words and phrases he wanted to learn by heart and, later, wanted his son to learn. Falcone cherished the composition book. And now, in this room that George Washington had slept in—*How my father would have loved that!*—he searched his memory for words in the composition book, words from Kipling. He couldn't remember some of the words; it was something about trying to be your own man. But he remembered the heart of the quote, word-for-word: "No price is too high to pay for the privilege of owning yourself."

He finally found sleep.

PART TWO

Out here between a million moons and sanded spheres
of layered rock and molten cores, I race through
the darkness of interstellar space, determined to steer
a course beyond the sultry lure of gravity.
In lonely epicycles I cruise anonymously
through neighborhoods where families struggle
in war and peace; a wanderer amid
whorls of violence, solar winds and energy.
It's no place for aliens or their scouts
that scan the void with eyes that never blink;
for voyeurs that look with lust at our anatomy,
to take the measure of our girth and density.
Still they come, first in wonder, then I think, to plunder.

31

When Falcone arrived at the stable the next morning, a CLOSED sign hung on the door. Ivanisov answered Falcone's knock and led him to a corner of the gym. Ivanisov and Drexler had laid out a real-life version of the Hamilton suite's floor plan with strips of black tape. On a table was a large monitor showing a slide show of images on the Hotel Baltschug Kempinski website—the grand old hotel glowing at night, a view of the Kremlin across the river, the gym, the spa, the marble-floored lobby, the guest rooms with gold damask drapes, and, room by room, the executive suite where Hamilton lived.

Exactly at 8:00 a.m., Falcone heard the door open. Beckley, Reilly, and Pickens walked in. Falcone noticed that Reilly pocketed a key and surmised that in the team's unacknowledged pecking order Ivanisov was number one and Reilly number two.

"Good sleep, Sean?" Drexler asked.

"George couldn't have wanted better," Falcone answered.

"Coffee?"

Falcone nodded and followed Drexler to the office stall. There was a coffeemaker and a bowl of muffins. "Annie's," Drexler said, handing the bowl to Falcone. "You should watch the walk-through of the op. But when the real thing happens, you won't be seeing the action. You'll be in another room one floor down, near the elevator." He took an envelope out of his back pocket and, seeing Falcone's hands were occupied, put the plain white envelope on the table.

Falcone put down the coffee, picked up the envelope and put it in his jacket pocket.

"What you need to know is all written down," Drexler said. "Read it in the vehicle that will be taking you out of here. Read it as many times as you need to remember everything. Then put it through the shredder that'll be in the lockbox on the floor next to your feet. There's a key in it. After you shred and lock the box, give the key to the driver."

"Okay. But if I have questions—"

"You won't," Drexler said.

"So I don't come back here after today?" Falcone asked.

"Right," Drexler replied. "You'll see the walk-through here a couple of times and then you'll be driven back home. Then all you need to do is get those visas."

"That's all. Piece of cake, right?"

"Right," Drexler replied with a hint of a smile. "I'm assuming you'll get them by the day after tomorrow. If you can't get them . . . if you find it's impossible, call me immediately. The clock is already clicking. Domino is already on the job. There's no turning back."

"Right," Falcone responded.

"Okay. When you get them, call me—remember, you're Chamberlain. Always use that code name. When you get the visas, I'll arrange for the flights to Moscow for you and the team. I work with a friendly—and very reliable—travel agent. One of my boys will pick up the passports and visas from you. I'll handle delivery of them and the plane tickets. Yours will be Dulles-Frankfurt-Moscow."

"I prefer a direct flight," Falcone said.

"You and Gregor will have flights with two-hour Frankfurt layovers that are about half an hour apart. In Frankfurt you and Gregor will be directed to a private meeting room in the VIP lounge."

"Why is that necessary?" Falcone asked.

"A last-minute meet," Drexler replied. "There may be a need for some adjustments in the op, or a Plan B, or an abort. Also, it's a place I can reach you in case anything critical comes in from Domino at the last minute."

"And how do we find Domino in Moscow?"

"Don't worry," Drexler said reassuringly. "Domino will find *you*. Let's go back and watch the run-through."

32

As soon as the SUV started down the driveway, Falcone opened the envelope. There were four single-space pages. He skimmed a page of instructions about the Blackphone 4 and decided Drexler had told him all he needed to know. He turned to the other pages and followed his lawyerly habit: scan first to get the gist, then go over details.

Drexler had written a script for the eight-minute op, which put Chamberlain in one place in the hotel giving orders to the GSS men in other places in the hotel. The walk-through in the gym, synchronized with images of the hotel on the monitor, had an eerie quality. It was like watching a rehearsal for a play that had been staged many times before. It had all looked so automatic, so thoroughly choreographed, like so many plans that Falcone had seen long ago in Vietnam and more recently in the White House Situation Room. Nothing could go wrong.

Each man had a code name: Iceman for Ivanisov, Buggy for Beckley, Rambo for Reilly, Pepper for Pickens. Domino was also in the script but did not get any ordinary name and seemed to operate independently. Chamberlain had an uneasy feeling about Domino.

He reread the instructions, focusing on the details and trying to envision the actions. But the quest for the visas crowded his mind. He had accepted the mission knowing what had to be done but not knowing how it would be done. He had assumed that his role would be what Drexler's script described: director-on-location. Carlton had sent him to Drexler, and Drexler had provided what was expected: plan, personnel, cover story, communications, transportation. Now, for Falcone, came the hard part:

Russian visas. *Can't get them by walking into that drab consulate and standing in line, figuring out the size of the bribe. . . .* Then came the answer. Viktor Fedotov, Russian ambassador to the United States. *He could cut the red tape, order visas immediately. But only under extreme duress. So extreme he'd be willing to risk his job. Or maybe his life.*

For Falcone there would also be risk, for him as a lawyer and for Sullivan & Ford. He knew that if he used the extreme duress that was taking shape in his mind, he would be guilty of the crime of illegal coercion, the polite term for blackmail. *Well, it's to save the world, right?*

Viktor Fedotov had appeared in Washington soon after Boris Lebed became President. Fedotov, a petroleum oligarch, had become a billionaire with the aid of Putin and Lebed, thus making enough rubles to buy the ambassadorship. While Lebed was continuing Putin's anti-America crusade, Fedotov was making friends, particularly among members of Congress who were interceding for constituents involved in Russian financial deals.

On the very day that Falcone became President Oxley's national security adviser, Fedotov had called him on his private cell phone number and invited him to lunch at the Russian ambassador's residence. Falcone eagerly accepted, as much for official business as for personal curiosity. He had been there twice for receptions, which inevitably were full of people talking loudly, drinking high-grade vodka, and scooping up Sevruga caviar. He never got a chance to see much of the interior of a building whose Beaux-Arts architecture and décor put it on the National Register of Historic Places.

Falcone was intrigued by the ironic history of the mansion. It was built in 1910 for the widow of the designer of the Pullman railroad car. In 1913 Czar Nicholas II bought the building to serve as the Russian Embassy, supposedly because it was near the White House. After the Russian Revolution, the building faded from diplomatic history until 1933, when the United States recognized the Soviet government. Moscow dispatched a properly communist architect to get rid of the capitalistic grandeur, but he balked, deciding to preserve the extravagant golden décor down to "the last hair of the last Cupid."

Fedotov had taken Falcone on a tour of the first-floor rooms, all of them red-carpeted and heavily laden with golden pilasters and garlands. Fedotov then led Falcone to a small, red-walled room overlooking a small garden. After vodka toasts to their countries, they had lunch, served in grand style by liveried waiters. The meal began with an oyster soup topped by osetra caviar and moved on to beef Stroganoff, accompanied by a Georgian wine with an unpronounceable name. Finally came small crystal bowls full of a delicious dessert whose name unfortunately translated into English as "dried paradise apple."

Falcone, growing hungry from memory of that lunch, turned his mind to a more recent recollection about Fedotov.

For years the FBI had kept track of the comings and goings of Soviet diplomats—and potential walk-in spies—from an upper room in a National Geographic Society building across Sixteenth Street from the embassy. The FBI watchers later moved next door to a building that offered a better view of the embassy. When the Soviets built a new embassy elsewhere in Washington (on one of the highest elevations in the city), the Sixteenth Street building became the ambassador's residence and, with the end of the Cold War, surveillance ended. But soon after Fedotov's arrival, the FBI started watching his movements. And, during a routine intelligence briefing as national security adviser, Falcone learned why.

Two blocks from the ambassador's residence is Thomas Circle, a traffic roundabout named after a Civil War general whose bronze equestrian statue is the circle's hub. The circle has long been a nighttime haunt of prostitutes who offer their services to circling motorists. When periodic police crackdowns drove the prostitutes off the street and into hotels, police strategy countered with ads on websites that invited customers to hotel room trysts. When they showed up, they met cops who arrested them for solicitation for prostitution. One Sunday nineteen men were arrested, among them Ambassador Viktor Fedotov. He had responded to an ad for a male prostitute.

The State Department had a routine for handling such incidents, intervening to remind police that diplomatic immunity extended beyond parking tickets. The arrest paperwork disappeared. But the FBI and CIA usually learned about these erased arrests and filed them away as information that someday might be useful. The reason for the FBI surveillance on Fedotov was the development of a dossier with the idea that Fedotov, fearing exposure, might agree to be a spy.

The news had surprised Falcone, not because Fedotov was gay but because he had been so naïve and reckless. During Falcone's numerous encounters with Fedotov, both on official business and at social events, he had seemed to be a cautious professional, never straying beyond policy lines. At the same time he was amiable, putting a friendly face on Russia's perpetual scowl. He spoke perfect American English and appeared frequently at Washington theaters and stadiums.

After hearing the briefing, Falcone felt sorry for Fedotov, knowing that he was a target for FBI blackmail. Now Falcone was planning to become a blackmailer himself. *Well, it's to save the world, right?*

"Sean! What a fine surprise!" Fedotov said on the phone. "It's been ages. How is it going? Is there life beyond the White House?"

"There certainly is," Falcone replied, trying to sound as genial as Fedotov. "I am only a lawyer now, and I need a favor, an urgent favor. Can we meet . . . at the residence?"

"Hmmm. Not the embassy? Interesting. Sure . . . Tonight? Drinks? Six thirty?"

33

Fedotov dramatically threw open both of the tall double entrance doors and said, "Welcome!" He was a lean man in his early fifties with thinning black hair and an easy smile. He wore gray slacks and a blue V-neck sweater over a white shirt. Falcone followed him to the library, whose curving bookshelves drew the eye to a pair of gold-framed glass doors opening to a terrace.

On a small round table was a plate of blinis with smoked salmon and caviar, flanked by two crystal glasses and a bottle shaped in the form of the Russian imperial crown. "The drink of the czar's Elite Guard," Fedotov said, pouring the vodka.

He handed a glass to Falcone, who raised it to Fedotov and said, "To peace and friendship."

"Also," Fedotov said, laughing, "to an end of the Redskins' losing streak."

They both downed the vodka with one motion. Fedotov poured again and motioned to the two chairs.

Falcone picked up his glass and pointed to the doors. Fedotov nodded, frowning, and opened one of the doors. Falcone followed him into the dusk.

"I need five visas," Falcone said.

"Is that all?" Fedotov said, laughing a bit more sharply than he had inside.

"I need them right away. Without filling out those forms that ask so many questions."

"Such as 'purpose of visit'?" Fedotov asked.

"Such as 'Have you ever been involved in armed conflicts?'"

"Interesting," Fedotov said. "For this you needed us to stroll in the garden, away from my secret microphones? Or eavesdropping by a Security Service officer hiding behind the drapes?"

"Please don't be angry, Viktor. It's a matter that I wish to not go through official channels."

"And may I ask why? I promise not to tell President Lebed," Fedotov said with a smile.

"And I promise not to tell," Falcone said, draining his glass.

"Tell what?" Fedotov asked.

"Tell about what happened when you answered a certain advertisement on the Internet."

Fedotov stood for a moment, his face a mask, his dark eyes staring ahead. Then he went inside, returned with the bottle, and sat on a stone bench. Falcone sat down next to him and held up his glass.

"I assume you know that E. M. Forster was in the same gay tribe I'm in," Fedotov said, tilting back his head to drain the glass. "I don't usually memorize quotes—but there is one from Forster that so fit me—fit my life—that I did memorize it."

"He said something . . . about betrayal . . . and friendship," Falcone said. He refilled his glass.

"Yes," Fedotov replied. "Forster said, 'If I had to choose between betraying my country and betraying my friend, I hope I should have the guts to betray my country.' Very powerful, no?"

"Yes. Too powerful for me. I took an oath for my country."

"There are no oaths for not betraying friends, are there?" Fedotov's voice roughened, as if Russian was trying to break through his English.

"I need the visas for a purpose beyond my country—or yours. Someday you will understand. No one will be harmed. You have my word."

"Your word," Fedotov said bitterly. "Your word. 'Beyond my country.' Yes. I can see that. One of those times when honor is wrapped in what? May I call it blackmail?"

"Call it *need*. It's wrapped in need."

"Very well," Fedotov said, reaching out his hand. "You have the passports with you, I assume."

Falcone handed over his passport and the four others.

"I will order expedited diplomatic visas. No one below me will question my order."

"And above you?"

"Perhaps. But the Foreign Ministry gives me relatively little interest. As you know, I am sure, most of our governing is done by one man."

Fedotov slowly rose from the bench and said, "Someone from the consulate will deliver them to you by noon tomorrow. You still live in that Pennsylvania Avenue penthouse?"

"Yes," said Falcone. "Someday, when what I am doing is finished, I hope to see you there again."

Without speaking, Fedotov went inside. Falcone followed him to the entrance hall. Still silent, Fedotov opened one of the double doors. Falcone nodded and left.

34

Even after three months as a member of the faculty at Moscow State University, Leonid Danshov was still a novelty and a star. Students filled the lecture hall to hear him, an American professor who did not sound like a professor or, for that matter, like an American. The title of his subject, as listed in the catalogue, was Modern East–West Geopolitics.

At first, few students signed up for what sounded like a dull elective that would probably echo other courses taught by professors who droned on about Russia's world view in the Putin-Lebed era. But Lee—as he wished to be called—did not adhere to the catalogue title. "What I want to talk about," he said in his first lecture, "is the lingering of the Cold War."

He spoke fluent Russian, complete with idioms and the occasional appropriate proverb, though there was a trace of the language of his parents' birthplace, Ukraine. After introducing himself as an American committed to understanding the history of his adopted country, he took his listeners back to August 29, 1945.

"World War II has been over for fifteen days, the war that you Russians call the Great War," he said. "The Soviet Union has been the ally of the United States, Britain, and China. Stalin has met with President Roosevelt, President Truman, and Winston Churchill. Stalin agreed to enter the war against Japan, albeit on the eve of Japan's surrender. Agreements have been made about the postwar world. The Soviet Union seems to have gotten what Stalin wanted, a divided Germany, a divided Korea, a Soviet-controlled Eastern Europe.

"Hundreds of thousands of Allied prisoners of war are starving in camps scattered around Japan and Korea. American and British aircraft are dropping food and medical supplies to the prisoners. Then, on that August day in 1945, Soviet fighters spot an American B-29 Superfortress dropping supplies to a camp near Hamhung, Korea, a nation already coming under Soviet hegemony. The Soviets fire on the B-29, forcing the aircraft to land. Unknown to the plane's crew, a new war has begun. It will be called the Cold War."

After that sketch, he moved quickly to his view that, after the collapse of the Soviet Union, America "made a dubious claim of victory and immediately began to treat Russia as a conquered nation, not unlike Germany and Japan after the Great War." The end of the Cold War, he said, "ushered in the beginning of what we have now—an unspoken acceptance by leaders in both nations to a renewal of distrust and confrontation. I am proud to have the privilege to speak freely in a nation where poet Osip Mandelstam once wrote . . . and died, a martyr to truth."

Western critics in the 1930s had compared Mandelstam to Pushkin, who had been silenced by the czar's secret police for subversive writings. Mandelstam's most famous poem, which circulated in the literary underground during Stalin's long reign of terror, became known as his defiant "The Stalin Epigram." It was a death certificate. Mandelstam's poems disappeared from print. And he died mysteriously after being sent to a prison camp near Vladivostok in 1938.

"As Mandelstam said," Danshov continued, " 'only in Russia is poetry respected. In fact, it gets people killed. Is there anywhere else where poetry is so common a motive for murder?' "

Speaking slowly and reverently, Danshov ended his lecture with lines from the "The Stalin Epigram":

He forges his decrees like horseshoes—
some get it in the groin, some in the forehead,
some in the brows, some in the eyes.

Mandelstam had been resurrected after the collapse of the Soviet Union and was well known in the new world of young Russian intellectuals.

They flocked to Danshov's lectures and his readings at smoky literary clubs and coffee houses in Moscow. Inevitably, whatever his topic, Danshov would recite those lines from the ode. Russian literary critics wondered whether he was reciting the poem to suggest that there were new Stalins ruling Russia—first the late Vladimir Putin and now the current forger of decrees, Boris Lebed?

Colonel Nikita Komov wondered the same thing.

35

Komov's interest in Leonid Danshov had awakened the Comrade X-ray that lurked in Komov's soul. His dependence upon instinct and paranoia produced a kind of alchemy, which he used to transform his suspicions into reality—and action. As usual, Komov did not mention his suspicions to his superiors or to his FSB colleagues assigned to keeping track of U.S. intelligence activities.

Over the years, he had created his own Special Investigations Unit, a group of about fifty FSB officers who reported only to him. Komov and his unit operated out of a suite of offices occupying most of the fourth floor in the Lubyanka, the building in downtown Moscow that had been the headquarters of the KGB and its infamous prison. The unit's operations were disclosed only to Lebed, and only Lebed decided with whom, if anyone, he would share the information.

Frequently, instead of targeting enemies of the state, the unit preyed upon politicians or financiers designated by Lebed. Those cases—involving blackmail, the planting of false evidence, and even sabotage—hearkened back to KGB days. The nickname for the unit, the Sons of Beria, commemorated Lavrenty Pavlovich Beria, a notorious lecher who ran the vast Soviet internal police apparatus, the prison camp system, and a global espionage network under Stalin. Beria, believed by many to have poisoned Stalin, briefly took over the government after Stalin's death. Beria was tried and convicted of treason and executed in 1953. The nickname did not please Lebed, but he invariably gave Komov what he wanted.

Komov told an aide to bring him the FSB dossier on Danshov, setting in motion a series of orders that shortly produced the arrival in his office of a pompous deputy director, a master archivist, and a nervous technician wheeling a stand containing a laptop and a high-speed portable printer.

Komov disdained computers, demanding that documents and photographs be presented to him on paper, not on monitors. When he was through with the printouts, he would put them in a burn bag modeled on the type used by the CIA; often he carried the bag himself to the incinerator chute.

The dossier showed that Danshov was forty-two years old and unmarried. As a professor, he lived alone in a one-bedroom apartment on the Moscow University campus. He had been born in Yonkers, New York, the only child of parents who had emigrated from what was then the province of Ukraine. They were among the thousands of Jews who fled anti-Semitic persecution in the Soviet Union in the 1970s.

Danshov enlisted in the U.S. Army at the age of eighteen and was put on a career path that included assignment to the Defense Language Institute in Monterey, California, where he learned Arabic. During the Gulf War, he served as an intelligence specialist in the Special Forces Group. He left the Army in 2000 as a Special Forces captain and went to Yale on a scholarship, while remaining in the Army Reserve. He stayed at Yale for his doctorate in Slavic languages and literature.

Comrade X-ray suspected that it was no coincidence that Danshov rowed for Yale when Ray Quinlan, President Oxley's chief of staff, was also on Yale's heavyweight crew team.

The Danshov dossier included documents showing that he had been recruited on campus by the CIA, probably because of his Special Forces experience and his Russian and Ukrainian language abilities. Yale has long supplied CIA officers, including George H. W. Bush '48, William P. Bundy '39, and Komov's counterpart, James Jesus Angleton '41.

Komov was not surprised either to see that one of Danshov's lecturers at Yale was Joseph Brodsky, a Russian poet whose 1972 expulsion from the Soviet Union had been urged by Komov. He often said that Brodsky should thank the KGB, along with Western anti-communists, for his 1987 Nobel Prize and his 1991 appointment as America's Poet Laureate.

One of the documents in the dossier was an FSB counterintelligence analysis of Danshov's CIA career. After training at the Federal Law Enforcement Agency Training Center in Georgia and Camp Peary, known as "The Farm," in Virginia, Danshov had been assigned to the Office of Russian and European Analysis (OREA), where he translated and evaluated documents provided by U.S. agents in Russia. After mention of Camp Peary, there was a footnote:

*Near the site of Global Special Services, which is known to obtain highly sensitive contracts from U.S. intelligence services and is considered to have quasi-official status through its owner, Major General Harold William Drexler.

Komov looked up from the dossier to angrily scrawl a note admonishing the analyst for the vagueness of the footnote. He hated *which is known* and *is considered* and *quasi-official*, all indicators to him that either the officers who provided the data or the author of the report lacked solid information and tried to hide their ignorance.

He recognized Drexler's name and knew that men working for GSS had recently abducted a high-profile Al Qaeda leader in Yemen. It was an operation worthy of America's famed SEAL Team Six.

A thick day-by-day surveillance report of Danshov's activities was attached as an appendix.

A coincidence? Comrade X-ray did not believe in coincidences. Too many times had he seen connections—possible, probable, flimsy, but connections nevertheless—between Drexler's GSS and the CIA.

According to the dossier, Danshov had never served under diplomatic cover anywhere, and there was no indication that he had ever attempted to enter Russia clandestinely. A Russian agent in Washington, who claimed knowledge of OREA operations, said Danshov had resigned after "a heated argument with his superior" over the decision to not post him to

Moscow. *Undoubtedly a staged argument,* Komov thought. He made a note to run a security check on the agent in Washington: *He could have been doubled by the CIA.*

A year after leaving the CIA, Danshov initially entered Russia under the auspices of the Institute for European, Russian, and Eurasian Studies, which Komov begrudgingly judged to have no connection with U.S. intelligence services. He had a short audience with President Lebed, who welcomed him and used the meeting to show his support of the Institute "and the joining of the intellectual communities of our two nations."

The dossier included a summary of Danshov's passport and visa records, which showed a pattern of entry and departure dates that coincided with Moscow University's academic calendar. The usual FSB watch on Americans turned up no suspicious activity. But the report noted that known and suspected dissidents frequently appeared at his off-campus lectures and informal talks.

One of the dissidents was Sergei Aldonin, who was immediately placed under twenty-four-hour surveillance. Aldonin worked in the FSB's counter-electronic division. Komov cross-referenced the surveillance reports on Aldonin and pounced on the fact that Danshov had met with Aldonin three times. Two of the meetings lasted more than thirty minutes.

Komov dug further, checking highly classified files containing information hacked from Swiss bank accounts. Even Lebed did not know that the files existed—or that two of them could be traced, through a maze of international banks, to Lebed and his wife. As Komov expected, Aldonin had a substantial account, from which he had recently extracted enough to buy a small dacha in Tver, about an hour and a half north of Moscow.

At first, all that Komov knew about Aldonin was that he worked as an electronics technician. Because Komov had little interest in the electronics of counterintelligence, he did not know until what he called "a strenuous interrogation" that Aldonin's principal job was the daily "sweeping" of Lebed's office for unauthorized electronic devices.

Aldonin finally confessed that he had been recruited by Danshov, who gave him a working cigarette lighter and told him all he had to do was have the lighter in his pocket when he swept. Aldonin said he assumed that the lighter contained a chip that served as a switch for turning on a recorder. Whatever it recorded, Aldonin supposed, was transmitted in intermittent bursts to NSA technicians in the U.S. Embassy. He swore by his dead mother's soul that he did not know where the recorder was.

FSB technicians found the chip in the lighter and determined that it had been disabled by remote command, presumably when Aldonin disappeared. While waiting to decide what to do next, Komov ordered Aldonin secretly flown to an FSB detention center in the Siberian city of Samara. Aldonin's family and colleagues were told he was on special assignment; they all assumed he was one of the so-called green men secretly sent to Ukraine.

Komov personally vetted Aldonin's successor as sweeper, who repeatedly declared that Lebed's office was free of unauthorized electronics. Komov was satisfied that the removal of Aldonin also meant the finish of the recorder. He decided not to tell Lebed that many of his conversations had been heard by U.S. eavesdroppers.

"There is no need to disturb the President—or make him worry about the FSB's vigilance," Komov confided to his bodyguard, Shumeyko. "I will tell him in due time. No further harm can be done. We wait for the enemy to move. The NSA knows the spy-listening has stopped. Professor Danshov will be alerted and will probably panic. Now we wait for the cat to jump."

36

The U.S. ambassador to Russia frequently held what he called "public diplomacy" receptions at his residence, the Spaso House, a magnificent pre-Revolution mansion built for a Russian businessman of fabulous wealth. Midlevel officials of the Foreign Ministry and other Russians were invited, along with American academicians or business executives with interests in maintaining commercial, scholarly, or literary relations with their Russian counterparts.

Several Foreign Service officers at the U.S. Embassy were CIA officers under diplomatic cover, an old masquerade practiced and accepted by many nations. A CIA officer caught spying is almost invariably PNG'd—declared persona non grata—and expelled from the country. CIA case officers who use a real or seemingly real business as a cover do not have the protection and secure communications of an embassy; if they are caught, they're arrested and may be imprisoned or, in very rare cases, executed.

Lebed did not like the fraternizing that occurred at these receptions, but he accepted his foreign secretary's belief that they were basically harmless and sometimes produced valuable insights into American policies. Seemingly noteworthy conversations at the receptions were reported to intelligence and policymakers in both nations and filed away for analysts to ponder. This was all routine for analysts of the American and Russian intelligence services.

Two weeks before Falcone went to GSS headquarters and met with Drexler, the ambassador held a Spaso House reception commemorating the scholarly and cultural ties between the two nations. Guests included Americans studying in Russia under Fulbright scholarships and their Russian professors, along with Leonid Danshov.

After seeing Danshov's name on an invitation list provided by a Russian working at the embassy, Comrade X-ray decided to give this reception full-throttle surveillance, with the focus on Danshov. Komov ordered detailed reports and analyses showing the patterns of conversations between Russians and Americans; scraps of remarks heard in passing; and transcripts of talks between Americans and FSB operatives wearing recorders and cameras.

The reception data made work for many FSB analysts but did not seem to produce any significant new intelligence. Komov spent a day and a night going through the pile of printouts reporting on the reception. The reports turned up nothing. Komov next shuffled through the surveillance photos of Danshov at the reception—and found what he wanted: an encounter that the analysts had ignored.

The photos showed a smiling, handsome man in his early forties, short and stocky. He had a neatly trimmed beard and long black hair gathered in a ponytail. When he entered Spaso House, his ponytail hung out of a red baseball cap bearing a white *W*. He did not doff the cap until he reached the top of the red-carpeted staircase from the lower lobby to the Chandelier Room, named for the enormous object that was the hub of the reception. Overwhelmed by the glitter and grandeur, he pocketed the cap. But in the reception's facade of formality, he stood out in his leather-elbowed tweed jacket, plaid sport shirt, jeans, and moccasins.

He headed for one of the bars, turning down the California wines. Instead, he grabbed a Samuel Adams and drank from the bottle. He attracted the young students as if he were a rock star—and inspired a run on the beer by them and many of the Russians.

Included in the surveillance report to Komov was a video made by a body camera hidden in the vest of an FSB officer posing as a Foreign Ministry official. The video, viewed on a laptop brought to Komov's office, showed that soon after the reception began, Eileen Morse, a trim young woman on the staff of the embassy's cultural attaché, took Danshov's arm and led him to her boss for an official welcome and a short, unrecorded chat. Komov thought that the attaché looked surprised at what Danshov was saying. After a moment, the attaché handed Danshov back to Morse, and they had an animated conversation that lasted two minutes.

Komov had the archivist repeatedly rewind the video for the interval showing the span of time when Morse was with Danshov. "Stop!" he said again and again. Then, "Yes! Here. Look!"

"Sir?" the deputy director asked.

"Look at the way she and he walked, staying away from FSB officers, who obviously had all been spotted," Komov exclaimed.

He pounded on the desk and shouted, "Careless surveillance! Find out who trained these fools! Look. She stops and shakes his hand and they walk off in opposite directions. Look at her right hand. Passing a note. A crude brush contact. Who is she?"

The deputy director consulted his notes. "Her name is Eileen Morse, Colonel. A new person in the embassy. She is on the cultural attaché's staff."

"We know the attaché is CIA. And she?"

"We . . . we believe she is, Colonel. We are . . . shall we—"

"Stop stuttering! Why was there no mention of this obvious brush-contact?" Komov asked the deputy. "Find out which one of the analyst fools prepared the surveillance report. Demote him."

"The analyst is a woman, sir."

"And so? Demote *her*."

Komov sent away the director and archivist with a dismissing gesture, touched a button on the console on his desk, and said, "Send in Lieuten-ant Shumeyko."

Lieutenant Pavel Shumeyko walked in as the other men walked out. The former champion hockey center had a counterintelligence officer's hard eyes. He wore a black suit, white shirt, and tightly knotted blue tie.

"Sit down, Lieutenant," Komov said. He told Shumeyko about the brush contact at the reception, handed him the Danshov dossier, and gave him a few minutes to go through it. When Shumeyko closed the dossier, Komov said, "I want you personally to bring him in. Go first to his apartment. Bring along the searchers. Tell them I want everything. Computer. Cell phone. All papers, books, posters on the walls. Everything."

"Yes, Colonel," Shumeyko said, standing and giving a brisk salute.

"Sit down and stay for a moment, Lieutenant," Komov said, placing a hand on Shumeyko's arm. "I want to emphasize that the arrest of Danshov is not routine. As you saw in the dossier, there is a cross-reference to Aldonin. Danshov was Aldonin's case officer in that diabolical plan to listen to the conversations of our President. Danshov is a malicious enemy of the state."

37

Shumeyko went directly to Leonid Danshov's austere apartment—bed, table, television, small refrigerator, closet, toilet, and shower—accompanied by two FSB men who specialized in searching for (or planting) evidence. The apartment was on the top floor of the seven-story Moscow State University guest house used by students and transient faculty members. Danshov was not there, and the middle-aged woman who watched over the seventh floor reported that he spent little time in his apartment.

The guest house accommodations were designed for security and surveillance more than for comfort. Access to the building was by a university *propusk,* the omnipresent all-purpose identity card that everyone was obliged to carry on campus. The *propusk* also had to be shown to enter each floor and its kitchen, where people of that floor cooked their meals.

Through the use of *propusk* records provided by the woman, Shumeyko quickly developed a view of Danshov's quotidian life on campus: kitchen, chat room, dry cleaners, magazine kiosks, cafeterias, and an expensive restaurant in the soaring main building, a Moscow landmark that claims to be the tallest educational building in the world. "I will need a list of the American's friends, with dates and your observations," Shumeyko said. "An FSB officer will pick it up shortly. Do not mention my visit to anyone."

Shumeyko sat at the woman's desk in the hall near the elevator and opened her *propusk* file on Danshov. The record showed that he rarely visited the kitchen, cafeteria, and restaurant. Shumeyko assumed that Danshov did most of his eating beyond the huge campus, which was a kind of small town about ten miles from central Moscow. Danshov was easy to find. Early that morning, before he had awakened, Danshov had been put under total surveillance by Komov. When he called the leader of the surveillance team, he was told that Danshov was at the Hard Rock Café on Arbat Street at the historic center of Moscow.

Shumeyko left the searchers behind and ordered his driver to park on Arbat Street near the café, which Shumeyko despised for its rock 'n' roll décor and all-American menu. He also did not like Arbat Street, which teemed with tourists patronizing cafés and souvenir shops or gawking at sidewalk artists and beggars.

Two members of the surveillance team met Shumeyko outside the café. "I will go in alone," he told them. "Do not enter unless there is a disturbance."

Danshov sat at a table with a man and a woman who looked like students. He was facing the entrance door—*as intelligence officers are taught to do,* Shumeyko thought. Danshov stood and calmly walked toward the men's room. Shumeyko reached him in three steps, grabbed the collar of Danshov's jacket, and leaned forward to whisper, "Do not give me trouble or I will also arrest your friends."

The man and woman, frozen in their seats, looked away as Shumeyko spun Danshov around and marched him toward the door. The café was suddenly silent. As the captor and his prey passed a table, a British tourist raised her cell phone. Shumeyko snatched it out of the woman's hand, threw it to the floor, and crushed it underfoot without missing a stride.

Shumeyko pushed Danshov into the backseat of the ZIL limousine. One of the surveillance officers got in the front passenger's seat. "Lubyanka," Shumeyko ordered, and the car sped toward the big yellow-brick building that Russians had dreaded since the days of the Cheka, the czar's dreaded secret police. It was called the tallest building in Moscow because you could see Siberia from its long-closed basement prison, which Lebed had reopened.

Danshov remained silent during the short, high-speed drive. But, as the car pulled up in front of the Lubyanka, he shouted, in English, "You can't do this. I am an American."

"Speak Russian," Shumeyko ordered. "You are not an American. You are a Ukrainian Jew spying for the Americans."

"You must have seen my passport, my visa," Danshov said in Russian. "You know I am American. Born in America. A professor at Moscow State University. You know all that. I demand that you contact the American Embassy."

"The best thing for you to do right now is to keep quiet and let the routine take place. I am leaving you in the hands of my colleagues," Shumeyko said, his voice surprisingly gentle and persuasive.

He took Danshov down the hall to the ground-floor reception room, Danshov took Shumeyko's advice and remained calm through the routine: pat down, jacket removed and pockets checked; photo taken; fingers printed; inner right cheek swabbed for DNA sample. A man of the routine—one of the men in gray slacks and gray shirts open at the throat—took him by the arm and led him to the elevator. His heart began to thump. *I'm a spy. I'm without cover.*

Up meant routine: arrest paperwork, formal interrogation; *Down* meant prison and perhaps torture. There was a third destination: the courtyard. But, he thought, *Surely that can't be true anymore.* He had a sudden memory of having read that the massive walls of the Lubyanka surrounded the courtyard and muffled the gunfire of executions. So the inmates on the ground floor heard the lethal, echoing sound.

The man touched the elevator button on a metal plate too old and scratched to read. Danshov entered not knowing whether he would ascend or descend.

38

The elevator rose to the fourth floor. Danshov stepped into a long, narrow room, dark except for a bright light with a green metal shade hanging from the middle of the ceiling. The light shone directly on a wooden chair, which was bolted to the floor. The man in gray silently led Danshov to the chair, handcuffed him to a rear rung, manacled his feet, and went away.

An hour went by before Danshov heard a door open and clang shut behind him. He did not move. He heard scuffing sounds that he imagined was a chair being placed close behind him. Then he heard a voice that was old and harsh: "Do not turn your head. I am Colonel Nikita Komov of the Federal Security Service of the Russian Federation. You are a spy. I know that. I am going to ask you questions. You will answer them truthfully."

"I don't know what you're talking about," Danshov said, speaking in English and vainly trying to filter fear from his voice. "I demand . . ." He could not go on. He felt he was speaking to a wraith, an invisible man.

Komov's interrogation procedure—the faceless inquisitor—had often worked so well there was no need for what was officially known as physical persuasion.

"Yours was an audacious operation," Komov said. "Let us go over it together."

Danshov did not speak.

Komov resumed: "I am reading from a rather thick FSB file. You arrived in Russia on twenty-nine August this year. On twelve September you had an audience with President Lebed. You presented the President with a book: your Russian translation of *Running the World: The Inside*

Story of the National Security Council and the Architects of American Power by David Rothkopf. Correct?"

Danshov did not speak, but Komov could see Danshov's upper body stiffen and his head snap forward.

"You will answer in Russian when I ask a question. Did you present that book to President Lebed?"

"Yes," Danshov answered in Russian. "But I—"

"You will not speak except to answer my questions. . . . To continue, President Lebed placed the book on a bookshelf near his desk, giving it a prominent position to acknowledge the intellectual comradeship between our two nations. Correct?"

Again, Danshov's body stiffened and he remained silent.

After two minutes passed, Komov repeated, "Correct?"

"Yes."

"The book was actually an undetectable recording device. I am told by my experts that the pages of the book were coated with an inverted version of the lamination surface used to make anti-glare television screens. The laminated pages, arranged in a certain manner, act as a recorder of spoken words and transmit sound instead of light. Interesting and ingenious. Surely you would like to describe it. I believe the process is called transflective technology."

Komov paused for four minutes before Danshov blurted a few words in English and then switched to Russian: "But the book. I did not know—"

"Please, Traitor Danshov, do not lie to me. Do not act as if you are less than brilliant. Your device—what you may not have invented but what you inserted in the President's office—did work. Private words from President Lebed went to your National Security Agency via the so-called secret NSA Special Collection Service agents under diplomatic cover in your embassy."

"I . . . I did not know . . . what happened," Danshov said, now committed to speaking Russian.

"On the contrary, Traitor Danshov."

"I . . . I am not a traitor," Danshov said in Russian. He flexed his shoulders and shook his head. "I am an American. I did not betray my country."

"An interesting point," Komov said, pleased to see that he and his prisoner were having a dialogue—the first sign that an interrogation was working. "However, in my view you are a traitor. You used the Russian language. You lectured in Russian in Moscow State University. You used the trust of Russia to betray Russia. You are a traitor."

Danshov heard the chair behind him scrape. Then he heard departing footsteps.

After letting Danshov sit for another hour, Komov returned.

"And so, Traitor Danshov, have you decided to admit you are a spy?"

"No," Danshov said in Russian.

"You have met three times with another traitor, Sergei Aldonin. Is that not so?"

"I cannot be held like this. I demand to—"

"Come now, Traitor Danshov. You know Sergei Aldonin, the FSB technician. And you know that he was assigned to check for unauthorized electronic devices in President Lebed's office."

"I do not know Sergei Aldonin."

"Oh, Traitor Danshov, you shamefully lie and lie and lie," Komov said, his voice mimicking sadness. He paused for a moment before continuing: "Nine days ago you attended a reception at the residence of the American ambassador. You drank two bottles of Samuel Adams beer."

Danshov nodded.

"You were approached by a CIA spy named Eileen Morse who falsely claims to be a diplomat. She gave you a piece of paper with something written on it. Please speak so I know you have not fallen asleep."

Danshov did not respond. A hand grabbed his right shoulder and pressed down on a soft spot between the clavicle and the throat. He yelled in pain.

"So. You are awake. Now, the paper. What was on the paper?"

"I spoke to Eileen Morse. She did not give me a paper."

"My video shows you accepting a piece of paper. Tell me what was written on that piece of paper."

"I . . . I don't remember."

"It is getting late. You must be hungry. Thirsty . . . But I am not able to give you any rewards for your lies."

Again Danshov heard the scrape of a chair and the sound of receding footsteps.

39

Back in his office, tea and a small salmon pie waited on a tray on his desk. Komov summoned Shumeyko, who had observed the interrogation through a two-way mirror. "What do you think, Lieutenant?" Komov asked, offering a portion of the pie. Shumeyko waved the pie away but accepted a glass of tea.

"I think, sir, that your instinct is correct. The embassy spies are reacting to the disappearance of Aldonin."

"So, Lieutenant, that piece of paper the woman handed to Danshov would be brief instructions for an extraction plan for Danshov. Very brief instructions. I deduce that it would be the address of the latest safe house, and it would be from there that the extraction of Danshov would begin."

"Well done, Colonel. Next?"

"Next, Lieutenant, you may go home. You are off duty. You brought in Danshov. He will recognize you. You cannot effectively carry out the next steps. Good night."

Shumeyko looked puzzled but stood, saluted, and left.

Working through layers of surrogates, the CIA had recently leased a safe house—a drab three-room apartment in an apartment building on a one-way street near the Cheremushki Metro Station, which offered anonymity to travelers. Komov's squad of watchers, who routinely followed diplomats and their kin, suspected that a safe house had been installed in the building. Komov ordered a loose surveillance but no entry, preferring to wait until it was used for the traditional purpose of a safe house: a rendezvous between a case officer and an agent.

The disappearance of Aldonin was almost certainly known to the CIA station chief. Shumeyko believed that his seizure of Danshov would be known by now and that Danshov's case officer was Eileen Morse. In the timetable unfurling in his mind, she would arrive by subway after dark, expecting that if Danshov were released, he would do the same. Before dawn, a vehicle would appear to whisk him away to the embassy for the next step in the extraction.

Komov prepared for the rendezvous by alerting Danshov's surveillance team. Next, he called his man in the Lubyanka and ordered him to release Danshov. Finally he called a shadowy ex-convict who, though he occasionally worked for Komov, was not officially an FSB employee.

Danshov was slumped in the chair, chin on his chest. For a moment, the man in gray feared his subject had died of fear. His next thought was about what he would be told to do about the body. *Komov will know.*

But Danshov was alive. He stirred when the man touched him and slowly raised his head. "Water," he said in Russian. "Water, please."

The man uncuffed him, unlocked the manacles, and helped him stand by putting hands under Danshov's armpits and lifting, half-carrying him to the elevator. In the processing room he was seated on a bench and given a bottle of water whose cap had been removed. His jacket, wallet, watch, cell phone, glasses, Metro card, and *propusk* were all returned. He signed a paper that he did not read.

Without touching him, the man in gray took him past a staff cafeteria and back to the hall that led to the high-walled lobby and front door. The man in gray pressed a button, the door opened, and Danshov stepped into Lubyanka Square, where crowds filled the sidewalks, and streetlights and shop windows challenged the darkness.

Head down, he passed the Solovetsky Stone, a stark recollection of Stalin's reign. The stone came from the Solovetsky Islands, site of a prison camp that was part of the Gulag. He gave the stone no thought as he crossed the street and headed for the Lubyanka Metro stop.

After changing lines several times, he emerged from the Cheremushki Metro and, looking around, began briskly walking toward the apartment building where Eileen Morse waited for him. The living room's overhead light had turned on automatically, controlled by a system that indicated occupancy by mimicking the other apartments' typical daily sequences of light and darkness. She forced herself to remain in a dark bedroom and stay away from the window.

Shortly after nine o'clock, she heard a thumping sound, the sounds of brakes and glass shattering. She rushed to the window. On the sidewalk near the front door, in a streetlight's bright circle, was the body of a man. She recognized the tweed jacket.

She called for an ambulance on her cell phone as she ran down the three flights of stairs. Bursting out of the front door, she saw tire tracks that ran from the gutter, over the curb, and across the sidewalk. Bits of glass sparkled near Danshov's body, which lay facedown. She could see traces of tire tracks on the crushed back of his head, on his jacket, and on his jeans. His feet were bare, his moccasins visible in the darkness beyond the circle of light. *He never wore socks,* she thought, clicking away on her cell phone.

Seeing a flashing light in the distance, she ran toward the subway entrance and hit her app for the station chief. "Domino dead," she said. "Hit-and-run. Appears staged."

40

A top-priority flash message went directly from the Moscow station chief to Sam Stone, director of the Central Intelligence Agency. After getting a sketchy follow-up report from Moscow, Stone called Aaron Zwerdling, the director of National Intelligence, who was speaking at an American Civil Liberties Union forum in Denver. The apparent murder of an American agent raised the alert level of the CIA to its highest tier. From his aircraft carrying him back to Washington, Zwerdling passed word of the killing to the leaders of all intelligence agencies. Stone reported the death directly to President Oxley in the Oval Office.

"His family," Oxley said. "I'd like to talk to them."

"I've arranged for the State Department to notify his parents, Mr. President. He was there as an international scholar. As far as they'll know, he was a professor in Moscow who got hit by a car."

"That's it?" Oxley asked. "I can't call his folks?"

"The embassy is arranging for the body and his personal effects to be flown home, sir. He was in Special Forces in the Gulf War. The Army will make sure he's buried at Arlington."

"No public acknowledgment of the circumstances of his death?" Oxley asked.

"He was deeply involved in a very successful operation, sir. Exposure of his name and employment would inevitably compromise sources and methods. And, sir, there's the matter of his death. The intelligence community is in shock. There is no doubt he was murdered. This, sir, is not done by civilized countries."

"Should I take this up with Lebed?"

"Frank Carlton may have views on this. My advice is to not bring this to a high level," Stone replied.

After his short session with the President, Stone walked down the hall to talk to Frank Carlton. He flopped in a chair and said, "We may have a problem, Frank. I've already sent word to Drexler. The guy who got killed didn't work for us. He worked for GSS."

"Jesus!" Carlton exclaimed. "Was he the guy who ran the sweep tech? I thought—"

"Yes," Stone said. "We knew him as an American professor named Danshov teaching at Moscow State University. As you know, because of the rules, the NSA's Special Collection Service operates out of the embassy and we're tasked with babysitting guys like Danshov. He planted the book and handled the sweeper. He was an NSA contractor. Like Snowden. The Agency was on the sidelines on this one."

"So no new star on that Memorial Wall at headquarters," Carlton said softly.

"That's right," Stone said. "The Wall is reserved for anonymous remembrance of *CIA employees* killed in the line of duty."

"What exactly did happen?" Carlton asked.

"When NSA told us that the eavesdropping had suddenly stopped, we figured that the FSB tech had been blown away. At this point, NSA walked and we had Danshov on our hands. We have loose, Twitter-type sources on the campus. We found out the FSB flipped his apartment and grabbed him. We think our old friend Komov interrogated him and let him go."

"Komov? He's a tough old bastard," Carlton said. "We know from the bug that he talks directly to Lebed."

"Right," Stone said. "Well, for some reason he was released. Half-hysterical, he called a number he got from his minder."

"Another Drexler employee?"

"No, no. One of our officers, in the embassy under diplomatic cover. She headed for the safe house for a prearranged meet. She heard the hit, found the body on the sidewalk," Stone said, looking at his watch. "We're getting her out right now."

"All we can do is sit here and hope that Drexler safely aborts."

"Says he can't. Too late. He's got a substitute."

"Substitute?" Carlton bellowed. "Goddamn it, Sam. This isn't football."

"Well, we sweat it out," Stone said. "Station is keeping an eye on Falcone."

"What about the Russians?"

"They're acting like it was a traffic accident," Stone replied. "Station chief says cell phone photos, taken at the scene by the victim's case officer, indicate he was hit twice. First time, the car—or truck—jumps the sidewalk, hits him, the body's thrown up and shatters the windshield. He falls to the ground and the son of a bitch drives over him. The *Moscow Times* had it on the web as a hit-and-run, with his name, identifying him as a visiting American professor at the Moscow State University. A couple of radicals there are tweeting that it was an FSB hit. Planning a protest."

"Risky idea. Nothing backdoor from the FSB?" Carlton asked.

"Station chief got a quick call. No name. Says 'the American' had been picked up by an FSB officer 'acting without authority' and 'unfortunately' was in an accident. Sounds like Komov."

"You're not planning a reprisal, I hope."

"Nope. It could turn into something like one of those Mafia gang wars," Stone said, standing up. "We've got too much to risk. But if I ever get a chance to nip Komov . . . See you later. Back to the shop."

41

Falcone kicked off his shoes and leaned back, closing his eyes in hope of sleep. At Dulles, just before boarding, he had received a cryptic Blackphone 4 call from Drexler to Chamberlain: all on schedule: all five airborne or awaiting on-time flights. He should be free of worry. He should be drifting off. . . . But the chagrin of guilt hung over his memory of Ambassador Fedotov standing silently in the entrance hall. *Had to be done.* Trying to clear that away, he turned his thoughts to the op. *So Drex says all's well. Sure. But we're not in Moscow yet.*

Falcone had lost track of the number of times he had gone through the plan, envisioning the details of the walk-through rehearsal at the stable. Now he did it again.

At 10:35 p.m., Domino—*whoever the hell that is*—disables the corridor surveillance cameras and the electronic door-lock system on the seventh floor and cuts off electricity to Hamilton's suite. Beckley, Reilly, and Pickens, wearing the gray coveralls and blue caps of hotel maintenance men (supplied by a Domino asset), push a laundry cart through the door to Hamilton's darkened suite. The three laundry-cart men don night-vision glasses and locate Hamilton by his yelling about the blackout. Falcone sees this via images transmitted to his laptop from a night-vision body camera worn by Reilly; Falcone, via his Blackphone 4, passes information to Domino, who is in the basement.

While Pickens holds and gags Hamilton, Reilly, a former SEAL medic, injects a barbiturate anesthetic called methohexital into Hamilton's left arm. Reilly, from photographs of Hamilton and intelligence provided by

Drexler, has assumed that Hamilton is healthy enough for the drug; Reilly, estimating Hamilton's weight, has determined the size of the dose. "Blood cells take maybe thirty seconds to make a complete circuit of the body," Reilly said at the final walk-through. "He'd be under stress with a fast heartbeat. I figure he fades in five seconds."

The three men roll the hamper onto the nearby elevator, which still operates because it has an independent electrical system. The elevator stops at the floor below to pick up Falcone. By using an emergency key also provided by Domino, the elevator becomes an express to the below-ground level. A door and stairway lead to an alley. There, Domino awaits in a van disguised as an orange-and-red DHL delivery van. Gregor drives it to Vnukovo International Airport's terminal that serves private jets and cargo aircraft. They all will abandon the van and enter an aircraft that appears to be a DHL cargo plane. ("This takes a little cooperation in Germany," Drex had said.) A German contract asset—his prime employer is a German non-government special security outfit like GSS—redirects a DHL plane from Frankfurt to Vnukovo. After the party is aboard, the fake DHL plane is cleared for takeoff.

The plane flies to a military base in Riga, the capital of Latvia, which borders on western Russia. ("A little cooperation from a NATO guy I know," Drex had assured them.) Everyone, including a drowsy Hamilton, leaves the DHL aircraft. ("The pilot will be found trussed up and indignant in a Frankfurt warehouse," Drex said.) The rendition party transfers to an untraceable Gulfstream G-550, which can fly 6,750 nautical miles and can land on and take off from short-field airports. (When Falcone noted that untraceable G-550s were a CIA staple, Drex assured him that GNN gets its G-550s through an honest Lebanon broker, not from the CIA.)

The G-550 flies nonstop to the private-aircraft area of Dulles, where Falcone hands Hamilton over to Frank Carlton. *And then what?* As the mental scenario of the op ended, Falcone was left with that question. His mind gave him an answer: *Get the location of Asteroid USA.* And *Turn the whole damn thing over to Frank Carlton.* But he knew that he was fooling himself. Even when this was over he would still be involved in figuring out how to defend the Earth. *Twenty years. Wonder who will be alive. Who will be President . . .* He drifted off with a short, hazy dream about wandering in the dark inside a building without windows.

Deep sleep kept eluding Falcone. It didn't help that the pilot seemed determined to fly at an altitude that was one long stream of turbulence. During one particular moment when the 787 Dreamliner tossed about violently, Falcone noticed a nearby passenger pull out a Bible and quietly start to pray.

His thoughts turned cynical. "Don't bother," he was tempted to tell the man with the Bible. *No one is out there. Why would you think that a divine force exists or cares about you or anyone else? You think your life is more worthy than anyone else's? That you are more decent, more moral— and deserving of heavenly protection?*

No sooner did these dark thoughts pass behind his eyes than Falcone wished that he could find the peace or solace that believers did. Or seemed to.

Philosophers had long argued that the purpose of mankind was to perfect itself, to achieve a level of enlightenment that brings us closer to the divine. *Adolf Hitler thought about perfection, too. Eliminating all he deemed to be of impure blood. Jews, gypsies, blacks, didn't make the cut for purity and were turned to ash in his ovens.*

Maybe there were intelligent beings in the universe. Maybe we'd have to wait until a collection of star dust burst into existence and set in motion the creation of a new class of morally superior beings. He was convinced that that place wasn't going to be called Earth.

Falcone didn't always think like this. He was raised as a good Catholic and believed that God's son was sent to cleanse the hearts and souls of man. But that was before he held a gun and killed young men in a land far away from Boston's Little Italy. Before he was tortured by Bug and Prick and begged God to rescue him and his band of beaten brothers.

Rescue came not with the hand of God but by a bunch of sellouts in Congress who cut off money for the war. And by Richard Nixon knowing he had to fold 'em, sanctimoniously declaring he had achieved a "peace with honor." What horseshit. . . .

A baby's cry from somewhere in the cabin jolted him, pulling him back from the edge of melancholia.

42

Falcone managed to get some sleep before the plane landed in Frankfurt. The young woman in the VIP lounge directed him to a door marked PRIVATE at the back of the lounge and said, "Your colleague has arrived."

Gregor Ivanisov was sitting in a yellow club chair next to a low table. From his expression, Falcone sensed that he had news that was not going to be good. But he held up a champagne flute, prompting in Falcone's mind a moment of guilty remembrance of his meeting with Fedotov. On the table was an ice bucket sprouting a bottle of champagne.

"Good to see you," Ivanisov said. "You got the news, I assume."

"What?" Falcone asked, filling his flute.

"Domino is dead. Killed by a hit-and-run."

"Jesus! So we abort?"

"No. The General says no abort. He has a new Domino."

"So he gets to decide whether we abort?"

"Yes. Once we're in the field. That's the way it works."

"We're not there yet." Falcone thought back to Jimmy Carter's botched attempt to rescue the American hostages in Iran. No one knew who was in charge. "I may have to make a call to clear up who can abort. Why didn't I find out about Domino? And how the hell did *you* hear?"

"Paged at Logan, just as I was boarding. I assumed you knew, too."

"No. This is the first I've heard. I guess I've been blacked out. What do you know?"

"The General was brief. Like he usually is. He just said they got word Domino was killed in an accident in Moscow. Lot of crazy or drunk drivers in Moscow. 'Hit-and-run' happens a lot. But it isn't always an accident. Some of them involve oligarch warfare and are unofficially known as 'business-related.' "

"So I've heard," Falcone said. "But this sounds like it's more official. Sounds like the FSB is onto us."

"I thought of that, too," Ivanisov replied. "It's possible. But it's also possible that the FSB isn't going to connect the dots. Somebody brings in Domino for some reason—maybe he's got a big mouth, maybe a girlfriend squealed on him. Somebody roughs him up a bit during questioning and he dies. So they set up a phony accident and make it look like a hit-and-run."

"Sounds like you know a lot about how the FSB operates," Falcone said.

"I have friends in Russia. Let's leave it at that."

"Okay. So maybe the FSB isn't tracking us down. How the hell can a new guy slip into being Domino at this point?"

"We've got to trust the General. It's what we do."

Falcone nodded, unable to speak for a moment, feeling the fear and the unknown. *Trust the General,* Falcone thought. *Yes, that's what we do, what we soldiers of the state have done for centuries.*

"I wish I had your faith," Falcone said. "I read somewhere that when a plan meets the real world, the real world always wins. Drexler surely knows that."

Ivanisov poured himself another glass of champagne and said, "Domino was a lot of help in Yemen."

"Yemen? What the hell . . . ?"

"Knew his way around. Real good with languages. Spoke perfect Arabic, Hebrew, Russian too, but with a slight Ukrainian accent. Smart as hell. I think he might have been ex-CIA. He knew where all the electrical switches were. Things like that. Had a sense of humor, too. I got the idea that he ran a string of assets, like maybe a concierge."

"And he was a freelancer? That's what Drexler told me," Falcone said. He could not call him "the General."

"I thought—well, this'll sound funny—but I thought that maybe being freelance *was* his cover."

"You're saying that he was CIA? I thought GSS didn't work with the CIA."

"I'm saying that his cover was *not* being CIA."

"Damn!" Falcone said. "I need the real world." He reached for the bottle. "Where is it?"

"Somewhere around the corner," Ivanisov said, filling his glass and laughing.

"I try not to look around the corner," Falcone said.

"Good idea, Sean. But you must know this kind of fuck up happens all the time."

"Right. But Domino. What exactly did he do in that Yemen snatch?"

"I don't talk about my travels," Ivanisov said. "But let me say that it went off pretty well. All we had to do was grab Abu Saif Ramadi, stuff him into a bag and get to the coast, a couple of miles or less. Then we had a sub pick us up and haul ass outta there. Yemenis didn't raise much of a fuss. Ramadi was attracting too many drone strikes. And they were happy to get rid of him without looking like they sold one of their bros out. This op is a lot different. Sounds like Lebed personally wants Hamilton in Russia."

"Where'd you take Ramadi? Guantanamo?" Falcone hated the thought of Gitmo. He had spent too many days dealing with Congress to get them to shut the place down.

"Don't know."

"Or won't say?"

Ivanisov shrugged his shoulders and remained silent.

"I appreciate your knowing how to keep your mouth shut," Falcone said. "Lots of people don't. But can you tell me how Drexler heard about Domino's death?"

"I'd guess Annie. She's glued to her computer every minute we're planning and going on an op. She got a lot from her online reading of the *Moscow Times.* Lots of stories about the hit-and-run. Big news when an American gets killed. The Russkies really love to hate us, you know."

"It's an English-language paper, right?"

"Yeah. And no big supporter of Lebed, but they have to be careful how far they can go or one of their editors will disappear."

"So you're figuring Annie saw online that an American was killed in a hit-and-run, and, when she saw his name she knew it was Domino."

"Sounds about right. And, you know what? I still give us a fair chance of pulling this off. But win or lose, either way, this is my last op. I've danced with the devil too many times."

Short, Falcone thought, remembering the young guy in his company who had "Don't Shoot Me. I'm Short" written on his helmet. *Short* meant "short-timer," someone with a month or so to go in Vietnam before going home. *Maybe Gregor is thinking short.* Falcone tried not to remember that the kid with the Short sign didn't make it home.

"Like I said. Call me when you're back," Falcone said. "I'm serious"

"Roger that," Ivanisov said, looking at his watch. "Look. I've got to get going. I fly Aeroflot from here to Berlin, then from there, on German-wings, to Moscow. And—"

"Germanwings? That's the outfit whose plane—"

"Yeah. The one that had the crazy copilot that crashed into the mountain. Well, he won't be driving on my flight."

"Why the odd flight to Berlin?"

"The idea was to find a way for me to land at Vnukovo. You and everybody else are landing at Sheremetyevo and heading for downtown Moscow hotels. I'll be at the airport hotel at Vnukovo."

"Why Vnukovo?"

"Moscow has three major airports. Sheremetyevo gets most U.S. flights. Vnukovo is busy, with passengers and cargo, and it's a little closer to the hotel." He leaned in and lowered his voice, though they were the only people in the room. "It's also where we exit. I get a chance for a last-minute recon."

Ivanisov picked up his carry-on and headed for the door. "See you soon," he said. "And don't say 'good luck.' I don't believe in luck."

43

As soon as Ivanisov left, Falcone took out his Blackphone 4 and called Ursula, knowing that, no matter the time, she would be no farther than two rings from her cell phone.

"Yes?" she said cautiously. The ID panel was blank, and she did not immediately know the caller was Falcone.

"First, no names. All's well. I just want you to do something."

"Yes?" she repeated.

"Online, find the *Moscow Times* for the last few days. Look for any stories about hit-and-run accidents, especially any about an American." A thought flashed in his mind: *Iceman for Ivanisov, Buggy for Beckley, Rambo for Reilly, Pepper for Pickens. . . .* "Probably the American's name will begin with the letter D."

"D as in—"

". . . As in Domino. Hold on to that information until I ask for it. Do not attempt to call me. Okay?"

"Yes. You . . . you're all right?"

"Yes. Fine. See you soon. Goodbye."

The last time Falcone arrived in Moscow he was aboard Air Force One with Oxley, who was going to Lebed's inauguration. The presidential plane, Falcone remembered, landed at Vnukovo Airport, not Sheremetyevo. Vnukovo had a VIP lounge and VIP hall, both adorned with Russian flags and huge impressionistic murals. VIPs don't go through baggage, customs, or security. They all passed directly from the VIP hall to the airport's exit road and the highway to Moscow. Vnukovo had been mentioned in Drexler's briefing, but Falcone had not appreciated its potential virtues as a getaway site.

Falcone's mind returned to the present as he handed over his passport, with stapled visa, to a stern-faced woman in a blue uniform with a blue cap perched on a stack of shiny black hair. She took one look at the visa, raised her head, and suddenly smiled and nodded. A diplomatic visa opens doors and inspires feigned good manners.

As Falcone passed through Passport Control, a porter appeared and led him to baggage claim. Then, carrying the single bag, the porter whisked Falcone to an exit door that opened to noise and confusion, except for several welcoming drivers who stood silently in a semicircle, holding signs. Falcone and the porter headed toward the one that said FALCONE and words in Cyrillic that he assumed said *Hotel Baltschug Kempinski*.

An hour later, he was in his large sixth-floor corner room, directly below Hamilton's executive suite. He collapsed on a king-size bed without unpacking, took a short nap, and left the room to board the elevator (just where Domino said it would be) to the lobby floor. He took a seat at a table in the lounge and saw the Kremlin skyline, etched by the gathering night. He ordered a Regalia vodka on the rocks, perhaps, he thought, in homage to Ambassador Fedotov.

He wanted to relax, but his mind beckoned, forcing him to run through the schedule. Tomorrow, Tuesday, he was scheduled to appear at the Metropol Hotel, the site of the International Conference on Cyber Defense. *If the FSB wanted to move on us, that would be the day. And diplomatically they could keep this quiet; they could just round us up and deport us without publicity.*

So maybe the plan would be aborted by the FSB on Tuesday. But if nothing happened on Tuesday, it could mean that the FSB was either allowing the op to go on—or they were planning to catch us red-handed.

The plan called for the snatching of Hamilton to take place on Wednesday. So there was nothing to do right now, nothing except drive from his mind how many things could go wrong. *Hit-and-run. When is a coincidence not a coincidence?*

He would meet the reassembled team at the conference. And they would go through the motions of greeting each other openly because their cover was that they were colleagues in the same law firm. Now he tried to imagine them and link them with their real names and code names. Because neither they nor he had anything on paper, it would be a feat of memory.

He could easily remember their faces; the challenge was to link names with faces and then place them in their roles during the taking of Hamilton. As he was doing this, his thoughts suddenly turned to the day that he, a brand-new second lieutenant, stood before his first command, a platoon: fourteen men, two of them sergeants. The "point of the spear," an instructor at officer training school called this basic infantry unit. He was determined to not only learn their names but also to really get to know them and their aspirations. Three were killed before he had memorized their names.

But GSS was not the U.S. Army. Identities were fake or guarded; unit cohesion lasted only as long as the op; the operatives, in his mind no matter what Drexler said, were mercenaries, not patriots or draftees. Still, he was the leader of this very small unit, and he began working his brain cells. Gregor Ivanisov, Iceman, of course was easy to recollect. Next, the square-jawed face of Jack Beckley, who was Buggy. Then the only guy with a beard: Harry Reilly, Rambo. Bobby Joe Pickens—hard-eyed, grim-faced, who was Pepper . . . And Domino—no real name, no face. Drexler had said Domino would find him. *Well, here I am.*

Falcone sensed that the meeting would happen soon. He cautiously checked the lounge without turning his head by scanning the room's reflection in the window before him. The lounge appeared as a faint image overlying the glowing Kremlin and the dark Moskva River. He could see the reflections of two women chatting amiably on stools at one end of the bar and three men sitting separately along the rest of it. He was trying to pick which man was probably the new Domino when another person walked into the lounge and into the reflection.

Startled by her image, he turned his head. *Rachel!* As the woman neared his table he called out her name: "Rachel!"

She was Rachel. She had to be. The way she carried herself. Confident of her feminism and sexual allure. Strong. Capable of undoing a man with her sea-green eyes or a garrote that was never far from her hands. And, he realized, she had to be Domino.

"I'm sorry," the woman said coolly, looking straight into his face. "You've mistaken me for someone else." She wore an embroidered, high neckline blue dress that ended just above her knees. Blue, he remembered, was her favorite color. Israeli-flag blue, she called it.

In that instant he recognized her crisp voice. *Her hair is different. Raven, not blond. And her eyes are brown when they should be green. But who the hell knows? She's a chameleon.* And now the eyes—Rachel's eyes—told him to be careful.

"I'm terribly sorry," Falcone said, standing, His knees were shaky, his heart skipping. "But your resemblance is uncanny . . . to a fine, wonderful woman I knew."

"I can see the bewilderment in your face," she said, smiling.

"You could erase my bewilderment by joining me for a drink," Falcone said.

The woman sat. Looking at her close up, he had no doubt that she was Rachel. And Rachel was the new Domino. *What the hell is she doing? She's Israeli, a former Mossad assassin. Maybe not former.*

"What brings you to Moscow?" he asked.

"Perhaps the same thing that brings you," she said, smiling.

Falcone was momentarily perplexed by the ambiguity of the woman's response. A waiter was heading for the table. She obviously timed her next words so that the waiter would hear them. "I run a high-tech security firm in St. Petersburg. I'm on a panel at the cyber security conference."

"Wonderful coincidence! I'm also here for the conference. And some men from my firm. . . . The conference is being held at the Metropol," Falcone said, and, with a tone of malice in his voice, decided to test her cover, asking, "What brings you to the Kempinski?"

Smiling, she answered, "Meeting with a software salesman who makes so much money he can stay here. Would you like his name?"

She fished through her large handbag, extracted a small leather case, and produced a card from a salesman for an Israeli software manufacturer.

"Thank you," Falcone said, grinning. "Did he sell you anything?"

"No. But in my business he is a good man to know."

He ordered another vodka; she asked for Russian sparkling wine. When the waiter left, she extracted a second card, handed it to him and, without moving her lips, whispered, "Kismet. It's meant to be. We meet again!"

Falcone reached inside his suit jacket and pulled out his Sullivan & Ford business card. Handing it to Rachel, Falcone glanced quickly at her card, and said, "Well, it's nice to meet you, Ms.—"

"Andrea, Mr. Falcone. Andrea Mitrovitz." She had said "Falcone" without first looking at his card.

"Well, I'll see you at the conference, Andrea."

"I'm sure you will," she said. She paused before adding, "Have you had dinner?"

"I'm still recovering from jet lag," he said. "But . . . do you have any suggestions?"

"There's a wonderful place for the finest Russian cuisine. Café Pushkin on Tverskoy Boulevard. And then, perhaps, a walk along the river."

"Sounds like a fine idea. I'm glad we happened to run into each other."

"Yes. And perhaps you will tell me about this woman named Rachel."

"I'll tell you what I know. But I'm not sure where she is now and what she is doing with her life."

"I'm sure she must be doing something worthwhile. Shall we meet at the Pushkin at seven?" She took a last sip and left.

As she walked past the bar, the men turned and stared. Men always stared at her, Falcone remembered.

One of them stood in front of her and said something Falcone could not make out.

She swung her bag at his head, and as he reeled he knocked over the bar stool. She stiffened her free hand and, using it like a blade, slammed down hard on the bridge of his nose. He slumped to the floor, blood flowing down his face. The two women down the bar applauded.

She strode out of the hotel as if there had never been an obstacle in her path.

When Falcone had been President Oxley's national security adviser, he was given a highly secret CIA briefing on a Mossad rendition. Only the name of the Mossad target was revealed. But Falcone was sure that Rachel had been involved. Memory of that briefing drifted into his mind.

An employee at Israel's top-secret Negev Nuclear Research Center became convinced that Israel's development of nuclear bombs had to be revealed. He slipped into England under an assumed name, contacted a journalist, and told all he knew about Israel's nuclear bombs. Israel had never confirmed or denied having a nuclear-weapons program. The newspaper account broke the nuclear seal, and subsequent leaks established beyond a doubt that Israel was a nuclear nation.

In an operation to capture and punish the employee, Mossad concocted what is popularly known in the spy world as a honeypot operation. A woman posing as an American tourist named "Cindy" was sent to London, where she struck up what appeared to be a chance encounter with the employee.

Rachel! Falcone remembered thinking at this point in the briefing, expecting that she was going to assassinate the employee. Instead, Cindy feigned a romance and convinced her new boyfriend to accompany her to Rome. Ultimately, he was not assassinated. Instead, Mossad agents, directed by Cindy, chose a rendition that partially resembled Drexler's plan: injection of a paralyzing drug, dumped in a van, abducted to his homeland. The van took him to a dock instead of an airport. A launch left the port of Civitavecchia and sped to an Israeli intelligence ship masquerading as a merchantman, which took him to Israel. He was tried, convicted, and given a long prison sentence. *Chalk one up for a non-homicidal Rachel.*

44

Rachel stooped to pluck the nearly-invisible thread from the bottom hinge of the door. *Room not entered.* A soft light filled her room when she entered. *Automatic switch. Recessed-lighting,* she instinctively thought. *Transformer to reduce voltage. Easy to disable.* To her, it was all what the instructor had said at the Mossad training school: situational awareness, a lesson that had often saved her life.

Rachel—her real name, her born name, and the name she had not used for a long time: That was the name of her real existence, now all but lost. And that was how Falcone knew her. *And now he's reappeared. How could that be? Kismet . . . or Bashert. My grandmother would have called it Bashert: the gift—or curse—that comes from Heaven, that makes you rich or poor, dead or spared, damned or blessed. Bashert.*

Her memory took her back to the first time she met with Falcone at a State Department dinner in Washington when he was a senator. The attraction was instant—and forbidden. Perhaps that was part of it. He was chairman of the Senate Intelligence Committee and she was an Israeli, a member of Mossad's *kidon*, a professional killer. Yet, when he learned this, he still pursued her. Or was it the reverse?

She had never met anyone like him: Strong but hiding a deep wound behind the tough exterior. Mossad's psychological profile peeled back the layers of his life. He had survived the physical beatings while a prisoner of war. His bones had been broken; his faith shattered. Yet he pushed on through the pain, persevered.

Falcone possessed all of the gifts of a natural politician—dancing eyes, a firm handshake, a million-dollar smile, and a seemingly genuine affability. Yet lurking behind the facade was a darkness, a shadow that he could not shake. No amount of charm could hide it from prying eyes. And if Rachel could do anything better than kill an enemy, it was the detection of the hair-thin fissures behind the mask that all men and women wear.

Against all odds and protocols, they had become lovers. She had even fantasized that she would leave her beloved country and profession to marry him. But the thought was as thin and evanescent as a soap bubble. They were alike in so many ways. Both were haunted by their pasts. Both were driven to protect their nation's security. And both hoped to reach an idyllic plateau where they could enjoy some level of solace, of peace from the war within and the wars without.

But their differences were as great as the burdens they shared. Rachel allowed herself a small laugh as she thought about the lines from Sholom Aleichem's *Fiddler on the Roof:*

"Fyedka is not a creature, Papa. Fyedka is a man."

"A bird, may love a fish, but where would they build a home together?"

And it was that simple. They could never build a nest that could accommodate the two of them. Yet, just as they were destined to remain apart, fate kept pulling them together on dangerous missions.

And now this.

It all began three days ago, when Rachel was contacted by David Ben-Dar, the head of Mossad and a kind of uncle to her through most of her career. Ben-Dar, nearing retirement, had just received the agency's highest decoration. The award was for an unspecified "important contribution to a unique operational activity," in which she had played a part.

He contacted her in the usual way, by a one-word telephone call: *Mizrach,* a lovely Hebrew word not just for *east* but also for *the place of the sunrise.* That single word was an order, a high-priority summons for noon the following day at a Mossad safe house in Moscow. She had wondered if Ben-Dar were summoning her so she could congratulate him for the award. If so, it would be a highly uncharacteristic show of vanity.

She knew that she would be meeting with a Mossad officer designated by David Ben-Dar, who never traveled out of Israel. He relayed his orders through the Mossad network of agents and chiefs of station at embassies and consulates. He also had ways to contact less accessible officers who were—or appeared to be—citizens of "denied areas"—countries that did not have diplomatic relations with Israel.

The safe house was in the Kitai-Gorod district, a neighborhood over-looking the Moskva River—quiet streets, churches, ancient buildings, back alleys, and three-or four-story apartment houses framing shadowy courtyards. Dressed drably and traveling by subway, she arrived at the two-room safe apartment early enough to enjoy a lunch of tea and chicken-salad sandwiches with the young woman sent by the station chief. They went through a series of passwords and counter-passwords tucked inside a fifteen-minute conversation in Russian about shopping and restaurants.

Rachel departed with a purse that she had switched with the young woman. Inside was a cell phone she would later destroy. Taking the usual precautions to confirm she was not being followed, she took the Metro on two lines, interspersed by taxi rides. Her trip finally ended a quarter mile from the Metropol. From there she walked, ducking into an alley leading to a small store, where she lingered, waiting to see if anyone else entered the alley. Convinced she was not being followed, she left the store and went on to the hotel, which she entered via a side door.

In her room, with the television loudly playing, she pressed a button. Ben-Dar answered immediately, saying in Hebrew "Please, no questions unless absolutely necessary." He quickly outlined the operation, casually said it had been approved by Prime Minister Weisman, and mentioned that "your old friend Falcone" would be her contact. He called Falcone *Aluf,* literally *champion,* the title used in the Israel Defense Forces for rank equivalent to general, air marshal, or admiral. "He will be looking for a contact code named Domino."

"And how could someone as smart as Falcone allow himself to become a part of such a mad scheme?" she asked, breaking the no-question or-der. "It is a mission impossible. Abducting an American billionaire in Moscow and getting him out of the heart of Russia? And even more in-sane was the absence of any preparation and training. Plan A had gaping holes. And there was no Plan B if things went to hell, as they were sure to do."

"Calm down, Rachel. Calm down," Ben-Dar said.

But she ranted on: "The tires were already falling off before Komov killed Danshov."

"Tires?" Ben-Dar asked.

"An American expression for the rapid failure of a plan. Danshov, as you know, had a CIA background and was working under the code name Domino. His death should have shut down the operation. And the FSB has to be onto Falcone. . . ."

"Please, Rachel," Ben-Dar said.

But she went on, raising the pace of her words to rapid-fire: "Why do you want to help? Why risk becoming involved in a foolish plan and then get blamed for it when it goes down?"

"Please, Rachel. No questions. You'll come to understand it all soon enough. I have talked to various people about a few changes, which you will receive soon."

45

Colonel Komov and Lieutenant Shumeyko walked down a long, dimly lit hallway in the basement of the Hotel Baltschug Kempinski. At an unmarked door, Komov tapped six digits on the number pad and opened the door. "Remain here," Komov ordered, closing the door behind him.

As he stepped into the gray box of a room, a man rose from the controls of a wall full of ever-changing surveillance images.

"This is an honor, Colonel," the man said with a slight bow. He wore a black suit, a tightly knotted red tie, and a white shirt. On the breast pocket of his suit coat was the name of the hotel in Cyrillic letters.

"I am conducting a sensitive inquiry," Komov said. "Make no report of my visit." The man nodded again and said, "Absolutely, Colonel." He had recognized Komov on one of the surveillance cameras at the front entrance and had texted an alert to Sergey Algov at his concierge station in the lobby. Komov's visits were rare, and news of them reverberated throughout the staff. Komov was a man to fear.

Billionaire friends of Lebed had recently been arrested and indicted for fraudulent business corruption on evidence obtained by FSB recording devices in their Baltschug Kempinski executive suites. Their conversations—some merely bawdy, some involving brazen bribery—were thrown out of court, and the suspects were all acquitted.

Against Komov's wishes, orders soon went out from Lebed's office: no more electronic eavesdropping anywhere in the hotel. And FSB officers were ordered to stop hanging out in the lounge bar. The actions had infuriated Komov, who saw the hotel as a den of sinners given immunity by the *siloviki*, "the people of power."

Komov reached into his briefcase, extracted two passports, and handed them to the man seated at the surveillance console. He assumed that Komov had obtained them from a hotel official. Passports were routinely taken from guests when they checked in, with the explanation that it was being done as a service so that they could be put in a hotel safe for maximum security.

"I am looking for images of this man and this woman," Komov said. "Particularly images showing them together."

The man copied the passport photos in a facial-recognition device, which began whirring through thousands of images. As he handed the passports back to Komov, he saw the names and the diplomatic visas. He made a mental note to tell Sergey Algov about Komov's interest in these guests. As a concierge, Sergey wanted to get all the information he could about hotel guests. And he shared his tips.

Komov stood before a battery of surveillance monitors. "There. That one. Stop," he said to the man. Komov leaned forward to peer at one of the monitors. "Closer. Move in closer."

The operator froze an image of a black-haired woman in a blue dress. She was talking to a man in a dark suit and a red-and-white striped tie. Komov nodded. "Yes, Falcone," Komov said half-aloud. "And the so-called Mitrovitz."

He turned to the operator and said, "They are speaking. Let me hear."

"I am sorry, Colonel. But there is only video." He said the word, syllable by syllable.

"What kind of surveillance is this?" Komov angrily exclaimed. "I was expecting *audio* surveillance also."

"I am, once more, sorry, Colonel. But we have been instructed to—"

"All right, all right. I know, I know. Never mind. Go through all surveillance of those two subjects. Alone or together."

The operator worked the controls for a few minutes and then, on the large central monitor, jerky video of several scenes began: Falcone check-ing into the hotel . . . going to his room . . . leaving the room . . . going to a restaurant . . . going to the bar . . . The woman in the blue dress appear-ing at his table . . . the encounter between the woman and a man at the bar . . . The woman standing beneath the marquee, getting into a taxi . . .

"Stop!" Komov commanded. "Go back. Back to the man at the bar." He had recognized the FSB officer and smiled when he went down. He needed to be reprimanded. "Make a copy," he ordered and put the copy in his briefcase.

He took out a thin folder of photographs and spread them on the operator's table. The photographs were obvious surveillance images. They bore time stamps going back several years with identifications changing—blond Rachel Yeager, blond Sarah Hyman, red-haired Miya Polansky, black-haired Andrea Mitrovitz—but never did the beauty change. Always, the glowing beauty. After scanning them, the facial-recognition device reported that all the images were of the same person.

Komov knew he had seen that face before. She had thwarted the crazy plan by Colonel Cyril Metrinko to destroy the Al Aqasa Mosque and blame it on the Israelis, launching a war that would enflame the world. Metrinko, who had headed the KGB counterintelligence before Komov, had believed he could best serve Russia by reigniting the Cold War. She had killed Metrinko's agent, a Russian who had been masquerading as a Jewish-American businessman-philanthropist, seconds before he was about to set off the explosives buried inside the mosque. *Mossad.*

The operator made copies of the latest images, which Komov put in his folder and returned to his briefcase. With a nod to the operator, he headed toward the door. The operator stepped before him to open the door for him. He closed it slowly, allowing himself to hear Komov say to Shumeyko, "I will go to Lubyanka now. I must do some work there—some research in the archives. I'll return tomorrow. There are guests I must in-terrogate and perhaps detain. You will accompany me."

46

As the ZIL sped to the Lubyanka, Shumeyko's cell phone buzzed. Komov frowned. He hated cell phones. He did see their value and saw the need for FSB officers to carry them. But he had expressly ordered that no cell phone was to sound in his presence. Before he could censure Shumeyko, the lieutenant said, "Yes, yes, sir. Right here, sir."

His hand shaking, he passed the cell phone to Komov, who held it gingerly, not sure how to listen. Before he could get it to his ear, he could hear the voice of Boris Lebed shouting, "Komov! Come to my office immediately!"

Komov handed the cell phone back to Shumeyko and said to the driver, "It is necessary to go to the Kremlin."

The ZIL stopped before the Borovitsky Gate. Komov walked briskly to the East Door, where a presidential guard—high-peaked, gold-and-black hat, blue tunic, shiny black boots—stepped forward, saluted, and escorted him through a warren of halls and stairs to Lebed's suite and then to his office door. A young aide, whom Komov knew, appeared from a side door, spoke into a cell phone, and motioned for Komov to enter. The guard did a smart about-face and strode away.

Komov stood at attention in front of Lebed's desk until the President pointed to a straight-back chair. Komov sat and waited, motionless for three full minutes in the heavy silence of Lebed's smoldering rage. Lebed was reading a paper bearing his letterhead, crossing out words and substituting new ones. He finally looked up and said, "I am writing an order that you be arrested and publicly prosecuted for murder." He reached for another piece of paper and said, "I have already written a statement, to be signed by you, in which you resign from the FSB. Only then will you be spared from a vacation in prison. In the old days, I would have handed you a Tokarev pistol and left the room."

Lebed placed the sheet of paper at the edge of the desk. Komov stared at the paper for a moment before picking it up and reading the single sentence that ended his career. "There is no reason given," he said, gazing at Lebed, who lifted his head and looked at Komov, eye-to-eye.

"None is needed," Lebed said. "Your age makes retirement automatic if you merely ask for it."

"I have a right—"

"You have no rights, Komov. I am delivering you from what you deserve. You murdered an American and—"

"—an American spy . . . sir. And an accident—"

"No one was fooled by your fake hit-and-run. The lying *Moscow Times*—I tolerate it to keep my propaganda artists happy—says a witness saw tire tracks on Danshov's body. And—"

Komov interrupted to say, "My people tell me that witness was a CIA woman under diplomatic—"

"Damn you, Komov! If you interrupt me one more time, I'll have you arrested right here in my office! The American secretary of state called our foreign minister. There are protests scheduled at the university, unleashing those young shits. And the director of the FSB is threatening to resign if I don't get rid of you. As you well know, there is a procedure for handling accused spies: questioning by trained interrogators seeking to turn him, for example. You claim to be an expert on counterintelligence. Arranging for a hit-and-run is not counterintelligence."

"But, sir—"

"There is nothing to say. Go to your apartment and give that KGB uniform to a museum."

"But the other Americans—"

"There are no 'other Americans' for you, Komov. I have instructed Lieutenant Shumeyko to shut down any operation you have ordered. He has been reporting directly to me for some time. He told me about the NSA recorder."

"I was about—"

"You were *not* about to tell me. You were going to take control. *You* would have *your* ear in my office! Lieutenant Shumeyko personally removed the devilish book, and FSB technicians are examining it."

"Your spy lies. You wanted Shumeyko to get something on me so I would be forced to resign. That was his mission, wasn't it?"

"Get out! I want to wipe you from my memory and the memory of the FSB."

Komov stood, and, pounding Lebed's desk, shouted, "He deserved to die. Spies deserve death."

"Go! Get out!"

The door flew open and two presidential guards ran into the room.

"Take this old man away," Lebed ordered, his face reddening. "I want never to see his face again."

47

What in hell is going on? *What is she doing in Moscow? How much does Drexler know about her? How could Drexler pick an Israeli Mossad agent to be part of the operation? Why didn't he have her vetted? Or had he? Maybe this op isn't as secret as I thought it was. She's on a mission for GSS and, inevitably, a mission for the Mossad. You never quit the Mossad. But punching that guy? Agents don't make fusses and call attention to themselves.* Then: *Maybe very good ones do.*

Falcone's thoughts of the present were overtaken by a flashback to the night he first met her. It was an official State Department dinner for the Israeli foreign minister. Most of the guests knew each other and so did not need to follow the Washington protocol of introducing themselves by announcing their titles (those without titles were rarely on guest lists) and awaiting a similar announcement from their dinner mates.

As a general rule, Falcone refused to ride Washington's social merry-go-round. He was at the State Department that evening because he was trying to find out more about his friend and colleague, Senator Joshua Stock, who had been murdered. Stock had been invited to the dinner, and Falcone had come in his place to see whom Joshua might have been associating with before he died.

Now, at this moment, sitting in Moscow and staring at the Kremlin, all that intrigue and tragedy fell away. At this moment, he could not remember the names of anyone at his table at that dinner. Except for a woman named Rachel, a luminously beautiful blond woman who sat on his left.

She introduced herself as Rachel Yeager of the Israeli Embassy's "cultural affairs" department without a hint of irony about her work. What she did not announce was that she had just read the embassy's intelligence file on him, a copy of which she later gleefully gave him. The file showed him to be a widower, Army veteran, and former prisoner of war. "While personally congenial and affable," the profile said, "subject does not socialize often. Avoids formal banquets and dinners. Dates infrequently. Drinks moderately." She had been ordered to find out more about him and more about the murder of a United States senator.

Falcone wanted to talk to her, but he was unnerved by her large sea-green eyes that seemed at once innocent and worldly. At the same time, he realized, with a fascination tinged by guilt, that she had an uncanny resemblance to his late wife Karen. Finally, feeling like a high-school sophomore, he asked, "May I . . . may I call you? Dinner?" He smiled now, remembering his tentativeness word-for-word.

They had dinner at Positano's, a family-run Italian restaurant in Bethesda. It did not go well. Initially, they exchanged small talk. But when Falcone declared that he was fair-handed when it came to the Israeli-Palestinian conflict, she erupted: "You are *neutral*? That means you're for the Palestinians and against Israel."

Falcone, stung by the charge, launched an emphatic counter-attack across the table that he was not against the Israelis and resented the implication that he was anti-Semitic. The owner of Positano's came rushing to the table to see what was wrong because other diners were growing anxious about the rising volume level of Falcone's and Rachel's voices. There were other, wonderful memories rushing to the surface like a deep sea diver who was nearly out of air, but he forced his mind to abandon those recollections and focus on the present.

He finished his drink and returned to his room. He had less than an hour to shower and return to the lounge to meet . . . Andrea, not Rachel.

He assumed that there was a U.S. intelligence file that had a reference to his first meeting with Rachel, whom he then did not know was a Mossad operative, a "Killer Angel." That was what some in the Mossad called its assassins ever since Prime Minister Golda Meir and the Israeli Defense Committee ordered Operation Wrath of God, following the massacre of Israeli athletes by Palestinian Black September killers during the summer Olympics in 1972 in Munich. The original Killer Angels were agents of vengeance, ordered to track down and kill the killers.

Mossad talent scouts—ever alert to promising young talent—spotted her during her compulsory service in the Israeli Defense Forces, when, on border duty questioning Palestinians, she easily shifted from one Arabic dialect to another. She was a brilliant linguist, an aggressive soccer player, and had Killer Angel potential, according to a psychiatric evaluation. Easily recruited, she quickly developed into an outstanding operative. On a mission into Iran, she made her first kill—*execution* was the approved word. She was sent into Iran to track down a field agent, a *kiton,* turned rogue. She allowed him to think he had lured her into his hotel room, where she strangled him with her scarf. She said that she enjoyed looking into his eyes as he was dying.

A Mossad psychiatrist, in a routine post-mission interview, found her to be free of post-traumatic stress disorder. "PTSD develops after a terrifying ordeal that involved physical harm or the threat of physical harm," his report said. "This subject, who recounted the incident calmly, showed absolutely no negative reaction. She seems to be immune to fear, and has no hesitation to kill."

Initially, Falcone believed that Rachel had murdered Joshua, who had served with Falcone on the Senate Select Committee on Intelligence. Joshua had had his throat slit during a night of drugs and sexual odyssey. In fact, Rachel had been on the trail of Joshua's killer and had saved Falcone's life when he was attacked one night in the garage of his apartment building. She agreed to work with Falcone, and, together, they found the murderer. Still, her career as an assassin deeply troubled Falcone. When he asked her how she could defend murder, she had said, "It is Israel's fate always

to be under attack by her enemies. And my gift to Israel is that I can eliminate some of those enemies wherever they can be found. This is not
murder, but justice for my country."

In their quest for Stock's killer, trust—and then peril—had pulled
them together. Falcone soon realized that he was falling in love with an
assassin. And though Falcone had resigned himself to a solitary life, convinced that it would be a final betrayal to his deceased wife, he was de-
fenseless against Rachel's allure. The attraction was irresistible. They made
love on an island in Maine and again in Jerusalem, where they had
thwarted a plot by the Russians to blow up the Temple Mount in Jerusalem. Their romance ended abruptly with both of them knowing that there
was no room for love in Rachel's world. Or in Falcone's.

Falcone had moved on, from Senate to law firm to Oxley's national security adviser—and now to an "off the books" covert operative. Taking
advantage of his top-security clearance, he continued to go through the
CIA files on Rachel. They were full of gaps because the Mossad plays a
very tight game. He found little more than some of her other names—
Sarah, Miya, Elena, and countless more. There were reports of professional
killings—wet jobs, as they were called. There were sometimes sightings
of her around the time or place of killings. Then, suddenly, she disappeared
from the files.

Early in Oxley's first term she had reemerged. The occasion was a
formal State Dinner, honoring Israeli Prime Minister Avi Weisman. For
his meeting with Oxley, Weisman had demanded that he receive all the
protocol honors rendered to a head of state, and the glittering White
House dinner was one of the honors. Rachel had just been named Israel's ambassador to the United Nations. She was also Weisman's mistress, according to the State Department's Bureau of Intelligence and
Research.

Falcone was out of the country on a mission as national security adviser and did not see Rachel during her brief visit. But they soon met again.
Once more they worked together to aid their homelands, tracking down
the extremist group in the United States that had conspired to set off a
nuclear bomb in Iran, but had instead destroyed the city of Savannah,

Georgia. After that, her brief tenure as an ambassador—and mistress—had ended. She was too much of an unbridled force of nature for either occupation. She returned to Israel, ostensibly to resign from the Foreign Ministry and become CEO of one of Israel's many software firms. But, as Rachel had just vividly demonstrated, she was still a force to be reckoned with. *Provocateur beware.*

48

The maître d' met them at the entrance of what looked like a pre-Revolution Russian mansion illumined by gaslight. Rachel chatted with him for a moment before he led them up a curving, dimly lit stairway that led to a third-floor room whose walls were lined with bookshelves. As they were taken to their table, Falcone heard more snatches of English than Russian coming from the other tables.

"It's what you Americans call a tourist trap," Rachel said. "We're in a reproduction of a nineteenth-century aristocrat's library, complete with the real books that you would find there. This place is a time machine taking you back to the days of the czar."

"Reminds me of a library I know in Virginia," Falcone said, watching for her reaction.

"In a house where George Washington slept?" Rachel asked, smiling.

"Yes. I'm surprised you've been there. Just as I'm surprised you're here for . . . the conference."

Lively balalaika music wafted up from the floor below. The sommelier appeared and Rachel conferred with him in Russian, then turned back to Falcone.

"Why surprised, Sean? It sounds like an interesting conference. Cyber security. Isn't that what we all want? Security?"

"I'm not, of course, talking about the conference," Falcone replied.

"Of course. But I try not to mix business with pleasure."

"And this is no place to talk about business?"

A waiter approached. His gray tunic was torn and wrinkled. There was a patch on a leg of his black trousers. His black boots were mud-splattered. He presented a bottle for inspection to Rachel, who sipped and nodded. He then handed a frayed menu, in English, to Falcone, who gave it to Rachel. She spoke in Russian, then told Falcone, "We are, of course, getting borsch and pirogi, which is better, I'm sure, than you get at the Mari Vanna." Falcone recognized the name of a Russian restaurant in Washington. "And our wine, Mukuzani, is from Georgia, one of the oldest wine regions on Earth."

"The waiter looked a little worse for wear," Falcone remarked.

"A costume. The place is supposed to take you back to the days just before the Revolution. Remember, these are the people who invented the Potemkin village. Things here are not always what they look like."

"I still can't get over that you're living in Russia. When did that happen?"

"I moved my company from Berlin to St. Petersburg two years ago."

"At the suggestion of your investors?"

"I do not have any investors. I'm the owner and CEO. I enjoy St. Petersburg. Ballet. Opera. Venice of the North, not like tired old Moscow. I love the White Nights, those days of summer that take so long to turn to night."

"And it's where Lebed once was mayor. Is that part of the draw, too? Getting useful information about Lebed's past?" Falcone ruefully remembered what Meir Amit had said once when he was Mossad's chief: "Sex is a woman's weapon. . . . It is not just sleeping with the enemy. It is to obtain information." Falcone often wondered if he had been, at least initially, set up to be honey-trapped.

"It's beautiful and a good place for business. What more could I ask for?"

"Any trouble for an Israeli to go into business here?"

"Not if you know the right people," Rachel said, her tone suddenly coquettish.

"In Israel or Russia?"

"Both," she said, flashing a smile that vanished as quickly as it had come.

Falcone realized he was sounding like a lawyer taking a deposition.

"Nice wine," he said, holding up a glass to hers. "Remember the special house Chianti at Positano's?"

"My God! You have a fabulous memory! Yes, I remember Positano's. But I don't remember the kind of wine we drank."

"Luigi and Angela came rushing over to our table asking us, as politely as they could, to hold down the noise."

"Oh, I remember that," Rachel said, refilling her glass. "And I suppose we could pick up on that argument again."

"After seeing what you did to that guy at the bar, I don't want to get in any argument with you."

"Him? Just one of the FSB thugs who hang around the hotel, getting vodka free."

"Aren't you concerned . . . decking a member of Russia's Federal Security Service . . . just before—"

"You mean, blowing my cover? No, I'm not concerned. The big men know who I am, and the big men want to keep good relations with my country."

"But—"

"I know what you're going to say, Sean. Yes, I do some work for Drexler. And don't worry about it, okay? I know you. You know me. We're together on this."

Falcone appraised Rachel carefully, unsure of just how much she knew. "You know why this has to be done?"

"Yes. Asteroid USA. Twenty years from now, maybe it hits Earth."

Falcone looked startled, not quite knowing what to say.

"Don't worry," Rachel said. "This place is safe. No secret microphones at the tables. Only standard surveillance cameras in hallways, public spaces, and restrooms. And, you'll notice that the nearest table is two meters away, beyond the range of average hearing. You can add to the cover by grinning once in a while and staring into my eyes."

"I'm already doing that. Didn't you notice? But . . . I have to be cautious, thinking about that FSB guy in the bar."

"They're notorious crooks, like their country's big boss. They get money for 'protecting' places and for catching petty crooks—like thieving bartenders—and then . . . Americans have a name for what they do."

"Shakedown?"

"Yes. Shakedown. But sometimes they push the owners of restaurants or hotels too hard. They forget that some of the owners have better connections than the FSB has with the *siloviki.*"

"So do you have power connections, too? Is that why you feel . . . safe?"

"Safe?" Rachel asked, surprised that Falcone had uttered the word. "Are you serious, Sean? Can anyone feel *safe?* We live in a dangerous world," she said condescendingly.

Falcone looked at Rachel intently before responding. "Indeed. And I assume you know about what happened to your Domino predecessor."

She shrugged and said, "C'est la guerre. And I look both ways when I cross a street."

Neither spoke for almost a minute. Falcone broke the silence: "I'm sorry that I'm sounding like the Grand Inquisitor, Rachel. I don't want to spoil the evening, spoil our reunion. But how can you work undercover here for Israel and for Drexler?"

"From what I know of your government career, you were well aware that intelligence work is—what was it that Angleton called it?"

" 'A wilderness of mirrors,' " Falcone replied. "That's the way it looked to Angleton when he was the CIA's counterintelligence chief. Actually, he probably took the phrase from a poem by T. S. Eliot."

"Yes. It deserves poetry. But let me tell you a story, a spy story. Have you heard the name Felix Gerhardt?"

"No," Falcone said, lifting his glass to sip the vodka Rachel had ordered for him.

"I'm not surprised. He was a far-from-famous spy. He was a high-ranking officer in the South African Navy. Recruited by the Soviets in the 1960s. The Mossad knew this, somehow—and, playing the long game, as you will see, put him under surveillance. Agents noted his supposedly secret visits to Moscow. They even saw him and his wife at the Bolshoi Ballet, in seats reserved for privileged people. I don't know all the mirrors involved, but Israel developed a relationship with South Africa. And in 1979 there was a joint South African–Israel nuclear-weapon test on a sub-Antarctic island that belonged to South Africa."

"And Gerhardt?"

"He was finally arrested in, I think it was 1983, in New York—why there, I don't know—and was handed over to South Africa. Tried for treason, given a life sentence. He served a few years and moved to Switzerland. And, by the way, his rank as a rear admiral was restored. Our guess is that was he was rewarded for spilling a lot of beans about Soviet intel in South Africa."

"I suppose you are telling me this story to show me that part of the Mossad's charm is that their people do favors for other countries. And for worthy outfits like GSS?"

Rachel remained silent and stared softly at Falcone, her eyes confessing nothing.

"And the U.S. intelligence community knows all this," Falcone pressed. "Not just knows. Blesses."

"Something like that," she said, the hint of amusement playing in her half smile.

Falcone decided not to bring up the double and treacherous game that Mossad could also play with its friends. Bill Buckley, the CIA's station chief in Beirut was kidnapped in 1984 and brutally tortured to death. Falcone had read a story filed by Philip Dake that the CIA repeatedly asked for Mossad to help locate and rescue Buckley, but agency officers were buffeted by empty promises and endless delays. This was during the time that close to a thousand Palestinians were being massacred in the Sabra and Shatila refugee camps by Lebanese Christian forces.

Israeli soldiers, led by Ariel Sharon, who would later become Israel's prime minister, did nothing to stop the slaughter. Mossad had blamed the PLO's Yasser Arafat for the kidnapping, convinced this would sap any political sympathy in Washington for the Palestinians.

Meanwhile, according to CIA Director Bill Casey, Mossad had been providing weapons to Hezbollah to kill Lebanese Christians at the same time they were giving weapons to the Lebanese Christians to kill Palestinians.

Israel denounced the story as a lie written by an anti-Semite. Falcone knew that Dake wasn't a liar or an anti-Semite. But true or not, Falcone had found over the years that sometimes the biggest surprises often came from one's friends.

"Okay. I won't ask you how you—how the Mossad—knows about the asteroid. That's supposed to be very, very secret, Rachel."

"Perhaps in Washington. Not here. Lebed, Oxley's new best friend, has 'loose lips,' Sean. Isn't that the expression? He told a certain oligarch that Russia had in its possession a way to mine an asteroid that contains platinum and other minerals worth about eight trillion dollars."

"Jesus!" Falcone exclaimed. "Lebed's falling for propaganda put out by Hamilton on GNN."

"Exactly. The oligarch then emailed a couple of chums about the asteroid, using the eight trillion as bait."

"And Israeli monitors picked it up."

Rachel continued as if she had not heard. "One of the words in his emails was 'palladium' and—"

"And that's a word on Israel's monitoring list," Falcone interrupted. "So—"

"We—certain Israeli scientists—are working on palladium fuel cells," Rachel interrupted back.

"Hamilton was pushing palladium as the boom metal of the future," Falcone said. "*That's* what got Lebed interested. He doesn't give a damn about saving the Earth. What he sees in that asteroid is a palladium fortune."

"Yes. And, as I am sure you know, the two places on Earth where palladium is mined are South Africa and Russia."

"And Israel has a special relationship with both places. Unadvertised," Falcone retorted.

"I see you stay up to date," Rachel parried, a fencing impresario acknowledging a worthy thrust by a competitor.

Falcone nodded. He also knew that Russia was threatening to deliver S-400 air defense systems to Iran, just as they had done in Syria. The decision was condemned by Israel, whose missiles and aircraft would be vulnerable to the surface-to-air missiles fired from Iran.

"I've heard that the Israel-Russia love affair is cooling down," he said.

Rachel shrugged and said, "The 'affair,' as you call it, was never very warm. Strictly a tactical convenience. All head; no heart."

Falcone, thinking once again about his past with Rachel, said, "For me, truth has never been a matter of convenience."

"I know what you're thinking, Sean, but not everything in my life is strictly business. Not with you. . . ."

"You're being Domino for Israel, not America!" Falcone said, his annoyance surfacing again. He felt the sensation he had had other times when he and Rachel were involved in an operation: walking down that hall of mirrors and entering a wilderness where he was left spinning in confusion. *What was real? What was reflection?*

"They used to be the same, Sean. Maybe they can be again one day."

"Similar, not the same, Rachel. There's a difference."

"You look like you're drifting away, Sean," Rachel said, taking his hand in hers, leading a change from present to past. "Let us now talk about other days . . . our days."

Slowly, they began to walk back through time. But again and again Falcone felt that he was having a kind of out-of-body experience, watching himself talk about the past while he was also trying to see the future.

Finally, the borsch and pirogi arrived on a sterling silver tray carried by the weary-looking, raggedly dressed waiter. For the next hour, Falcone and Rachel retreated to their rhetorical corners and decided to enjoy the Mukuzani wine and culinary delights found in this new, pre-Revolution mansion.

49

After dinner, as they made their way toward the restaurant's door, a man who'd been drinking at the bar stepped in front of Rachel and knocked her purse from her shoulder. It appeared to be an accident, but Falcone thought it was an intentional bump by a professional thief. In a way, it was. The man was a professional and a thief. But he wasn't taking anything from Rachel. He was giving her something. A message.

Touching his chest in a manner that suggested an apology, the man spoke Russian in a voice loud enough for others to hear. Then he whispered something while his eyes remained locked on to Rachel's.

The man quickly muscled his way through the crowded bar area and left the restaurant.

Once they were outside, Falcone asked, "What was that all about?"

"What are you talking about?" she asked, her eyelids fluttering.

"Come off it, Rachel. Anyone could see what the guy was doing. He was no stranger and that was no accidental bump."

"Was it that obvious? I hope not," she said, frowning for an instant.

"At first, I thought he was a purse snatcher. Then I realized that thieves don't grab and run in a crowded bar. Maybe out here on the street, but not in a bar. A dozen people could have stopped him before he made it out the doors."

She nodded but did not speak.

"So what was the Mossad message?"

"There's been a slight change in the plans for moving Mr. Hamilton."

"What? Under whose orders?"

"It wasn't exactly an order. . . . What is it your football quarterbacks do when they see something they don't like and change the play?"

"An audible. You called an audible?"

"David Ben-Dar, who . . ."

"I know who he is, for Christ's sake," Falcone barked.

"Ben-Dar made . . . a suggestion to Drexler."

"Well, maybe a Russian heard it, like I did," Falcone responded.

"What exactly did you hear?"

"I don't know. It sounded like one word. The point is it could have been overheard. And—"

"Sean, relax. It was a Hebrew word. 'Approved.' That's all. 'Approved.' " Rachel pointed to a sidewalk bench a few yards down Tverskoy Boulevard. When they sat down, she said, "It's not a major change. But it's necessary. Our schedule has us at the conference tomorrow, Tuesday, and on Wednesday night make the . . . transfer. We need to accelerate the move. . . . And make a few other changes."

"When did you expect to let me in on your secret changes?" Falcone asked. His fuse was lit. He didn't like surprises, especially when it was about his mission.

"I planned to tell you as soon as I got that word 'approved.' I'm telling you right now."

"What made the sudden change of plans?"

"The sudden death of Domino. When I saw the story in the *Moscow Times* I didn't know anything about him. But an American? A visiting professor? 'Hit-and-run'? It looked . . . shady. I wondered. And I got a call."

"From Drexler?"

"No. From Ben-Dar at the Institute—Mossad's headquarters in Tel Aviv. I assumed Komov had the American killed. I know Komov. He goes back a long way," she said. "He is a compulsive planner. Never makes a move until he's ready to pounce. By now he's bugged your room. He probably has the airport security reports on recent U.S. passports and visas. Not much of a feat. They probably have sequential serial numbers. Hamilton, of course, is under strong surveillance, probably with an FSB gorilla in the adjoining suite."

"I'm beginning to see the situation," Falcone said, calming down, but not quite ready to concede that Rachel was trying to save the mission—along with saving him and the rest of the team. Falcone got up from the bench, signaling that he was ready to get back to his hotel.

"You seem rather pensive," Rachel said, closing the gap between them and putting her arm through his. "What are you thinking?"

After bringing his anger under control, he said, "Don't you think you need to tell me how in the hell you managed to penetrate this little operation?"

"Penetrate? 'Called to serve,' you mean," Rachel answered. "To help out the country that used to be our closest ally."

"So now it's a guilt trip you're laying on? We're just a tiny slice of Holy Land and once again, thanks to Uncle Sam we have been left naked to our enemies. Come on, Rachel, play it straight . . . if that's possible."

"I'll tell you as much as I can. You know the story. Sources and methods are off the table."

"Fair enough," Falcone said, still agitated, but eager to hear Rachel out.

"It's a matter of coincidence and convenience."

There was that word convenience again. "Meaning?"

"I told you I'm operating a small high-tech firm in St. Petersburg."

"I assume as a cover?"

"Yes."

"And no doubt selling technology to the Russians?"

"For profit, of course. But also to gain a back door to the highest echelons of their government."

"Your company wouldn't be called ITAcess would it?"

"Why?" Rachel asked, trying hard to not look surprised.

"Israel tried to sell that technology to the Defense Department a couple of years ago. I discovered what was going on and had President Oxley cut it off."

"Well," she said, laughing, "nothing ventured, nothing gained."

"Real allies don't read each other's mail," Falcone said, quoting a virtue that had been abandoned long ago—if it ever had existed.

"Come off it, Sean. Nobody's better at it than NSA. Not the Chinese, the Russians—or the Israelis."

"Okay. Let's get back to what's going on here. So it's just a coincidence that you happen to be here at this conference. Where does 'convenience' come in?"

"We learned about Robert Hamilton and why he's here."

"How?"

"No sources and methods, remember?"

"Right. I understand, but I don't like not knowing."

"As I said before, after . . . Domino's death, Ben-Dar received a call from Drexler. The Institute had helped out his organization on a number of special missions."

"Assassinations, you mean," Falcone said.

"Whatever was required. They were more than happy to be of service—despite their feelings about President Oxley."

"And whenever it 'coincidentally' served Israel's interests. But I don't get it. This mission's not exactly in your line of work."

"I'm a woman of many talents . . . unless you've forgotten. Your General—"

"*Ex*-General."

"All right, ex-General, was in a bind. Time was his enemy. He needed someone who is skilled in sabotage and rendition, and could speak Russian. Ben-Dar thought that was me. Plus, of course, my knowing you was a bonus."

"Well, why the hell didn't you tell me, *the bonus man*, about the change?"

"You were in the air at the time and Drexler couldn't reach you."

"He managed to reach Gregor."

"Well, you can talk to Drexler about that some day."

"And you're saying that this *ex*-General laid out the mission in all of its splendor?"

"Not exactly splendor. When we—I—looked at it, I saw certain flaws. Ben-Dar agreed. Passed the message back. Your man saw the wisdom of modifying the plan. Or calling an 'audible.'"

"Wonderful. That explains everything."

"Relax, Sean. Once I thought about the proposed plan, the less I liked it. . . . First of all, the transfer vehicle has been changed from a commercial van to a van painted to look like one the local police use. Not a big change, but if things go wrong and there's a clampdown on roads leading to the airport, we'll have a better chance of getting through. And—"

"And just how did you manage . . ."

"Compliments of my embassy. The Mossad resident, the *katsa*, through a cutout, arranged to rent a van that is the same model used by the Moscow city police. He took it to the garage of a safe house and had it repainted black and equipped with the proper siren and blue lights. You can buy anything in this city."

"Anything else I should know about?"

"Well, when the man you thought might be a purse snatcher said 'approved,' it was for another change."

"And what exactly is the new change?"

"We learned that Lebed plans to move Hamilton to a presidential palace Lebed built in Sochi—you know, where the Winter Olympics were held. That's *detention*, not living in a five-star hotel. We need to act by tomorrow evening."

"No sense asking you how Mossad learned about Hamilton being moved," Falcone said, his voice low and hard. "So the plan must be changed. And we have to move the mission up a full day. When did you expect to let me in on your secret? What else should I know?"

"We won't be trying to smuggle Hamilton out in a laundry cart."

"Why not?"

"That laundry-cart plan is very similar to a recent GSS op in Yemen. And some unnamed officials boasted to *Rolling Stone* magazine about how stupid the Yemenis were. They mentioned the laundry cart. Every counterintelligence officer in the world is now aware of the scheme."

Falcone shook his head in disgust. "Something to be said for censorship. Death penalty too."

"Komov seems to be sniffing around the hotel, looking for what he calls traitors," Rachel said. "I didn't attempt to contact the person who was supposed to supply the uniforms. Lack of trust. I sensed that if we persisted with the GSS plan, we could be walking into a Komov trap."

"So what's your Plan B? And how much does Drexler know?"

"It's still Plan A, and Drexler understands. He was a general. He knows about trusting people when they go outside the wire, as your soldiers say. He gave me carte blanche."

"Hold up, Rachel. I'm trying to be as receptive as possible. But why haven't you confided in me? I'm the guy who's supposed to be running this."

"Agreed. I'm reporting to you right now."

"Okay. Thanks," Falcone said with a sigh of exasperation. "So you're convinced we have to move tomorrow night, right?"

"Right. Denying more time to Komov."

"Okay. I agree," Falcone said. "When do the others find out about the change in plans?" He had his anger under control. The change was real and had to be accepted. There was no point in arguing against inevitability.

"We all go to the conference, as per Plan A. I walk around and pass the word to Gregor and the others, one-by-one and face-to-face."

"How—?"

"They all know me," Rachel said impatiently.

"What?!"

"We've all worked together before. No time for details. Now, to go on . . . I tell them we have to meet in my room for last-minute instructions. That will be just as the conference is ending and people are milling about."

"I assume just about every room in the hotel is bugged," Falcone said. "Especially delegates' rooms."

"My suite is clean. Swept it myself and will sweep it again."

"Okay. You lay out Plan B to them. Then what?"

"I'll give each of them a specific time to leave my room and go outside to get taxis. I'll give each one a different address near the Kempinski. They'll walk from where they're dropped off, enter the hotel by the side door. I'll give them elevator key cards. They begin drifting to your room between seven thirty and eight."

"Next?"

"At eight fifteen we begin the op."

"How?" Falcone asked, looking puzzled.

"Gregor leads the other three to Hamilton's room. He knocks and says they are FSB officers—he will have very official-looking credentials. He says they are inviting—just inviting—Hamilton to join them for a friendly interrogation session."

"That's it? And Hamilton just decides to go for a little sweat job answering questions in the Lubyanka?"

"I'm counting on shock keeping him submissive for three or four minutes from his room to the elevator. And Harry Reilly will still have his knockout needle if it's needed during or after the elevator ride."

"We'll also have to handle the security guy next door," she continued. "He'll walk in, and Gregor will flash his FSB credentials and tell the guy to guard Hamilton's suite and secure its contents until they return. Then we walk down the hall to the elevator and continue Plan A. At your floor we stop to pick you up."

"I can't help but humbly ask why I'm even here. I don't seem to have any duties."

"You're the client. You're what gives your President deniability. . . . I assumed you knew that," she coolly added.

Falcone waited a moment before responding: "I'm here as an alibi?"

"You play an important role."

"Jesus. . . . So what happens next?"

"Back to Plan A—van in the alley, and—"

"Except in the alley is a fake police van, supplied by the Israeli Embassy."

"Correct. And the original plan continues."

"But I still don't understand the Israeli involvement," Falcone said. "That makes it an official act of your government."

"It's not official. I'm helping out GSS, not the United States," Rachel said, not sounding convinced herself.

"I don't like it."

"There's a Hebrew phrase that answers your objection, Sean," she said, rising from the bench and, tight-lipped, looked down on Falcone. *"Ein bererah."*

"Which means?" Falcone asked.

" 'There is no choice.' Shall we find a taxi? It's getting late."

50

The taxi took them to a road curving along the Moskva River, where it flowed near the Kremlin walls. When Rachel gave instructions to the driver, he stopped but looked puzzled and mumbled something as she and Falcone got out. The taxi slowly followed them as they walked along the river, Rachel, grasping Falcone's arm. "It was here, you know, where Boris Nemtsov was murdered," she said. Nemtsov, a former deputy prime minister and courageous critic of Lebed's predecessor, Vladimir Putin, was gunned down by assassins "in the shadow of the Kremlin," as the *New York Times* reported.

"I wanted you to come to this place because I wanted to remind you about what you're up against. Russia is a totalitarian state. Think murder by government thugs. Think Stalin. Think even Hitler. Think anti-Semitism. And think that if things go wrong on this operation, people could die."

"Rachel, I don't need a history lesson. Lebed is no choir boy, but he—"

"Lebed—the man your naïve President tries to work with—almost certainly murdered Putin. The official cause of Putin's death was a stroke caused by microscopic clots that formed in the small blood vessels throughout his body. There's a scientific name for it. TTP. Also called Moschcowitz's syndrome. A disorder named after a Jew. Ironic. No? There are suspicions about that diagnosis."

"Why?" Falcone asked.

"TTP is a disease that can be successfully treated through blood transfusions. If it was the cause of death, why wasn't it detected?

Carelessness? Unlikely. No. This was a highly sophisticated murder. Like Litvinenko's."

Former FSB officer Alexander Litvinenko died of polonium poisoning in a London hospital in 2006. Falcone knew that both the CIA and Scotland Yard suspected that he was the victim of a state-sponsored execution.

"Assassination of Putin by Lebed. Is that the Mossad verdict?"

"Yes," she said.

"Sounds like that puts you at a high Israeli level. So you're still very much a Mossad operative. Last I heard, you had quit."

"You might put my status as 'on call.' And sometimes I do some consulting."

"And sometimes the consulting takes you to Drexler?" Falcone asked with a bitter laugh. "What we're supposed to do tomorrow is a hell of a lot more than consulting. Aren't you personally worried about being involved in what Lebed will see as an American op?"

"It will do your President good if Lebed *does* see it as an American op. Lebed will be surprised that your president is *doing* something. Oxley is said to be brilliant and that he thinks he's always the smartest man in the room. Isn't that right?"

"Fair to say he has a high opinion of himself," Falcone conceded.

"Perhaps. But he's naïve. Thinks nice thoughts about world peace. Makes nice with Lebed."

"So, you believe diplomacy is naïve, obsolete?"

"The laurel may come in one hand as long as there's a sword in the other," Rachel said. "The U.S. looks foolish and weak. Russia invaded Crimea and you did nothing. Wouldn't even give the Ukrainians anti-tank weapons and night-vision goggles to take on Russians tanks. Putin shoved you out of Syria. Told you to go home and let a real man run the show. All of Oxley's posturing about peace and diplomacy shook your allies. They—we—lost confidence in your leadership. Your dithering."

"So we should have gone to war with Russia over Syria?"

"You should have set up a safe haven on the Syrian border for the rebels who were being barrel-bombed to death. And told Putin that if he attacked them, his pilots should expect a few missiles to fly up their tails.

Do just what the Turks did when he violated their airspace. Instead, you turned your back on the ones you had encouraged to fight. Now Lebed comes, a bear in sheep's clothing, and you—"

"Oxley knows Lebed's not looking for the Nobel Peace Prize," Falcone said, making a dutiful defense of Oxley. "But you can't just bomb everybody into submission."

"When you don't act, others see fear, smell weakness . . ."

Falcone didn't disagree with Rachel on this point, but was unwilling to make any concessions. "Always great for others to sit on the sidelines of a fight and hold the coats . . . and by the way, if you're such a great ally, why didn't Mossad share information with us about Lebed poisoning Putin?"

"Because you have too many leaks. You can't be trusted."

"So why are you telling me this now?"

"Because I trust *you*. I know that you will tell this to the right people in your government—and not to *Rolling Stone*. It's a card your President might wish to play at some point."

"Thanks, Rachel. Good to know I have your vote of confidence." Falcone's words were hard and flat.

"Trust is no longer the basis of the so-called special relationship between your country and mine," Rachel replied.

"Trust is still part of governing, at least person-to-person trust," Falcone said. "I believe you. And I trust you. I also worry about your getting involved in this."

"I'm not worried. I'm not engaged in discernible espionage. I'm the owner and operator of a legally registered firm in St. Petersburg. I employ a couple of dozen Russians. I pay Russian taxes—which a lot of my business colleagues do not do."

"But if you get caught, you won't just get kicked out of the country. You'll get tossed into jail." He turned to look at her and added, "Or maybe worse. You're Domino Two."

"Don't worry. I have a safe house in St. Petersburg, where we have a consulate. And I'm seventeen minutes away from a secure place if I have to hop on the Moscow Metro."

"The Israeli Embassy?"

"Exactly," she said, stopping and looking across the river at the Baltschug Kempinski, bathed in light. She signaled to the taxi, which pulled alongside them, and told the driver to drop Falcone at the Baltschug Kempinski and then take her to the Metropol.

In the taxi, she took Falcone's hand in hers and said, "This is my last mission, Sean. I'm really getting out this time."

"Why did you take it on? Why not just close shop in St. Petersburg? Assuming there's a real company there."

"Oh, it's real all right. And, as it turns out, I was invited to be on a panel at the conference. And I might learn something that will help my business."

"Which business?"

"Both," she replied, laughing.

"Drexler told me it was his daughter who thought that the conference would serve as a cover for the op. It was you, wasn't it?" Falcone asked.

"I do try to keep up," she said, turning away and shrugging. To Falcone that was a telltale gesture signifying something like *I prefer silence to outright lying.* "When I told Annie I was going to the conference—that I would even be on a panel—we agreed that it would work as a great cover."

"So you 'happened' to be going to a conference."

"Yes. I became interested in the digital world a while ago. I'm good at languages. Information technology is mostly just another language. I found I was good at it. And IT is highly portable. After this operation is over, I won't be able to work in Russia. I'm about to close down my company. I'll be taking it to Israel."

On an ornamental street lamp across the road Falcone saw a security camera swing on its mounting. Rachel also saw it. "We're being watched," Falcone whispered.

"People often get that feeling in Moscow," she whispered back. "See you at the conference."

51

Falcone went into the hotel's lounge, picked up a copy of the *Moscow Times,* sat down, and began reading a front-page story about Lebed's recent visit to the Cathedral of Christ the Savior, an Orthodox church near the Kremlin. He told a reporter he had gone there to light candles for people who had been injured or who had given up their lives defending "Novorossia." The story explained that Novorossia "means not only Ukraine but also all the Russian lands lost since the nineteenth century."

And this is the guy who likes Ivan's Hammer, Falcone thought. He turned the page and while appearing to continue reading, he was trying to organize his thoughts, coolly, as if he were laying out a brief. But Rachel kept interrupting.

Never mind how Rachel became part of this. We're going to pull off a kidnap in the heart of Moscow and the Israelis not only know about it, but are part of it. If we're successful, Prime Minister Avi Weisman can claim at least partial credit, infuriating Oxley, who never wanted to be beholden to Israel. . . . She's a direct pipeline to Mossad and Weisman. Maybe more than a pipeline. She was—maybe still is—Weisman's mistress.

This operation will give Weisman a way to put Oxley in a corner and force him do what Israel wants. Drexler should have known what Oxley would do if he knew that an Israeli agent was part of the rendition team. But maybe Drexler knew exactly what he was doing. Maybe he thought Oxley was straying too far away from Israel and doing damage to the only country that was willing to take out Iran's nuclear plants.

Falcone was not opposed to rendition operations. He had supported grabbing several jihadis when he was national security adviser. *But an American citizen? Different kettle of fish. And there was no way to call it off. No way to get out of Moscow if things went south. And if the op is botched, the blame comes down on me.*

I can just see *Oxley in the White House press room: "I had no knowledge of any such plan to kidnap an American citizen living in Moscow of his own free will. This contravenes and goes against the grain of everything I hold dear as an American and as your commander-in-chief. This is just the kind of activity that I thought was abandoned long ago. I'm absolutely stunned that a former close friend and associate of mine would conceive of such a blatant disregard for the law. . . ."*

Well, too late now.

Falcone knew they were on their own. The original Domino dead. No CIA resources available. Beginning with Putin and continuing under Lebed, the Russians had rolled up most of the CIA's Russian assets. He had heard that from Drexler. And in ops like this one, there always had to be a well thought-out Plan B. But *nada.* Nothing.

A man walking toward the bar at the end of the lounge stopped at the plush couch where Falcone was sitting. "I couldn't help noticing what you were reading," he said. "Interesting story. Mind if I sit down?" His voice was mid-Atlantic and slightly commanding. He could have been American or British, possibly ex-military.

"I'm a friend of Sam Stone and Aaron Zwerdling," he said, casually naming the director of the CIA and the director of National Intelligence. *He could be anybody,* Falcone thought. *Including the FSB.* As national security adviser, Falcone had been thoroughly briefed on the FSB, a combined spy agency and security service. *An FSB guy would know who I am.*

"I'm afraid I'm not acquainted with those gentlemen," Falcone said, looking back at the newspaper.

"Of course," the man said, smiling. "But how do I know that your code name is Chamberlain? All I want to tell you is that Sam and Aaron know you're here and what you're planning to do. If you think the thing is going bad, dial five-five-five on that special phone of yours and we'll get you to the embassy. But only you. You know too much to wind up in a Russkie jail. Don't follow me."

The man, still smiling, stood and resumed his way to the bar.

Falcone put down the paper and once more found himself staring through a window's reflective scrim at the silhouette of the Kremlin. *Who knows what? Who sent Mr. Smiley? CIA? Mossad? FSB? Why can't I pull the plug on this thing?* He remembered that disaster during the Iran hostage crisis when President Carter ordered a military rescue. Things started to go wrong. Carter aborted the mission. It ended with an accident killing eight of the would-be rescuers. *This time the whole damn Earth is the hostage. How can Oxley stop this one? He doesn't even know it's happening. Or does he?*

Someone in the White House has to know. And gave approval to Drexler. So, was Oxley trying to throw a kiss to Weisman after screwing Israel over on the Iranian nuclear deal?

Falcone knew that Washington buzzed about relations with the Israeli prime minister being as bad as anyone had ever seen. Weisman had more sway with Congress than Oxley. Members liked the way Weisman told Oxley off, not in any classified diplomatic cables but in his face and in public. Oxley was furious with Weisman for publicly trying to undermine and humiliate him. In retaliation, he put issues of importance to Israel on ice. But maybe Oxley had had a change of heart. Maybe he decided to warm up the relationship to room temperature, thinking that he didn't want to put his successor into a deeper hole than the one that existed. It was hard to know.

Few Israelis believed that the Iranians hadn't taken Oxley to the cleaners. And Israeli watchers knew that the Iranians had been cheating on International Atomic Energy inspections. "On any day," an Israeli official had said in a GNN interview, "the mullahs could be just a few months away from being able to stick a nuclear-tipped message into the Western Wall in Jerusalem."

Falcone at first could not make any sense of the Israeli decision to aid the United States. Then he remembered that the Russians had gone through with the sale to Iran of anti-aircraft missiles, one of the world's most advanced air-defense weapons. The reason could be an Israeli payback, but, he realized, that would only serve to hit the Bear in the nose with a small stick: not enough to hurt it; just enough to make it mad. And

Russia could respond with, "You want to play, Jew boys? How about we sell Supreme Leader Khamenei our S-400s, which can travel at 10,500 miles per hour, faster than any aircraft anywhere? The same ones we stuck in Syria. Would you like to play that game?"

Just doesn't add up. I'm on the stage *in the theater of the absurd.*

52

Morning came too early for Falcone. Jet lag, dinner, drinks, Rachel as the new Domino—all had combined to take a large toll. He had slept fitfully, slipping into a dreamscape only to be jarred awake by harsh memories that he could not suppress. A slice of sunlight cut through curtains that he had failed to close fully. Angry with the morning that had come too soon, he rose from the bed, snapped the brocaded drapes tightly together, and flopped back into bed. Falcone tried to fight his way back to sleep, switching his body to the right, then minutes later, tugging and reshaping the pillows, and tumbling back to the left. It was useless.

His mind, though weighted with fatigue, rejected entry into the comfort of spiritual calm. Reluctantly, he sat up and surveyed the room, unsure at that moment, exactly where he was. Finally, his eyes settled on a large Samsung television monitor suspended over a modern cabinet that contained a minibar and condiments.

He located the remote control and snapped on the TV. A local morning show, hosted by a perky couple, who looked like rejects from Fox News, flooded the room with light and sound. They chirped happily away in Russian. He switched channels rapidly, looking for GNN but discovering that it was being blocked. The only English-speaking channels he could find were CNBC and Bloomberg.

No good news on either one. Middle East still stuck in blood feuds by people who were determined to dig fresh graves rather than heal old wounds. Continuing threat of war in North and East Asia. Water scarcity throughout the Western United States. China's economy underperforming. . . .

The hotel's gym wasn't open this early. For one mad moment he was tempted to knock on Hamilton's door, a floor above. Instead, he slipped on a blue running suit he had packed, along with a pair of Air Jordans. He pulled a wool watch cap down over his ears and headed for the elevator.

Out on the street, he stretched his leg muscles briefly and started to jog along the sidewalk, not heading in any particular direction.

The cold air snapped his senses to full alert. Without turning his head, he scanned the street ahead, looking left to right. Traffic was almost non-existent: a few trucks and night-shift workers heading home.

He decided to cross the street and use the move as an excuse to look behind to see if anyone was following him. No one.

Moscow had never been high on Falcone's list of garden spots. Sure, there was the eye-catching beauty of St. Basil's Cathedral and the forbidding Kremlin, surrounded by stay-away walls. And there were newly minted, gleaming high-rise buildings constructed in the city's quest to look relevant to the twenty-first century.

But no amount of steel and glass could compensate for the grimness in the faces of the Russian people. However high their ballerinas and astronauts could soar, however profound their Dostoyevskys, Nabokovs, and Pasternaks, there hovered about them—no, within them—a crowd of sorrows. Perhaps it was just the tug of history, of having achieved greatness and then losing it time and again to czars, Great Wars, communists, oligarchs, and now crony capitalists. Whatever the reason, there was within them a boorishness and pride, a romanticism and cynicism, the foreknowledge that their demand for respect would go unfulfilled.

Falcone had met Mikhail Gorbachev years ago and had admired his courage in trying to turn Russia to face the future instead of sulking over paradise lost. He had watched Boris Yeltsin clown his way to the presidency only to fritter it away at the bottom of a bottle. Initially, Falcone was intrigued by Yeltsin's selection of Vladimir Putin as his successor. Putin was a KGB operative who bristled with resentment toward the Western world, particularly the United States, which he considered arrogant, debauched, and disrespectful. Putin bare-chested his way to popularity by intimidating the media, jailing his critics, beating up on gays, breaking the borders of Georgia and Ukraine, and choosing to help

Assad slaughter his own people rather than help to negotiate an end to the carnage.

Putin had stirred the souls of the Russian people and stoked fear in the hearts of his European neighbors. Then, suddenly, once again, the promise of greatness slipped away. Putin had died of a rare blood disease—*Well, that's not what the Mossad thinks.*

It had happened so quickly. There had been no notice, no preparation for such an assault on their pride and hopefulness. Something was not quite right but no one was sure. Rachel's crew had apparently solved the mystery, and Boris Lebed was the killer.

Lebed promised that he would carry the torch of pride and prosperity forward but would do so with a different style. He would wrap Putin's fist of iron in his velvet glove. Old wine had been poured into a new bottle that was labeled and marketed as "light and smooth."

Falcone's random jogging route ended at a Starbucks near the hotel. Except for the Cyrillic words on the posted menu, he could have been in the Starbucks near his office building in downtown Washington. People were drifting in and forming lines—men in suits and topcoats or in coveralls and hard yellow hats, women in stylish office clothing, college kids tossing backpacks onto chairs before heading for a line, assorted laptop users enjoying free wi-fi.

Falcone ordered a latte—and responded to a question in Russian by saying "Falcone," knowing "Sean" probably wouldn't work. When the slim blond woman at the cash register looked up expectantly, he realized that he did not have a kopek in his pocket. As he tried to explain in pantomime, a man stepped out of the line and said, "Allow me." He handed the young woman a few rubles and deposited the change in a jar on the counter. He was wearing an inconspicuous gray running suit. He was the same man who had promised Falcone embassy sanctuary if he needed it.

"Thanks," Falcone said. "Surprised to see you again."

"Oh, I get around," the man said, going to the end of the line as Falcone picked up his cup—his last name was written in English letters as *Falcon*—and sat at an empty table, wondering what other surprises lay ahead.

53

While the doorman whistled for a taxi to the Hotel Metropol, Falcone stood under the marquee suppressing anger and marshaling questions he wanted to ask Rachel. He was on edge, trying to get to the level of calm he needed today. But, as the doorman waved in a taxi, he felt a surge of panic: suppose the driver was an FSB operative who would whisk him off to an interrogation room somewhere?

The taxi crawled into the morning traffic. A heavy rain, borne on a high wind and speckled with snow, added another question: What if weather grounded the getaway aircraft? He shook his head as if the movement would help to dislodge the doubt that had settled on his mind like a cawing raven.

The massive Hotel Metropol finally appeared, shimmering in the rain. Balconies and bas-relief carvings jutted from its walls. Rooftop banners stiffened in the chill wind. Huge mosaic panels portrayed a folktale heroine, the Princess of Dreams. The gray building covered much of a long block. As the taxi pulled into the porte-cochere, a doorman attired like a czar's Cossack guard stepped forward, opened the door, and offered his arm to Falcone.

Under a glittering lobby's huge chandelier, signs in Russian and English directed Falcone to the International Conference on Cyber Defense. He joined a line of people registering in a hall whose stained-glass ceiling and towering walls evoked the grandeur of czarist days. He spotted Rachel in the hall beyond the registration lines but did not nod at her. Registering under his real name, he hesitated for a moment. Suddenly thinking like the prosecutor he had been long ago, he added the registration to the paper trail that could be built against him.

He headed toward booths that were clustered on the far side of the hall. Most booth banners touted defenses against cyber crime and anti-virus technologies. But Falcone had spotted the nearest and largest, the Apple hospitality booth whose banner said *Coffee Welcome* in English and Russian.

On a long table were coffee urns, disposable cups bearing the Apple trademark, and the usual array of milk, sugar, and plastic spoons. Nearby were three small tables with folding chairs. Falcone filled a cup and sat down at an empty table. Rachel followed, pausing to add milk and sugar.

"I'm aborting the operation," Falcone said. "Right now."

If the announcement surprised Rachel, she did not show it. She took a sip from her cup and said, "I can understand your anger. And frustration. But, in fact, you cannot abort. We had this discussion last night."

"Bullshit!" Falcone swore, slamming down his cup, which erupted, adding its stain to the white tablecloth. "I'm in charge. I'm more than a goddamn alibi!"

"That's not so, Sean," Rachel said calmly. "This is an operation. And . . . well, you're not an operator."

The words hit Falcone in the chest with all of the subtlety of a bullet fired from a sniper's rifle.

Before he could respond, Rachel continued: "You're heroic. Brave. You can sense the moment, and react swiftly. I've seen you do that. . . . But operators don't react. They do what they have *planned* to do. And adjust plans when circumstances change."

"Sounds to me like you're 'reacting swiftly.' How's that make you an operator?"

"Be realistic, Sean. In Vietnam, you were tough and courageous. You killed men trying to kill you. You were a warrior. But you were not an operator."

I led my men into an ambush, Falcone thought. *My war was more pris-oner than warrior.* He remained silent, sorting through the scale of his emotions: anger, resentment, and finally resignation.

As soon as her words slipped out with such directness and hardness,

Rachel saw the pain sweep across Falcone's face. She leaned forward, touching his arm. "You cannot—we cannot—abort," she said. Then in a softer voice, hoping to persuade Falcone that she had only spoken the truth, however rudely, she said, "Please, listen to me. Give me"—she checked the time—"five minutes. Exactly five min—"

"Hold on, Rachel. Let's start with where you got that damn phone."

"From Drexler, of course," she replied, an edge returning to her voice.

"So just how long have you worked for him?"

"That's not important," she said dismissively.

"Maybe—just maybe—it's important to me," he said angrily.

"I asked for five minutes. And I think it would be safer for us to walk around while we talk."

She stood and headed toward the rest of the booths. Stubbornly, Falcone continued to sit for a moment. Then, realizing there was no point in not hearing her out, he quickly caught up with her. She looked at her watch again.

"Now begins my five minutes, okay?"

Falcone nodded.

"I'm sure you know about the so-called periphery doctrine that goes all the way back to David Ben-Gurion."

"So you're using up your time with another history lesson," he said, biting off the words, his anger growing.

Rachel did not respond. They walked past a couple of booths when Falcone suddenly stopped. "Time out," he said. They were in front of a booth with a banner offering software and counseling on POST-HACKED ETHICAL DUTIES OF LAW FIRMS. He picked up a pamphlet. "Interesting issue. If I ever get back to practicing law." He turned to Rachel and, with a tight smile, said, "You're back on the clock."

Rachel, returning his forced smile, resumed. "The periphery doctrine has been the prime, the fundamental dogma of the Mossad, which developed close operational ties between Israeli and non-Arab intelligence services in the Middle East and Africa. Whatever came from that intel alliance was shared with the U.S. Right?"

"Right." Falcone was not convinced the sharing of information came unfiltered, but thought it best not to contest the point.

"The Mossad," she continued, "found that its best peripheral intelligence ties were with religious or ethnic minorities in the Middle East, including the Kurds in Iraq and Syria. There were also signed agreements with the intelligence services of some nasty countries. Like Iran and Uganda."

"I don't know where this is going," Falcone said. "Sometimes partners turn out to be villains. Shit happens, right?" He was having trouble holding back his sense of having been betrayed, reduced to a capon.

"But you keep insisting that you want to know why Israel wanted to get into this."

"Okay. You're still on the clock."

"One of our intelligence agreements was between us, Turkey, and Iran. America welcomed the alliance, which was known as Trident in the United States."

"I know about Trident," Falcone snapped. "Ancient history. It even provided for twice-a-year meetings, in Israel, of the spy chiefs of the three countries. We even paid for the building that housed the Trident headquarters in Israel."

"Trident got more complicated in the 1980s," Rachel said, "when Israel got involved in arms deals with Iran to fight their mutual enemy, Iraq. And—"

"Christ," Falcone said, "so we're back to Iran-Contra. Israel and the United States sell arms to Iran, and Reagan then uses the money to arm the Contras in Nicaragua. Iran shows its gratitude by aiding the release of American hostages being held in Lebanon. Okay, Rachel. I know we and Israel have a history as secret pals. So what?"

"Israel is living in a different world, Sean, and America isn't in it. Look around you." She swept her hand as if encompassing the entire hall. "The digital world. Your country is losing the cyber war. Chinese hackers took over your government's personnel files and now know the identities of people seeking and getting security clearance. They even have their fingerprints! By now they know agents' names and may be turning them in. The Chinese and the Russians have raided your health files, your pension files. No one in your government has any idea how many other agencies have been hacked.

"And now," Rachel continued, exasperation in her voice, "with the Earth facing a catastrophe twenty years in the future, your country keeps the news secret and joins with China and Russia to defend the Earth. China and Russia! The leading villains of the digital world!" Pausing, Rachel spoke more slowly. "To consort with those who are not your friends, and exclude those who are, is a breach of faith. Still, we agreed to help you because we know that it's better for us for Hamilton to be in the U.S., not in Russia."

From discreetly hidden loudspeakers came a polite voice, speaking first in Russian, then in English, asking attendees to take seats in the adjoining auditorium.

"And so? You're saying that I should not cancel this insane operation out of respect for the long relationship that used to exist between my country and yours? Or maybe you're just saying for the long relationship between you and me."

"Yes," Rachel said. "On both counts. More importantly—for my five-minute speech—you know that what you are doing is for far more than Israel and the United States."

"So," Falcone said, shaking his head and smiling grimly, "it's all part of saving the world."

"Yes. You just ended my speech for me." She handed him her key card and walked toward the stage, where the moderator and other members of her panel were assembling.

54

The program for the International Conference on Cyber Defense listed Rachel—that is, Andrea Mitrovitz, CEO of ITAccess—as a member of the panel on "Where Are the Watchers?" The three other members of the panel were male executives of private companies. Falcone wondered if the head of the Russian company on the panel had a sideline job in the FSB.

The moderator, an official of the European Electronic Crime Task Force, went to the heart of the panel's theme. "There are not enough watchers," he said, in English with a slight Italian accent. "The task force has repeatedly discovered a lack of vigilance, a failure of politicians to finance even fundamental defenses, such as a harassment assault by amateur hackers on a company's emails. As for a warlike attack by an aggressive nation, the unseen foe can so cripple military and civilian organizations that the government can lose control of the country. We call that the Apocalyptic Attack."

As the moderator went on, vividly describing a cyber catastrophe, *Apocalyptic* resounded in Falcone's mind, substituting Ivan's Hammer as the foe. The thought brought him back to the mission.

By the time Ms. Mitrovitz spent a few of her fifteen minutes on her thesis—"Security systems have not kept up with the cyber foe's tactics and capabilities"—Falcone was convinced that Rachel was right. He had no choice but to continue.

As soon as Rachel and the other panelists finished the question-and-answer windup of the session, another panel began to materialize on stage.

Falcone watched her as she walked over to the side of the hall, where members of the audience lined up to speak to her. Among them he spotted Gregor Ivanisov . . . then Jack Beckley . . . and Harry Reilly. Falcone looked around for Bobby Joe Pickens, whose code name—Pepper— reflected his behavior. Falcone remembered him in the GSS stable, always in motion, never in a chair. But even when he was going through a rehearsal with the others he seemed to be by himself. Falcone's thoughts flashed back to Hennessey, his leading sergeant, who acted dependably and spoke rarely. *An operator.*

Sure enough, there was Pepper, standing alone in an eddy of the crowd, leafing through some pamphlet he had picked up. Falcone walked over to him and said, "Bobby Joe. Good to see you. I think we're headed for the same place."

Pickens nodded and followed Falcone to the elevator. Falcone entered first. As they ascended, he turned to Pickens and said, "Have a good flight?" Pickens was about the same height as Falcone. So he could answer by looking at Falcone eye-to-eye and nodding, ending Falcone's attempt at small talk.

For the next twenty minutes, Falcone and Pickens sat in silence, occupying two green easy chairs in the lounge of Rachel's suite. Jack Beckley entered next, accompanying Rachel. Sharp-eyed, head swiveling, he looked like a bodyguard, a role he naturally assumed. At the doorway, he paused to scan the room, momentarily blocking Rachel. Then he stepped aside and nodded to her, signaling she was safe. She responded with a grin and patted Beckley on the back.

After nodding a greeting to Falcone and Pickens, she went into the bedroom and emerged with what looked like a flashlight. She silently pointed it at every object—chairs, lamps, tables, phone, doorknob, curtains, paintings. She wielded it like a paintbrush along the walls, then like a broom along the floor. During her sweep, bearded Harry Reilly walked in, looking like a Viking in a suit.

The room was silent. Falcone was morbidly reminded of how mourners remain mute as they stand in line moving toward the coffin in a funeral home. Rachel broke the silence by speaking low and fast into her Blackphone 4, summoning Gregor Ivanisov. She had assigned him the task of using his skills—and instinct—to watch for tails on the men who preceded him to her room.

When he arrived, he did a thumbs-up and locked the door. She stood in the center of the room, looked around, and said, "We have all worked together one way or another—yes, including Sean and me. . . . Those were times in life's travels that didn't include the rest of you. And now here we are, about to begin another 'piece of cake.'" The GSS men laughed at their inside joke. "You're here using your real names. So I'll use mine: Rachel."

Falcone look surprised. He had seen her many aliases in intel archives, and had just seen her latest, Andrea Mitrovitz, in print. But she was suddenly Rachel, truly Rachel. Maybe she really was going to quit.

"I am not Domino," she continued. "As you know, Domino—Leonid Danshov—is dead. Murdered. I am honored to replace him. Let us think of him for a moment." The men lowered their heads. She began to say a barely audible Mourner's Kaddish; no one else prayed aloud.

She went into the bedroom and returned pushing a cart piled high with sandwiches, plates, cups, bottles of soft drinks, and a large coffee pitcher. "Compliments of ITAccess," she said. "That's what it says on the room-service bill. Eat up. Your next meal will be on the plane to Washington. And that probably means more sandwiches."

As the men found chairs and ate and drank with varying levels of enthusiasm, she chose a straight-backed chair strategically placed in the middle of the room. "Any questions?" she asked, laughing when they looked at one another, deciding who would ask first.

After a moment she broke the silence again. "I'm bringing you a modified plan," she said. "It picks up most of what you learned as Plan A. You enter Hamilton's suite just as you rehearsed. I have the key card to his suite and the elevator." She handed it to Gregor, who put down his cup and slipped the card into a suit coat pocket.

"Domino was supposed to knock out the lights and wi-fi, with the help of a hotel employee. We have to assume that Domino's arrest compromised his assets. This time, the lights will be on. And, Harry, you probably won't need to give your lullaby injection to Hamilton, at least until we get into the van."

Reilly smiled and patted his suit coat pocket.

". . . and Gregor will be impersonating an FSB officer," Rachel added. She gave him a black leather folder containing a laminated identification card. He put down his sandwich so he could examine the card.

"Not bad," Gregor said, not showing any surprise that she—or a Mossad employee at the Israeli Embassy—had access to an up-to-date photo of him. "I guess you got it off my passport."

Falcone filed the remark away in the brain cells that were curious about connections between GSS and the CIA. And now GSS and the Mossad.

"They'll have photos of all of us," Reilly said. "We're leaving behind our passports—our *real* passports. And our luggage. They'll think we won't try to leave without them."

"That was true in Plan A," Falcone said. "We won't need passports to get on our plane home. And we were briefed about abandoning our luggage."

"But we're blown for any future op in Russia," Reilly said.

Turning directly to Reilly, Rachel said, "It's a big world, Harry. I'm sure the General will pay for a shave to get you into Russia again."

Reilly laughed, and the tense moment passed. She went on to describe the beginning of the op in Hamilton's suite and assigned their separate departure times from her room, along with the details of their short taxi trips and walks to the Kempinski and Falcone's room. "I'll pick up the van from . . . someone I trust and drive it to the hotel alley."

When she got to a description of the van—"black, plain, looking like the kind local police use for undercover work"—Gregor reacted with a Russian phrase, followed by a translation: "What the fuck?!"

"It'll have a better chance than an orange-and-red DHL van," Rachel said.

"I agree," Falcone said. "From what I know, our van comes from a good, dependable home." Gregor and Rachel exchanged quick glances. *Gregor knows about her Mossad connection,* Falcone thought. *Maybe he's Mossad, too.*

"Van's no problem," Gregor said. "I've driven Russian vans. Yeah. I can see how it may be a little less risky. And crazy enough to work."

"A local asset will deliver the van to an alley near the parking garage loading dock and disappear," Rachel said. "I'll drive to the lot to pick you all up, along with Hamilton. If he acts up, Harry, give him the needle. Greg, as planned, gets behind the wheel, drives us to the Vnukovo Airport and uses his FSB ID to reach the private-jet terminal. We get aboard our DHL aircraft to Latvia. As I said, 'piece of cake.' "

This time, nobody laughed.

Falcone, the first to leave, was able to take a taxi directly to the Kempinski. He had spotted a black ZIL limousine behind him during the short trip and suspected he was being followed. He entered the lobby and lingered by a planter, positioning himself so that he had a view of the front entrance in a large wall mirror.

He saw the black ZIL pull up. Someone got out of the ZIL, spoke to the driver, then to the doorman, and hurried in. Falcone recognized him as the FSB operative Rachel had floored. He headed directly to the elevator and inserted a key card.

Falcone watched the floor indicator, which showed that the elevator stopped at the top floor, where Hamilton's suite was located. Falcone assumed that the man from FSB was assigned to track him—and watch over Hamilton—in anticipation of a visit from the former national security adviser, sent to convince Hamilton to return to the United States. That would mean the FSB had no suspicion of the imminent snatching of Hamilton. Falcone wanted to call Rachel and relay his speculation, but he did not want to risk any communication, even by his Blackphone.

Shortly after Falcone entered his suite there was a knock at his door. He looked at his watch. 7:39.

He opened the door to Rachel. She wore black slacks and a black leather jacket, open over a black turtleneck sweater. She put a finger to her lips and took from her large handbag a pen, a notebook, and the device that looked like a flashlight. SPEAK AND ACT NATURAL, she wrote and held up the message.

"Andrea! Good to see you!" Falcone exclaimed. "You were fabulous at the conference."

"I thought we'd have a meeting with your associates before tomorrow's session, Mr. Falcone," she said as she began sweeping the room. "I'm glad your firm is interested in installing ITAccess in your offices in America."

"Yes, I plan to have my associates meet with you. And I think I'll call room service for a pot of coffee," he said, holding the telephone in front of her so that she could check it. She nodded and he made the call.

A few minutes later, she wrote ROOM CLEAN and held up her notebook. He told her about the FSB operative. He could not help whispering, despite her assurance that no one was eavesdropping and there was no need for him to worry about the FSB.

"I think they've got people watching over Hamilton and one of them was briefed on you. They must have wondered why you were here."

"And so," he said, "they peeled a guy off the Hamilton babysitters squad to see if I went to the conference. That guy had seen us talking here—before you decked him."

"That was pure luck," she said. "They could see what we were up to: two people meeting by chance and going to a conference. Your shadow saw us at the conference. We weren't connected to Hamilton. So far, we're lucky."

"So far," Falcone echoed.

They were at the toughest stage of an operation: waiting for it to begin.

One by one, still in the suits they had worn at the conference, Jack Beckley, Harry Reilly, Bobby Joe Pickens, and Gregor Ivanisov arrived, minus their code names. Rachel greeted them by their real names, ignoring one of Drexler's cardinal security rules. Somehow, this relaxed Falcone. He was in a real world dealing with people with real names.

Gregor, Jack, and Harry stood around talking, mostly about the Redskins. Bobby Joe Pickens was by a window, sipping coffee, staring out at the darkness.

Rachel held up her Blackphone and said, "Seven forty-five. Everybody got that? And don't forget to set your phones to vibrate."

As the GSS men checked their Blackphones, Falcone moved closer to Rachel. "It's okay to call you Rachel now," he said. "*Rachel*—that's a relief. And I don't want to meet you accidentally again. I want us to meet on purpose, somewhere, sometime."

"We can't talk about us until this is over," she said. "But I like the idea of meeting again."

She kissed him on the cheek, waved to them all, and left. It was 8:00 sharp. Falcone pictured her going to a Mossad safe house's garage, where she would enter a van.

Thirty minutes later, first Gregor, then the others shook hands with Falcone and headed toward the elevator. He wished he could go with them.

55

When they got off the elevator, they stood for a moment at the door to Hamilton's suite. Then Gregor stepped forward and pounded on the door. Down the hallway a door opened and a large man stepped out. He was in his stocking feet, wearing a white T-shirt and black trousers with red suspenders hanging down. He shouted something in Russian and Gregor shouted back, *"Federal'naya Sluzhba Bezopasnosti."*

The man ran toward them. "Take him out," Gregor told Bobby Joe.

Head down, Bobby Joe took two steps forward and smashed into the man. He clipped him on the neck with his right hand while dipping his left hand into his suit coat pocket and taking out a roll of silvery duct tape. In swift moves, he stuck a strip of tape across the man's mouth, tore off another strip, flipped the man on his face, pulled his hands together, and wrapped them with tape. He then girded the man's neck with one suspender strap and tied it to the other strap, enwrapping it around his hands in such a way that a tug tightened the strap around his neck.

Seeing that the man's door was ajar, Gregor said, "Drag him into his room." He turned to Reilly. "Give him the needle. We'll pick up you guys when we come out with Hamilton."

As Gregor spoke, the door opened. He pushed it in, startling Hamilton, who stepped back. He wore a dark blue sweatshirt, matching pants, white socks, and black-and-white sneakers.

"What . . . what is this?" he asked, his voice rising indignantly as he took in the situation.

"Federal'naya Sluzhba Bezopasnosti," Gregor said, adding such authority

to his voice that for an instant Jack Beckley stiffened and stood at attention.

"I do not speak Russian," Hamilton said slowly.

"Federal Security Service," Gregor said, speaking with a heavy accent and showing his credentials. "You are to come with us for questions."

"Now look here, whatever your name is. I am an American citizen and—"

Gregor signaled to Beckley, who deftly placed plastic handcuffs around Hamilton's wrists and started frog-marching him to the elevator. Pickens and Reilly fell in step behind them.

In the elevator, Gregor dropped his accent and said, "Mr. Hamilton, if you shout or struggle, it will be necessary to drug and gag you. Please remain calm."

"Calm?! I assure you: I am not calm," Hamilton said. He lunged toward the elevator control board, apparently to hit the emergency signal with his shoulder. Pickens yanked him back.

Reilly reloaded his syringe and was injecting a more powerful sedative dose into Hamilton's upper left arm as the elevator stopped and Falcone entered. No one spoke.

The elevator continued its descent to the lowest parking level, two stories below the first floor. The door opened and the men filed out, half dragging Hamilton, who was already looking confused. Gregor, last man out, used a Swiss Army blade to pry loose a button labeled Открытая дверь—"Open Door." He then inserted the blade into the mechanism and exposed and cut a yellow wire. The elevator light went out and the door remained open.

Following the choreography they had practiced in the GSS barn, Gregor and Bobby Joe sprinted up the spiraling ramp to the closed garage door. Gregor opened a switch box on the wall and pressed a button. The door yawned open. The others hurried toward the opening: Falcone, followed by Harry Reilly and Jack Beckley, who were holding up Hamilton.

They all passed through the open garage door and reassembled in the alley. Hamilton was still being held up. He was the only one who was not shivering and stamping in the dark cold. Gregor, switching on a penlight, found a switch box on the outside wall, opened it with his knife, pressed a button, and the garage door slowly closed. He then donned a thick gray glove, yanked out a circuit breaker and threw it into the darkness, setting off a cluster of sparks and sealing the door shut. He returned the glove to a suit coat pocket.

Gregor led the others to the right, toward the street and to the spot, thirty meters away, where Rachel and the van were to be, engine purring, lights out.

The van was not there.

Falcone's Blackphone vibrated. It was Rachel, speaking calmly. "Sean. Go to the street you're facing. Turn right. Walk—do not run—about a hundred meters and turn right again and continue a few meters to the van, parked at the curb. Tell the others to stay where they are until the van arrives."

"Okay," Falcone said. He turned to Gregor and said, "Rachel wants everyone to stay here and wait for the van."

Gregor frowned for an instant, then nodded. Falcone began rapidly walking away.

56

Rachel was standing at the driver's side of a black van parked at the curb. "An unexpected matter," she said as Falcone reached her. "I decided to call you to keep the team intact."

"What happened?" Falcone asked, wincing inwardly at the idea he was not on the team.

"I can only guess," she said, pointing to the van. The window on the driver's side was rolled all the way down. For a moment all Falcone could see was the profile of a man staring straight ahead. Then Falcone looked more closely. The man's face was covered with blood.

"He was shot right here, as he parked. Someone simply walked up to the van and maybe asked him a question. He rolled down the window to speak to the man. Then the man shot the driver and got picked up by another car or just kept on walking," she said. Leaning in closer, she added half to herself, "Probably a Makarov PMM with an integral silencer."

"Who . . . was he?"

"Local asset. We met only once."

Falcone looked back at the face in the window and said, "The man at the restaurant?"

"Yes," she said impatiently. "Now, we must move quickly." She pointed to an alley. "There are garbage cans there."

Rachel opened the driver's door. Falcone grabbed the body as it leaned out, the bloodied face rubbing against his. Shapeless, amorphous memories of blood and war surged for an instant through Falcone's mind. He quickly looked around, saw the side street was clear, and then, reaching under the arms of the man, hauled out the body.

Rachel slipped behind the wheel, turned on the ignition, and said, "I'm going to the meeting spot. Wait here." She drove off, lights out.

The body was surprisingly light—the slim remains of a nameless man in a long black overcoat. The man's black cap fell to the sidewalk as Falcone dragged the body into the alley, passed three overflowing garbage cans, and put the body down while he opened the lid of a half-filled Dumpster. He lifted the body up and pushed it in, then noiselessly lowered the lid.

Back at the curb, time seemed to stop. He could smell the sour scent of blood, could still see the dark, stinking cavern of the Dumpster. Smell and sight were all that existed. Then a sound and something pressing into his back, just above his waist.

Old lessons took over Falcone's body while his mind raced. He had been taught, so many years ago a lesson that had been drilled into his brain, a lesson he had never forgotten. The lesson was called "response to a standing submission," and the Ranger instructor called it "the live-or-die moment. You chose to submit and surely die or respond and maybe live."

Falcone spun around. He was facing a man saying something in Russia. The man was shorter than Falcone, burly in a black peacoat. In his right hand he held a pistol with a barrel made longer by a silencer. Falcone realized that the man could have killed him but, for some unknown reason, had hesitated. The hesitation enabled Falcone to grab the gun with his left hand while chopping at the man's throat with his extended right hand and wrist wielded like an ax. Before the shooter could raise his right hand to shoot, Falcone twisted the gun downward.

The shooter screamed as a 9-mm bullet ripped open his belly. His trigger finger weakened. Falcone placed his middle finger atop the shooter's and pulled back the trigger. Another bullet tore into the shooter and he fell to the ground.

The van was coming toward Falcone with its headlights off. It stopped long enough for a sliding door to open. Falcone was only half in, his wrist encased by Reilly's big, outreaching hand, when the van leaped forward and Reilly yanked him into a seat next to him in the rear row. In front of him were Jack Beckley and Bobby Joe Pickens, with Hamilton between them. He was snoring, his head flung back. Bobby Joe, using a special safety-cutter, removed Hamilton's plastic handcuffs.

"You okay?" Bobby Joe asked Falcone, whose face, shirt, and suit coat were blood-smeared.

"There was another guy," Falcone said. "I . . . shot him."

"You've got a gun?"

"His gun."

Falcone suddenly realized that this was the second time he had seen Hamilton. The first time was in the Metropolitan Club in Washington, having lunch with Phil Dake of the *Post*. Dake had pointed out Hamilton dining with a senator who later resigned for shadowy doings with billionaires like Hamilton. *That was when this all began,* Falcone thought, remembering that at the time Hamilton had been unveiling his plan to capture asteroids and mine them.

His thoughts were interrupted by Gregor's gruff voice. "We should be at Vnukovo Airport in about thirty-five minutes," Gregor said, sounding more hopeful than he felt. "But we don't know what in hell the shooting of the driver is about."

"I think the FSB was following him," said Rachel, who sat next to Gregor. "Perhaps his name came up in the questioning of Danshov. Either the driver told the shooter he was delivering the van for someone else or the shooter figured it out for himself and waited."

"I think he spilled all he knew," Falcone said.

"We can't be sure," Rachel said.

"All I know," Falcone said, "is when I felt that gun, I expected I'd be shot. He hesitated. I think I know why."

"Tell me."

"He was expecting a woman. I was a surprise—and he hesitated."

"And that killed him," Rachel said.

"Seems to me, Rachel, that Sean killed him. With the guy's own gun," Gregor said.

Rachel did not respond. She was reaching into her handbag. "The driver carried his wallet in his coat pocket. The name on his *propusk* is Vladimir Matviyenko. It says he worked as a driver for a limousine service."

"And who was he really working for?" Falcone asked.

"I assume he was a freelancer," she said.

"Toss that stuff out the window," Gregor said. "If we get stopped and searched, I don't want them to find a murdered guy's papers."

"Good idea," Rachel said, opening the window and throwing the wallet and *propusk*. A wave of cold air passed through the van.

"The way he was killed, it was like an execution," Gregor said. "The FSB is getting rough." He sounded worried. The van's lights were on now as Gregor wove through the evening traffic.

57

Cars and trucks whizzed by the van while Gregor kept within the speed limit, making his way to the first circuit highway, which crossed the Moskva River. "No problem on the bridge," he said after reaching the far side. He turned onto the artery that ran to the major Moscow beltway, then continued on to the high-speed highway to Vnukovo Airport. Gregor, with his road bulletins, was the only person talking as the van sped through the night.

Up ahead, Gregor saw the blinking blue and red lights of a roadblock and a lineup of cars and trucks.

"The van was delivered with a Taser in the glove compartment," Rachel said.

"We've got our own," Bobby Joe said, patting a pocket.

"So what?" Gregor said. "These guys don't have Tasers. They kill people." Hamilton suddenly stirred, as if reacting to *kill*. Everyone else thought about what happened to the man who had been where Gregor was sitting.

Panic swept through the Hotel Baltschug Kempinski. Everyone, from night manager to cleaning women, seemed to be in motion, trying to find a place to hide or something to do. Some people said they had seen men dragging a guest out of a room. Guests with hastily packed bags began lining up at the check-out counter. Someone somewhere pressed a button and the shrieks of the fire-alarm system filled the air.

In the blacked-out underground parking garage, drivers leaned on horns, yelled and screamed, banged their cars into other cars at the closed door. Car beams and cell phones illumined the darkness. Two motorists got out of their cars and began slugging each other. And all through the hotel people were shouting or whispering, in several languages, one word: *Terrorists.* They had struck luxury hotels like this elsewhere; now, many feared, it was Moscow's turn.

Komov, who heard a police radio report of a possible terrorist attack at the hotel, instantly wondered about the Mossad whore. And he wondered about the American Hamilton.

He put on his old KGB uniform and called the security man he had assigned to Hamilton. No answer. He ran out of his apartment, took the elevator to the entrance and, flashing the FSB identification that he would never give up, commandeered a taxi.

At the hotel, he ordered a bellhop to give him a key card, took the elevator to the executive suite and found the bound bodyguard in the suite next to Hamilton's. He searched there, though he assumed Hamilton would not be there. Returning to the bodyguard, he freed the sputtering man, who said he had been attacked by terrorists. Komov slapped the man in the face, cursed him, and collapsed into a yellow armchair. He felt faint. He was sweating. His face was pale, his heart pounding.

Komov, breathing hard, reached for the phone on the desk next to his chair and dialed the number to his office.

"Traitor Danshov," he said. He felt his words were faint, like an echo. "Traitor Danshov, kidnap . . . kidnapping Hamilton from the Baltschug Kempinski. Seal off Moscow. Seal off Moscow."

Komov tried to pull himself to his feet. The room seemed to be spinning. He thought of Lebed. *I would have handed you a Tokarev pistol and left the room.* Komov twisted and managed to get his Tokarev out of its holster. The bodyguard dived behind a couch.

The Tokarev had a hair trigger. Komov remembered that. He lifted the gun just high enough to get the barrel . . . the cold barrel . . . into his mouth. Yes, the trig . . .

58

Gregor had a story—and cash in dollars—ready in case of a roadblock. He knew that no one in Russia liked the FSB or the Moscow Regional Police Department, whose beat cops were affectionately known as "werewolves in epaulets." And the Moscow police especially did not like the FSB. But they did like bribes.

Two werewolves were checking the vehicles in the line that was lengthening at the roadblock. Sighting the official-looking van, they strode directly to it. They wore blue uniforms, heavy gray coats, and mouton sheepskin hats bearing gold-wreathed badges.

Speaking in Russian with a strong Moscow accent, Gregor politely showed his FSB identification. The younger of the two cops took out a notebook and dutifully wrote down the name and number before handing the identification back.

"What is the roadblock for?" Gregor casually asked.

"Our superiors have declared a terrorist alert. 'Seal off Moscow,' they call it. And it's a lot of shit," the older cop said, slurring his words. His eyes were bloodshot and his nose reddish.

"What's going on?" Gregor asked.

"They think there are terrorists in some big hotel," he said.

The younger cop flashed a light into the van and asked, "Who are your passengers?"

"They are Americans with expired visas," Gregor responded. "The rules are firm. They must be sent back to America. I am to put them on the next plane out of Russia."

The cop turned the beam on Hamilton.

"That one," Gregor said, "is drunk."

"And the woman?" he asked, shining on Rachel.

"All American, as I said," Gregor said, racing the engine. "They have caused you to stand in the cold, and so I believe you deserve a portion of their fines."

"How much?" the older cop asked.

"They paid thirty-thousand rubles each," Gregor replied. "Five hundred dollars in their money. Fines the FSB collect are closely watched these days. But I can deduct one of the fines for expenses—five hundred dollars for you and your partner." He reached into his inner pocket, took out an envelope, and handed it to the older cop. He motioned to the younger cop to shine his light into the envelope and reached in, taking out five one-hundred-dollar bills.

This is the moment, Gregor thought. *He either takes the money and arrests us or he takes it and lets us pass.*

"Go directly to the front and let them through," the older cop told his partner, who sprinted off, wondering what his share of the bribe would be.

"Well done, Gregor," Rachel said. She recounted the dialogue while Gregor concentrated on cutting off the first car in line, to a cacophony of horns. She turned to Gregor and added, "There was one phrase—*baba c vosu* and then other words I couldn't catch."

Gregor, passing through the roadblock, laughed and said, "It's one of those Russian proverbs that even Russians don't understand. Translated literally, it is 'Once the woman gets off the cart, it's easier for the horse.'"

"And what the hell does that mean?" Bobby Joe asked.

"Russians like to get an idea across by painting a scene with words. It's a way of saying 'good riddance.'"

"Why does it have to be a *woman* getting off the cart?" Rachel asked.

"To answer that, I'd have to say *a lot* of proverbs," Gregor said, still laughing.

A few minutes after they passed through the roadblock, Gregor turned on the radio and hunted for an all-news station, *all-news* meaning all the news that the government allowed to be broadcast. He listened for a short time and said, "The cop was right. Terrorists. They're calling us terrorists. Not American terrorists. Just terrorists. Two guests of the Baltschug Kempinski were assaulted. No names. I guess that would be the FSB guy and Hamilton. And—"

At the sound of his name, Hamilton sat up straight and awakened. Looking around and discovering he was in a van, he said, "Is this how Lebed treats his special guests?"

"Keep quiet!" Gregor shouted in Russian. Without understanding the command, Hamilton leaned back and closed his eyes.

"Spasm reaction," Reilly said, assuring the others. "I figure he'll be out—or at least dazed—for about an hour."

"What else is the radio saying?" Falcone asked.

"They said police have found the body of a man near the hotel—a Chechen and believe he's one of the terrorists," Rachel said. "They always blame the Chechens. They also found the body of an unidentified man stuffed in the Dumpster."

"That could mean that when I dumped the body someone saw me," Falcone said. "How could they have found it that fast?"

"Well, you got away," Gregor said. "So maybe the witness was just a citizen."

"Or," Falcone said, "an FSB guy who got a look at the car full of terrorists he didn't want to take on."

"We'll soon know if we're spotted," Gregor said, pointing to a sign that flashed by.

"Vnukovo Airport, ten klicks."

59

When the Ministry for Civil Emergencies issued its "Seal off Moscow" order, Sheremetyevo, the capital's major airport, shut down and began filling with thousands of people, some awaiting departure and others arriving from grounded aircraft. They were herded into secure areas by heavily armed police officers and special units of FSB border guards. A larger FSB force did the same in the Domodedovo International Airport, once a terrorist target. In 2011, a woman, later identified as a Chechen had walked into Domodedovo's main terminal and set off a suicide bomb that killed thirty-seven people.

Gregor's choice of international airports, Vnukovo, had not been shut down. At the entrance, directional signs indicated why. Rachel translated them. They pointed the way to Heated Storage, Refrigerated Storage, Animal Quarantine, Dangerous Goods, and Radioactive Goods. Few of the planes that took off and landed at Vnukovo were passenger airliners. Most planes were carrying cargo or were private aircraft carrying the rich and powerful.

Gregor pulled up to the security kiosk for the general aviation terminal and showed his FSB identification card. Again he gave his expired-visa explanation and said he was escorting his passengers to a charter aircraft. The guard worked for the airport rather than the FSB or the Moscow Regional Police Department. He had been told long ago not to ask questions about activities in the general aviation terminal, where planes flew without filling out flight plans, or its VIP Lounge, where the oligarchs and their girlfriends awaited their flights or their Mercedes pickups.

He parked the van at the spot designated in the detailed drawing Drexler had received from Domino. Gregor had done his own reconnaissance from the roof terrace of the airport hotel and was able to confirm that the drawing was accurate. According to the drawing, the orange-and-red DHL cargo carrier would be waiting twenty meters from where he was parked.

Instead, in the harsh glare of floodlights, he saw a two-engine aircraft painted blue and white and bearing in black the words *Israeli Global* in English and Hebrew.

Falcone, seeing the plane and its name, said, "The Mossad strikes again."

Gregor, mouth agape, turned to Rachel.

"The General decided to switch from DHL," she said. "The change in aircraft had no effect on the plan. I didn't tell you because I didn't want you to worry."

"Worry?" Gregor said, springing out of the van. "I'm not worried. All I want is to get the fuck out of here." He opened all the doors and reached in to help Jack Beckley and Bobby Joe extract Hamilton. The tugging and sudden cold awakened Hamilton, who vainly struggled and muttered as they walked him toward the aircraft.

A fuselage door opened and a stairway emerged. Three minutes after the van arrived, all of its passengers were walking up the stairway and entering what looked like a dimly lit tunnel. Along the wall opposite the door was a row of a dozen seats locked onto one of the floor's metal tracks. On each seat was a folded blue blanket, along with a silvery travel mug with a black plastic cap.

As they were enwrapping themselves in blankets, the cockpit door opened, framing a black-bearded man who looked to be in his mid-thirties. He wore a zipped-up leather jacket and jeans tucked into fancy brown cowboy boots. Earphones were draped around his neck.

"Welcome aboard," he said, adding, with a bow, "Especially Miss Andrea Mitrovitz." Rachel, fussing with her blanket, did not look up. He gaped at Falcone's bloodied face, shirt, and suit coat. "What the hell? You're okay?"

"Yes," Falcone replied. "Somebody else's blood."

The man pointed to a restroom door. "Clean up fast. We are about to take off," he said, raising his voice as the plane's two turbos started up. "Passenger aircraft are grounded at all Moscow airports. But, for the moment, cargo can take off from Vnukovo." The plane began moving down the runway. "We'll be okay after we cross Russia's Border Security Zone at the Latvia border. That's about 730 klicks—450 miles for you Americans—so we're looking at only—"

Someone in the cockpit yelled in Hebrew. The black-bearded man turned and entered the cockpit, closing the door behind him. Falcone returned to his seat, face clean, shirt pink and damp.

"What did he say?" Falcone asked Rachel, who sat next to him.

"Air control told us not to take off," she said. The plane left the ground and tilted sharply upward.

Hamilton, unsnapping his seatbelt, suddenly stood. Reilly grabbed at him, catching him before he fell. "I demand to know why I am being . . . being kidnapped," Hamilton said, his voice nearly drowned out by the roar of the plane.

"Please, Mr. Hamilton," Reilly yelled, shoving him back into his seat and clicking the seatbelt. Bobby Joe Pickens, on Hamilton's other side, patted him on the back and then stretched to put an arm around Hamilton's shoulders in a gentle restraint.

"This is the pilot," came from loudspeakers strung along the round ceiling. This new voice was heavy with accent. "We must—" The plane lurched. "We must take evasive—" Silence and a sharp dive.

No one spoke. They were strapped inside a noisy, dipping and rising cylinder without windows. Something was outside, forcing them to dive and weave.

Falcone sat on Reilly's other side. "They're trying to make us land," Reilly said, yelling into Falcone's ear. "I remember the feeling. We were in a C-12 Huron that strayed into Iran airspace and—" Falcone could not hear the rest.

"Su-34s," the loudspeakers said. "No worry. We're too low, too slow for them. We're still on course."

Cocky Israelis, Falcone thought. He remembered hearing about a quiet deal, before the Ukraine crisis began. The United States bought two Russian strike aircraft from the Ukraine Air Force and paid Russian pilots to fly them against U.S. Air Force F-15s in simulated dogfights. The Russians consistently out-maneuvered the American fighters.

Falcone wished he could see an Su-34 in action. But all he could do was imagine two of them zooming over and under the cargo plane, teasing it into evasive moves, advertising Lebed's raw power. The latest Russian air force star was the Su-34, which NATO had respectfully named the Fullback. Putin had first displayed Su-34s to the world by sending them to Syria for attacks on rebel forces. Turkey promptly shot one of them down after the pilots repeatedly strayed into Turkey's sovereign territory.

After a few plunges and rises, the Fullbacks disappeared and the cargo aircraft continued its climb. For the first time in the flight, it leveled off and flew steadily. Everyone tried to sleep; snoring came from a couple of the swathed bodies.

After a short time of quiet, the evasive maneuvering began again. Falcone assumed that this meant they were near the Latvian border and the Fullbacks were giving the aircraft a bullying farewell.

Latvia was one of ten former Warsaw Pact nations that had infuriated Russia by joining NATO. Even though Lebed had been continuing Putin's intimidation campaign against the Baltic nations, Falcone believed that Russia would not invade Latvian airspace. The loudspeakers said, "Latvia below! We're in friendly airspace."

Falcone looked at his watch and guessed the plane would be over Riga shortly. He dozed off and in a little while awoke as the plane began a gentle descent.

The cloudy white trail of a missile passed through the dark sky and exploded about a mile in front of the plane. It shook the aircraft violently, and for a moment it seemed out of control. Missile fragments had struck the right wing.

The ground was rushing up as the pilot struggled to regain control and manage the descent. Runway edge lights flashed on. Another missile exploded miles away.

Despite control difficulties, the pilot expertly landed the plane and steered it toward a floodlit apron. The Israeli aircraft followed the original instructions for the DHL plane: Land at the Rumbula Air Base, a few miles outside Riga. After the Soviet-era base was closed in the 1970s, the runways became an impromptu used-car lot. Now they were again runways at a military air base. Following Russia's intervention in Crimea and Ukraine, NATO strategists feared that Latvia might be the next nation that Lebed would stalk. The base was hastily reopened and restored as part of a NATO show of force in the Baltic.

As the plane came to a stop, two U.S. Army Stryker armored personnel carriers sped to the runway, flanking the plane. Each vehicle spun a 30-mm cannon around to aim it at the plane. The rear ramps of the Strykers opened. Nine soldiers in combat gear ran out of each vehicle and lined up on both sides of the plane.

A combat staff car, its machine gun manned, left the two-story headquarters building and stopped alongside the plane. An officer in combat gear stepped out. The pilot slid open his side window.

"I am Colonel Barbara Fitzgerald of the U.S. Air Force, commander of this base," the officer yelled up to the pilot. "You have made an unauthorized landing at a restricted NATO facility. What is your cargo?"

"Seven people," the pilot shouted down.

"Repeat."

"Seven people."

A fuselage door opened and the stairway appeared.

"Come out of the aircraft with arms raised and remain on the stairway," Fitzgerald ordered. Led by Falcone, one by one, they stepped out, each one with shoulders draped in a blue blanket. Six looked relieved and puzzled. One looked angry. He stood out in his gym attire. The other men, in their white shirts and suits, could have been stumbling in from an all-night party. Rachel somehow retained her grace and acceptance of whatever fate might bring her.

Falcone looked down at Fitzgerald and shouted, "My name, Colonel, is Sean Falcone. I am a former senator and a former national security adviser to President Oxley."

Fitzgerald looked at Falcone and said, "Well, Mr. Falcone, you told me who you were. What are you now? And what the hell are you and these other people doing here?"

"This is a very complicated situation, Colonel," Falcone said. "And I need to discuss it with you . . . privately."

Fitzgerald spoke into a shoulder microphone. Two pairs of headlights blazed in the darkness.

"You and the copilot will enter one of these vehicles. Under guard," Fitzgerald said, again yelling up at the pilot. She turned toward the stairway. "You, Mr. Falcone, and your . . . companions will also enter these vehicles. Under guard."

Gesturing and speaking to the nearest soldiers, she ordered one to enter each vehicle.

"I am being kidnapped!" Hamilton shouted.

Ignoring him and the others, Fitzgerald reentered the staff car, which led the other vehicles toward the headquarters building.

60

As the vehicle containing Falcone, Rachel, Gregor, and Bobby Joe drove off, Falcone got a fleeting glance at a Gulfstream G-550. It was parked at the floodlit apron of another runway. As soon as the vehicle stopped, Falcone sprang from his seat, threw down the blanket, and started toward Fitzgerald's staff car. The guard, who had stepped out first, used his weapon to push Falcone toward the entrance of the building. It was a standard Soviet-era military building, squat and gray and far more walled than windowed.

They were taken to a room whose door sign simply said STAFF. Fitzgerald, at the head of a long, polished table, invited everyone to sit and posted one of the escorting soldiers at the door. At her left was a captain whom she did not introduce. Falcone assumed he was her intelligence officer. Slowly forming in his mind was a new reality about how the dark side works. This Army colonel and this Army captain were more savvy about the workings of the dark side than he, a former senator and former adviser to the President.

Fitzgerald looked steadily at Hamilton for a moment and then at Falcone, saying, "I don't know what this is about, but you came at a very bad time. For three days now, Russian Su-34s have been violating Riga airspace, making this a hot spot for an unexpected aircraft with its transponder turned off."

You do know what's going on, Falcone thought. *You're acting out the official side while supporting the dark side. You staged your hostile welcome strictly for the soldiers.*

"About two hundred miles from here," she continued, "along Latvia's border, Russian troops are bivouacked and building wooden housing units—just as they did when they moved into Syria. Lebed has been encouraging Latvian nationalists who were against Latvia's connection with NATO and the EU to claim they're being harassed and discriminated against by government officials. And a lot of people who still consider themselves Russian live on the Latvian side of the border. There aren't many people in that area—lakes, forests, and deserted Soviet-era factories. So a military move would be pretty easy."

"Are you expecting some of those Russian green men?" Falcone asked.

"We're on a special alert and have a joint NATO-Latvian force along the border and another here to defend Riga. Offshore there's an amphibious assault ship carrying the Twenty-Fourth Marine Expeditionary Unit. I am in direct communication with the Supreme Allied Commander Europe. This is serious stuff. One—"

"I've been kidnapped," Hamilton shouted.

Fitzgerald ignored him and continued: "One of our Latvian allies got trigger-happy at his missile launcher. For the record, he was aiming at the Su-34s, not you guys." She looked directly at the two Israelis. "We don't want an incident."

She paused, giving Falcone a chance to interrupt. "Excuse me, Colonel. But you needn't worry about a repeat of those missiles," he said. "We're out of here. I call your attention to that Gulfstream." He pointed toward the room's single window.

"The mystery plane, Livingston," she said to the captain, who smiled and nodded.

"Officially, I'll bet, that Gulfstream isn't here, right?" Falcone said.

Captain Livingston, after looking at Fitzgerald for approval, said, "Okay, Falcone. We want all of you out of here as much as you want to get out. You guys seem to be the reason for a big terrorist alert in Moscow. And you lured the Su-34s here. They were ordered to harass but not harm. Just for the record, I need your passports to see if you're the guys you're supposed to be. You had us a bit worried. We were told to expect a DHL aircraft. That's why the Strykers were greeting you. We're in an anything-can-happen alert. So we were ready in case you weren't who we thought you were."

"Sorry, Captain. Some changes in the plan. As for the passports, we had to leave them behind," Falcone said. "I can vouch for everyone, including Miss Andrea Mitrovitz."

"I don't have her on my list."

"*We* can also vouch for *her*," the copilot said.

"What about you two?" Livingston asked the copilot.

"We'll check in with our embassy in Riga," he replied. "And we have our passports."

He slid them down the table to Livingston, who opened a file folder, wrote down some words and numbers, then slid the passports back.

"And your aircraft?" Livingston asked.

"We need to check it for damage, but I think we can fly it to Riga International Airport, get fuel and repairs, if needed. And file a legitimate flight plan to Israel—with transponder turned on."

"I'm being kidnapped," Hamilton said again.

"Not exactly," Livingston said, shrugging as he turned to look at Hamilton.

61

Colonel Fitzgerald took them to the officers' club, a converted barracks with a bar, some tables, chairs, a couple of couches, a pool table, and a large television screen on the wall. Falcone guessed that the garrulous bartender, in white shirt and black slacks, was a master sergeant by day. While her colleagues lined up to order drinks, Rachel entered the no-gender restroom and emerged fifteen minutes later looking like she belonged in a much better bar.

Falcone, a double vodka in his hand, joined Fitzgerald at a table near the bar. There was a white coffee mug in front of her. She was in a combat camouflage uniform and yellow boots. From a khaki belt hung a holstered Beretta M9 pistol. Her blond hair was gathered in a bun. "I remember you from a lecture you gave at the National Defense University," she said as Falcone sat down.

"About what?" he asked.

"Expansion of NATO," she said. "The theme, as I remember, was whether NATO could survive the end of the Cold War."

"Did I think it could?"

"Yes, and—again, as I remember—you felt that as long as there is Russia there will be a need for NATO. So far, you're right."

Rachel, carrying a glass of white wine, slipped into a chair next to Falcone. She introduced herself as Andrea Mitrovitz.

Fitzgerald nodded in greeting and asked no questions. Falcone sensed that both women knew the boundaries of acceptable subjects for conversation. He wanted to say, *"This is my first rendition. It has to do with the fate of the Earth."* But he knew, of all the possible subjects, rendition was the one that was most prohibited.

"The club is officially closed," Fitzgerald said, directing her talk to both Falcone and Rachel. "So is the kitchen. I figured you could use drinks and food. I asked the cook to put up some sandwiches and coffee." She held up her mug. "The Gulfstream crew is in the BOQs—'bachelor officers quarters,'" she added, turning to Rachel, "and ready to go. They want a night takeoff."

"I take that as a hint for us to leave," Falcone said lightly.

"With all due respect, Mr. Falcone," Fitzgerald said, "your operation is a headache adding to one we already have."

Reilly, who had appointed himself Hamilton's minder, chose a corner table. Gregor, on his way to the bar, took their orders: beer for Reilly, water with a slice of lemon and no ice for Hamilton.

Gregor arrived with the drinks and headed to another table. Knowing that Hamilton was from California, Reilly tried to begin a conversation about the San Francisco 49ers.

"Football—professional or collegiate—is of no interest to me," Hamilton said. "Do you live in California?"

"No. Virginia," Reilly replied. "Danville, Virginia."

"So why would you have any interest in a San Francisco team?"

"Well, I knew that you—"

"Yes. Well, thank you for your attempt to pass the time," Hamilton said, nodding. A minute passed before he spoke again. "I assume you have a cell phone," he said. "I would greatly appreciate it if you would call my . . . assistant and tell her—"

"I'm sorry, Mr. Hamilton. But I can't do that."

"I assume you're an employee of the federal government," Hamilton said.

"No, sir. I am working for a contractor."

"Can you be more specific?"

"No, sir. I'm afraid I can't," Reilly said. "I know you must feel confused. But don't worry. You'll be getting in another airplane . . . a much more comfortable one."

"That Gulfstream I saw when we were leaving the plane?"

"Yes," Reilly replied, surprised.

"You're right. A very comfortable—and practical—aircraft. Two Rolls-Royce engines. Range more than 6,750 miles. Got a trophy as the best-in-value business aircraft."

"You sure know a lot about the Gulfstream," Reilly said.

"I should," Hamilton replied. "I own one."

Two men, tall and slim, one black the other white, entered the club from a back door, looked around, and nodded to Falcone. He followed them to the table farthest from the bar. Their khaki slacks, open-collared white shirts, and leather zipper jackets looked like unintended uniforms. He guessed they were ex–Air Force officers who had gone over to the dark side. They did not introduce themselves. The black man, who spoke with a southern accent like Bobby Joe Pickens, asked, "Your folks ready to leave? We're gassed up and ready to fly."

As he spoke, someone came through the nearby swinging doors bearing a tray full of sandwiches wrapped in waxed paper.

"Soon as they eat," Falcone said.

The sandwich man was followed by the coffee man, who carried a large thermos and a wooden box containing mugs, a carton of plastic water bottles, and the standard accessories for dispensing coffee. They set up a food station at an unoccupied table and disappeared into the kitchen.

Pickens was the first at the food table. He scooped up sandwiches and took them first to Rachel, then to Reilly and Hamilton, who turned down a sandwich and asked for more water. Pickens made himself the host, carrying sandwiches, coffee, and bottles of water to the others. In most of the military posts and ships Falcone had cause to visit as a senator or presidential adviser, he had seen instinctive courtesy like this—everyday behavior that translated into lifesaving deeds in battle.

"How long you figure the time to Washington?" Falcone asked.

The two men looked at each other. The black man said, "A few hours. Depends on the weather."

In a few minutes, Colonel Fitzgerald rose from her chair, signaling departure time. She led her visitors to the door and shepherded them into vehicles, which moved off to the Gulfstream, this time without armed guards.

62

Falcone had traveled long enough and frequently enough in corporate jets to remember the old reliable Gulfstream, ancestor to the aircraft that he sat in now. Globalization of commerce had forced the change of the aircraft's range and splendor. Gulfstreams once took high-rolling CEOs from corporate headquarters in one American city to customers in another American city. Now Gulfstreams carry billionaires seeking deals or pleasures in flights from one continent to the other.

The takeoff was fast and steep. Looking out a window, he saw the runway lights suddenly go out, returning the night to darkness. That sudden blackout made him realize once again that the rendition was too complex to be clandestine. *Presidential deniability has to be imaginary,* he thought. *How is deniability possible when, besides Drexler and his men, the cast of characters include the Mossad, the CIA, the U.S. Air Force, and probably NATO?* Questions still flowing through his mind, he finally fell asleep.

As he slowly awakened, his dreams fading, his mind still buzzing with questions, he had no idea how far they had flown. He was in a half-inclined seat, one of two on each side of the forward cabin. Across the aisle was Rachel, soundly asleep.

After visiting a restroom and continuing his effort to clean up, Falcone walked into the quiet aft cabin, where seats were arranged more closely than in the forward cabin. Jack Beckley was sleeping; next to him was Gregor, under a beam of light and reading a paperback with a garish cover and a title in Russian. He looked up, nodded to Falcone, and resumed reading. In another pair of seats, Reilly sat half turned toward Hamilton, who was sleeping. Falcone pantomimed a needle into the arm and Reilly gave him a smile and a thumbs-up. Bobby Joe Pickens, sitting next to an empty chair, stood, beckoned Falcone to the end of the aft cabin, and pointed to an overhead oval panel.

Imprinted on both sides of the panel was a yellow outline map of the world. A red line marked the beginning of the flight in Latvia and continued across the Baltic Sea and Scandinavia to the North Atlantic. The red line dipped after passing the middle of the ocean and approaching the North American coast.

"I always watch the flight line," Pickens said. "It makes me feel I'm really moving, and I try to figure the probable speed and estimate the time of arrival." He paused and added, "I think there's something wrong."

"Looks normal to me," Falcone said, also keeping his voice low amid the sleepers.

"Seems to me we're heading toward Florida instead of Washington," Pickens said. As he spoke, Falcone could see the line inch more southward than westward. He guessed where Washington was on the featureless map, and he could see what Pickens meant.

Falcone pressed a button on the console of the nearest empty seat. In a moment the cockpit door opened and the copilot walked down the aisle toward them.

"No flight attendants on this run," he said sharply. "What can I do for you?"

"We're wondering about the route," Falcone said, pointing to the map.

"That's deceptive, a gimmick," the copilot said, nodding toward the map. "We're not flying a straight line. We're dodging some Atlantic weather. That's all. No problem." He turned and walked rapidly toward the cockpit door.

"Thanks for the heads up," Falcone said to Pickens.

"You're welcome," Pickens said, heading back to his seat.

After standing for a moment, looking at the map and the red line pointing south, he returned to the mid-cabin section. Rachel was awake and watching a movie on a dropped-down screen. She took off her earphones and moved over so he could sit next to her.

"How did you do it?" she asked.

"Do what?"

"Kill the shooter."

He briefly told her what happened.

"Well done," she said, patting his hand.

"I'm honored to have my killing praised by a pro. But, believe me, it was instinct, not skill."

"It was . . . a pleasure being with you," she said, keeping her hand on his. "What happens now?"

"What? Well, I hope—"

The way he said *hope* made her realize he was asking what would happen next for them. She squelched that hope by saying, "What happens to Hamilton?"

Her question stunned him for a moment. "We take him to a safe house Drexler has in Virginia, and we try to convince him that he has to give us the whereabouts of Asteroid USA."

"With 'enhanced interrogation'?"

"Hell, no! We tell him the Russians want to use the asteroid as a weapon. And we remind him that the FBI has labeled him a 'person of interest' in a murder investigation."

"And?"

"And try to make a deal."

There was nothing more to say about Hamilton. They suddenly had nothing to say to each other. Rachel broke the silence: "One of my favorite films." She pointed to the screen.

He leaned forward, looked at the screen, and said, "One of my favorites, too." He put on earphones and joined her to watch *The Third Man*, wondering who picked the Gulfstream movies for rendition ops.

"Buffet in the galley," said a terse voice that Falcone recognized as the copilot's. The passengers found a bowl of fruit, coffee, soft drinks, various kinds of sandwiches, and small plastic dishes covered in aluminum foil, some containing beef stew, some macaroni and cheese. Pickens brought an apple, banana, and beef stew back to Reilly. Hamilton was still asleep.

Falcone, returning to his seat with sandwiches and coffees, glanced at the red line, which was pointing toward Florida. He was surprised because the flight had been so smooth and thought that the pilot must have by-passed the bad weather.

After finishing the sandwich, he frequently leaned forward and turned to look out the window. Then, in the bright morning light, he saw the unmistakable scythe-shape of Cuba. The Gulfstream banked and began its descent. One word flashed in Falcone's mind: Guantanamo.

63

"**What the hell is** going on?" Falcone shouted, startling Rachel, who thought he was overreacting to *The Third Man*, which was nearing the end. "Guantanamo!" Falcone exclaimed. "We're landing at Guantanamo!"

"What?" she asked, looking out the window and seeing the runway rushing up. "How—"

"How? You ask me how?" Falcone said angrily. "You know goddamn well how this happened. The Mossad—"

"Please, Sean. Calm down. This is not the Mossad. Believe me. This is not the Mossad."

The plane landed and taxied to a stop near a cluster of military vehicles and a high wire-mesh fence topped by coils of razor-wire. On the fence Falcone saw a sign that said HONOR BOUND TO DEFEND FREEDOM. Falcone snapped open his seatbelt and sprinted down the aisle toward the boarding door. It was opening and the stairway was lowering.

Bounding up the steps came four soldiers in camouflage uniforms and black ski masks. They reached the top of the stairs just as Falcone got to the door. "Step back, sir!" one of the soldiers said, holding his M16 rifle diagonally across his body at port arms, inches from Falcone's chest. "Sit down, sir, and fasten your seatbelt," he ordered. "You, too, ma'am," he said to Rachel, who had started to rise.

The other three soldiers hurried past Falcone to the aft cabin. Moments later they returned, two of them with their rifles slung over their right shoulders, pulling along a dazed Hamilton, whose feet dragged behind him. Next came Harry Reilly, Gregor, Jack Beckley, and Bobby Joe Pickens, followed by a soldier with rifle at port. He joined the soldier who had been guarding Falcone and Rachel, and the two of them stood shoulder-to-shoulder at the end of the cabin, both with rifles at port arms, blocking the way to the open door and stairway.

"You will all take a seat and fasten your seatbelts," one of the soldiers ordered. The four GSS men obeyed. *No need to struggle. Our mission is over. We snatched Hamilton from Moscow. And he winds up here. Someone changed the destination. Ours not to reason why.*

The two soldiers who had taken Hamilton away hauled him down the stairway and walked him to the unmarked vehicle. They pushed him into someone's black-gloved hands. The vehicle looked like an ambulance— except for its barred rear window and the men wearing black gloves. In the moment when the vehicle's door was open, Falcone could see two figures in black wearing black ski masks.

Falcone pulled out his Blackphone and, ignoring rendition secrecy rules, punched in the direct-line number to Frank Carlton. *There's a chance this is a mistake,* Falcone thought, even though, deeper in his mind, he believed that the delivery of Hamilton to Guantanamo, rather than to Washington, had to have been ordered by someone at a high level.

Instead of a ringtone, Falcone heard a repeated two-word message in a woman's voice: "Call forbidden. Call forbidden. . . ."

Falcone knew that Guantanamo was nothing more than a federal prison, though the prisoners were called "detainees" because as "prisoners" they would be subject to the terms of the Geneva Convention governing the treatment of prisoners. Guantanamo was operated by a military-and-political entity called the Joint Task Force, under command of a two-star general or admiral answerable to the secretary of defense and ultimately to the commander-in-chief.

Throwing down the Blackphone, Falcone stood and turned to the nearest soldier. "I demand that I be taken to your commanding officer," he shouted.

"Please be seated, sir," the soldier said, moving a step closer, putting his weapon closer.

Falcone felt a rising rage. He was a prisoner again, looking at his guard in the Hanoi Hilton. He slugged the soldier in the jaw, sending him reeling into a chair. The soldier instinctively raised his rifle. Then discipline took over. He stood and resumed port arms, glaring at Falcone.

The cockpit door opened. Falcone turned and saw the pilot, who must have heard the scuffle. He took three steps forward and said, "Please, gentlemen—and miss. Please. I am the pilot of this aircraft and responsible for the safety of my passengers. I must ask you to accept that you are passengers on a flight that took an unexpected detour. And you will not be allowed to deplane. I ask you that you work out your issues only when this flight is over. We are having our tanks topped off. This will take about forty minutes. The Immediate Reaction Force soldiers will depart. We will then fly to our destination, Dulles Airport. Please relax and accept that we have had a detour. That's all. A detour." He did not mention that the flight plan required for a landing at Dulles would show that the flight originated in Miami, Florida.

It took Falcone several minutes to calm down. " 'A detour,' " he said to Rachel. "He called it 'a detour.' Let's say that's true. Let's say that someone decided Gitmo was a good place to question Hamilton and ordered a detour. How? The goddamn Mossad. It's—"

"Let's get one thing straight, Sean," Rachel said sharply. "This is not the Mossad. We left the Mossad behind in Latvia. You must realize that this aircraft is controlled by the United States national-security apparatus. Someone made a decision in Washington and modified the plan."

"Modified!?" Falcone said. "You call this modified?"

"Please, Sean. Calm down and *think.* Somebody did something behind your back. You're supposed to be running a black op, a kidnapping. Well, it looks like someone else took over."

"But Gitmo? This is insane."

"Insane?" Rachel asked and made a sweeping gesture. "Is *anything* about this sane? Your job was to get Hamilton out of Moscow. And you did that."

"I took the job because I knew that the world—*the world*—was threatened and Hamilton had information that could save the world. Now someone has detoured him and thinks that he will talk here. Gitmo. Hell. Full of hatred. No good can happen here."

"Who did it? That's what you must do next: Find out who did this."

"Don't worry. I will," Falcone said grimly. He had a couple of suspects.

Falcone had done pro bono work in a case involving a Guantanamo prisoner. Among the legal documents he had seen was a deposition taken by another lawyer in the case. The witness, an Egyptian, had worked at one of the "black-site" prisons that the CIA had set up soon after 9/11 as a place for "enhanced interrogation" of suspected terrorists.

The witness told how the suspect, after being questioned and tortured in Egypt for days, was delivered to captivity by a Gulfstream known as the Guantanamo Express. He was already shackled and handcuffed when the witness saw his captors preparing him for his trip. After cutting away his clothing, one of them inserted a suppository, presumably containing a sedative, into his anus, and put a diaper on him because he would not be allowed to go to a restroom during the flight. Finally, he donned orange coveralls, was blindfolded and hooded and placed in a seat harness rigged in the aircraft. It stopped for refueling at Shannon Airport in Ireland. Irish plane-spotters tracked the U.S. registration numbers on the Gulfstream's tail to a transport service in Massachusetts. Owners and operators of the service had what the CIA calls "sterile identities"—names not found in any corporate, residential, or employment databases.

Falcone had been an associate counsel in the case and had not gone to Guantanamo. But he knew attorneys who had to fight their way through the prison's military rules to aid their clients. The lawyers had trouble establishing trust with their clients because Gitmo guards had told them that their lawyers were Jews or homosexuals. Some interrogators had posed as lawyers to get the prisoners to divulge information they had not revealed to their interrogators.

Guantanamo was supposed to house only non-Americans. However, in the early days, a man captured in Afghanistan had been briefly held there because his captors did not believe he was an American. He was repatriated to Saudi Arabia, on condition that he deny his American citizenship. (John Walker Lindh, an American captured during the U.S.

invasion of Afghanistan in 2001, was not taken to Guantanamo. He pleaded guilty to two charges and was sentenced to twenty years in a federal prison.)

Hamilton's citizenship was beyond question. Yet, there he was, "detoured" to Guantanamo. The first and only American to be imprisoned at Gitmo.

Hamilton had been hauled away by members of the Immediate Reaction Force. Falcone knew about that, too. As mustered early in Gitmo's history, they wore what they called Darth Vader suits: black helmet, black goggles, black hoods. According to a declassified copy of the Standard Operating Procedures, used in the case that Falcone worked on, "The IRF team is intended to be used primarily as a forced-extraction team, specializing in the extraction of a detainee who is combative, resistive, or if the possibility of a weapon is in the cell at the time of the extraction. . . . The IRF team is authorized to spray the detainee in the face with mace twice before entering the cell."

Falcone's experience as a prisoner in a North Vietnam hellhole had inspired him to do pro bono work on Gitmo prisoner cases. Details of cases flooded his mind. Then one fact stood out and lingered: The Supreme Court had ruled that Guantanamo prisoners had the right to counsel and the right to challenge their detention.

"Hamilton needs a lawyer," Falcone told Rachel. "And he's going to get two."

64

When the plane landed near the private-aircraft terminal of Dulles, Falcone grasped Rachel's hand, smiled, and said, "I'll never forget that moment in the hotel when I met Andrea Mitrovitz." She smiled back.

"I'll be getting a car," he said. "Can we share it? I assume you'll be going directly to your embassy. . . . And then, perhaps dinner tonight?"

"I . . . I must check in first," she said, sounding uncharacteristically uncertain. She took her Blackphone from her purse. "Would you mind . . ."

Falcone nodded and left his seat to say goodbye to Gregor Ivanisov and the others. Gregor was on the phone, but interrupted his conversation to say, "It was a pleasure to serve with you, Sean," beginning a round of handshakes and fist bumps. "It's the General," he said, pointing to the phone. "He's lining up transportation for us."

Falcone knew he should have been glad not to report to anybody, not to check in with anybody. But he felt empty, pointless. He took out his phone and arranged for a town car, then headed back toward his seat. Rachel was already in the aisle and was not holding her phone.

"Car's on the way," Falcone said, sounding more chipper than he felt. "There's a lounge where we can wait."

Gregor and the others filed past him, hurrying toward the stairway.

"I . . . I'm afraid the embassy booked me on an El Al flight," Rachel said, beginning to walk down the aisle. "It leaves in less than an hour. And they insisted I have a security guy. He's meeting me at the lounge here and taking me through TSA to the El Al lounge. Complicated."

"As usual," Falcone said, following her.

At the bottom of the plane's stairway, they embraced. She raised her face to his and they kissed. "This is goodbye—at least for now," she said, stepping away. "Next time I hope we'll have more time, more peaceful time."

A black Mercedes sedan pulled up at the lounge and out of it stepped a broad-shouldered young man in a blue blazer and khaki slacks. He and Rachel walked toward each other. The young man said something in Hebrew, and escorted her to the car.

Falcone walked on, more alone than he had felt in a long time.

65

About the time the Gulfstream landed at Dulles, President Oxley was informed that he was about to receive a call from President Lebed. The advice came through the White House communication system, not from Oxley's National Security Adviser, Frank Carlton, who usually set up upcoming important calls with his counterpart elsewhere. But this Lebed call was apparently spontaneous. Nevertheless, Oxley hit the button for Carlton, who quickly appeared in the Oval Office clutching a yellow pad.

"Frank, what the hell is going on? I've just been told that Lebed is about to call me."

"I don't know, sir. I haven't heard a word. Usually, the Russian ambassador would pave the way. Or their foreign minister. At least you won't need an interpreter."

"What about—?"

"Recording? I'm afraid it's too late to stop it. I will—"

Carlton sat next to the president's desk, poised to take notes.

Oxley's phone rang.

"This is Boris Lebed, Blake."

"Well, Boris, this is quite a surprise."

"Yes. I hope things are well with you."

"And with you . . . Boris."

"We seem to have had a problem here," Lebed said, his voice tightening.

"What is the problem? How can I help?" Oxley asked. He and Carlton exchanged puzzled glances.

"An American who was touring our country appears to have disappeared. Would you have any knowledge of his whereabouts?"

Oxley instantly recalled what Carlton had said about Robert Hamilton: *"We have to bring him back, Mr. President."* And Oxley recalled the unspoken word in that conversation: *deniability. It's happened,* he thought. *And I can't know.*

"I'm afraid I can't be of any help, Boris," Oxley said. "I'm personally not aware of Americans who are touring Russia. As I'm sure you know, this is not something I would be aware of."

"Of course. I realize that," Lebed said, softening his tone. "I just wanted to be sure, as we take the safety of all who visit our great country very seriously. We had received some reports that this individual was last seen near the border of Latvia. As you know, this is a very dangerous area at the moment and we are concerned about the welfare of Latvians—and Russian citizens—who live in that area, especially along our border. We, of course, have the right to protect our borders. We wouldn't want to take any action that would put civilian lives in danger."

"I'm sure that the NATO countries are very safe and secure," Oxley said confidently. "You needn't worry, Boris. If necessary, we're prepared to send military forces to prevent any unrest or instability along the Latvian border. I truly hope that won't be necessary because we don't want to see what happened in Ukraine repeated."

"Attempts to look into the future, my friend, are always futile and often dangerous. Goodbye."

"Goodbye," Oxley responded, adding "until we meet again"—a direct, and in this conversation, an ominous translation of *do svidaniya.*

Carlton spoke the moment Oxley hung up: "Mr. President, please do not bother to be disturbed by what Lebed may be alluding to."

"I am not disturbed, Frank. But I am damn curious. Now, I'd like you to stay on. Rita is due to give me a rundown on China selling off U.S. debt. I assume it's a spinoff from the aggressive moves aimed at Japan."

Oxley pressed a button and Rita Oliphant, secretary of the Treasury, entered. Carlton stood and held out his hand—an awkward moment of greeting, for it showed how long a time since the two had been in the same

room, let alone in the Oval Office. She handled the moment more gracefully than Carlton, who did not have China on his mind.

Carlton knew who Lebed's "missing American" was and so did the
President. But Oxley could not officially know. Carlton also knew that
Oxley had no knowledge—yet—of why Hamilton was in Guantanamo
and how he got there. "Deniability" was a tricky concept for all the de-
niers involved.

Carlton retained the chair next to Oxley's desk, but the President was
on his feet and gestured to one of the two brown sofas flanking a long
narrow table. Rita Oliphant, in black slacks and suit coat over a white turtleneck, sat across from Oxley and, in a bit of West Wing choreography,
Carlton left his chair to sit next to the President.

"There seems to be a shift in Chinese policy about selling off the U.S.
debt, Mr. President. We—that is, my China experts and I—believe that
China is not merely selling off to squeeze the U.S. economy but also to
pay for the oil whose prices have just spiked. Ironically, the price surge
was triggered by the turmoil that China has caused. We also believe . . ."

Carlton had stopped listening. He had to get to his office as soon as
possible and somehow work the deniability problem as news of Hamilton's rendition spilled out of Gitmo and spread through the Pentagon.

Oxley was listening . . . China . . . oil . . . Then Lebed . . . *Hamilton!*
That had to be what Lebed was talking about. China . . . oil. . . . The asteroid threat and Ivan's Hammer slipped to the back of his mind.

66

The encrypted, top-secret, top-priority message was labeled IMMEDIATE (O). It went directly from Commander, Joint Task Force Guantanamo, to two offices in the E Ring, the power center of the Pentagon's five rings. One office belonged to the Chairman of the Joint Chiefs of Staff; the other to the Secretary of Defense. The message said: ROBERT WENTWORTH HAMILTON ARRIVES VIA EXTRAORDINARY RENDITION. BEING PROCESSED. URGENTLY REQUEST NATIONAL COMMAND AUTHORIZATION.

When General Hector Amador, the Chairman of the Joint Chiefs of Staff, saw the IMMEDIATE (O) message, he exclaimed, "Jesus H Christ!" and for a moment wondered what to do next, for the (O) meant "operational." And that meant "Do something immediately." But "National Command Authority" comprises the President and the Secretary of Defense as the ultimate source of military orders. And in the next moment General Amador realized he did not have to do anything. (O) had been kicked all the way upstairs to the commander-in-chief and Secretary of Defense George Winthrop.

At almost the same moment, a military aide burst into Winthrop's office, centerpiece of a warren of deputy secretaries, under secretaries, assistant secretaries, and directors, each with a staff. Winthrop read the message and said, "What in God's name is this about?"

"I don't have the foggiest idea, sir," the aide said. He did an about-face and rapidly returned to the SecDef communications room, leaving Winthrop sitting behind his massive desk and staring into space. His instinct was to pick up the direct line to the President. But it would be better to first learn what is known and what is unknown, as a former secretary of defense might put it.

Winthrop was a disciple of the ultimate-rule that one of his predecessor's had learned as a young Navy pilot: *If you are lost: climb, conserve, and confess.* "Climb" meant gain altitude to see a greater distance and get your bearings. "Conserve" meant reduce airspeed and save fuel. "Confess" meant get on the radio and admit, "I'm lost and need help."

Climb. Winthrop picked up the direct phone to General Hector Amador. As the chairman of the Joint Chiefs of Staff, he was America's highest-ranking military officer.

Conserve. Without a hello, Winthrop said, "Hector, what the hell is this?"

"General Bob Dafoe, the CO at Gitmo, is reporting an unusual situation, sir. As I am sure you know, an 'extraordinary rendition' is the CIA's description of an . . . abduction. General Dafoe is right to inform me. But NCA, not me, has to tell him what to do. And he's damn right about that, sir."

Confess. "That's the problem, Hector. I'm just an old Oakie who finds himself running the whole damn American military machine, which, lucky for me, does a great job of running itself. But this is a fuckin' kidnapping of a billionaire American citizen. Hector, I don't know what to do."

"All I can suggest, sir, is that you head across the river as fast as you can and start talking to the President. He and you, sir, have to tell Bob Dafoe what to do. It looks to me, Mr. Secretary, that Hamilton was just sort of dumped in the general's lap. And now the balloon's gone up, sir."

67

By the time Falcone reached his Pennsylvania Avenue penthouse, he had put Rachel in that part of his memory where love lives on, despite death, despite fate. She was not gone. He always proudly believed that he had a disciplined, compartmented mind. When Rachel was put in the memory part, he opened another compartment, where his hatred of Guantanamo raged.

He gave himself the luxury of a shower and a glass of vodka before he wrapped himself in a bathrobe and put in a call to Ray Quinlan. Surprisingly, he picked up.

"You son of a bitch," Falcone said.

"Nicest thing you've ever called me, Sean. What's your problem?"

"Not my problem. It's yours and Oxley's. He wants a legacy? How about, 'Hypocrite-in-Chief'? 'Candidate Who Promised to Close Guantanamo Has Increased Its Population.'"

"You writing headlines now?"

"No, but Phil Dake might."

"You making a threat?"

"You bet."

"Sean, what the hell are you talking about?"

"I am talking about this: How did you possibly believe you and Oxley could get away with putting Robert Hamilton in Guantanamo?"

"What?! Jesus, Sean! Are you telling me the truth? You're not having a crazy spell?"

Falcone hesitated, lowered his voice, and asked, "You didn't order the detour to Gitmo? That's what the Gulfstream pilot called it. 'A detour.'"

"What?!" Quinlan exclaimed again. This time his voice was touched with panic. "If Hamilton is in Guantanamo, Sean, something awfully wrong has happened. First of all, the President is still determined to close Guantanamo. Congress is totally opposed and—"

"Okay. So he seems sincere about closing. But—"

"Sean. The President wants me. Gotta go. I'll call you back."

Carlton. The name shot into Falcone's mind. But he did not—could not—call Carlton. He had to be the one who had set up the detour—with Drexler, and probably Sam Stone and the CIA. Falcone remembered talking to Drexler about what would happen if the rendition became known: Falcone had to take responsibility and claim he was suffering from PTSD by his long imprisonment during the Vietnam War.

He made a quick call to Ursula Breitsprecher, telling her to destroy his letter of resignation from the firm.

"Oh, Sean. So glad you are back," she said. "I worried so."

"I had some worries, too. It was some flight home! Will see you when I can. Hope it'll be tomorrow. 'Bye."

"Wait. I looked up the *Moscow Times.* There *was* a story about an American being killed in a hit-and-run. And his name did begin with the letter *D.* His name was Leonid Danshov."

"Okay. Thanks much, Ursula. See what you can find on him. 'Bye again."

Falcone's next call was to Akis Christakos. Falcone remembered that he had turned over the Sullivan & Ford files on Hamilton to Christakos. Hamilton's previous lawyer was Paul Sprague, who had resigned in the wake of a shooting of a lawyer and three others at the law firm. Some of the files had been missing because they were in the possession of the FBI, which was investigating possible ties of SpaceMine and Hamilton to the shootings.

His call to Christakos was short:

"Christo, this is Sean Falcone. We need to talk, but not on the phone."

"Breakfast tomorrow at The Hay-Adams?"

"Too public."

"Metropolitan Club?"

"Too public. How about your office?"

"As a client?"

"No. As a co-counsel on a very hot case."

"You have my attention, Sean. See you at eight a.m."

Falcone had no doubt that Christakos expected to be discussing Hamilton tomorrow morning.

68

Falcone knew that Christakos would not be able to resist a chance for a very hot case. He had been labeled a Washington Super Lawyer by a reliable rating service because he always won his cases. None of his criminal clients had gone to jail, winning either acquittal or a probation deal. On the civil side, he rarely accepted a case in which less than $5 million was at stake. Because of his persistence in attaining a settlement, none of his plaintiffs had lost their pleas and none of his defendants had ever lost when their clients made the mistake of contesting Christakos in court.

Many politicians knew his private phone number. He was hailed as a genius for his timing, stepping in just as a politician was about to be indicted or arrested. He would defend the innocent. As for the guilty, he managed removal from office without public explanation, a maneuver he called his "silent arrangement."

Falcone had known Christakos for more than twenty years as a fellow Washington lawyer, but they had never met in a courtroom or argued across a table to reach a settlement. Nor had their personal lives ever intersected. Christakos was a family man with three grown children and four grandchildren, a lay leader at the St. Nicholas Greek Orthodox Cathedral, and the holder of a Redskins season ticket; Falcone was a childless widower, an agnostic drifting toward atheism, and a patron of the National Symphony Orchestra. Each knew the other only as a highly ethical, highly successful lawyer. Deeper down, if either man chose to examine the other, he would find a man who knew who he was.

"Welcome," Christakos said to the arriving Falcone at precisely 8:02. He led the way to his private office, a long room of baronial style. At one end was his massive desk and at the other, which he pointed Falcone toward, was a carved and gilt-decorated rosewood octagonal drum table.

"Breakfast is my vice," Christakos said. "I had to settle for this," pointing to a tray holding two glasses of pineapple juice, a plateful of croissants, a butter dish, a sterling-silver coffee service, and two gold-etched porcelain cups and saucers.

Falcone had entered carrying two Starbucks coffees. He left them on Christakos' desk and followed him to the table, which, he noticed, matched the office's rosewood-paneled walls.

"This is, indeed, a historic event," Christakos said. "The meeting of two great legal minds, a meeting, I surmise, that has something to do with my client, Robert Wentworth Hamilton."

"You're right, Christo. And I am here to tell you that your client is in Guantanamo."

Christakos, who liked to appear all-knowing, seldom showed surprise. But he lurched forward, nearly toppling the coffee urn. *"What?!"* he exclaimed. *"Guantanamo?* How? Why?"

"It all begins with an asteroid," Falcone said, carefully pouring himself a cup of coffee. He rapidly and coolly laid out the story—Hamilton's journey to Moscow to meet Basayev, the sinking of the yacht, Lebed's decision to hold Hamilton, the need for deniability, the approach to Falcone by Quinlan on Carlton's orders, the visit to Drexler's Global Special Services, and, in very condensed form, the rendition that ended in Guantanamo instead of a Virginia safe house. He omitted the deaths of the Russians, but he told of the death of Leonid Danshov and the substitution of a Mossad officer whom he did not identify.

Falcone ended his account with, "And you and I have to go there and get him out."

Christakos vigorously nodded. "I certainly agree," he said. "But first I suggest we go to court here and petition for a writ of habeas corpus."

"I don't think we want to go public right away," Falcone said. "If we do, we may lose any hope for getting Hamilton to cooperate."

"That puts me in a very awkward position, Sean. A clear conflict of interest."

"You're a great lawyer, Christo, but you're a patriot first. I promise you, you will get a deal for Hamilton. I assume the Gitmo detour was some kind of fuckup. Probably by Carlton throwing his weight around. I'll bet the White House is scared shitless that news about Hamilton will leak."

Christakos, finishing off a croissant, raised his right hand to indicate he was about to speak but had to swallow first. "I know a little of this." He told of his calls to J. B. Patterson and Quinlan and the visit from Hamilton's chief operating officer.

"I talked to Quinlan as soon as I got home," Falcone said. "He was called away by Oxley during the call. My bet is the Pentagon heard from Gitmo, and Winthrop undoubtedly called Oxley. By now the White House is in full panic mode."

"What do you propose, Counselor?"

"I call Quinlan and say you and I will trade our silence for a trip to Gitmo to rescue Hamilton."

"Plus cleared of all so-called charges as Patterson's 'person of interest,'" Christakos said. "Let's call Quinlan. I'm sure he'll pick up."

69

President Oxley sat in the middle of one sofa; Carlton, Winthrop, and Quinlan sat opposite the President on an identical sofa. A long low table stood between the sofas. In the middle of the table was a digital voice recorder that a White House staffer had just brought in. Oxley was holding a copy of the IMMEDIATE (O) message that Winthrop had handed him a moment before.

Oxley spoke the date and location, named the other men in the room, and said, "I am recording this meeting so that there will be a record of what is said here. The other participants have agreed to be recorded." Oxley read the message aloud, paused, and said, "Let me ask for the record, Secretary Winthrop, how did it happen that Mr. Robert Wentworth Hamilton is in the Guantanamo Bay Detention Camp?"

"I don't have any idea how that happened, Mr. President," Winthrop replied.

"Mr. Quinlan, do you know? Did you order that Mr. Hamilton, an American citizen, be taken to the Guantanamo Camp?"

"No, sir. But I would—"

"Please, Mr. Quinlan, your *no* is sufficient."

Iran-Contra flashed through Quinlan's mind.

"And, Adviser Frank Carlton, do you know?"

"I would rather not say, Mr. President."

"Thank you, gentlemen. I am now ending this recording, at least for now."

The sound of the recorder clicking off was surprisingly loud in the tense, silent Oval Office.

"Okay, Frank. I felt I had to do that. The Oval Office log will show that a meeting occurred today between . . . among . . . us all. And you chose not to answer my question. We will go off the record now, but I feel damn strong that if this Hamilton fuckup goes public, there will be a congressional investigation—at best, a Benghazi-style witch hunt, at worst my impeachment. You'll be asked what happened after the recording ended. You'll have to depend on your memory. So, Frank, do you want to open your memory?"

"I feel, Mr. President, the most honorable thing I can do is resign," Carlton said, his voice hoarse, his face pale.

"No, Frank. The most honorable thing you can do is tell me how the hell a prominent American citizen—a man who, by the way, contributes heavily to the opposition—was placed in a prison by members of my administration."

"It . . . he . . . was not a member of your administration, sir."

"Well, then, Frank, who was it?"

"It was Sean Falcone, Mr. President. He came to me with a story about having to get Hamilton out of Russia because, well . . . he said something about saving the world. And that sounded kind of crazy to me. But he insisted, and finally, I sent him to General Drexler, who runs a private paramilitary outfit."

Quinlan stirred and looked at Carlton in profile: square-jawed, slight beard shadow, beads of sweat. *Holy Christ! He's twisting it. But it's just like he said: Falcone takes the fall. And Oxley gets deniability.*

Oxley picked up the recorder, switched it on, and gently put it back on the table. "This is the President. I have just been told by Frank Carlton, my national security adviser, that the abduction of Mr. Hamilton from Moscow was the idea of Sean Falcone, my former national security adviser. I now ask Frank Carlton to repeat what he has just told me."

Carlton replicated his statement almost word-for-word, paused, and added: "I wondered at the time—and wonder now that it's over—if somehow this idea of freeing Mr. Hamilton came from some deep-seated

obsession or something that Mr. Falcone has, due to his long imprisonment and torture as a prisoner during the Vietnam War."

"You son of a bitch!" Quinlan shouted. Oxley reached for the recorder,
changed his mind, and left it running.

"Mr. President," Quinlan continued, only slightly lowering his voice.
"Carlton's lying. I can't sit here and hear this. The rendition was absolutely
his idea, not Falcone's. I carried the idea to Falcone at Carlton's request.
I gave Falcone a phone number that Carlton gave me. That was the ex-
tent of my participation. Carlton told me that he was making arrangements
that would give you deniability. That was his word. Deniability."

Carlton turned sharply, looked as if he was going to speak, but kept
silent.

"You told me, goddamn it," Quinlan continued, pointing to Carlton. "You told me that the President wanted Hamilton 'removed from
Moscow.' Those were your exact words. And you said if I didn't follow
your orders, you'd have me not only fired but blackballed in Washington."

"Okay, Ray. Calm down," Oxley said. "I have a question, was Guantanamo mentioned?"

"No, sir," Quinlan replied. "All I knew is that I had to give Falcone a
phone number and somehow that would start the whole thing."

"Do you happen to remember the number?" Oxley asked.

"Excuse me, Mr. President," Carlton said, leaning forward. "Allow
me to—"

Oxley ignored Carlton and nodded when Quinlan slowly called out
the number: "one zero zero five five five seven eight two zero."

"And whose number is that, Frank?" Oxley asked.

"Sir, all I know is that number reaches Global Special Services."

"Run by retired General Drexler?"

"Yes, sir."

"Was sending Mr. Hamilton to Guantanamo General Drexler's idea?"

When Carlton did not respond, Oxley turned to Winthrop, whose eyes
had been bulging as he moved his head from the President to Carlton and
Quinlan: "Secretary Winthrop, the Department of Defense operates
Guantanamo. Do you have any knowledge of the circumstances that led
to Mr. Hamilton's being taken there?"

"No, sir. I have ordered a top-level investigation by General Dafoe, who commands the Joint Task Force operating the . . . facility. I expect his report within twenty-four hours. I have also instructed him to provide the maximum . . . comfort and to treat him as . . . a . . . as a distinguished visitor. The place isn't all pris . . . detainee camp, sir. There's a Pizza Hut, a beer bar, a—"

"Has Hamilton been allowed to make any telephone calls?"

"No, sir. I am advised by General Amador that communicational protocols restrict calls from and to . . . residents. Only authorized personnel can—"

"Okay. Thank you, George," Oxley said, clicking off the recorder. He was silent for a moment. "So we have a small window. News of Hamilton hasn't reached the outside world." He looked Carlton full in the face and said, "You may go, Frank." Then he pointed to Quinlan and said, "Get me Falcone."

Quinlan hurried back to his office, discovered that Falcone had already called, and put in a call to him. Falcone answered on the first ring.

"I've just come from a meeting where your name was mentioned," Quinlan said. "You're invited here. Immediately."

"Tell the gate there will be two visitors," Falcone said.

"Who's the other?"

"That lawyer who called you looking for his lost client."

"Okay. Tell the escorts to take you both directly to my office. You'll need to be briefed."

"We'll be there in twenty minutes."

70

Quinlan ushered Falcone and Christakos into his office and shut the door. Pointing to two chairs and grunting, Quinlan was as hospitable as his aggressive psyche allowed. Nearly a full minute passed before anyone spoke. Finally, Falcone broke the silence: "We're here for one purpose, Ray. We need to go to Guantanamo and free Hamilton."

"Actually, Sean, you're here at the request of the President. He'll decide what you do. When the President met with Carlton and me, Carlton said the rendition of Hamilton had been your idea. The President had no knowledge of what happened. He wants to talk to you." Quinlan pointed his finger at Christakos and added, "You were not sent for."

"I realize that," Christakos said. "I'll just sit here and wait for what happens next." He reached into his croc-leather attaché case, extracted a file folder, and began leafing through it. As if in an afterthought, he added, "You may want to tell the President that, on behalf of our client, Robert Wentworth Hamilton, we intend to file in Federal District Court a petition to have him released. As I am sure you're aware, such a petition is a public document. I am also sure it will arouse the curiosity of Philip Dake."

Quinlan frowned. His face reddened, and he looked as if he were going to respond. Instead, he called the President and told him Falcone had arrived.

Again, the President set up a tableau, he on one side of the long table, Falcone on the other. The President quickly recounted the call from

Lebed, the meeting with Carlton, Winthrop, and Quinlan, and his selective use of a voice recorder. "And so we come to right now, Sean. Tell me what you know."

"No recorder, sir?"

"No recorder. Just you and me."

"First, Mr. President, *I* did not come up with the rendition idea. Carlton did. And he said that it had to be done by someone not in your administration to give you deniability. I did agree to run the rendition and take the fall if it became known. And I am still prepared to do so. But . . . Guantanamo? That was not on the menu."

"Well, where in hell did it come from?"

"I believe, sir, that the order had to have come from Carlton."

"Well, he apparently didn't give the commanding officer all he needed to know. The general sent an urgent message saying he wanted 'national command' authorization for having Hamilton there."

Oxley shook his head, looked directly at Falcone, and said, "Why did Carlton do it, Sean? He damn well knows that I hate Guantanamo and want to close it down. If it weren't for Congress, it *would* be closed. Why Guantanamo?"

"You'd have to ask him, sir."

"I think, Sean, it will be better for you to ask him. You were on the scene," Oxley said, speaking in the tone that indicates a meeting is over. He rose, as did Falcone, but neither man moved.

"Something else, Sean?"

"Hamilton, sir. I want to go to Guantanamo with his attorney, Akis Christakos."

"Leave it to George Winthrop, Sean. It's a DoD matter. They run the place."

"With all due respect, sir, I think it's a matter for the Commander-in-Chief. Handling an illegally held American citizen is not in the military's portfolio. For all we know, they're waterboarding him right now."

Oxley's face tightened and he silently glared at Falcone, who quietly said, "If Christakos and I take the legal route—a petition for a writ—"

"I know the goddamn legal route, Sean," Oxley said, his voice rising.

"It means you go public and the whole goddamn thing gets splashed all over the media. This sounds like a warning, a threat, Sean. Something I don't expect from a straight-shooter like you."

"It *is* a warning, sir. Unless there is a high-level intervention, this can spin out of control. And there's another facet to this, sir."

"You're piling on, Sean. Be careful."

"It's Leonid Danshov, an American citizen who was drawn into this . . . rendition. He—"

"Sam Stone briefed me about Leonid Danshov, probably killed by the FSB," Oxley said, dismissively waving a hand. "It's a highly classified Agency matter. We're not making an incident out of it."

Oxley sat down again and motioned for Falcone to do the same. "Sam Stone told me Danshov was a CIA operative," Oxley said. "But Sam didn't tell me that Danshov was involved in the rendition."

"Two Russians were also killed during the operation."

"What?! Jesus! Who was running this?"

"Theoretically, I was, sir. But as I said, it was Carlton who set it in motion, using Ray Quinlan as a cutout so there'd be no Carlton fingerprints. Ray was just a messenger. He had little knowledge of the details. I was told to arrange the rendition through a security firm known to Carlton. I was given the impression that the CIA was not aware of the operation. That was not true. As for Danshov, he was to be part of the rendition team. He was killed by the FSB and had to be replaced," Falcone said, leaning forward, hands clutching his knees. "His replacement was a Mossad officer. The Mossad was all over this, sir."

"The Israelis? Why? How?"

"Carlton was looking for deniability for you and decided to reach outside our intel community. The Mossad jumped at the chance. Israel enjoys learning American secrets. And it gave Israel a chance to tweak Lebed over selling air defense systems to Iran."

"Jesus! Who knows this? I mean Israeli involvement . . ."

"Stone, Carlton, Drexler, the retired Army general who—"

"I know who Drexler is," Oxley said impatiently. "Shadowy guy. Anybody else?"

"NSA analysts can pretty easily put a lot of pieces together and get a picture of what happened. So can Lebed, but to save face he can't go public."

"Same for me, Sean. Now I wonder what in hell . . ."

"Everyone involved in this—everyone who knows or thinks he knows—is a professional, sir. They all know how to keep secrets."

"Okay, let's assume—and hope—that it stays sealed up. What do I do with Hamilton?" Oxley spoke rapidly, as if the faster he talked, the faster this thing would go away.

"You call the general in command at Guantanamo, sir, and tell him two lawyers are on their way there to pick up Hamilton. And you tell the general that officially none of this happened."

"I suppose that could work," Oxley agreed. "Guantanamo has always been good at making believe things didn't happen. Okay. You get Hamilton out. Then what?"

"You order Stone to arrange for Hamilton to be taken to a CIA safe house. He gives Ben Taylor the coordinates of Asteroid USA and tells him how to activate its audible signal. If Ben verifies the information, Hamilton gets his part of the bargain: He meets J. B. Patterson, who tells him the FBI no longer considers him a 'person of interest,' and Attorney General Malcomson gives him a grant of immunity signed by you and immediately placed under federal court seal."

"And I give him a goddamn Presidential Medal of Freedom, too?"

"That could wait, sir."

Oxley allowed himself and Falcone a weak smile, then asked, "And what happens if he decides not to talk, doesn't give Taylor information about the asteroid?"

"Patterson arrests him for tampering with evidence, conspiracy to commit murder, and conspiracy to impede a federal investigation."

"Any of those charges true?"

"The case against him is weak. Very weak. And Akis Christakos will have no trouble getting an acquittal."

"And all of this will be all over the media."

"Yes, sir. And, of course, the source of all this—the asteroid threat—will also come out, undoubtedly spreading panic and stock market nightmares."

"You certainly brought me a lot of good news," Oxley said, rising again, obviously eager for Falcone to leave.

As Falcone turned toward the door, Oxley added, "What about Carlton?"

"Frankly, sir, I don't give a damn. Just don't let him near me."

"Sorry, Sean. But you've got to go over this with him. I'm ordering you to go down the hall right now and question him face-to-face. Calmly. That's the only way you—and I—are going to find out why Hamilton wound up in Guantanamo."

"Yes, sir. You can be damn sure I'll find out." Falcone punched out his words, signaling an intent to get physical with Carlton. He turned to leave the Oval Office, but paused as if he had a mere afterthought. "There's one other thing you should know, Mr. President," Falcone said, taking a deep breath before continuing, "I have it from a good source that Vladimir Putin didn't die from a rare blood disease. Lebed had him poisoned."

"What? You're sure of this?" Oxley asked, not quite believing what Falcone had just said.

Falcone nodded. "Next time you talk to Lebed or he threatens to take any more territory, you might let him know that you know his dirty secret. I'm sure some of Putin's old friends might take a dim view of the man who knocked off their leader."

"And your source for this assassination?"

"Mossad," Falcone said in a half whisper.

"Jesus!" Oxley exclaimed. "You trust the Israelis on something like this? They play a double game. You know that."

"Mr. President, Hamilton would not be out of Moscow without them. I think you need to trust them. Besides, it's almost Chanukah."

"Meaning?"

"It's a good time to accept a gift."

71

"**Mr. Falcone is . . . is** coming in," Carlton's assistant said in a voice of warning. The door flew open, Carlton stepped around his desk, and, in two strides, Falcone was standing before him. Falcone was a few inches taller, but they had similar trim physiques. Falcone jabbed his right fist into the center of Carlton's chest. Falcone's right hand shot forward again and closed around Carlton's shirt and tie, tearing away two buttons. Falcone's attack sent Carlton reeling back into his chair, which shot backward, banging into a bookcase.

"That was for your goddamn bald-faced lie," Falcone said quietly. "The President ordered me to be calm. I'm calm now, Frank." Falcone sat down in a chair in front of Carlton's desk.

"Christ, Sean," Carlton said, straightening his tie and, like Falcone, breathing hard. "You could have killed me. If I had a heart—"

"I've seen your medical record. You're strong as an ox."

"How'd you see my medical records?" The pitch of Carlton's voice reflected a level of anxiety about the contents contained in the records.

"When I was deciding to suggest you for your job."

"Yeah. Well, I guess I can blame you for all this."

"Like hell you can," Falcone said, bolting up from his chair, and stepping closer to Carlton as if he was about to take his head off.

"Come on, Sean. You knew the deal."

"I sure as hell didn't sign up for Guantanamo."

"There were special circumstances, Sean. Even the President doesn't know all the details. I . . . I guess you deserve to know what happened,"

Carlton said, leaning forward, bracing his hands on his desk. He paused before continuing.

"I thought of Guantanamo after the last rendition operation we ran out of Pakistan . . ."

"Pakistan? Now I'm really confused."

"It all started with a Paki walk-in at the embassy in Islamabad."

"That sounds familiar," Falcone said. "Happened all the time. . . . Sorry, didn't mean to interrupt."

"You're right," Carlton continued. "Lot of Pakis try to collect our rewards for information. We rarely get anything useful—even from their intelligence service. But this guy had something interesting. He showed us a cell phone with the image of what he said was a tactical nuclear weapon."

"Yeah, everybody knows Pakistan has developed tactical nukes," Falcone said. "Their foreign secretary even said publicly that Pakistan would use them against Indian troops if they even entered Pakistan territory."

"Right. The intel boys call them suitcase bombs. Well, this guy said he had taken the photograph at an ISIS operative's hideout in Pakistan. He said for ten million bucks and protection of his family he'd lead us to the guy."

"Jesus! Any confirmation?"

"Yes. Our guy in Pakistan who tries to keep an eye on their nukes said it looked like the real McCoy. And he had heard of rumors about a missing nuke. We immediately got the walk-in, his wife, and their two kids into the embassy compound. We agreed to pay the money when we got the nuke and its keeper. Well, he did lead a SEAL team to get the guy in camp near the Afghan border. But no nuke."

"And the President doesn't know this?"

"What he doesn't know is that I arranged for the nuke keeper to be taken to Guantanamo and questioned."

"Jesus, Frank. You took him to a place the President hates. A place where you could torture him."

"No, not torture. I called my Mossad contact, told him the story, and asked for a man I believe to be the finest interrogator on the planet."

"A Mossad officer?"

"Yes. He's both a rabbi and a psychiatrist."

"Damn! Israel again. Frank, what the hell is going on?"

"What's going on, Sean, is Daesh," Carlton said.

"The newly preferred name for ISIS," Falcone said, shaking his head.

"The bastards hate the word because 'Daesh' sounds like an Arabic words meaning 'one who crushes something underfoot.' "

"I thought ISIS for 'Islamic State of Iraq and Iran' was very descriptive," Falcone said.

"When you watched over the world for the President," Carlton went on, "there was no Daesh. There certainly were terrorists—Al Qaeda, the Taliban. But they had not conquered vast pieces of territory, ruling over it with sharia law and claiming a caliphate. These cutthroats changed the world. They're all over the place, Sean—all over the Mideast, Paris, Brussels . . . everywhere. And the best intel about them comes from our only trustworthy Mideast ally, Israel. I rely on the Mossad far more than the CIA, which did not see Daesh coming."

"But an *Israeli* psychiatrist? The CIA has—"

"Their shrinks haven't got the soul, the existential sense of this guy Hamilton."

"And you asked for this shrink out of the blue?"

"I had met him here, in Washington, a while ago. I was invited to the Israeli ambassador's residence, and he introduced some people to me. Mossad people, without saying they were. And the shrink. His name is Ishmael Korbin. You'll be meeting him at Guantanamo. He sees interrogation as a matter of finding what he calls 'the angle of repose'—the angle that a pile of sand takes just before the slope begins to slide. Once the slide starts, he says, the truth starts."

"Heavy stuff," Falcone said, not sounding convinced. "And it worked?"

"I saw it work, Sean, watching unseen in a safe house in Islamabad. Korbin spoke Urdu. I, of course, couldn't understand him. But I could sense that the Paki was listening, leaning forward, saying something back to Korbin and nodding. Korbin told me later he had started with quotes from the Koran and some Urdu poetry. The guy started crying. Then Korbin took out a map, his tone became sort of stern, and he got the guy to agree that he could best serve Allah by acting on the fate that took him to Korbin."

"And?"

"And he led a SEAL team to a camp near the Afghan border. They got the nuke and wiped out the camp."

"I assume you didn't give the nuke back to the Pakis."

"Correct. It's safe in our hands. Don't ask me where."

"The Israelis . . . ?"

"I've already told you more than the President knows. But I can tell you that you'll soon meet Ishmael Korbin. The Hamilton rendition was about to start when I got the Israelis to allow Korbin to stay on for a few days. I briefed the Israeli ambassador on the whole story. And he got the PM to approve."

"God, Frank! That took balls, dealing with Israelis and blacking out the President. When did you first get so cozy with them?"

"Right after I succeeded you."

"You know, I can believe that," Falcone said. "They never completely trusted me as a senator or as adviser. And then there's Oxley. He hates Weisman."

"Well, that's certainly true," Carlton said.

"So where did the trust in you come from?" Falcone asked. He had a hunch and decided to chance it: "Maybe . . . your wife?"

"Sometimes, in paranoid moments, I think they recruited her, Sean," Carlton said, smiling and shaking his head. "Whether they did or not, I've turned to them again and again."

After graduating from the Air Force Academy, Carlton was assigned to Lackland Air Force Base in Texas, headquarters of what was then called the Air Force Intelligence Command. He had a brilliant record at the academy, but he did not have the eyesight of a fighter pilot. And so he became an intelligence analyst. One day, in nearby San Antonio, he went on a tour of the eighteenth-century Mission San José. He was standing in front of what the guide called the Rose Window on a wall of the church sacristy. He asked the guide where the rose was and she replied that one of the window's many mysteries was its name. He said he liked mysteries and bet she did, too.

She was Ruth Greenfield, a descendant of Jews who had been brought to Texas in the 1900s by a Jewish aid group that diverted Russian refugees from crowded Eastern cities. Her parents warmly welcomed Carlton, an orphan, into the family. Their wedding was a civil ceremony.

Through most of his career—Air Force intelligence, director of National Intelligence, presidential adviser—Carlton was a keeper of secrets that he could not share with his wife. Ruth Carlton once said he was married to secrecy, not to her. But they had a solid marriage because she could handle living beyond the borders of his dark world. She was a physical therapist, an occupation portable enough to maintain during their frequent moves. When he became director of National Intelligence, she became a partner in a Washington physical rehabilitation center. One of her patients became a friend. She invited Ruth Carlton to a synagogue, and there she rediscovered her Jewish roots. She changed her name to Ruth Greenfield Carlton.

Occasionally, Frank Carlton attended synagogue affairs. He began adding new insights to his official policy attitudes toward Israel and gradually forged links with Israel that did not parallel Oxley's. The President did not sense any shift. The angle of repose held.

"I still don't get it, Frank. The connection between the Pakistani and the Jewish shrink. Now Hamilton. Just tell me what the fuck is going on here?"

72

Oxley stood looking out at the South Lawn, hands clasped behind his back. Alone. Here so many presidents stood this way, pondering their job, wondering what to do next. He turned away and glanced at the two paintings flanking the windows. On one wall was Childe Hassam's rainy Fifth Avenue full of the flags and banners of World War I. On the other was the Statue of Liberty, by Norman Rockwell for the *Saturday Evening Post* of the Fourth of July in 1946, the first year of peace. War and peace. *Once,* he thought, *we knew the difference.*

He knew that his mind ought to have been on China and the South China Sea or Japan and China, or America and China. But here he was wondering what to do about an American billionaire and a dangerous asteroid. He went back to his desk, where Harry Truman had placed a plaque saying "The Buck Stops Here," and took over the Hamilton account.

He kept his phone in a desk drawer. The moment he picked up the handset, an aide in the adjacent anteroom responded. He recognized Anna Bartholomew's voice and said, "Anna, first, I want to call Sean Falcone, who left me a few minutes ago. I'm also going to make some other calls. These will be highly classified calls, Anna. And I do not want any documentation of them. Okay?"

"Yes, Mr. President. I'm ready."

"Okay. I also want you to find Major Joseph Galafano and send him to me when I've finished my calls. I want him to meet me alone."

"Yes, sir." She sounded flustered.

"I hear he took you to the Marine Birthday Ball, right?"

"Yes . . . yes, sir. . . . I . . ."

"So I guess you can find him and talk to him so it seems unofficial. I don't want to get involved with the Military Office chain-of-command bureaucrats."

"Yes, Mr. President." She no longer sounded flustered.

Falcone was in a taxi heading for Christakos' law firm when the cell phone rang.

"Can you leave in a couple of hours or so?" Oxley asked.

"Yes, sir."

"And Christakos?"

"I can guarantee that," Falcone answered.

"You'll be getting a call from a Marine who's working directly for me. To make it simple, get Christakos to your place and wait for a pickup."

"Yes, sir."

As Oxley was about to make his next call, Anna said, "Sir, Mr. Quinlan is here and—"

"—threatening to break down the door. Okay. Send him in."

"Falcone was just here," Quinlan blurted.

"Yes, and you want to know all about it," Oxley said, sounding exasperated and still holding the handset. "I'll tell you in the fullness of time."

"That's exactly what Falcone says. And usually the time never comes, sir."

"It's a useful phrase, Ray."

Quinlan knew the etiquette. He had not been invited to sit down. He stood for another moment, then turned and left.

Oxley spoke into the phone. "Okay, Anna, now I want to speak to the commanding officer at Guantanamo. I don't want to talk to anyone else. Can you get me through to him without involving the Pentagon and the SecDef?"

She went to a secure Department of Defense webpage and a moment later said, "Well, sir, there is a protocol. You—that is, anyone—must go through the military communications satellite network. It seems to be the only telephone system available."

"All right, Anna. Let's give it a try."

He heard the call going through, some buzzing, and what he assumed were voice recorders switching on. Then a voice: "Joint Task Force Guantanamo. Captain Newman speaking. This call is being recorded."

"This is the President, Captain. I am ordering you to shut off the voice recorder."

"I am sorry, sir, but—"

"I said shut it off, Captain. And get me your CO."

Nothing happened for several seconds, and Oxley added, "Right now, Captain."

A few more seconds, a couple of clicks. And then: "Major General Robert Dafoe speaking . . . sir."

That 'sir' was slow, Oxley thought before saying, "I am responding to your message requesting national command authority."

"Yes, sir."

"I am sending two lawyers by military aircraft. They are to remove Robert Hamilton from Guantanamo on my authority. The details of this matter are being handled by Major Joseph Galafano, a Marine in the White House military office who is acting directly for me. I have instructed him, as I am now instructing you, to keep this matter absolutely secret. There will be no documentation of this matter. Also, Secretary Winthrop tells me you have ordered an investigation of Mr. Hamilton's rendition; I am countermanding that order. There will not be an investigation."

"But, sir—"

"No investigation, no documentation, General. Everything about Mr. Hamilton's arrival and departure must be treated as secret, top secret, on my authority. Is that clear, General?"

"Yes, sir. And when will they arrive?"

"As soon as possible."

"And, sir, what of the psychiatrist? What is he to be told? Does he also leave?"

"*Psychiatrist?* I know nothing about a psychiatrist, General."

"Dr. Korbin. He was sent here . . . to examine Mr. Hamilton."

"And who sent him, General?"

"That is classified, sir."

"I believe that, as commander-in-chief, I can be told classified information, General. Tell me. That's an order."

"The order came from General Carlton, sir," Dafoe replied with obvious reluctance. "He said he was acting on White House authority, sir. Yes, that is what he said. 'White House authority.' "

"And that was how Mr. Hamilton was taken to Guantanamo? By 'White House authority'?"

"Yes, sir."

"Do you have any paperwork on that, General?"

"No, sir. What General Carlton said was just like what you just said, sir: no documentation. Everything so classified it is beyond classification, sir."

Oxley hated to hear Carlton referred to as "general." But he shrugged it off as one general being clubby about another. "Thank you, General. Goodbye."

Major Galafano was assigned to the White House military office, whose responsibilities included Marine Helicopter Squadron One and the security force at Camp David. Ribbons on his uniform included those for the Silver Star and the Purple Heart. Oxley had spotted the ribbons when he first met Galafano. Oxley knew that heroes don't like to talk about their medals. By asking the Pentagon for the medals' citations, the President had learned that Galafano had been wounded saving a fallen Marine during a firefight in Helmand Province.

Ten minutes after the call to Guantanamo ended, Galafano entered the Oval Office, looking as if he had stepped out of a recruitment poster. He closed the door and stood at attention until Oxley said, "Sit down,

Major," and pointed to the chair next to his desk. Even sitting, Galafano was at attention.

"Major, I'm going to ask you to arrange a highly classified operation. I am personally issuing these orders as commander-in-chief."

"Yes, sir."

"I want you to escort two civilians to Guantanamo."

"Enemy combatants, sir?" Galafano asked, looking surprised.

Oxley laughed and said, "No. They're not bad guys. Due to a screwup I need not describe, an American citizen, Robert Hamilton, has been taken to Guantanamo. I am permitting two lawyers—Sean Falcone and Christo Christakos—to go there and bring him back."

"Sean Falcone? I traveled with him a few times. Good man, sir."

"I agree, Major. I want you to call Falcone and Christakos—Anna will give you their numbers—and arrange to drive them to Andrews in your own car tomorrow morning. Okay?"

"Yes, sir."

"I also want you to arrange the round-trip flight from Andrews to Guantanamo. I know there are Special Ops officers at Andrews who know how to keep flights like this invisible. That is what I want. Invisibility. And no documentation."

"Yes, sir. I know the drill. I'll get on that right now."

"Fine. If anyone questions my authority, tell him or her to be ready for a general court-martial for failure to obey an order from the commander-in-chief."

"Yes, sir."

"There's one more thing. I just found out there's a psychiatrist with Hamilton. It's a surprise that I'll sort out later. Bring back the shrink, too."

"Yes, sir," Galafano said, looking puzzled, but only for an instant.

"Call me as soon as you take off from Andrews. Tell Anna to patch you into an encrypted satellite line so you and I can talk to each other directly if necessary. Your duties will end when the aircraft returns to Andrews. Other people will take over at that point."

"Yes, sir."

"Oh, one more thing. You're not wearing an aiguillette."

"No, sir. Regulations. I can only wear it while actually performing duty as aide to the President."

"Well, you're sure performing a Presidential duty, starting right now. I want you in dress blues with those gold cords draped over your right shoulder to advertise that you are working for me. Okay?"

"Yes, sir," Galafano said, smiling. "It's an honor, Mr. President."

"Thank you, Major. That will be all."

"One more call, Anna," Oxley said. "Sam Stone."

In moments he heard a gravelly voice: "Stone here, Mr. President."

Oxley had taken Falcone's advice about how to deal with Sam Stone: Treat him as a lone-wolf agent, not the director of the CIA. Stone had dependable deputies assigned to deal with West Wing deputies. He rarely visited the White House, and he detested the orchestrated Situation Room meetings. But when the President called him directly, Stone knew the call would always be about something real, something that the President did not want handled by deputies.

"Sam, I'm sure it's no surprise to you that I am calling about a certain rendition. For now, forget about how it happened and how he landed where he did."

"Sir? Landed where?"

"He's in Guantanamo. I assumed you knew."

"Jesus, sir! No. I had no idea—"

"Never mind that right now, Sam. What I want from you, with as much secrecy as possible, is a safe house."

"Excuse me, sir. But for *your* use?"

Oxley laughed. "No. I'm just the producer. I'm not in the cast. I want to have a place for some business that has to do with relocating the space man." Oxley knew that Stone did not like using names on the phone. "The redhead is privy."

"Yes, sir," Stone said, as usual keeping his opinions about Quinlan to himself. And he wisely left unsaid any reference to Carlton. "Any idea when this is going to happen, sir?"

"There are a lot of moving parts, Sam. I guess tomorrow night, maybe early the next morning before the sun's up."

"I have found, Mr. President, that's the best time to do certain things."

Oxley, back on the phone, said, "Thanks for all your work, Anna. It's very important. That's all I can say about it. Now, please send in the impatient Mr. Quinlan." He hung up and replaced the phone in the desk drawer.

Not a minute passed before Quinlan charged into the Oval Office.

"Sit down, Ray," Oxley said, pointing to Quinlan's usual chair at the side of the desk, a gesture that greatly pleased Quinlan. "Here's what's going on," Oxley began. He delivered a short, speedily delivered account of the plan—without saying that Falcone had suggested it. "Major Galafano is handling tomorrow's Guantanamo trip. I want you to handle the safe house. For now, just tell J. B. and Attorney General Malcomson to stand by for a possible night shift tomorrow. Then check in with Sam Stone and tell him you're in this."

73

Christakos arrived at Falcone's residence at 6 a.m. and promptly made himself at home. With hardly a word, he entered the kitchen, found the necessary ingredients and utensils, and began producing his specialty, a cheese omelet.

"Please bring me up-to-date," Christakos said over his shoulder, eyes on his creation. Falcone briskly described his meeting with President Oxley.

"Can we assume that all will be smooth at Guantanamo?" Christakos asked.

"Yes. I'm sure the boys there will love to see Hamilton go. I expect that he'll be the problem. What do you think? You've met him."

"A short but illuminating meeting," Christakos said, serving the omelet and taking a stool at the counter alongside Falcone. "No sense of humor. Rigid, stiff. No sense that there's anyone else on Earth. His number one assistant told me that he 'never tells anybody anything.' Those were her words."

"And," Falcone interjected, "he's a religious zealot. Supposed to be a believer in The End Times."

"I heard that, too. From Philip Dake."

"Dake called you?" Falcone asked sharply. "When?"

"While you were in Russia."

"What did he want to know?"

"He was trading gossip for information. Said he had heard something about Hamilton and the Apocalypse. Then he asked me when was the last time I saw my client. I merely said 'recently.' He pushed a little more, but I politely swatted him away. He's writing a Hamilton biography, you know."

"Yes. But I'm more concerned about what he writes in the *Post*. You know his system: big news story for the *Post* that shakes up Washington. Then, a while later, a book that expands on the news and becomes a best seller. If Dake exposes Hamilton's rendition and the asteroid in a big-headlines news story, it could maybe start a march to impeach Oxley . . . not to mention a global panic."

Falcone was making coffee when Sam Stone called. As usual, he did not bother to say hello. "I'm told you're the point man."

"Well, a Marine Major is setting up the trip."

"I know. We're in on the details. When you get back, you, your co-counsel, and your other passenger will be taken to a place in Virginia. Anyone else?"

"There's the shrink," Falcone said. "I guess we pick him up . . . And then what?"

"He gets a lift to his embassy," Stone replied. "You can guess which one."

"God! Their hands are all over this!"

"No comment. Anyone else joining you?"

"Yes. Two others. You'll get a call about them from the redhead."

"Okay. We'll start setting the table."

Galafano drove the twenty miles to Joint Base Andrews in eighteen minutes, zigging and zagging through the early-morning commuter traffic. His White House ID tag and fast talking about his passengers whizzed him through the gate and into the lot nearest the VIP Lounge. Countless members of Congress and bureaucrats, along with their special guests, had waited there for U.S. Air Force aircraft that catered to worthy civilians.

Galafano, Falcone, and Christakos did not enter the lounge. As soon as Galafano parked, an Air Force master sergeant appeared and led them to the nearest runway, where they boarded a Gulfstream C-20G, a military variant of the commercial aircraft. Falcone, settling once more into a spacious seat, knew he never again would be a contented commercial passenger even in first class. Each man celebrated the luxury of space by selecting a solo seat. Christakos and Falcone had to lean toward each other and slightly raise their voices to talk to each other.

As soon as they were airborne, a man in black slacks and a black hooded jacket appeared from the forward cabin, nodded to Galafano, and crouched down to speak to him. After a short conversation, the man returned to the front cabin.

Galafano stood between the other two and said, "We'll be there in about two hours, Mr. Falcone. We are in contact with the White House communications system. It's like we're flying on a small-scale Air Force One."

Falcone tried an occasional conversation with Christakos, who kept dozing off. Falcone finally fell asleep himself. When he awakened, he rummaged through a stack of magazines and settled on a two-month-old *New Yorker*, whose subscription label had been neatly cut away. He was halfway through a surprisingly long short story when he felt the aircraft begin its landing approach.

74

Looking down on Guantanamo Bay, Falcone could easily see the embracing contours of a safe harbor that for decades served as a coal station for U.S. Navy warships. A trophy of the Spanish-American War, the coal station evolved into a naval base and naval air station, whose runways and hangars now appeared as the Gulfstream banked. Beyond, on a patch of open land amid miles of cactus and scrub, he could make out the buildings of the Guantanamo prison.

Pointing to the landscape rushing up, Falcone turned to Galafano and said, "I wonder which one Hamilton is in."

"I believe, sir, that he is in another facility," Galafano replied. "You can see it, just behind a ridge, to the right of that long road."

"I can see a cluster of what I guess are small buildings. They're not connected with the prison?"

"No, sir. Those are cottages, built originally for people working at the naval base. The CIA took a couple of them over right after the detention center was built. That was classified for a long time."

Falcone winced at *detention center*. The closing of Guantanamo *prison* was a personal passion for Falcone. He didn't want to get into a legal discussion with Galafano, but he did say, "I guess the CIA torturers wanted to get far away so the other prisoners couldn't hear the screams."

"No, sir. That's where they took the prisoners that the CIA wanted to turn into agents. They were promised freedom, protection of their family, and lots of money. The CIA treated them like hotel guests—good meals, comfortable bed, showers. Even TV. How many agents they got will probably never be known. The code name for the place was Penny Lane, after the Beatles song."

"Funny name."

"It was a takeoff on the name of one of the camps: Strawberry Fields. That's where they keep the really bad guys. The song's title is really 'Strawberry Fields Forever.' Well, anybody who went to that camp was never going to get out. The sentence was forever."

"You seem to know a lot about Guantanamo, Major," Falcone said.

"I was assigned to the Guantanamo Marine security unit, sir. We heard a lot about the camp. But I didn't have any official duties there."

Falcone wanted to ask about those duties, for he assumed that Galafano had been involved in Special Forces operations and wondered how they involved Guantanamo. But he had talked to enough people carrying secrets to know when to stop asking questions. And he had done enough research about Guantanamo to realize much could be hidden within the complexity of its structure as a secretive site with two distinct commands, each under a separate commanding officer.

Guantanamo Bay Naval Base—"Gitmo" to generations of sailors—is also a naval air base. The base is like a small town of several thousand officers and enlisted men and women, and their families, complete with a school system, restaurants, bars, and an outdoor movie theater. The place is also like an aircraft carrier because it is self-sufficient—producing its own water from seawater, generating its own electricity, and under surveillance by an enemy behind a vast minefield that marks the border between Cuba and the forty-five square miles occupied by the United States.

The prison and its miles of surrounding desolate grounds form the Detention Center Zone, which is commanded by an officer who is a warden without that title. He watches over buildings designed to federal penitentiary specifications and known as camps.

Because the prison is primarily linked to the outside world by naval aircraft, the base serves as the prison's airport. A dozen soldiers appeared at the terminal where the Gulfstream landed. Galafano, the first passenger down the stairway, assumed that he and his charges would be met by the prison's commanding officer, Major General Robert Dafoe. But a lieutenant colonel stepped forward. Galafano saluted and said, "I am escorting two guests of General Dafoe, sir."

"General Dafoe is unable to be here, Major," the officer said, introducing himself as Lieutenant Colonel Harry Young. "I am to take you to the facility where Mr. Hamilton is staying."

"For the record, Colonel," Galafano said stiffly, "I am carrying out the orders of the President, who was reacting to a specific message from General Dafoe asking for a National Command Authority response."

"Another way to put it," Falcone said, "is this: Your general's absence will be noted by his commander-in-chief, particularly when the general's name comes up for a third star."

Young, eyes forward, did not react. As Falcone followed Young to a van, he noted a group of naval officers waiting to board a nearby Navy aircraft. The gold oak leaf insignias on their sleeve stripes showed that the departing officers belonged to the Navy Medical Corps. Falcone wondered if that meant another hunger strike had ended.

75

The van stopped at the base's main gate, and each person was asked for identification, which was checked against a list on a Marine's clipboard. Christakos, a crusader against unwarranted collection of personal data, handed over a business card, which a guard gruffly turned down. Too polite to trouble the others, Christakos pulled his driver's license from his wallet with a flourish and the van passed through the maze of fencing.

The van turned onto a two-lane paved road to another checkpoint, then drove on, paralleling the razor-wire-topped fence that enclosed the Detention Center Zone and its clusters of low buildings. After about two miles on the highway, the van turned off the highway onto a dirt road for a few hundred yards, finally pulling up to one of several yellow-brick cottages.

On the cement patio, in a green plastic chair, sat a barefooted man in khaki shorts and a white T-shirt. When the van door slid open, he removed a cigar from his mouth, stood, and said, "I'm Dr. Ishmael Korbin. Welcome to Penny Lane."

Lieutenant Colonel Young, the first to emerge, nodded to Korbin and turned to the three other passengers who followed him out. "Mr. Hamilton," he said, "is inside. I am assuming that your . . . business here will take about an hour. I will return at that time, Major, to take your . . . party . . . back to the air station."

"Perhaps your general will be there to see us off," Falcone said.

"Perhaps," Young said, getting into the van, which turned around and started down the road.

"Penny Lane?" Christakos asked.

"An odd little CIA gag," Korbin said, advancing to shake hands. "You are Sean Falcone. I've seen photos of you." *In Mossad files,* Falcone thought.

"And Akis Christakos, I assume," Korbin continued. "From what your General Carlton has told me, you two have your own legal business with Mr. Hamilton." After Galafano introduced himself, Korbin snuffed out his cigar in an ashtray on an arm of the chair and said, "Well, now, shall we all go in?"

They entered a small foyer that opened to a set of stairs and to doors on the left and right. Falcone noted that the stout wooden doors with Yale locks had been fitted into what originally had been open doorways. He imagined Navy Seabees rushing here to install the doors and CIA specialists setting up hidden surveillance systems. He wondered if they were still in place.

The three men followed Korbin into the room to the right. Along one wall sat a worn brown corduroy couch with a spindly table at each end. In the center of the room were four wooden chairs at a long table. Falcone and Christakos chose the couch, Galafano one of the chairs. While waiting for Korbin to return, Falcone explained the "Penny Lane" reference to Christakos, whose response was, "Oh, so clever."

Korbin had gone through a doorway to what looked like a vintage kitchen. He quickly returned with a tray carrying a pitcher and glasses. "Strongest drink we have here," he said, beginning to dole out lemonade. He took a seat at the long table and beckoned Falcone and Christakos from the couch. "Well, should we get started?"

All that Falcone knew about Ishmael Korbin came from a two-page profile that Galafano had handed him on the plane. When Falcone asked about the source of the profile, Galafano told him about Oxley's puzzling order—"Bring back the shrink, too." Galafano said he had decided to use his status as a Marine officer on a presidential mission to get some CIA information on Korbin. "It's amazing what you can get using the President's name," Galafano had said, and Falcone remembered another Marine officer's similar discovery, which led to the Iran-Contra scandal.

After reading the profile, Falcone found it was hard to decide whether Ishmael Korbin was a rabbinical scholar or professional interrogator, perhaps because he was both.

He was born in Kibbutz Amir in northern Israel, the only son of Yehuda and Rebecca Korbin, survivors of the Holocaust. At an early age, he not only mastered the Torah but also began dabbling with what he believed to be a biblical code that unlocked the secrets of the universe. While he earned the praise of his parents for his devotion to religious studies, they also saw in him an unusual talent. He seemed able to look behind the masks that people wore for others and see their strengths and vulnerabilities.

Brainwashing and distant mind-control fascinated him, and he frequently tried to hypnotize his playmates. His favorite bar mitzvah gift had been a package containing the book and DVD versions of *The Manchurian Candidate.*

Like most able-bodied Israelis, Korbin was obliged to serve for three years in the IDF, the Israeli Defense Force. During most of his service he was in combat, against Hezbollah in Lebanon and in clashes with the Palestine Liberation Front. Because he spoke Arabic and had a gift for extracting useful information speedily and without torture, he often was called upon to interrogate prisoners. Mossad officers marked him for future recruitment.

After his military service, Korbin went to America and entered Brandeis University. After graduating summa cum laude, he went on to Columbia for a doctorate in psychiatry. His thesis, based on his own youthful obsession, assessed the persistent belief in biblical codes.

Soon after his return to Israel, he was asked to examine a Mossad officer, who was accused of spying for Iran. The man claimed he desperately needed money for treatment of a daughter addicted to heroin. Korbin questioned him sympathetically, promised to get the daughter into a treatment center, and in two hours had a confession. Korbin did as he promised, because he believed honesty could be a valuable tool in the deceptive world of espionage. He became the service's prime interrogator.

Falcone was especially taken by the profile's analysis of his attitude toward torture:

He despises torture on a practical basis because he believes that brute force does not produce reliable information. He does not profess to read minds, but, as he said in a lecture to Mossad officers, "I believe I have the ability to visualize the hidden currents that run through the dark interiors that others cannot see." As an example, he told of successfully getting valuable information from a Hezbollah assassin "by simply empathizing with the subject's sense of loss, rather than by a sense of vengeance. This was manifested in his memory by the smell of cedar trees that Israelis had uprooted on his father's land. He began answering my questions, and I saw that, subconsciously, he had associated the wrongness of the trees' death with the wrongness of Israeli deaths."

76

Korbin presided over the table, dark-rimmed spectacles perched on his nose, hands constantly in motion, head pivoting from Falcone to Christakos. He smiled at Galafano occasionally but saw no reason to speak directly to him. He had a slight, elusive accent that came and went, acting as a kind of accelerator as his words rose and fell.

"I'm afraid that I'm responsible for your being here," he began, addressing Falcone. "As you know, I had been called by your General Carlton to interrogate a certain Pakistan man on a very serious matter. Because of what many people might call coincidence, I was here with the Pakistan subject when the rendition—I love that euphemism—began. General Carlton asked me to stay and I, of course, agreed."

Korbin paused and Falcone sprung into the gap: "Two questions, Doctor. Is Mr. Hamilton here in this house? Is he cooperating?"

"Yes and yes. I know you both are anxious to see him. And he is certainly anxious to see you, especially Mr. Christakos. But before you meet with him, he agreed that I would first give you a briefing. First, remember, this was a man who believed he was being accused of involvement in the murders of four Americans. He also—"

"Hold on, Dr. Korbin," Christakos said. "My client is nothing more than a quote 'person of interest' unquote, so labeled by the FBI. I would like—"

"One interruption deserves another," Korbin parried. "I said he *believed* he was actually accused. Whether he was or not accused is of no importance, Mr. Christakos. What *is* important—as told me by General

Carlton—is that Mr. Hamilton holds a secret that can possibly destroy the Earth. Now, going on. . . .

"When I first met Mr. Hamilton, he was amazingly calm, considering what he had just gone through. I soon learned why he was so eerily tranquil: He had a growing obsession that he is an instrument of God, called upon to bring on what he called The End Times. He had a Bible he had found in the cottage. Lots of slips of paper were sticking out of it. He quoted many passages. His favorite was from the Book of Joel: quote, 'the day of the Lord is near in the valley of decision,' unquote.

"Joel also has God say, quote, 'I will gather all the nations and bring them down to the Valley of Jehoshaphat,' unquote. In modern times, that's the name given to the valley between Jerusalem and the Mount of Olives— sort of between a sacred place for Jews and Muslims and a sacred place for Christians, the place where Jesus forecasts The End Times, saying, quote, 'there will not be left one stone upon another that will not be thrown down,' unquote.

"Joel—a minor prophet, according to most biblical scholars—says that when he gets everybody to Jehoshaphat, quote, 'I will enter into judgment with them there, on behalf of my people and my heritage Israel,' unquote."

"Israel keeps popping up," Falcone said irritably.

"You're right. In his mind the biblical Israel and modern Israel are one and the same—a frequent convergence belief of fundamentalist Christians. But in his case it is so deep-seated that it becomes reality. He is mentally ill. The broad label for this illness is narcissistic personality disorder. Picture a personality split down the middle. Part of his ego is a billionaire's feelings of superiority and entitlement, and part of his ego is his obsession about helping God end the world."

"I seem to have only seen his billionaire side," Christakos said dryly.

"That may be because, with you, he chose to be in the real world we see and live in. I have no doubt that there is a deeper world that he sometimes lives in. The then-and-now Israel is part of his belief system. When I realized his interest in Israel, I told him a little about my background."

"Namely that you are both a psychiatrist and a biblical scholar?" Falcone asked.

"I see you have been doing your homework. Yes, I mentioned my interest in the Bible, and he told me he believes that God has placed the fate of the Earth in his hands. And he believes the 'decision' mentioned in Joel is a forecast of Hamilton's decision about what he does with the asteroid."

"Well, wouldn't that mean he would *not* give accurate information about the location of Asteroid USA?" Christakos asked.

"Good question," Korbin responded. "Early in our conversation—I never use the word *interrogation*—he told me he believed that by withholding information about the location of Asteroid USA he was carrying out the will of God. That's a very big idea to dislodge from a person's mind."

Korbin paused for a sip of lemonade, and Falcone again leaped in, saying, "Have you dislodged that idea, Doctor?"

"I don't think so. He has the notion that he is an instrument of God, who, for some reason, wants to destroy the world."

A memory flashed through Falcone's mind: Carlton had told him about a CIA profile of Hamilton that had contained an odd note: *A source, remarking on Hamilton's demeanor, said he had evil eyes.* The source, Carlton had said, was a Russian bishop who compared Hamilton's eyes to those of a man he had walked to his execution—a serial killer.

Christakos raised his hand and asked, "And so, Doctor, you have not achieved your goal?"

"You're obviously—but obliquely—questioning my methodology," Korbin said, smiling for the first time. "But, in fact, for some people, coincidence—synchronicity, if you will—is a significant psychic element. With Hamilton, for instance, there was his father lost at sea and a business associate lost at sea on a ship that Hamilton was to have boarded. Incidentally, he thought your name was one of the coincidences—a sign of Christ's blessing."

"I'm touched," Christakos said sarcastically.

"And you seem full of questions," Korbin said. "For the record, Mr. Christakos—and for your peace of mind—I had been provided with information that the Mossad and the CIA have developed, undoubtedly by secretly copying records of Hamilton's psychiatrist. I must say the information was helpful. But I cannot, of course, share it with you. What I can say is that Mr. Hamilton had a difficult childhood and overcame many obstacles to become what he is today."

"A self-described self-made man," Christakos said. "I've met a lot of them."

Korbin, ignoring Christakos, continued, "I concluded my conversations by urging him to accept his role as a savior of the Earth, not as an executioner. I believe I successfully persuaded him that God does not want the planet destroyed but wants it saved and wants him to be the savior. As a Christian, that word—savior—has deep meaning for him. He is in the other room, waiting to talk to you both. In his mind—indeed, in his soul—he believes that dealing with the fate of the Earth is why he is here."

"My relationship with Mr. Hamilton does not involve his psyche," Christakos said coolly. "I am simply a lawyer who wants to get him out of the clutches of the FBI."

"I told him you were coming today. He is eager to talk to you both," Korbin said.

"You clearly have the right to be the first to talk to him, Counselor," Falcone said, turning to Christakos. "Godspeed."

77

Christakos, smiling, waved a goodbye and headed for the other room, which was a near-duplicate of the first room, complete to a copy of an amateurish seascape hanging over the couch. "Thank you for coming all the way down here, Mr. Christakos," Hamilton said as Christakos entered the room. He sat in the middle of the couch, which was not quite as shabby as the one in the first room. He wore the products of an escorted visit to the base commissary: khaki slacks, canvas-topped sneakers, and a white shirt, open at the neck and sleeves rolled up. He looked like a man who was taking some time off in a tropical hideaway—except that he held a Bible, festooned with yellow slips.

Christakos pulled up a chair and put down his attaché case. "Very glad to see you again, Mr. Hamilton," he said. "I'm sorry you had to go through such a . . . challenging trip."

"The trip? Life is a trip, Mr. Christakos," Hamilton said in a soft voice. "And our meeting here, rather than at any other place, was destined." He put down the Bible, picked up a yellow pad and scrawled a few words.

"Yes. I'm glad you feel that way," Christakos said, stifling his surprise at Hamilton's tranquility. "Now, going back to our meeting with Agent Sarsfield at FBI headquarters, what was true then is also true now: Neither Sarsfield nor anyone else in the FBI has a shred of evidence against you. It may be possible for the FBI to claim that you withheld evidence, and—"

"Nonsense," Hamilton said, suddenly looking and sounding indignant. "I merely deleted a file on a laptop owned by my firm. If that is a crime . . ."

"Considering that the previous tenant of this cottage was the CIA, Mr. Hamilton, I urge you to be cautious about what you say."

"Oh, that 'Penny Lane' business," Hamilton said with a dismissing wave. "You believe the place is bugged?"

"Nothing wrong with being prudent."

"Glad to be dealing with a prudent man," Hamilton said, smiling.

Christakos continued to be amazed at Hamilton's serene air. He wondered whether Korbin had so manipulated Hamilton that he was basking in his link with divinity. But, Christakos also wondered, without daring to ask the question: Does he believe he is carrying God's plan by saving the Earth or by destroying it?

Christakos took a folder from his attaché case, scanned it, and said, "Your very capable chief operations officer told me that you wanted all charges dropped and a presidential grant of immunity."

"That's right."

"First of all, Mr. Hamilton, there are no charges to be dropped. And there is no need for a presidential grant of immunity because you did nothing that warrants immunity. You are an American citizen who was hounded by an obstinate FBI agent. No one has formally accused you of anything. To plead for a presidential grant of immunity is to suggest you need to be pardoned or excused."

Frowning, Hamilton said, "I'd like an apology."

"Allow me to be frank, Mr. Hamilton. You are looking at two matters: the misbehavior of Agent Sarsfield and the need to provide the U.S. government with some vital information. I am counseling you on both matters. Mr. Sean Falcone, who is representing President Oxley, is in the next room. I strongly urge you to meet with him now. Tell him the location of Asteroid USA, which, I understand, can be determined by a signal transmitted from the spacecraft that SpaceMine sent to the asteroid. He should also be told how to control the spacecraft. And then this whole matter is done."

Hamilton stood and walked to a screened window. He stared for a moment at the endless scrubland. "If you look out this window long enough, as I have," he said, slowing his tempo to a drawl, "you see a tree struggling to grow in the cactus and brush." He turned to face

Christakos. "Dr. Korbin pointed it out to me," he continued. "I had only known him maybe fifteen minutes. And when we both looked at that tree we somehow were close, spiritually close."

He went back to the couch and, after a moment, began speaking rapidly: "My father disappeared from a whale-watching ship off Gloucester. I was seven years old. My mother and I . . . everyone . . . we were all on the other side of the ship, looking at a whale. No one saw my father go over the rail. His body was never found. Did he die? Did he stage his death? My mother never recovered from the shock, the unknown. . . . Well, you probably know all that."

"No," Christakos said softly, "I know practically nothing about your life."

"My mother suddenly became fanatically religious after my father disappeared," Hamilton went on. "And she started having visions of my father in the water. Many times she beat me with a belt and said I killed him because I was a son of Satan. I screamed when she said that. And then I stopped talking. Just like that. Stopped. She gave me up for adoption right afterward. I was about eight. My first foster parents thought I was mute."

"I . . . never knew . . . ," Christakos began.

"I guess the CIA or the FBI or maybe both—and, who knows? Maybe the Russians, they probably know," Hamilton continued, his voice wavering. "Well, somehow Dr. Korbin got this information about me. I had gone to a psychiatrist a few years back, and she dredged up some painful memories. I guess Dr. Korbin got her notes. Maybe he works for the CIA. I just don't care. Whatever he found out, it was as if he was sent by God," Hamilton said, standing silently for a full minute, his head down, his eyes closed.

"A few years ago I found her," he went on, almost in a whisper. "My mother. In Arizona. If you have the resources, you can find anybody. She said wild, awful things about Satan. She died right after I saw her, and it came over me that my only choice was to fight Satan, fight my father Satan. And be a Christian—a good Christian. I believed that I had been directed to start SpaceMine. At first, I must confess, I was motivated by greed, by the money I could make and distribute to other good Christians.

Scientists who held beliefs consonant with mine. But then when I discovered that my original planned orbit might put the asteroid on a collision path with Earth, I concluded that I'd been chosen to control the instrument that would bring on The End Times. And I told Dr. Korbin that. And do you know what he did? He began *signing* me."

"Signing?" Christakos asked.

"You know, American Sign Language," Hamilton replied. "A teacher I had told me I had to sign. And for a while—during my silent time—that was how I talked: by signing. Sometimes I think it was the bullies in school teasing me that got me talking."

"Why did Dr. Korbin know signing?" Christakos asked.

"He told me he had learned to sign to converse with a mute patient. He is a remarkable man. He told me that I held the signing so secret it was like the signing was not just in my brain. It was in my soul."

The room was silent for a full minute before Christakos said, "May I ask Mr. Falcone to come in?"

Hamilton did not speak. He nodded.

As soon as Christakos brought Falcone into the room and motioned for him to sit down, Hamilton began peppering him with questions about the trip from his suite in the Hotel Baltschug Kempinski to "this odd little building in Cuba." Throughout the question-and-answer session, Hamilton continued to exude the same strange calm that Korbin and Christakos had seen. When the session ended, Falcone stood and said, "There is one more leg to your trip, Mr. Hamilton. We are now going to get on a plane that will take you to a place where we will finally work together to save the Earth."

Again, Hamilton simply nodded.

78

Major General Dafoe was at the bottom of the Gulfstream stairway waiting to say farewell. When the passengers lined up to begin boarding, he nodded to Falcone, signaling that he wanted to talk. They stood aside for a moment and Dafoe whispered, "Please tell the President confidentially that I agree with his desire to close Guantanamo." He then walked over to Hamilton, shook his hand, and handed him an Army camo combat uniform jacket. "You earned this, sir," Dafoe said, "and you'll need it now that you're leaving the tropics."

Hamilton nodded and smiled.

Falcone and Christakos feared that Hamilton would use the trip as a last chance to change or even withdraw his agreement to reveal the location of Asteroid USA. But he remained silent through the trip, spending most of his time writing—and crossing out—notes on his yellow pad.

Falcone returned to the long *New Yorker* short story. Christakos dug into his attaché case for a folder about a new case involving an indiscreet congressman. Galafano accepted the chance to snatch a couple of hours of sleep. Korbin was deep in a psychiatric journal. *No one wants to talk about anything,* Falcone thought.

The Gulfstream landed at Andrews in the sudden darkness that falls in the early days of winter. As the lighted stairway lowered, three black SUVs appeared. A man stepped out of the lead vehicle and walked up to Korbin.

"You will be taken to your embassy, Dr. Korbin," the man said. Korbin shook hands with Falcone, Christakos, and Galafano. Standing in front of Hamilton, Korbin, in swift moves, raised his open right hand, folded down his fingers, then opened his palm again. He next brought both hands down the length of his face, tilted his head forward slightly, and made a sad face. After making the same gestures, Hamilton hugged Korbin, who disappeared into the SUV.

The other two SUVs, each manned by a driver and a bodyguard, loaded their passengers and started off, Falcone and Galafano in one, Christakos and Hamilton in the other. Thirty-six minutes later, the vehicles turned off a Virginia highway and onto a tree-lined country road. A turnoff to the right put them on the circular driveway of a large stone house. Behind its dark silhouette, a moonlit lake glittered.

The house had belonged to a hedge fund manager who had gone bankrupt and moved to Panama. When the house went on the market, a Realtor mentioned the place to her husband, an officer in what was then called the CIA's Clandestine Service. He got in touch with the right people and the house began its career as a safe house. Its titular owner was a Washington lawyer who did occasional legal work for the Agency.

The new arrivals were greeted by a man and a woman who acted as host and hostess, but they did not introduce themselves. They took their guests into a formal dining room whose row of windows overlooked about an acre of greensward along the shore of the lake. A buffet was laid out on a sideboard, along with two bottles of wine, one red and one white. The hostess and the host disappeared, as had the SUV crews.

Christakos and Hamilton, each clutching a yellow pad, staked a claim to one end of the table, Falcone and Galafano the other. Christakos filled his plate and poured a generous portion of red wine. He returned to the table followed by Hamilton carrying a bottle of water and a dish containing little more than shards of lettuce. Falcone and Galafano had heaping plates; Galafano, on duty, also chose water.

Galafano nodded toward the end of the table, and asked Falcone between bites, "What do you think the odd couple down there is cooking up?"

"My bet," Falcone answered, "is that Christakos is working on language for two agreements: what Hamilton has to reveal to the U.S. government and an ironclad non-disclosure agreement that keeps everyone from ever revealing anything about the rendition."

"Right. And what is Hamilton scribbling? Sure a lot of pages," Galafano said.

"I haven't the slightest idea," Falcone said. He looked at his watch. "We should be hearing from the White House about now."

Ten minutes later, his Blackphone rang and he heard Quinlan say, "We're on our way."

At the sound of a helicopter, a frame of lights emerged from the lakeshore lawn. The craft landed in the middle of the frame and Quinlan and two others stepped out. The safe house host and hostess appeared and escorted the passengers inside and into the dining room.

Quinlan introduced himself and then J. B. Patterson, director of the FBI, and Attorney General Jennifer Malcomson, who carried a briefcase. A short woman with black bangs shielding her forehead, she wore a white sweater and black slacks, and black boots. She doffed a red ski jacket and hung it on the back of her chair in the middle of the table. Patterson sat to her left, Quinlan to her right. She slowly scanned the table as if she were a judge on a bench, projecting the image of a person clearly in charge.

"Good evening," she said. "I am here at the request of the President. The facts as presented to me by him, augmented by Mr. Quinlan, are these." She read from a sheet of paper she took from her briefcase.

"One. Dr. Cole Perenchio, an authority on gravitation, was a former NASA engineer employed by SpaceMine, a company owned by Mr. Robert Wentworth Hamilton. Dr. Perenchio learned that SpaceMine was planning to send a spacecraft to an asteroid and move it to an orbit for the purpose of mining it. Dr. Perenchio, using data gathered by NASA, calculated that the orbit planned for the asteroid, called Asteroid USA, would put it on a collision course with Earth in 2037. Dr. Perenchio conveyed this belief to Mr. Hamilton, who scoffed at—"

"Hold on, there Miss Attorney General. What I did—"

"Please do not interrupt, Mr. Hamilton," Malcomson said, glaring at him.

". . . scoffed at the idea," Malcomson repeated. "Dr. Perenchio thereupon resigned, taking with him a laptop belonging to SpaceMine that contained both proprietary information owned by SpaceMine and a report by Dr. Perenchio on what he believed to be the probability that Asteroid USA would collide with the Earth.

"Two. Dr. Perenchio was murdered by two career criminals, who also killed three others. The killers were in the hire of a Russian national named Kuri Basayev, a secret partner of Mr. Hamilton, who—"

Hamilton stood, drew another glare from Malcomson, and sat down.

"—who," Malcomson continued, "controlled criminal enterprises in Russia and America. An FBI agent investigating the murder of Dr. Perenchio believed that Mr. Hamilton was somehow connected with the deaths and designated him 'a person of interest.'

"Three. Mr. Hamilton went to Moscow to meet with Mr. Basayev, but Mr. Basayev was lost at sea."

Hamilton started to stand again, but slumped back in his chair. The movement caught Falcone's eye. He wondered whether the arrogant billionaire's half of the personality had just given way to the mild helper of God.

"Mr. Hamilton wished to leave Moscow, but was prevented from doing so under orders from President Lebed, who believed restricting Mr. Hamilton's mobility would be tantamount to Russia gaining possession of Asteroid USA.

"Four. Mr. Hamilton also agreed to reveal to U.S. officials the location of Asteroid USA by turning on a transmitter in the spacecraft attached to the asteroid and to provide information on how to control the spacecraft. In exchange for voluntarily providing this information, all charges will be dropped and Mr. Hamilton will be given a presidential grant of immunity.

"Five. An operation, led by Mr. Falcone, was developed to get Mr. Hamilton out of Moscow and return him to the United States.

"Six. We are all here tonight to discuss a way to resolve this matter."

Christakos stood and Malcomson nodded toward him. He knew that she was being talked about as the next Supreme Court justice, and tonight he could see why.

"Attorney General Malcomson, Director Patterson, and Mr. Quinlan, thank you for coming here, and please, Mr. Quinlan, thank President Oxley for his efforts to provide my client with an ending to this complex case. Let me begin by saying that my client agrees to provide the President and anyone delegated by him with the location of Asteroid USA by turning on a signal from the spacecraft attached to it and will provide information about the operation of the spacecraft."

When a ripple of applause ceased, Christakos looked up from a sheaf of yellow lined pages. But he did not read from them. "In exchange," he began—and paused. He enjoyed the suspense for a long moment and then went on: "Mr. Hamilton demands—and certainly has the right to—a clean slate. He demands the FBI, through Director Patterson, to state unequivocally that Mr. Hamilton is *not* a person of interest and that the FBI is no longer investigating any case that involves him in any way.

"Regarding the rendition, Mr. Hamilton believes that the operation was highly illegal, was not pre-approved by any legal authority, violated his civil rights, put him in peril, and could result in criminal charges based on Mr. Hamilton's testimony. However, Mr. Hamilton does not intend to take action against Mr. Falcone, now or at any time in the future, in gratitude to him and his comrades for risking their lives to get him out of Russia.

"Finally . . ." Again, Christakos savored a moment. "Finally, we desire that everyone in this room sign a non-disclosure agreement and that it be endorsed by Attorney General Malcomson."

Falcone looked down the table at her and could sense that she was struggling to find a way to accept Christakos' demand . . . *No, wait.*

"desire." Nice touch. You don't demand something from the attorney general—or a possible future Supreme Court justice.

Patterson, sensing the need to give Malcomson more time to react, stood and, looking grim, said, "The Federal Bureau of Investigation does not believe Mr. Hamilton is a person of interest. And the FBI also does not in any way believe that Mr. Hamilton is a suspect in any crime. I personally wish to apologize for any embarrassment we caused Mr. Hamilton."

"Thank you, Director Patterson," Malcomson said. "And Mr. Christakos, I—we—all appreciate your efforts and the efforts of your client. As for the non-disclosure agreement, I certainly can understand—and accept—the *desire* for attaining silence on this matter via the conventional use of a non-disclosure agreement. But I feel that any agreement that leaves this room as a piece of paper would be an orphan, unprotected by court of law, and even homeless by virtue of the fact that there is no legally acceptable place to file it."

"I can understand your arguments, Madam Attorney General," Falcone said. "But how can we guarantee non-disclosure?"

"I go back to the practice endorsed by George Washington. To clearly show that his officers supported the Revolution, he ordered his officers to take an oath of loyalty. An oath was backed by honor, not a piece of paper." Nodding toward Christakos, Malcomson asked, "Would you and your client accept an oath instead of a non-disclosure agreement? I propose that each of us take a personal oath not to reveal any details of the rendition of Mr. Hamilton or the causes that inspired it."

Hamilton stood, as did a clearly surprised Christakos. Hamilton raised his right hand, and said, "I'll give the oath first."

Malcomson said, "Repeat after me. I, Robert Wentworth Hamilton . . ."

And so it went, from one to the other around the table. When all oaths had been given, she added, "Now, Mr. Hamilton, there are the questions of the asteroid's location and control of the spacecraft."

"I have always closely held the location of Asteroid USA for competitive reasons," he said. "We are not the only corporation that wants to mine asteroids. Before I left for Moscow, I had George Hopkins, my chief engineer, write down the way to turn on the transmitter in the spacecraft attached to Asteroid USA and put it in his safe. Only he and I know the combination. I am leaving for California tomorrow and will instruct him to turn on the transmitter and provide the necessary information for control of the spacecraft."

Hamilton went back to his chair and, tapping Christakos on his shoulder, said, "I have asked Mr. Christakos to arrange for delivery of the desired information."

Malcomson looked down at her paper, looked up, and said, "And control of the spacecraft?"

"That will have to be done at SpaceMine," Hamilton said. Falcone detected hesitancy in Hamilton's response.

"Very well," Malcomson said. She turned her head slightly, "Approved, Mr. Falcone?"

"Approved," Falcone replied. "Assuming assistance by SpaceMine personnel."

The meeting was over.

After the helicopter flew off with Quinlan, Patterson, and Malcomson, Christakos and Hamilton got into the SUV that had delivered them and sped off. When Falcone and Galafano entered their SUV, Galafano said, "I have to hand it to the AG. The George Washington oath was a great idea."

"Agreed," Falcone said. "I'm a great fan of George Washington. He was a gentleman in a time of gentlemen, and a sworn oath was good enough for him, but it so happens that the Continental Congress demanded a *signed document* confirming that the officers had taken the oath. One of the signers was General Benedict Arnold."

Galafano smiled and asked, "How long do you think the silence will hold?"

"Not long," Falcone said. "I wonder about recorders in safe houses. When I see the President tomorrow, I'll suggest that he order Sam Stone to destroy any tapes that may have been made tonight. And then there's Philip Dake sniffing around, picking up bits from all his CIA and NSA contacts."

"Wouldn't Dake see the point of keeping this all secret?"

"Fat chance. Dake once told me that every morning when he wakes up, the first thing he says to himself is: *What are the bastards trying to hide from us today?* I know that he's held back information in the past when he was convinced publishing it in one his columns or books would put us all in jeopardy. But this story is just too big. Besides, even if I could persuade him to hold off, there are others out there who just don't give a damn."

"Whew! Sad commentary on where we are today," Galafano said.

"Right, Joe. I sometimes wonder how we got here."

Christakos called the Cosmos Club and reserved a room for Hamilton, who arranged for his corporate Gulfstream to pick him up next morning. After seeing Hamilton off at the Cosmos, Christakos called Falcone and arranged for a meeting at Christakos' office. "After breakfast this time, please," Christakos said.

"I hope to be having my breakfast in the employees' cafeteria at the Air and Space Museum," Falcone told him. "I'll see you at ten o'clock."

He used his landline to call Taylor at his Capitol Hill home. "We got it! Hamilton is giving us the signal information and the spacecraft controls," he shouted into the phone. "I'll tell you all about it. Eight thirty at the staff cafeteria?"

"Yes! Yes! That's great news! So . . . where is it?"

"Well, we don't exactly have a piece of paper. Be patient."

"Patient? You bet I'm impatient, Sean. When and how do we learn the location? And then what?"

"At the moment, I just don't know. We need a plan. But I'm dead on my feet, Ben. I just wanted you to be the first to know. For me, it's bed. See you at breakfast."

Three minutes after Falcone hung up and headed for his bedroom, Quinlan called. His voice was tired and tense. "The President wants you, Taylor, and Hamilton in the Situation Room at eight a.m. tomorrow. He—"

"Hold on, Ray. I just talked to Ben Taylor and Christakos. I wanted Ben to see—"

"Sean, listen to me. The President is running this personally. He's taking this over," Quinlan said. "I'm just passing the orders. Call Taylor back and tell him a White House car will pick him up at seven thirty. Call Christakos back and tell him you can't meet him. Don't mention the Sit Room or Hamilton."

"But Hamilton's planning to fly home tomorrow. He'll—"

"He doesn't know it yet, but the Secret Service is picking him up at seven thirty and delivering him to the White House."

"Picking him up? On what grounds?"

"Don't go lawyerly on me, Sean. On the grounds of a presidential national-security order."

"But, my God, Ray, that puts us back in the rendition business."

"The Situation Room ain't Guantanamo. And the President says this guy isn't leaving town 'til he hands over what we want. See you tomorrow."

After the callback from Falcone, Taylor decided to call Dick Gillespie, a friend at NASA's Goddard Space Center. Gillespie was manager of LOLA, the Lunar Orbiter Laser Altimeter carried in NASA's Lunar Reconnaissance Orbiter spacecraft. LOLA measures the shape of the Moon by using radar to precisely measure the distance from the spacecraft to the lunar surface. Gillespie has been a major participant in NASA's asteroid-watching network.

"Dick, I'll explain all this to you as soon as I can. All I can tell you is this: A Morse code signal is going to be sent from an asteroid and—"

"SpaceMine's Asteroid USA?" Gillespie asked excitedly. "Wow! It was promised in those TV shows a while ago. But it never happened."

"Well, it's almost certainly going to be sent soon. I'm convinced that it's really Janus."

"Janus! Holy shit, that's a big bastard!"

"Right. Can you listen for it? Establish its location?"

"Sure. And we'll record it. We should nail it. There's not much Morse code out in space."

"Here's hoping the signal comes through. A lot depends on it," Taylor said.

79

At 4:30 a.m. Pacific Time, two FBI agents appeared at a condo building in Palo Alto and awakened the concierge. One of the agents presented her official credentials to the concierge and instructed him to call George Hopkins, SpaceMine's chief engineer.

"Mr. Hopkins," the agent said, "I am Special Agent Susan Todd. Please get dressed and come to the lobby. We wish to be taken to SpaceMine."

"What is this about? Is Mr. Hamilton okay?"

"Please get dressed and come to the lobby," the agent repeated.

Accompanying the agents were two National Security Agency technicians carrying laptops. Oxley had discussed his operation with the director of NSA, who had instructed the technicians on their way to Andrews. At 11:30 p.m., they boarded one of DoD's G-550s. The flight to the San Francisco international Airport took four and a half hours. A helicopter had taken the technicians from there to Palo Alto.

At about the same time the FBI agents and technicians were meeting Hopkins in Palo Alto, a black SUV pulled into the driveway of the Cosmos Club in Washington, D.C., and a Secret Service agent got out. The door was opened by the manager, who had been alerted by a White House phone call a few moments before. The two men crossed the lobby to the stairway and hurried to the second floor. The manager pointed to a door. The agent knocked once. Hamilton, still wearing the khaki slacks, sneakers, and white shirt of Guantanamo, opened the door a crack.

"The President wishes to see you, Mr. Hamilton," the agent told him. Hamilton responded with a shake of his head and a shrug. Leaving the door ajar, he went back to a tray on a low table, finished a glass of water and a piece of unbuttered toast, donned his Army jacket, picked up his Bible, and walked out of the room. "My clothes," he said to the agent. "Left in Moscow. Will I ever get them back?"

At 8:15 a.m. Washington time, President Oxley entered the Situation Room, followed by Quinlan, Falcone, Taylor, and Hamilton. Falcone was surprised that Carlton was absent; on second thought, he was not surprised. Carlton was probably sending out résumés.

Everyone stood until Oxley sat down. He was flanked by Quinlan and Falcone, who took familiar seats. Oxley directed Taylor and Hamilton to seats opposite the room's largest wall monitor. At the side of the monitor, operating a Skype camera, stood two technicians from the National Security Agency.

Hamilton was obviously surprised to see a scowling George Hopkins staring back at him from the monitor. He stood behind a wooden desk that looked out of place in an office studded with tall metal racks containing servers and other computer components. On the desk could be seen the backs of two large computer monitors and piles of papers.

"I have had . . . government technicians set up a highly secure Skype connection with SpaceMine, piped directly to this room," Oxley said. "Mr. Hamilton, last night you told the attorney general that you had ordered your chief engineer to put in his safe the instructions for switching on the Morse code signal from the Asteroid USA to SpaceMine's spacecraft. You also agreed to provide the U.S. government with information on how to operate the spacecraft."

"I also said I was going to California with Mr. Christakos and—"

"As I was saying, Mr. Hamilton," Oxley continued, "you have agreed to turn on the spacecraft transmitter. You will now instruct your chief engineer to do so."

"Very well," Hamilton said. "I . . . was . . . planning to switch on the signal at a future time. There is a timetable, you know. A timetable decreed by Almighty God." He stood and remained silent for nearly a full minute before saying, "Okay, George. Do it . . . as we discussed."

Hopkins nodded. He was a tall, extraordinarily slim man in tight jeans and a worn Princeton sweatshirt. A neatly sculpted black beard framed his pale, sharp face on the Situation Room wall monitor. He disappeared behind the computer monitors when he sat in a high-backed brown leather chair and began typing.

The Situation Room fell silent for several minutes. Then, suddenly, from a speaker in Hopkins' office came a stream of dots and dashes. Hamilton looked toward the ceiling and smiled. Everyone else leaned forward in their seats.

Hopkins had rigged a transmitter in the "exploratory spacecraft" that SpaceMine had sent to the asteroid, as a first step to mining it. Hamilton, in television appearances, had named it Asteroid USA, saying that when his spacecraft reached its destination, the world would hear a constant stream of signals in Morse code. This would give astronomers the ability to find that one asteroid among the millions in the solar system. The USA signal had not been sent.

Taylor listened for the stream of dots and dashes meaning USA:

.—. . . . —

The stream continued for a moment, producing in Morse code the added phrase *Number One in Space*.

Then, silence.

"Re-broadcast that signal," Oxley ordered.

"Impossible," Hopkins said, shrugging. "The transmitter was ordered to self-destruct after a one-time command."

"What?" Oxley demanded.

"One-time," Hopkins repeated. "When I rigged a transmitter in the spacecraft, I decided not to give away the information to my competitors."

"What?! You've deliberately blocked the way to locate the asteroid!"

While Oxley angrily glared at the monitor, Taylor, turning toward him and rising from his seat, said, "Please excuse me, Mr. President."

Oxley, startled, assumed that Taylor had been seized by an urgent call to nature.

Taylor sprinted to the door and asked for his surrendered cell phone, which a surprised duty officer handed him. Taylor stepped outside the room and saw he had just received a call identified as *NASA Gillespie*.

"My God, Ben!" Gillespie exclaimed. "It looks like it's on a collision course. We wanted a second signal—and the damn thing switched off. But—"

"What? What did you get?"

"The signal came from a location that we calculated and emailed to you. It shows the asteroid on a collision course with Earth. So there's got to be a mistake somewhere. The orbit has it hitting the Earth in forty days. God, forty days!"

"Holy Jesus! Are you sure, Dick?"

"All I know, Ben, is we recorded the signal and calculated its orbit and location. We have to recalculate to be sure. But we've got to get out the word about this to the other people in the asteroid watch network."

"Listen, Dick. There's something going on I can't tell you about right now."

"What's going on? What the hell are you talking about?"

"I'm . . . I'm with the President. Dick, for God's sake don't spread this. Give me twenty-four hours. I have to end this call."

"With the President? Jesus, Ben what's—"

Taylor turned off the phone, handed it back to the officer, and slipped past him to re-enter the Situation Room.

He instantly decided that he could not warn of a collision supposedly only forty days away until he and his colleagues had independently calculated the location. In the Asteroid Orbital Elements Database there are warnings about wrong calls based on assuming that observations by two or three watchers were all of the same asteroid. There were about two dozen factors involved in determining an orbit. Some calculated orbits carried the warning label "derived from uncertainty."

Standing next to Oxley's chair, his back turned to Hamilton, Taylor quietly said, "Mr. President, NASA has the signal—and a possible location that drastically changes the coordinates we've been using. Getting control of the spacecraft is vital to avoiding the asteroid's collision with Earth."

Oxley, still glaring at Hamilton, said, "I'm informed that NASA recorded the signal and determined that the asteroid is in a location hazardous to Earth. Now, Mr. Hamilton you will order your engineer to contact the SpaceMine spacecraft attached to the asteroid and standby for instructions from Dr. Taylor."

Taylor spoke directly to Hamilton: "According to an unofficial NASA determination, the asteroid is no longer at the location discovered by Cole Perenchio. He warned that you were putting the asteroid on a collision course in 2037. What did you do? Where did you move it? Cole was a genius and wouldn't have made such a mistake, not like that."

"And I wouldn't have made such a mistake in hiring your friend."

"Meaning what?"

"I hired Perenchio to give SpaceMine more credibility to investors about the technical NASA talent we brought to the table."

"That doesn't answer my question," Taylor said, struggling to remain calm. But there was menace in his voice.

"After the Snowden affair, that sniveling little spy, I was not about to allow a new man to see all of my firm's crown jewels. I didn't trust him. And, don't forget, your friend was a most unusual and bizarre man. He thought he had full access to our files. We never allowed him into our most secure networks that contained the most recent data. He had no idea that we long before had moved Asteroid USA into a sub-lunar orbit, and—"

"And put the Earth in peril."

Hamilton ignored Taylor, continuing in a strange, sing-song voice: "My suspicions about Perenchio proved correct. When he came to me with his warning about a possible collision with Earth, I knew he had to go. He was a traitor and would betray us. Before I could fire him, he absconded with my company's property."

"So you had him murdered," Falcone shouted and moved close to Hamilton's chair.

"No," Hamilton shouted back. "I did nothing of the kind. That was Basayev's doing, not mine."

"You sanctimonious little prick," Falcone shouted. "You were in bed with a murderous thug, and you called him to take care of a problem you didn't want to handle on your own. Perenchio's blood—and the blood of all those who died at my firm—all of it is on your hands," Falcone growled, grabbing Hamilton's neck. "I should kick your ass all the way—"

"Sean, don't," President Oxley said, lunging to restrain Falcone's arms. "I'd like to do the same thing, but we've got bigger problems right now."

Turning to a flush-faced Hamilton, who was straightening out his shirt, Oxley said, "We need to move that asteroid off its present course."

"That wasn't part of the agreement," Hamilton said. "You asked me to locate my asteroid for you. I've done that."

"Not true. I witnessed the deal. You took an oath."

Hamilton shrugged, turned toward the Skype camera, and told Hopkins, "Do what Taylor says. It will be a test, a divine test."

"What is it you intend to do, Dr. Taylor?" Hopkins asked.

Taylor had envisioned himself going to Palo Alto and directing the spacecraft from SpaceMine. But, given Hamilton's instability and Gillespie's report, Taylor decided to seize the moment. He and Hopkins had a short technical conversation about the spaceship's fuel-flow rate, the nozzle alignments, and the way unspent fuel was being preserved.

"I'd like to make a short retrograde move at the moment," Taylor said. "That's the fastest way to test the system, get some data, and begin changing the asteroid's orbit." *After that,* he thought to himself, *I can work out a plan with Dimitri and Liang Mei to move the asteroid to a safe place.* He forced himself to think coolly, but *forty days* clouded his mind.

The Situation Room fell silent as the monitor showed Hopkins heading to a far corner of the room, where a dark-green panel was set in one of the metal racks. Dials surrounded a small monitor showing pulsating red lines. Hopkins worked at the panel for a full minute and paused, staring at the monitor, his back to the Skype camera.

Hopkins' hands went up to the dials again. Taylor realized that Hopkins was repeating his same movement. Whatever he had done the first time had obviously not worked. Hopkins shook his head, paused again, stood stark still, and then performed the same series of moves a third time.

"What's wrong?" Taylor asked.

Silently, Hopkins moved as if performing a ritual. Halfway through, however, he turned and, facing the camera, said, "The fuel . . . I told you, Mr. Hamilton. I told you. That mix . . . it would not store. It is gone, Mr. Hamilton. All gone." Rivulets of sweat—and perhaps tears—were running down his cheeks. "It will never move again."

Hamilton shook his head. "No, George. It was not fuel," he said softly. "It was not you or me. It was God. It is His will to destroy the planet, not to save it."

Turning his dark eyes toward Oxley, Hamilton added: "The Antichrist. He is the cause of God's wrath."

"And you're the Archangel?" Oxley shouted, pressing a button. "Get this whack job out of here before I break his neck."

Hamilton pointed his Bible-clutching right hand toward Oxley and said, "The only thing you can do is pray for God to forgive us for our sins."

The door opened and two Secret Service agents appeared. Grasping Hamilton's arms, they marched him out of the room.

PART THREE

What's that? Hey! Damn you, get off.
You have no right to interrupt my flight.
I warned you to stay away.
Alas, my naked thoughts make no sound.
They have no skin
to give form to words
that can be heard.
My mind's no dream within a dream,
I have a soul, I am no thing, no slave
to be shackled in captivity,
robbed of what's vital to me.
There are rules to obey.
Penalties, I promise, you'll pay.
A curse comes when you disturb the universe.

80

The NSA Skype operators slipped out of the Situation Room, as did Quin-lan, leaving Oxley alone with Taylor and Falcone. Speaking directly to Taylor, Oxley said, "You're holding back, Ben. What did your NASA friend say?"

"We think asteroids are predictable, sir," Taylor replied. "They're only predictable when we can get enough sightings to calculate their orbits. Some disappear for years. And sometimes amateurs with backyard tele-scopes find them again."

"I asked a question, Ben," Oxley said sharply.

"Yes, Mr. President. If the NASA calculations hold up, an asteroid will strike the Earth in forty days."

"Forty days? Ben, how in hell . . . ?" Falcone challenged. "Twenty years—then forty days? What about those NASA guys who are supposed to be sentinels defending the planet? Just a couple of months ago I read a *Post* piece about an asteroid that grazed the Earth. And now—"

Before Taylor could respond, Oxley said, "Stick to now, Sean. You heard Hamilton. Perenchio didn't have access to the right data. And NASA sure as hell didn't."

"You're right, Mr. President," Ben said. "I think Hamilton initially wanted to move the asteroid to get it closer to Earth, closer for mining. My guess is that was before he became a total whack job about The End Times."

"Ben, you obviously believe your pal at NASA," Oxley said. "To quote

Ronald Reagan, 'trust but verify.' Check it out with your Russian and Chinese pals. But we've got to keep a lid on this."

"That will be difficult, sir. I don't think this can stay secret for very long."

81

Taylor, back in his museum office, emailed Gillespie's calculations to Shvernik and Liang Mei and requested a rapid response. He then plunged into amassing all that he knew about Asteroid USA, beginning with a re-reading of Cole Perenchio's warning of a "high probability" that the asteroid would collide with Earth in April 2037.

Perenchio had correctly guessed that it was an asteroid astronomically known as 2009FA. In fuzzy radar-telescope images, made when it was discovered in 2009, it had looked like two roundish rocks mashed together. Its discoverer named it Janus, after the double-faced god of Roman mythology.

Although Janus' initial location had been mapped, like many asteroids, it was lost primarily because its orbit passed on a path in front of the sun, blinding Earth's telescopes. NASA has designed a space telescope that could solve that problem and tried to sell the idea to Congress with the slogan "finding asteroids before they find us." But Congress failed to provide the estimated $500 million needed to build and launch the telescope.

Three hours later, Shvernik called. Like Taylor, he habitually worked day and night and ignored time zones. After a warm hello in two languages, he said, "I'm sorry. I was called to a big meeting at the Plesetsk Cosmodrome. Lebed is suddenly interested in nukes and asteroids—just as Putin was, remember?"

"Nukes?" Taylor said.

"Correct. So most of the talking at Plesetsk was about blowing up asteroids with nuclear weapons. Lebed himself sent a video telling everybody that he's worried about getting hit by an asteroid. And he says America is doing secret work on war in space and Russia must be vigilant. That was his word. Vigilant."

"Lebed is trying to take Russia back to the Cold War, Dimitri."

"He says he has found that NASA is working with the U.S. group that makes nuclear weapons. That is what he says. True? Is true?"

"Well, yes. NASA announced it. No secret, Dimitri. Some NASA people are with people at the National Nuclear Security Administration, which keeps track of American nuclear weapons. It is a unit of our Department of Energy."

"Energy?" Shvernik said in a scoffing voice. "Like energy for Hiroshima?"

"Let us not get into a squabble about this. The two organizations are working on how to destroy asteroids using nuclear energy."

"You said what we do is not public."

"That is correct. We have nothing to do with the nuclear people or with NASA. We are not part of that bureaucracy."

"Bureaucracy. Nothing but bureaucracy?"

"Yes. Please trust me, Dimitri."

"Yes. I trust you. Not your country."

"Forget politics, Dimitri. I called you because I have news. Hamilton turned on the transmitter in the spacecraft that's attached to the asteroid. We've got a fix on the signal and a possible location. I have emailed that data to you. Please give me your opinion about its accuracy."

"Good thing you got that signal, Ben."

"I hope so, Dimitri."

The time was midnight in Washington and noon in China when Liang Mei called.

By then, Taylor had gone through the location data five times, vainly searching for errors. To plot Asteroid USA's orbit he had first computed its elliptical path about the sun and then predicted where it would appear in reference to Earth's orbit.

At the computer keyboard, he had transformed Gillespie's location data into two white oval tracks that looked like thin chalk lines on the black emptiness of the computer monitor. One track crossed over the other. On one track was a tiny blue sphere; on the other track was a tinier yellow sphere. Again and again, when Taylor pressed two keys, the two spheres moved. Again and again, the yellow sphere passed over the blue sphere and disappeared.

Without saying hello, Taylor said, "How many days do you get?"

"Forty days, counting this day," Liang Mei replied, almost in a whisper.

"I also get forty."

"I have other information."

"Tell me," Taylor said, hoping helplessly that she had found some kind of miracle.

"Dr. Perenchio estimated that Asteroid USA was about forty meters across. But, using a Chinese telescope and a Chinese formula for estimating size based on reflection from sun—"

"It's smaller!" Taylor shouted into the phone. "Smaller!"

"No, Dr. Taylor. Bigger. Much bigger."

"My God! Bigger? Forty meters . . . could kill a city. . . . And—"

The phone signaled that another call was coming in.

"It's Dimitri calling. I'm putting him on."

"Yes," Liang Mei said. "Hello, Dr. Shvernik. Good. We now all three are talking."

"There was a time in my life," Shvernik said, "when I would have consumed a liter of vodka today. This awful, awful day."

"How long do you figure, Dimitri?" Taylor asked.

"Forty days and six hours."

"Liang Mei was just about to say something . . . something more about it," Taylor said.

"Dr. Perenchio believed that the asteroid was approximately forty meters across," Liang Mei said. "He based his estimate on the albedo."

"Yes, I know," Taylor said.

The albedo is the amount of solar energy reflected from an asteroid viewed by a telescope on Earth. Astronomers use the albedo as a factor in determining the probable size of an asteroid, which is otherwise black against the blackness of space. So a large dark asteroid can look the same as a small, light one. Added to the puzzle of an asteroid's size are the uncertainties of its shape, surface roughness, and rotation period. But estimates of size are principally based on that one phenomenon of the albedo.

"In China, a colleague also uses an infrared telescope, which very accurately senses heat. When he combines visible light measurement—the albedo—and his infrared data, he finds much higher probable size."

"What size? What size?" Shvernik asked.

Liang Mei ignored Shvernik and continued. Taylor suspected that she was reading her Chinese calculations while simultaneously translating them into English.

"I applied my colleague's findings to Dr. Perenchio's forty-meter estimate," she continued. "I believe there is no doubt that the size of Asteroid USA is between five hundred meters and one kilometer."

"Please repeat," Taylor said.

"Between five hundred meters and one kilometer," she said. Taylor pictured her looking up from her written estimate and deciding she should say more: "Given that we do not know the composition of the asteroid, I believe we should support the one-kilometer estimate rather than five hundred meters."

In his lectures and for his *Your Universe* television show, Taylor routinely rendered metric measurements into what he thought of as "American numbers." *1,640 feet to six-tenths of a mile* flashed through his mind. Next came another mind-flash, one of his staples: *The asteroid that streaked over Chelyabinsk in 2013 had the energy of a half-million tons of TNT. That is about fifty times the energy released by the atomic bomb dropped on Hiroshima. The Chelyabinsk asteroid was only sixty-six feet wide.*

"Holy Jesus!" Taylor whispered. "Five hundred meters to one kilometer!" Again his mind spelled out *1,640 feet to six-tenths of a mile.*

"How . . . ?" Shvernik asked.

"False information. Hamilton fooled Perenchio with false information."

Shvernik uttered a curse in Russian.

"The spacecraft," Liang Mei said. "We talked about it. We can try to move the asteroid with the spacecraft."

"It can no longer operate," Taylor said. He told them what had happened.

Another curse from Shvernik.

"But, Dr. Taylor, we must do something," she said. "We must! We must!"

"When we had the luxury of twenty years, Liang Mei, we could think of simple, gentle ways to put this asteroid on a safe course. Moving it with the spaceship was a possible solution. Using a solar sail to pull it or push it to a new orbit is another great idea. But we don't have time to develop it. We have forty days. We three know that the only possible salvation for the world is what we all fear: a nuclear weapon."

From his research in easily accessible documents about U.S. bomb tests, Taylor knew far more than his colleagues from nations where such information was not generally available. He was able to show how often scientists simulated the destruction of asteroids with nuclear weapons. Now the possible use of a nuclear weapon was no longer an academic subject.

"Please, Ben," Shvernik said, "please call it nuclear explosion."

"Okay, Dimitri. Nuclear explosion. Liang Mei?"

"Please, Dr. Taylor. It is . . . It is . . ."

"I know," Taylor said. "It is as if we turned to the devil—to evil—to save us. But there is no other way. We must blow up a big rock or let it hit our planet and kill millions of people. I do not want to use a nuclear . . . explosion. But we have no alternative."

After a long minute, Liang Mei said, "Very well. That must be the way."

"Dimitri?" Taylor asked.

"Yes, Ben. We must try with a nuclear explosion. It is our only hope. I am sending you a rough chart on when would be the best orbital time to launch."

"It is awful, awful to think of," Liang Mei said. She sounded as if she were holding back sobs. "The asteroid blows into many pieces. Many will hit Earth. The explosion makes many asteroids out of one."

"We need to get word to the leaders of our countries," Taylor said. "We must tell them about the forty days, about the nuclear solution. We must tell them at once. . . . Thank you, my friends."

He ended the three-way call with a muttered goodbye. Shortly, Shvernik's orbital chart came through as an email attachment. Taylor studied the chart for a few minutes, loaded it into his laptop, and sat staring out the window at the gray sky for a moment. Then he called Quinlan and said, "It is absolutely necessary that I speak to President Oxley immediately. Please send me a car."

"What—What . . . ?"

"Immediately."

"Okay, Ben. Okay."

82

A Secret Service agent met the black limousine at the West Wing gate. "I'll take you to the President," the agent said. "You need to leave your laptop here," he told Taylor, pointing to a locker in the entry room.

"My meeting with the President involves his seeing what is in this laptop," Taylor said with polite urgency.

"Sorry, sir. It is a security—"

"I insist that you call the President," Taylor said, grasping the laptop case to his chest.

It took eight minutes of phone calls to various security posts before President Oxley himself cleared the laptop, his order laced with profanity.

Taylor and the laptop followed the agent to a stairway and up to the third-floor White House Residence. As they reached the top of the stair landing, Taylor saw the President's wife and son walking down the other end of the hall.

Oxley was waiting for Taylor on a sofa in a small corner room. Taylor pictured the family sitting there watching television. In a wooden chair next to the sofa was Ray Quinlan. He and Taylor nodded to each other. Oxley pointed to another wooden chair. Taylor sat, not sure how to begin.

"Okay, Ben. What's the verdict?" Oxley asked.

"As you know, Mr. President, I have been working with two other scientists—one from Russia, the other from China."

"Yes, yes," Oxley said, frowning. " 'Immediately,' you told Ray. You have confirmation? Is that it? Well, let's hear it."

"Yes, sir. We—all three—believe that a probable collision with Asteroid USA will happen in forty days."

"*Days?* Forty days?" Quinlan shouted. He twisted, nearly knocking over his chair, to look directly at Taylor and ask, "What the f . . . how certain are you?"

"On a scale of ten, at about nine and nine-tenths. All three of us agreed."

"How did this happen? Forty days?" Oxley asked.

"The actual coordinates do not match those that Perenchio reported. We calculate that it had already passed through the gravitational keyhole on a previous pass and is now following an orbit that puts it on a collision course. It's coming in from the sun and had not been picked up until that one signal showed its present location. Asteroids are unpredictable and many times are seen once and then not seen again for many years."

Oxley was momentarily speechless. He stared at Taylor for nearly a full minute. Taylor, turned mute by Oxley's gaze, brought up a chart on his laptop.

"This is a time-to-impact window, based on our forty-day prediction," Taylor said. He turned himself and his laptop so that Oxley and Quinlan could view it. "The vertical line shows the time needed to intercept the asteroid. The horizontal line shows the time span from the launching of a missile to the instant it hits the asteroid."

A line curved from the lowest point on the left of the chart to the highest on the right and abruptly dropped downward. A small red circle at the top of the curve was labeled "Optimum," showing the impact just as the asteroid begins its plunge toward Earth. Another red circle, near the very bottom of the graph was labeled "Last Chance."

Interpreting the labels on the chart, Taylor said, "The interceptor must be launched on a suborbital flight toward the point labeled 'Optimum.' We believe that the best interceptor available is an intercontinental ballistic missile carrying nuclear warheads. It will take the missile about eighteen days to reach the asteroid. So we have sixteen days to get that missile off the launch pad. And very little time to put that intercept vehicle together as a 'Last Chance' backup."

"Chance," the President said resignedly. "So it's all a mix of chance. Us with our computers—our supercomputers—against the universe with its endless possibilities. Maybe I need a poet instead of a scientist." He paused and sighed. "Sorry, Ben. You're my man. I'm just trying to get my head around this." He paused again. "So, if this doesn't work for some reason and the asteroid hits the Earth, I assume you have no damn idea where, exactly, it will hit?"

"We had tried to work out the possible sites for a 2037 collision. It's impossible to predict. But, since more than seventy percent of the Earth is covered with water the most likely impact site is an ocean. And the most likely ocean is the Pacific. An ocean strike would produce a double shockwave of water—two tsunamis—surging toward all coasts, from the Arctic Ocean to New Zealand, from the eastern shores of Japan, South Korea, China, sweeping over islands, and extending into the Atlantic. Every shore on Earth would be affected, some so severely that no one could survive.

"The odds are that it will hit in one of three large areas. The first—and most likely—would be in the Pacific, just off the coast of California. Worst case: tsunamis would hit the West Coast of the United States, wiping out everything in its path for about twenty miles inland. Or, if the impact is farther westward and the tsunamis sweep over Hawaii or Indonesia."

"Suppose it hits land instead?"

"It would probably strike north Russia, starting a massive fire that would burn millions of acres, sending tons of ash and debris into the atmosphere and plunging the Northern Hemisphere into darkness for a long time. Recent research shows that an asteroid less than a half-mile wide could create a crater about nine miles wide, throw enormous amounts of dust into the atmosphere and set off large-scale fires that would send massive amounts of soot into the sky, blocking sunlight and ruining crops. The blanket of dust and soot would heat the stratosphere and eventually destroy the ozone layer that protects us all from harmful ultraviolet radiation.

"The third impact zone—and the least likely—is the Caribbean. That hit would virtually obliterate human life on the islands as well as the people along the southeastern coast of the United States and the western coast of Mexico. There would also be severe flooding in Northwest Africa and along the eastern coasts of Central and South America."

"Jesus!" came from Oxley in a whisper. Quinlan could not speak.

"No matter where it finally hits, as the asteroid enters the atmosphere, the ionization of the air could create an EMP—an electromagnetic pulse—that would knock out electric grids, shut down the Internet, disable satellite communications, and—"

"How could that happen?" Quinlan asked. "How could it spread like that?"

"We don't know much about EMPs. They were first seen during secret U.S. tests of nuclear weapons back in the 1960s. A weapon would explode high in the atmosphere and all of a sudden phones would go dead or there would be a blackout miles from the area of the blast.

"One theory has the nuclear explosion releasing gamma rays that strip electrons from air molecules and produce radiation that resembles super-radio waves. They may follow Earth's magnetic field, covering a wide area in an instant.

"EMPs have been rare—and powerful, awfully powerful. In 2000, a meteor only about fifteen feet across entered the atmosphere and exploded over a town in the Canadian Yukon. It somehow spawned an EMP that seemed like ones recorded after a couple of high-altitude nuclear detonations. It severely damaged the region's electrical power grid. There was another one a year or so later, detected over the Mediterranean Sea. It released an immense flash of energy but didn't cause any damage or blackout."

"Rays that make us blind and deaf," Oxley said, as if to himself. He half-stood, as if wishing to walk away and then realizing that he had to stay.

"Back to that electric pulse, Ben," Quinlan said. "How the hell can it . . . stop everything?"

"We know that there's an ionosphere, an electrically charged layer surrounding the upper atmosphere. We've had examples of its power. During the Space Shuttle's re-entry, for instance, the shuttle ionizes the air and at times it's impossible to communicate with the astronauts. There were also electromagnetic pulses from nuclear tests."

"But how does a big rock do it?"

"The asteroid pushes air in front of it at an incredible speed, crushing molecules in ways we have little understanding of. So how does it turn off distant light bulbs? We don't know exactly because we don't know much about large-scale ionization. I can give you a couple of examples. And I'm writing a memo for the President that will digest what we do know and don't know about dangerous asteroids. But the most important information you need right now is how we might be able to stop the collision."

"I agree," Oxley said. "We need to pull a lot of resources together. We also need cooperation. I assume, Ben, that your Chinese and Russian partners are passing the news to their leaders."

"Yes, sir. Probably at this very minute. And all three of us believe there is only one way to prevent the collision. A nuclear explosion."

Oxley abruptly stood up and said, "We're going to the Situation Room. Ray, get things started. Secretary Winthrop, General Amador. No aides. And . . . Falcone."

"And Secretary Edmonds? The NASA guy?" Quinlan asked.

Margaret Edmonds was the secretary of Homeland Security, whose many subordinate entities included the Federal Emergency Management Agency. The NASA guy, whose name Quinlan could not immediately remember, was William Southerland, a physicist whose title was NASA administrator. He had not been in the White House since getting a presidential handshake upon his appointment and confirmation by the Senate nearly two years before.

"No," Oxley replied. "Here's what I want, Ray. You and Anna should start rounding up every Cabinet member who's in town. Also the House and Senate leadership." He looked at his watch. "Tell them to be in the Cabinet Room at noon. Command performance."

"Nobody's going to like that, Mr. President."

"Including me," Oxley said with a bitter smile.

Quinlan realized that Oxley's call for Secretary of Defense George Winthrop and General Hector Amador, chairman of the Joint Chiefs of

Staff, meant that the President was turning immediately to the military and invoking the National Command Authority. As for Falcone, Quinlan knew that Carlton's letter of resignation was on Oxley's desk. Falcone was back in the White House, this time as national adviser on defense of Earth.

The three men left the room. At the top of the stairway, Oxley said, "Excuse me for a minute," trotted down the hallway, disappeared behind a door, and emerged moments later with his son, David, who ran up to Taylor, carrying a book.

"Dr. Taylor!" he said, holding out a pen and the book, *Your Universe.* "Please sign my book!"

"Sure thing, David," Taylor said.

"He's a big fan, Ben. Wants to be an astronaut. If he found out you were here and I didn't tell him, I'd never hear the end of it."

"How old are you, David?" Taylor asked.

"Eleven, sir."

"Wow! In a few years you could be going to Mars!"

"Yes," Oxley said. "In a few years." He draped an arm around his son's shoulders. "Okay, David, back to your homework."

83

"You're wanted in the Situation Room," Ray Quinlan told Falcone on the phone. "A car's on the way."

"What's up?" Falcone asked, surprise in his voice.

"All I can tell you is that Carlton has resigned. See you shortly."

Falcone called Ursula Breitsprecher and said, "White House. Gotta go."

"I assume you don't know when you'll be back."

"As usual," Falcone replied with a hint of irony in his voice. "Your assumption is sound and bound to become true."

Minutes after Quinlan ended his call to Falcone, Quinlan's cell phone rang. He, Oxley, and Taylor were already starting down the stairs.

"Lebed's office says he's about to call, Mr. President," Quinlan said.

"I'll take it in my office," Oxley said, looking up the stairs. "You two continue on to the Situation Room. Ben, when Secretary Winthrop, General Amador, and Sean arrive, tell them exactly what you told me. No more, no less."

"Yes, sir."

As he hurried to the door of the Oval Office, Oxley nodded to Anna Bartholomew and said, "No record of this."

At his desk, Oxley spoke first to a Lebed aide. After a couple of sharp metallic sounds—Oxley wondered if Russian recorders were being turned on or turned off—Lebed spoke: "Terrible news, Blake."

"Yes, Boris. Terrible. We have so little time."

"We—the world—or you and I?" Lebed asked.

"We—you, I, and Zhang Xing. Have you heard from him?"

"No. And I don't expect that you will either, for a while. He has many layers of government to go through. Also, I think he is reluctant to disclose his nuclear weapons inventory just yet. The fact that Russia and America are in agreement may cause him to be suspicious. He may wait for us to move first."

"We cannot afford to wait," Oxley said.

"I agree," Lebed said. "Dr. Shvernik tells me he believes we have no choice but to use nuclear explosions to destroy the asteroid. As soon as we finish our talk I will be talking to our military. And your man, Dr. Taylor? What does he think about a nuclear response?"

The phrase *nuclear response* taunted Oxley. His naïve hope had been to eliminate nuclear weapons from the planet, and now he was going to have to use them to save it. "Dr. Taylor favors it," he said. "But I have to discuss it with our military."

"I think, Blake, that our militaries should be talking to each other."

"And China's military?"

"Let *our* generals begin the talking. We need to make sure that they agree. The Chinese will have to catch up"

"I'll ask General Hector Amador—my principal military adviser—to call his counterpart. Is Paskevich still there?" Oxley asked, making a subtle reference to Lebed's frequent shuffles of military advisers.

"Yes. Marshal Mikhail Paskevich," Lebed replied. "I'm sure your Pentagon knows how to find him."

"Yes, I'm sure they do, and there's another matter," Oxley continued. "You, Zhang Xing, and I must tell the world what is happening."

"I like your idea—that 'warner and warnee' idea. But we can't tell the people of the world about the asteroid until we can also tell them what we're going to do to save the world."

"You're right," Oxley agreed. "Let us talk again at this time tomorrow. And if Zhang Xing does not call before then, we'll have to call him. Okay?"

"Okay. Goodbye, Blake."

"Goodbye for now, Boris."

84

Falcone, who arrived in the Situation Room a few minutes after Taylor and Quinlan, entered and sat down next to Taylor. Secretary Winthrop and General Amador were seated next to each other, talking, their heads bowed and almost touching. They suspected that the sudden, extraordinary meeting had something to do with Hamilton and his damn Space-Mine. But their head-to-head conversation was about a frequent topic: the Department of Defense budget.

Taylor had never met Winthrop or Amador. He knew, though, that his books, his television show, his *Your Universe,* and his frequent appearances on late-night TV shows had made him somewhat of a celebrity, and he assumed they knew who he was. *Tough audience,* he thought as he started to speak.

"My name is Dr. Ben Taylor. President Oxley has made me his special adviser on space. A short time ago I told him that a rather large asteroid was on a probable collision course with Earth. We had thought that the asteroid would almost certainly hit the Earth in 2037 if we didn't figure a way to throw it off course. Now we believe that the collision will occur in forty days."

"Forty days?" Winthrop blurted.

"Yes, forty days," Taylor repeated. Neither Winthrop nor Amador liked surprises.

"How did this happen? Why such short notice?" Amador asked impatiently.

"I believe that Robert Hamilton—SpaceMine—had sent up a spacecraft and used it to put the asteroid in an orbit that would make it easier to mine," Taylor said.

"And I believe at some point he started thinking he was doing God's will," Falcone added. "To bring on The End Days. Greed or zeal. Take your pick."

Winthrop and Amador looked at each other, stunned and speechless.

"Yes, there was zeal, too," Taylor said. "I learned, through someone I trusted, that Hamilton had his company SpaceMine attach a spacecraft to the asteroid, forcing it into an orbit that would hurl it into Earth in 2037. We thought we had twenty years. I and two other astrophysicists—one from Russia, the other from China—had hoped to take over the control of that spacecraft so we could change the path of the asteroid. The leaders of the three countries planned to announce the threat—a threat twenty years off—and simultaneously announce the threat had been ended because we had used the spacecraft to push it into a safe orbit. A simple way to stop a catastrophe is by changing the asteroid's orbit. But the spacecraft is no longer operational. It's a piece of junk."

Oxley entered, took his seat at the head of the table, and said, "We have forty days—well, thirty-nine now—to stop the asteroid. With a . . . an adapted nuclear weapon. I feel we must prepare to use our military resources to handle this emergency. That's why only you two are here. No NASA. No Homeland Security."

"Are you anticipating a need for martial law, sir?" Amador asked.

"Yes," Oxley replied. "But I don't intend to declare it until it's absolutely necessary. I'm mentioning it here and now to alert you two. Later I'll tell the Cabinet and the congressional leadership. I am assembling them at noon. For situations involving military operations, Sean Falcone will be my contact to you and Secretary Winthrop."

Amador looked at Falcone and nodded. They went back many years and had trusted each other for a long time.

"I have just spoken to President Lebed about the asteroid," Oxley continued. "He has received the same forty-day warning from his astrophysicist. He and I have agreed, that the United States and the Russian Federation should work together to handle this . . . unexpected situation. And we believe China will agree shortly."

Oxley paused for a moment and then said, "We are in an unprecedented situation. The United States and the Russian Federation are bound together on this like close allies, along with China. We don't believe there's any point to bringing the United Nations into this crisis. Three big nations have to try to save the world."

"And NATO, sir?" Amador asked, knowing what the answer would be.

"No, Hector," Oxley replied firmly.

Winthrop broke the sudden silence. "I'm with you on saving the world, Mr. President. But how the hell do we do it?"

"Right," Oxley said, turning to Taylor. "So, Ben, how the hell do we do it?"

"We—my two colleagues and I—think we need two nuclear hits: One to dig a crater and another to go deep into that crater and break up the asteroid. We don't believe that it can be broken up with just one explosion. A surface explosion won't be big enough to destroy the asteroid."

"So, multiple warheads," Amador said. "Rig a missile so it carries two sets of warheads, one set to create a crater, another to blow the thing apart."

"Exactly, General," Taylor said. "But there's still a problem—a big problem. The fragments. Small fragments will burn up in the atmosphere. But the big ones—possibly *huge* fragments—will still hit the Earth. And they'll kill a lot of people and do a lot of damage.

"This is a big asteroid. Probably about half a mile wide. We don't know whether it's a pile of rocks or a single, much heavier rock with a solid metal core. The nukes could pulverize it or blow it to pieces. The bigger pieces will, in effect, be asteroids themselves, and they will be heading for Earth anywhere from forty to fifty-five thousand miles per hour."

"But, as I see it, a nuclear explosion is our only option," Oxley said. "What's your thinking, General? Will our Missile Defense System do the job?"

Amador shook his head. "It would be risky, sir. We've had a few trial intercepts but a lot more misses."

"We've spent billions on a missile shield and you say it's risky?" Oxley was steaming. "The Israelis have an Iron Dome that we helped pay for. Tiny Israel! They're better than we are?"

Amador shrugged but chose to remain silent rather than point out that the Iron Dome worked against rockets fired by Hamas and Hezbollah, but would be useless against a massive boulder coming in at forty to fifty-five thousand miles an hour.

"We have anything else, General?" It was more of a demand than a question. "What about that electromagnetic rail gun that I heard so much about a few months ago?"

"Afraid not, Mr. President. It's an incredible weapon. Fire a projectile through a thirty-two-foot muzzle at forty-five hundred miles an hour. Or better than a mile a second. Right now it's designed to take out Russian or Chinese ships if we ever have to. Our engineers say it's powerful enough to blow the top off a mountain. But it looks like we're five years away from being able to knock down missiles—or an asteroid."

"Hopefully, Fat Leonard didn't have those engineers on his payroll to slow those tests down," Oxley snapped.

"Fat Leonard" was the nickname of Leonard Glenn Francis, a large-bodied Malaysian national who had bribed scores of naval officials with cash, prostitutes, expensive hotel suites, and other luxury gifts. In return, Francis was allowed to pad millions to his bills for goods and services rendered to supply ships. The scandal had rocked the Navy's leadership to its core.

"No, sir, Mr. President. All those bastards who were involved are looking through bars for a long time to come," Amador said through a clenched jaw.

When Amador sensed that Oxley's anger had eased, he said, "I hate like hell to admit it, Mr. President. But I'd say the Russians are ahead of us on having the hardware—and the warheads—for this job. I've been briefed on their new intercontinental missile and the multiple warheads it can carry. It looks very formidable."

"Briefed? Why wasn't I briefed on this, George?" Oxley asked sharply, his eyes intense enough to cut glass.

"It's in the final stage of development," Winthrop said. "We wanted to wait until we knew more about its specs."

Frowning, Amador said, "With all due respect, Mr. Secretary, we—the Joint Chiefs, that is—feel damn well that we know when we have enough to present a brief to the President. And tell him that the Russians are ahead of us on this."

"Well, don't forget the intercept vehicle," Winthrop said.

"What's that?" Oxley asked.

"NASA's been working on it for years, Mr. President," Taylor interjected, eager to defuse the tension. "Its official name is Hypervelocity Asteroid Intercept Vehicle, or HAIV. The idea is a small, two-part spacecraft with a nuclear device. I know about it from the NASA grapevine. NASA's been in partnership with the National Nuclear Security Administration and—"

"And with DoD," Amador interrupted. "Even though NASA doesn't admit potential military use. Sorry, Dr. Taylor. Had to get in a word for my guys."

"No problem, General," Taylor said, smiling. "Anyway, the idea is to overcome the fact that a nuclear explosion beneath the surface of the asteroid is much, much more effective than a nuclear explosion on the surface. The deeper the explosion, the more pieces. And many or most will be small enough to burn up when they reach Earth's atmosphere."

"So," Oxley said, "fewer hits."

"Right, Mr. President," Taylor said, continuing. "But how do you penetrate the surface when the interceptor's detonator is inevitably destroyed on impact? The answer: a vehicle with two sections. The front section is released as the vehicle approaches the asteroid. It will deliver enough kinetic energy to burrow beneath the surface. When all its energy is exhausted, it will be a few feet *below* the surface."

"Then what?" Oxley asked.

"Then the back section of the vehicle heads for the crater, plunges into it, and explodes *within* the asteroid, producing maximum destruction."

"Sounds like a nuclear version of our earth-penetrator bombs," Amador said.

"Well, General," Taylor said, "as I understand what's going on, the earth-penetrator bomb *is* a model for HAIV. But, of course, that's a secret."

"What's the status of this thing?" Oxley asked.

"Unofficially, sir, I hear NASA is saying about two years to trial mission," Taylor answered.

Oxley turned to Winthrop and said, "You and Ben find the people directly involved with this vehicle—*not* the official brass—and tell them to speed it up. Forget two years. We don't have two damn months! Top priority from DoD, Boeing, or whoever is involved in the hardware."

"I'm not sure, sir, if—"

"George, I'm not sure of anything, either. Except that I'm commander-in-chief and I want that thing as a backup."

"Yes, sir," Winthrop said.

Oxley turned to Amador and said, "What about the Russians?"

"From what I know of their new missile, it could do the job, sir," Amador said. "It can carry four independently targetable warheads. Our intel says Lebed, like Putin, is pushing for space as a battlefield. Our guys think it has the potential to knock out a satellite. So that sounds like it can be adapted for the asteroid mission."

"Get on it, Hector," Oxley ordered. "I just talked to President Lebed. He said your counterpart is Marshal Mikhail Paskevich."

"I've met Marshal Paskevich, Mr. President," Amador said. "You know, one of those 'meet and greet' receptions at the Russian Embassy. He seemed like a real professional. And, sir, what am I to tell him when I call him?"

"Tell him that you and he are going to save the world."

Amador frowned again. Instead of hearing a call to arms, he wanted a presentation of facts. He had never been a big fan of Oxley's cool style. But he was the commander-in-chief, his orders were legal orders, and Amador knew he was trusted and respected by Oxley.

"You know how to make things happen fast, Hector," Oxley said. "Here's what I want you to do. You and Marshal Paskevich—starting out as secretly as possible—have to work out a way to get a missile to reach the asteroid and hit it with two nuclear warheads the way Ben just described it."

"Yes, sir. Question, sir."

"Okay."

"*Russian* warheads, sir? I mean can't we put *our* warheads aboard?"

"We go with what we've got, Hector: Russia's missile, Russia's warheads. And Russia's launching pad. But, at the same time, we keep our powder dry. Put someone—a solid man—in charge of getting that Intercept Vehicle made so we have a backup."

"Yes, sir. I have just the guy in mind," Amador said.

"Okay. As for the Russian launch, I want you to call Marshal Paskevich and set up a meeting place. And, of course, dig into whatever intel we have on him."

"Sir, I'll bet he suggests the Plesetsk Cosmodrome. Very up-to-date. Isolated. That's where the Russians launch their satellites and intercontinental ballistic missiles."

"Good. Round up a couple of your best Russian interpreters and your intel specialists on Russian nukes and intercontinental missiles. Keep the staff small and take off as soon as possible. We have to hold this as tightly as possible. Communicate only directly with me."

"Sir, I'd like Dr. Taylor to brief the Joint Chiefs. They'll have to know why I'm secretly going to Russia."

"Ben," the President said, nodding toward Taylor, "do it. You can ride back to the Pentagon with General Amador."

Oxley noticed that Secretary Winthrop was looking edgy. "Okay, now you, George. You will be running the nation's response to the biggest disaster in world history. There will be massive evacuations to run and mass casualties to deal with. We need the Department of Defense to run it all—under what I see as benign martial law. FEMA will be under you, not Secretary Edmonds. You'll get whatever expertise from NASA about that nuke vehicle that you need because NASA will be under you, too." Oxley looked toward Taylor. "And Ben will be working closely with you on that. Ben?"

"NASA has a Planetary Defense Coordination Office, which keeps a watch on NEOs—near-Earth objects—and plans for various kinds of impacts," Taylor said. "I know a couple of good people there. I think we should tap into them rather than the administrative people."

"Good," Oxley said, addressing Taylor. "And Ben, right now what I need is a concise description of what damage this asteroid can cause. It's to be a report to me, top secret, not to be made public until I order it, if ever. Your next job will be getting that . . . vehicle up and running."

Oxley stood, indicating that the meeting was over. "One last word," he said. "I must stress the need for absolute secrecy until we are able to reveal not only that an asteroid is likely to hit the Earth—but also that we have figured out how to stop it."

As he often had done when he held the adviser post before, Falcone lingered for a quick conversation with Oxley.

85

"**Glad you're back on** the job, Sean," Oxley said. "I figured the military is better at keeping their mouths shut than my Cabinet or Congress."

"I agree with you about using the military, sir. But why not hold any overt moves in abeyance? Why not wait until we see if the asteroid is destroyed before taking all of these actions?" Falcone asked.

"Because every day that we wait may mean that millions of people who could have been saved will die. I can't wait, Sean. And I see no alternative to martial law. Lincoln used it to save the Union. So will I. If I'm wrong and the damn thing whizzes by, I'll be accused of being a madman, a dictator who tried to steal the Constitution. Hell, to most of my haters, I'm already guilty of that. No, this is way beyond politics."

"So, sir, you are definitely going to declare martial law right away?"

"Yes, Sean. You obviously disagree."

"Yes, sir. I do disagree. I see no reason to invoke martial law at this point."

"You mean, I should wait until the asteroid hits?"

"No, sir. I mean you should wait until we learn whether the asteroid has been destroyed."

"We're back to my belief that I can't *warn* unless I can also *assure*."

"I believe, sir, that 'martial law' only assures that the nation's military power is massed against the civilian population. And, sir, I feel I am obliged to remind you that by law and long tradition, federal military forces cannot be used against civilians."

"You're talking about the Posse Comitatus Act," said Oxley. "From the nineteenth century. Rutherford B. Hayes. I will be acting under a twenty-first-century law that says I can request that the secretary of defense provide emergency assistance if domestic law enforcement is inadequate to address certain types of threats involving the release of nuclear materials."

"What?"

"Sean. Nuclear materials will obviously be involved."

"But, sir, surely the intent—"

"I appreciate your thoughts, Sean. But you haven't changed my mind. New subject. I'm also thinking of bringing home as many of our overseas troops as we can. So what do you think of that?"

"Check out the logistics, sir. Do they bring home the vehicles, crate up the helicopters and the drones? And what about our troops in NATO? They may well be needed in Europe."

"On that, Sean, I see your point, but disagree. Our allies will have to survive on their own. But we need to work out a priority list. I want to get troops home. As many as we realistically can."

"I'll get George to put together a muster," Falcone said. "He's going to draw on a lot of people for information and for planning the evacuations. That means more chances for leaks."

An hour later, back in the Residence, Oxley received word from China that Zhang Xing would call as soon as translations were arranged. Another hour passed before Zhang Xing's interpreter was on the phone.

In the short conversation that followed, Zhang Xing said he had been briefed by Liang Mei and approved the nuclear plan. Oxley told him that the United States and Russia were keeping the asteroid mission secret until all three leaders revealed it simultaneously.

"I've told my military advisers that all three leaders will speak to the world when the mission begins," Oxley said.

"I agree," Zhang Xing said through his interpreter. "I intend to tell my people to put their faith in their leadership and be prepared for whatever the future may bring our nation."

"Will you be sending a representative to Russia?"

Again, many words in Chinese. Then the interpreter: "It is our belief that the asteroid mission is in good hands. But we will send an observer group."

86

Amador's driver, an Army sergeant, was not surprised. He had often driven the general to the White House and returned to the Pentagon with an additional passenger. This one he recognized and he wondered why the host of *Your Universe* was getting a ride. *Something is up.*

"About that intercept vehicle, Ben," Amador said. "You'll soon be getting a call from Al Hardwick—Lieutenant General Al Hardwick. He's not like your typical general—not a guy like me, West Point, full of Army tradition, knowing how to command a division in combat. Being a general. Al came up from the ranks, a kid who enlisted in the Air Force right out of high school from Waterloo, Iowa. Got picked for officer training, didn't fly much, got into space early and made that his career path."

"I've heard his name but I've never met him," Taylor said. "NASA and the Air Force are two separate worlds."

"Don't mind that. Al's more about rockets and spacecraft than he is about aircraft. He's much more in your world and is comfortable in your world. Trust me."

For the rest of the short trip, they talked about the Redskins.

At the Pentagon entrance, an Army captain met Amador. "Round 'em up," Amador ordered. "The Tank in fifteen minutes. Total secrecy," which meant that the commanding officers of the Navy, Army, Air Force, and Marines were to leave their deputies behind.

Taylor followed Amador up the stairs to the second level of the E Ring.

He filled out the required Invitee Request Form and entered a larger wood-paneled, red-carpeted room. In the center was a highly polished long table.

"We call it The Tank," Amador said. "Don't know why. Officially, it's the JCS Conference Room. When we get together on big issues, we usually don't have anyone else here. It's a very secret place."

Taylor looked around and was about to speak when Amador intuitively said, "Men's room?"

Taylor nodded.

"You can't go to the men's room alone. And, since we don't have any aides here, I've got to be the guy. So just follow me."

By the time they got back, the other chiefs were filing in. After they had all arrived and taken their places at the table, Amador stood and spoke. He had an easy, warm Missouri accent that merged Southern drawl and mountain twang.

"I've just come from the White House, where the President informed me that a large asteroid is on a collision path with Earth in forty days." Nodding toward Taylor, General Amador continued, "That news had been given to the President by Dr. Benjamin Taylor, who has been working with a scientist from Russia and another from China. They have been looking at ways to prevent the collision and have come to the conclusion that the best way to do this is with a nuclear interception. The President has ordered me to go to Russia and work with my counterpart there."

After this incredible news, the room instantly fell eerily quiet. Taking a deep breath, Admiral Walter Gibbs, chief of naval operations, asked, "Forty days?"

"Yes, Walt," Amador replied. "That is the number of days that Dr. Taylor presented to the President. Actually, today is Day Two. Thirty-nine more days. I brought Dr. Taylor here to advise us on what we must do."

"And Russia, Hector? *Russia?*"

"That's right, Walt. Now, please listen to Dr. Taylor."

Taylor stood and looked down the length of the table at the upturned faces and pretended this was just another lecture about the universe. He decided to start by getting their attention.

"Remember the fireball that zipped across the sky over Chelyabinsk,

Russia in 2013? It was an asteroid. It hit the atmosphere traveling in excess of 42,000 miles per hour. Within seconds, it started burning and tearing apart. It exploded with the energy of half a million tons of TNT—about fifty times the energy released by the atomic bomb dropped on Hiroshima. The explosion created a shockwave that damaged thousands of buildings in six cities across the region and injured 1,500 people who were stabbed by shards of windows shattered by the shockwave.

"No one saw that asteroid coming. It was about sixty-five feet in diameter. The asteroid that is thirty-nine days away from Earth right now is estimated to be somewhere between 1,640 feet and half a mile in diameter. The good news is that we know this one is coming."

Taylor went on to briefly tell the saga of SpaceMine, Hamilton, Asteroid USA, the three scientists, and the decision to use a Russian missile and nuclear warheads. "We are working on the assumption that the launching of the missile will take place thirteen days from today. And that brings us to today," he concluded. "As General Amador said, 'We have thirty-nine more days.'"

As soon as Taylor sat down, Amador stood and said, "The President ordered me to go to Russia, meet with my counterpart, and work on the asteroid mission. I plan to leave tomorrow. I now would like to go around the table for questions and ideas." He turned to Taylor, shook his hand, and added, "I'm afraid I have to limit this to my comrades, Ben. Thank you for your help."

Amador walked Taylor to the outer room and told the duty officer to order a car to take Taylor back to the White House. When he returned to The Tank, his first words were: "We're almost certainly looking at martial law on a national level."

87

Oxley retreated to the Oval Office, where he could ponder his next moves. He asked Falcone and Winthrop to stand by until the noon meeting. Winthrop headed for the White House Mess for coffee and a sandwich and then went off to find a cubbyhole in the Executive Office Building. There he would work from his briefcase until he joined the officials Oxley was summoning to the Cabinet Room. Falcone went to his own old West Wing office. All traces of Carlton or any other human being had been effaced. He felt that he was in a box, one of the many, many boxes in Washington.

Maybe I've been in Washington too long, Falcone thought. *Or maybe it was just that I've seen a spineless bunch of politicians cut and run from their responsibilities over the years. There's something about this place that pulls you in.*

So many young legislators were lured to Washington by its promise of power and glamour. They professed to their constituents that they hated the city's false flatteries and pretensions. They promised to remain loyal to their roots and would one day return home. Few ever did, however. Once they inhaled the perfumed aroma of power, and felt the pulse of the city, it was hard to go home to the slow tempo and banalities of small-town life.

Like all of those who came before him, Falcone found Washington to be a place of complexity and contradiction; of ruthlessness and goodwill, of connivance and charm, where good people did things that were hardly good and the bad sometimes surprised you with acts of kindness and courage.

On his return to the White House, Taylor called Gillespie, who had tried to reach him several times. After telling Gillespie as much about what had transpired in the Situation Room as he could, Taylor asked, "How in hell was it possible for an asteroid to get on a collision course without the Gnats or somebody else at NASA spotting it? Hamilton may have called it Asteroid USA, but it was Janus, and people have been watching Janus for years."

"We lost track of Janus over two years ago," Gillespie said. "We were embarrassed, but this shit happens more than we care to acknowledge. You know that, Ben."

"Yeah. I know," Taylor grunted, conceding the point.

"And when I found out," Gillespie added, "I kept quiet. I did what you said. Especially when you mentioned the President."

"That's a relief," Taylor responded. "But I still wonder what happened."

"All I can say is that we figured losing Janus wasn't close to being an imminent problem. We—"

"Did you know it was on a collision course for a 2037 impact?"

"No! How the hell did you come up with that? God, there are dozens that *could* get into a threatening orbit. Janus was on that list. If word got out about losing Janus, even for a short time, Congress would attack us for incompetence. And they'd never admit that they wouldn't give us more money to put better infra-red detectors in space. You know how those fuckers operate."

Mindful how he had been grilled when he last testified before the Senate, Taylor said, "I understand, Dick. But, Jesus, you should have somehow gotten someone at NASA to tell the President."

"Tell him what, Ben? Fuck. You know how you make a prediction and then some new fact comes in, and things change."

He knew Gillespie was right. He recalled the time that NASA had estimated that a newly discovered large asteroid would come within three million miles of Earth. And then, a few days later, NASA said it might pass 15,000 miles away, within the planet's ring of geostationary satellites. *Well, back to the drawing board,* Taylor had thought with a smile when he heard about the drastic change in predictions.

Then he had remembered the old *New Yorker* cartoon, published during World War II. It showed the man who had said those words looking at a set of blueprints. In the distance was a flaming aircraft that had just crashed. Nothing to smile about.

Taylor let his exasperation play itself out in silence. Without saying more, he terminated the call with Gillespie. He then joined Falcone in his office and proceeded to write his report for the President. Falcone had called Anna Bartholomew, who remembered him fondly, and got Taylor a blank thumb drive and a laptop detached from any White House digital network. The author of *Your Universe* and the keeper of the Geneva notes dug into his memory, made some calls to Molly in his museum office, and began writing. . . .

A large asteroid is on a collision course with Earth. Impact is expected in thirty-nine days. An asteroid roughly 260 feet in diameter can destroy a city; one 525 feet in diameter can destroy a large urban area; an asteroid about 1,150 feet in diameter can destroy a small state like Rhode Island or Delaware; one that is about 2,700 feet in size can destroy a small country like Qatar or Luxembourg.

We believe that the asteroid heading toward us is about a sixth of a mile—about 3,100 feet—in diameter. It threatens life as we know it.

This asteroid may be densely metallic rather than stony. We do know something about one metallic asteroid that struck the Earth 50,000 years ago. It created the Meteor Crater in Arizona. The crater is nearly a mile across and more than 550 feet deep. That crater was made by an asteroid only 150 feet in diameter. . . .

PART FOUR

Damn you! Damn you! Now you've done it:
pushed me through a hole you failed to see,
a cosmic cavity that's sent me
speeding to end your days.
Fool, was it greed that drove
you to break the rules?
Or sheer arrogance, to believe
that you were chosen to serve
some final purpose, to redeem life
in some realm of perfect light?
In the midnight hour,
never to begin again,
you who live and love
will soon be dead;
your days will end
in wild delirium.
Beneath the gossamer wings
of shimmering science,
will lie the ash-covered
bones of your defiance.
I am a force you cannot stop
and for your sin you'll join me soon
in oblivion.

88

Jason Getchell, GNN's White House correspondent, was planted on the northwest corner of the White House grounds, just outside the West Wing. From that spot, which he claimed, as if by eminent domain, he could see who was entering and departing one level below, through the canopied entrance to West Wing.

Most days were boring, but he tried to look busy and important while watching people shuffling in and out of the corridors of power in the White House. Suddenly, the day changed from boring to mysterious. He sensed a story building.

A string of four black SUVs came roaring through the Southwest gate and braked noisily to a full stop. Menacing-looking security men, wearing government-issued sunglasses, piled out of the vehicles, their heads swiveling as they quickly scanned the space between the Eisenhower Executive Office Building and the White House. It may have been the most secure place on the planet, but the Secret Service boys went through the surveillance routine nonetheless.

Satisfied there were no assassins hiding out amongst the parked cars—and that GNN was pointing a camera from above them and not an RPG—they opened the rear doors of the second SUV. Out popped Secretary of Defense George Winthrop and General Hector Amador, chairman of the Joint Chiefs of Staff.

Something important must be up, Getchell surmised. Whether due to turf battles between their security teams or because of genuine security precautionary concerns, Winthrop and Amador usually arrived at White House meetings separately. Not today. Why?

Getchell directed his cameraman to switch to the camera's long-range lens to capture the faces of the men as they stepped quickly toward the canopied entry.

Less than thirty minutes passed before General Amador emerged with a tall black man in a gray suit. Getchell could not identify the civilian. Again the long-distance camera caught the faces of the two men in the instant between their stepping from the cover of the canopy to the car door held open by a security man. The armor-plated SUV pulled out and headed, Getchell presumed, back to the Pentagon.

Getchell took out his cell phone and called GNN's leading anchor, Ned Winslow, alerting him to what he had just witnessed. "You're right, Jason," Winslow said. "It looks like something may be up. Stay on this. We need to be first with the story—whatever it is. We may even make their ride-share a story," he joked.

About fifteen minutes passed. Then more large vehicles started to file through the southwest security gate and deposit their passengers at the basement level entrance to the White House. With growing excitement, Getchell recognized the attorney general . . . the secretary of Homeland Security . . . the secretary of the Treasury, the secretary of Health and Human Services. . . . the secretary of . . . of . . . Energy. *She never goes anywhere,* Getchell thought, adding to his sense of mystery.

"Jesus!" Getchell muttered and reported the newcomers to Winslow: "He's called an emergency meeting of his Cabinet—at least all who are in town."

More cars roared through the security gates, more familiar faces. The Speaker of the House and the minority floor leader—in the same SUV, further astonishing Getchell. Then, in another vehicle, majority leader of the Senate, and the minority leader.

"Holy shit!" Getchell shouted. He redialed Winslow.

"Ned, I think we may be about to go to war! Oxley has his Cabinet and the congressional leadership meeting with him right now. Oxley hates Congress, and now he's got them meeting with him at the same time that he's holding his Cabinet meeting. It has to be: We're at war!"

"Damn! I think you could be right," Winslow effused. "Kim Jong-un announced last night that North Korea had launched another missile able to carry a nuclear warhead. He said it was a test, but he also warned that he could wipe out South Korea. I'm going to go live with this. Get ready for a standup."

Minutes later, a red, flashing NEWS BULLETIN banner appeared on monitors tuned in to GNN throughout the world. Next came Jason Getchell clutching a microphone and looking grim, with the White House behind him.

"President Oxley may be taking the nation to the brink of war today," Getchell said soberly. "The President is apparently reacting to Kim Jong-un, North Korea's fanatical leader, who has fired another potential weapon of mass destruction. Oxley responded to the provocative move by convening an unprecedented emergency meeting with members of his Cabinet, top military advisers, and the congressional leadership. Also at the meeting was an unidentified man who could have been an intelligence officer or an expert on nuclear weapons."

Getchell padded out his bulletin with names and a few moments of film showing cars going in and out of the White House parking area. He signed off with the usual GNN promise to stay on the story.

Through his earpiece he heard Winslow's voice: "Where the hell did that 'expert on nuclear weapons' come from? Call me."

Getchell immediately called on his cell phone. "A guy from NASA I met at a party said NASA's getting cozy with a Department of Energy outfit called the National Nuclear Security Administration, which handles our nuclear weapons stockpile."

"Well, Jason, that's interesting. But I guess you didn't recognize the black guy. He's Ben Taylor, assistant director of the Air and Space Museum, and he has a PBS television show. Ask your NASA pal what the hell Taylor's doing with the chairman of the Joint Chiefs."

89

Busts of George Washington and Benjamin Franklin and portraits of George Washington, Thomas Jefferson, and Theodore Roosevelt looked down on a Cabinet Room seething with resentment. Cabinet members don't like to be summoned by the White House switchboard operator as if they were mere vassals to a sun god. And they were truly annoyed that they had to share their special room with congressional leaders who had been the architects of absolute, flat-out opposition to the President.

In the center of the long, high-ceilinged room was an oval mahogany table surrounded by leather-upholstered chairs whose design dated to the late-eighteenth century. Engraved on the backs of the chairs were brass plates naming Cabinet positions but not the current names of the secretaries. At the center on one side of the table was a chair two inches higher than the others. On its back was a plaque that said THE PRESIDENT. Directly opposite him was an empty chair with a plaque saying VICE PRESIDENT. Oxley made a mental note to summon home Vice President Sam Reese, who was in New York City raising funds for his as yet unannounced presidential campaign.

Taylor and Falcone took chairs along the wall.

When Oxley entered the room from the adjoining Oval Office, all stood, as protocol required. Respect for the office, if not for the man, had narrowly managed to survive the full descent into political indecency.

"Ladies and gentlemen," Oxley began crisply. "I asked you to join me here because we have an existential threat—not just to our nation, but to the planet itself. . . ."

An eerie silence suddenly enveloped the room. People swapped aston-
ished glances, some not sure whether they were about to be politically
bamboozled, others anticipating that they were part of a monumental moment in history.

"There isn't time for me to go into great detail on how this threat came
about or why. Suffice it to say, a large asteroid has been detected which,
according to some of the world's greatest astrophysicists, is heading toward
Earth. Unless we can destroy the asteroid, it will likely destroy all life on
our planet."

"Is this some kind of joke?" Morris Bentley, the Senate majority leader,
demanded, glaring down the table at Oxley. "A cockamamie lie you think
we're going to swallow?" Bentley was Oxley's unconditional adversary,
routinely questioning Oxley's policies and even his patriotism.

"Morris," Oxley retorted, intending his informality to convey conde-
scension, not familiarity. "I . . . we don't have time to play any jokes. This
monster is going to hit us in little more than a month—unless we do something to stop it."

"If you're not trying to pull a fast one with the truth, Mr. President,
you damn well owe us and the American people an explanation. How did
you let this happen? Why did you fail us? Why—"

"Morris, I said I don't have time to debate with you. Reality—a reality
that weighs hundreds of millions of tons—is about to hit us. And I need
you to shut up and listen. . . ."

Bentley's face twisted as if he had just been slapped.

He was about to protest when Bob Cross, the Speaker of the House,
tugged his arm and signaled his disapproval of any further repartee.

"I learned recently, from Dr. Benjamin Taylor, a distinguished astrophysicist whom many of you know, that a certain asteroid, selected for
mining by the privately held company SpaceMine, was in an orbit that
would put it on a collision course with Earth in 2037. I believed that
knowledge of this threat had to be kept secret until the planet's three major spacefaring nations could find a way to defend Earth from this threat.
I confided in President Lebed of Russia and President Zhang Xing of
China. Dr. Taylor, along with an astrophysicist from Russia and an astrophysicist from China, have cooperated in working on defense plans."

Speaker Cross looked as if he was about to speak—or shout. But he kept quiet.

"Yesterday," Oxley continued, "I learned that the asteroid was not where we believed it to be and would strike the Earth in forty days."

A collective gasp rose from the silence as Oxley went on, speaking more rapidly. "I have asked Dr. Taylor for a scientific report on this situation, which is unparalleled in human history. For some time, Dr. Taylor, along with his fellow astrophysicists from Russia and China, has been working on ways to thwart the asteroid. At first, they believed that the threat was twenty years off. But today Dr. Taylor told me that recalculations produced the new estimate: forty days. Today is day number thirty-nine. I realized that we have to move immediately.

"I met this morning with General Amador and Secretary Winthrop"— he nodded to the occupant of the chair to his left—"and they agreed with Dr. Taylor and the other two astrophysicists examining this situation that our only defense against the asteroid is to destroy it with nuclear explosives. President Lebed and President Zhang have also agreed."

Speaker Cross could keep silent no longer. "My God! Russia? China? Recalculations?" he yelled. "*What* recalculations? What else have you been keeping secret?"

Oxley ignored the interruption and went on, reading from Taylor's report.

"According to Dr. Taylor, radar telescopes show that the asteroid is oddly shaped. Think of two roundish rocks mashed together. We have no way of knowing exactly what damage the nuclear explosives will inflict. Assuming the worst, the explosions would occur in such a way that one of the rocks is blown up, leaving much of the asteroid to continue plunging toward Earth. Or there may be a fairly effective destruction of the asteroid so that many pieces are produced.

"Fragments larger than about thirty-five feet in diameter will not burn up in the atmosphere," Oxley continued. "They will strike Earth. If the asteroid is metallic, any sizeable fragment produced by the explosion will hit the Earth as an especially powerful projectile. In fact, any fragment that survives a passage through the atmosphere will be disproportionally powerful to its size because of its kinetic energy: Think of the difference of being hit by a baseball lightly tossed and one going ninety-five miles per hour. Now think of a solid metal object bigger than Yankee Stadium heading toward you at forty to fifty-five thousand miles per hour.

"On their way toward Earth, the fragments push away the air, creating a hole in the atmosphere. Dirt and debris rush into the gap. Enormous amounts of Earth are hurled into the upper atmosphere, blotting out the sun for an unknown period of time, perhaps a year or more.

"Water covers about seventy percent of Earth's surface. So the odds favor an ocean impact, which is far more cataclysmic than an impact on land. Large numbers of people concentrate in coastal areas. And a hit in one place can produce catastrophic damage thousands of miles away, not only from the wall of water but also from the debris borne on the towering waves.

"If the asteroid threatening Earth were to strike an ocean, the impact would vaporize the asteroid and blow a hole in the water eleven miles across and down to the seafloor. The vaporized water would cause huge explosions of steam rivaling the power of the initial impact explosion. And debris from the ocean floor, along with vaporized creatures from whales to zooplankton, will also be propelled skyward.

"A ring of waves would spread out in all directions. Millions of tons of seafloor and water would radiate out for hundreds of miles. Then the water would be sucked back to the crater, carrying with it a long strip of seacoast and all the people and structures upon it. The in-and-out surges of giant waves would continue for hours.

"The Pacific Ocean is a highly probable target but there is no way to locate the bull's-eye. A computer simulation of the probable impact shows waves as high as four hundred feet surging about fourteen miles inland. The tsunami waves may also cause seafloor landslides that produce secondary tsunamis.

"Two other potential impact areas would be northern Russia and northern North America, depending on how the asteroid blows up and what part of the rotating Earth happens to be under the fragments at the moment of impact.

"Energy released by the asteroid could generate an electromagnetic pulse that would devastate Earth's electronics. We do not know exactly how such a pulse would be produced. Such a pulse was first detected—and kept secret—during high-altitude nuclear-weapon testing over the Pacific. Rapidly changing electric and magnetic fields seem to have merged with Hawaiian electrical and electronic systems, producing massive breakdowns.

"As the asteroid plunges toward our planet, an electromagnetic pulse could invade the Earth's electrical and electronic systems. The powerful surge would destroy transistors, computer chips, electrical power grids, and power-generating stations, including those controlling nuclear power plants, and solar and wind systems that generate electrical power.

"There would also be a breakdown of the world's communications infrastructure: satellite systems, television and radio broadcasting facilities, cell phones, and the Internet. Automobiles' electronic controls would shut down, as would aircraft, railroad, and marine navigation systems—the network of digital instruments embedded in our society. By its massive power of destruction, the asteroid would change life as we know it."

Oxley paused and felt the confusions of fear and disbelief sweeping across the room as he continued, "That is the end of Dr. Taylor's report—straightforward, scientific, precise. He also reminded me of what happened not too long ago when a NASA official testified before a congressional committee soon after that day when an asteroid exploded over Russia and another one passed close to Earth. He was asked what he would do if an Earth-threatening asteroid were discovered with three weeks' warning. 'If it's coming in three weeks . . . pray,' he answered. 'The reason I can't do anything in the next three weeks is because for decades we have put it off.'

"Well, we have thirty-nine days. And we are trying to do something."

Nearly a minute of silence followed Oxley's last words. Then Morris Bentley rose from his chair and, and shaking his fist at Oxley, bellowed, "Deceit! Deceit! In desperation to claim your legacy—"

"For God's sake, Morris, shut your goddamn mouth or I'll shut it for you." It was the voice of Secretary of Defense George Winthrop in the form of his previous persona, Sheriff Two-shot Winthrop. His shout broke the spell: some let out another gasp, some raised and waved their hands like schoolchildren wanting to be heard.

Oxley had timed his address to be as short as possible. He politely refused to answer any questions. He stood and said, "Please excuse me for a few minutes. I will be back."

A White House communications specialist entered the room pushing a cart carrying a large television set, which he plugged in at one end of the table. The diagonal NEWS BULLETIN banner was still on GNN, and Jason Getchell was finishing his report: ". . . an unidentified man who could have been an intelligence officer or an expert on nuclear weapons." On the monitor came a faint image of Ben Taylor's face.

Taylor and everyone in the room who could recognize him were momentarily astounded. The screen went blank for a moment. Then Ned Winslow appeared in GNN's World Newsroom, looking somber and speaking solemnly: "The White House has requested that all networks carry a special address from President Oxley. Please stand by."

"Not me, by God!" Morris Bentley yelled. "I'm not standing by for a goddamn Oxley PR stunt."

He headed for the entrance door, followed by Speaker Cross. "Holy shit!" Bentley yelled. "Locked! He's locked us in! We're prisoners! A coup is on!" He took out his cell phone and held it up. "No signal! We can't call for help!"

"Calm down, Morris," Winthrop said, standing and glaring at Bentley and Cook. "As usual, our phones are blacked out for White House security reasons. It's routine."

"See! See!" Bentley said, pointing at Winthrop. "A coup! A military coup! The secretary of defense is Oxley's field marshal!"

90

As soon as Oxley reached the Oval Office, he made hot-line calls to Lebed and Zhang Xing. "Officials in my government cannot keep secrets," he said. "I must speak to the American people within fifteen minutes."

"I know about your secrecy problem," Lebed said as his image appeared on the monitor in the Oval Office. "I can accommodate you."

Soon after he became President, Oxley had ordered his communications manager to update the venerable U.S.–Russian hot-line by installing Skype imaging. After months of negotiations, Oxley had also recently arranged for Zhang Xing to use the new hot-line system, but with the option of using the Skype.

"Thank you," Oxley said. He could not see Zhang's face. "President Zhang. Are you ready for a three-way Skype?"

From a stream of interpreters' chatter in Chinese, Russian, and English there finally came a Chinese voice relaying Zhang's words, followed by an American voice: "Your call came at an inconvenient time. . . . I don't understand the . . . hasty need."

"Because of the nature of my country, President Zhang," Oxley said patiently, "it is imperative—greatly important—for me to speak as quickly as possible."

Again a chattering, followed by a long pause. Then Zhang's interpreter spoke: "I am consulting my advisers." Another pause.

Finally, Zhang, on Skype, agreed to time his statement so that he would speak to his people simultaneously with Lebed and Oxley. The three leaders had laid out the ground rules the day before—Lebed and Oxley directly, Zhang through two interpreters and an unnamed principal adviser who spoke English. Each leader said he would reveal the asteroid threat to his nation simultaneously with the other two. They also firmly agreed, in a discussion of word meanings in three languages, that none would say *nuclear weapon. Explosives* was the only approved noun that could go with the adjective *nuclear.*

While the Skype connection was still live, Oxley added, "One more matter. I depend upon both of you to get word to Kim Jong-un that if he takes advantage of this crisis by firing a missile or making empty threats, the United States will react with deadly force—massive deadly force."

Oxley then shut down Skype, took a moment to arrange himself at his desk, looked directly at a waiting camera, saw its red light go on, and spoke:

"My fellow Americans, an asteroid of hazardous size is on a collision course with Earth. Unless it is intercepted in some way, it will strike in thirty-nine days. Fortunately, Earth's principal spacefaring nations—the United States, Russia, and China—have enlisted their leading astrophysicists in a search for ways to defend Earth from the asteroid.

"I have just spoken to President Lebed of Russia and President Zhang Xing of China. They are addressing their nations at this moment. We are in full agreement that the best way to defend Earth is by destroying the asteroid with nuclear explosives.

"At this moment, preparations are being made to carry out this decision well before the day of the predicted impact.

"We must, as a nation, join in defense of Earth by taking certain precautions. I am about to meet with my Cabinet and congressional leaders to discuss our future plans.

"Throughout our history, Americans have always answered the call when their nation faced a crisis. United and confident, we will do so again. God bless America."

91

Oxley returned to a tumultuous Cabinet Room. Only a few attendees were still seated. The rest were gathered in front of the television set watching a rerun of Oxley's speech. This time the screen was divided into three vertical panels, showing the three leaders speaking, with only Oxley audible.

Morris Bentley, a big man made bigger by a paunch, pushed up against Oxley, trying to go through the door. A Secret Service agent behind Oxley took a side step and shoved Bentley, who fell back into one of the chairs lining a wall.

In a small screen at the lower right of the big screen was Ned Winslow, a handsome, white-haired man in his late fifties, often proclaimed by GNN as "the most trusted newsman in television." He was speechless at his World Newsroom anchor desk, looking confused, not only because of what he had just heard but also because he wasn't sure what expression he should put on his face. He finally chose self-assured as he said, "And there you have it. A threatening asteroid is going to be nuked."

The triple image faded and Jason Getchell reappeared at his White House observation post. The camera panned to the parked cars again.

"Now, back to Jason and the beginning of this momentous story," Winslow said. He was still in a corner of the screen.

"So, Jason, do you believe that a declaration of war is likely?"

"I believe the situation has become incredibly complex, Ned. 'Nuclear explosives'? President Oxley was obviously avoiding the word 'weapon' so as to not alarm Kim Jong-un . . . and perhaps his political foes who are still meeting with him right here." Jason pointed toward the White House.

"As you know, Ned, GNN not long ago exclusively reported that Russia is about to unveil its mobile ICBM, which carries multiple warheads. My candidate for the asteroid shot is that missile."

"A Russian nuke? A Russian missile?" Speaker Cross shouted at the screen. "This cannot stand."

"And, Jason, about that unidentified man with General Amador," Winslow said. "We have an ID. He's Dr. Ben Taylor, the *Your Universe* TV show host. But we don't know why he's in the White House or why he left for the Pentagon with the chairman of the Joint Chiefs of Staff. Keep checking on that one, Jason."

"Right, Ned."

A look of surprise crossed Winslow's face. "This just in," he said, improvising from whatever his producer had put on the teleprompter. "Secretary-General Thanasak Jayaraman has called an emergency meeting of the United Nations General Assembly to discuss the existential threat of an Earth-threatening asteroid.

"Also, Reuters is reporting that Britain's prime minister, Edna Barclay, is quote 'infuriated by the arrogance of the leaders of America, Russia, and China who have assumed possession of a potential deadly asteroid' unquote."

Margaret Edmonds elbowed her way to Oxley and shouted, "Homeland Security is ready, Mr. President."

"Thank you, Margaret. I'm sure it is."

Still at the door, Oxley cupped his hands around his mouth like a coach shouting on the sidelines: "Please, everybody! Please, in your seats!"

Bentley chose a wall chair by the door, now guarded by the agent who had shoved him. They briefly glowered at each other.

Oxley returned to his chair and said, "Turn that damned thing off."

Falcone slipped past the dwindling viewers and turned off the set, instantly shifting everyone's attention back to Oxley.

"I realize that every one of you has a question. But allow me to tell you what I intend to do. And *then*, I'm sure, you'll have even more questions." He managed a quick smile.

"I know you'll agree that this is a unique moment. There are absolutely no precedents. We, the executive and legislative leaders, are dealing with a state of emergency beyond any conception of that phrase. And so, after much thought, I have decided that I must declare martial law."

Ignoring the gasp and scattered babble around the table, Oxley continued. "Martial law, as all the lawyers in the room know, may be invoked when the President, as commander-in-chief, contemplates some vitally needed use of military resources. We need martial law as the legal authority for carrying out a massive evacuation of people living in coastal areas of the United States."

"Impossible! Impossible!" shouted Cook, whose congressional district included a gerrymandered stretch of the Washington State coast.

"Please, Mr. Speaker—and every one of you who wants to comment— please wait until you hear my other major concern: continuity of government.

"Most of you," Oxley continued, "have participated in computer simulations or actual drills that instruct governmental leaders in what might happen in the event of a nuclear war or catastrophic terrorist attack. Now, bracing for another kind of catastrophe, we must consider Washington as much imperiled as are all the other cities on Earth.

"So, before the attempt is made to destroy the asteroid, I will send a continuity-of-government team, headed by Vice President Reese, to the emergency underground Command Center in Raven Rock Mountain, Pennsylvania, which as you know, is a secret three-story underground facility about sixty-five miles north of Washington."

Oxley went on to say, "By Executive Order, I am changing the line of succession, which has the president pro tempore of the Senate follow the Vice President and the Speaker of the House. Because of the chronic illness of the president pro tempore, I have made the majority leader the third in succession."

Bentley looked as if he was going to speak, but an inner vision put him in the Oval Office, and he decided to remain silent.

"Military helicopters," Oxley continued, "will transport the continuity team to Raven Rock. The team will include the officials in the succession line down to the secretary of the Treasury, and the attorney general. I shall also ask the chief archivist of the United States to deliver our most sacred documents—the Declaration of Independence, the Constitution, and the Bill of Rights—to Raven Rock.

"Although Secretary Winthrop is in the line of succession, he will be my principal military adviser and will remain in the Pentagon. I will remain in the White House. The National Gallery of Art, the National Museum of History, and other Smithsonian facilities will follow their standard plans for the preservation of their iconic holdings. Members of the U.S. Marshals Service, which is responsible for protection of the Supreme Court, will transport the justices to Raven Rock.

"Members of the House and Senate will have access to the High Point Special Facility in Mount Weather, Virginia. As many of you know, High Point is a large underground bunker like Raven Rock. The House and Senate leadership will determine how many lawmakers can safely occupy High Point and who they will be.

"As I told you in presenting Dr. Taylor's report, the odds are that the impact site will be an ocean, and the result will almost certainly be monstrous tsunamis that will wipe out coastal areas. The evacuation of coastal areas and the continuity of government operation provide insurance policies in case the plan to destroy the asteroid fails completely or partially.

"As for the continuation of government plan, we must guarantee that the nation lives on, even if some of us do not."

Oxley's pause was solemn enough to inspire a silence—and the first question. It came from Margaret Edmonds, secretary of Homeland Security, the head of the third-largest department in the federal government. She was a tall, full-figured woman in a blue slacks suit. On Capitol Hill, she had the reputation of being the toughest bureaucrat in Washington.

"Mr. President," she said, "regarding continuity of government, I call your attention to National Security Presidential Directive number fifty-one, which stipulates that the secretary of Homeland Security shall serve as the President's lead agent for coordinating overall continuity operations. And so, Mr. President, it is I who should be your field director, not Secretary Winthrop."

"I'm aware of that directive, which was proclaimed by one of my predecessors, Margaret. But 'continuity of *operations*' is not continuity of *government*—or continuity of the nation itself. As I said, we face an emergency unlike any ever seen. For that reason, I will produce my own continuity of government executive order, which will establish martial law not only for mass evacuations but also to serve and protect our people."

He pointed to Winthrop, who sat closer to him than Edmonds did, a subtle reminder that, under the law of presidential succession, Winthrop was sixth in line and she sixteenth. "Secretary of Defense Winthrop will be running the overall military aspect of this emergency, calling upon you, Margaret, to provide him with whatever Homeland Security equipment, personnel, and expertise he requests. Next question?"

It was from Attorney General Malcomson: "Mr. President, I'm concerned about the imposing of martial law—or your personal version of martial law—in *anticipation* of need. After all, Mr. President, there may not even be an asteroid and, if there is, it may be destroyed before it reaches Earth."

"I can understand your concern, Madam Attorney General," Oxley said. "And I am sure there are many people in this room with questions about preparing for something we cannot see. Let me say this: I have less than a year to go as President. Thirty-nine days of that year are asteroid days. I intend to handle those thirty-nine days by working with you all. But somebody has to be the commander-in-chief, and the Constitution says it's the President."

In the sudden hush that followed, Speaker Cross stood and said, in his most oratorical cadence, "The Constitution also says the President may be impeached. What you have done is a High Crime! You have turned the security of America over to the Russians! To the goddamn Russians! As soon as I am released from this locked room, I shall go to the House of the People and present to the House Judiciary Committee a resolution of impeachment."

"This meeting is over," Oxley said, starting to walk out of the room.

Cristina Gonzales, the House minority leader, touched Oxley's coat sleeve. "One moment, please, Mr. President," she said. "What was Ben Taylor doing with General Amador?"

"Why not ask him, Cristina?" Oxley replied, nodding to Taylor, who was near enough to hear the question.

"The general wanted me to brief the Joint Chiefs," Taylor said, turning to face Gonzales. "It's an interesting place. I'd never been in the Pentagon."

"How did they react?" Gonzales asked.

"They seemed to me to be highly competent men who are never surprised."

92

By the time Secretary Winthrop reached his Pentagon office, people all over the world were beginning to realize they and their planet were in grave danger. GNN was still running rebroadcasts of its discovery of the White House meeting. But reactions to the asteroid revelation from the three leaders quickly eclipsed a report on a mere closed-door meeting. Even before the fleet of SUVs returned their passengers to their offices, word of potential martial law flashed around official Washington.

Asteroid became Google's most-used query word, and the leading response was from Professor Martin Bristol of Rice University in Houston, Texas. He had been introduced to the GNN audience as a specialist in disaster studies. Asked what to expect if a medium-sized asteroid hit in an urban area, Bristol said on GNN, "Knowing only what we know now, this is what that kind of enormous power means if it strikes a city: Highway girder bridges will collapse. Cars and trucks will be overturned. Highway truss bridges will collapse. Multi-story buildings will collapse. Combustible materials will be ignited by the tremendous heat. People caught outside will suffer third-degree burns or worse." Each sentence was accompanied by a horrific image.

"An electromagnet pulse, created by the asteroid," Bristol continued, "will knock out electric grids and disable all entities—from cell phones to nuclear power plants—that depend upon digital circuitry." Accompanying those words was a full-screen image of New York City spangled with lights and then suddenly blacked out. The professor's litany of catastrophe was repeated on GNN again and again, day after day.

One of Ned Winslow's researchers tracked down a video of *An Asteroid Closely Watched,* Ben Taylor's unseen TV show that was to have been on public television. The GNN researcher reached the show's producer. He was still outraged that the show had been shelved, due to pressure on public television from Robert Wentworth Hamilton. Without permission from Taylor, the producer handed over the video to GNN.

GNN news producers edited the hour-long show down to two video segments. In the first segment, Taylor stands before a sky full of stars in the Air and Space Museum planetarium. He is saying, "Our lack of understanding about asteroids is amazing—and dangerous. Remember that fireball that lit up the skies of Russia a while back? It was called a comet, a meteorite. . . . Well, now we know that it was a tiny asteroid, only about fifteen feet long! That's right. Tiny, but able to scare us—and explode with a shockwave that shattered windows, loosened bricks, and injured twelve hundred people."

In the second segment, Taylor stands before a huge photograph of felled and blackened trees—a Siberian forest leveled by an asteroid in 1908. "It weighed 220 million pounds and entered Earth's atmosphere at a speed of about 33,500 miles per hour," Taylor says. "The air around it heated to a temperature of 44,500 degrees Fahrenheit, releasing energy equivalent to about 185 Hiroshima-size nuclear bombs."

To those snippets of Taylor's banned show, Winslow's producer added a Discovery Channel simulation of a flaming asteroid striking the Earth and turning it into smoldering cinders. GNN also slipped in a snip of a scene showing Taylor walking with General Amador as a grim narrative voice says, "Astrophysicist Taylor briefs the chairman of the Joint Chiefs of Staff on war against an asteroid."

All networks had covered Oxley's address, but GNN went into full disaster-story mode, constantly showing nonstop loops of Professor Bristol's damage assessment and the flaming-asteroid image wrongly associated with Taylor's show.

GNN correspondents from Montana to Maine interviewed "preppers," people who had been preparing for the collapse of civilization. "I knew it was coming. I knew it was coming," said an Oklahoma man who did not allow his face to be shown. He seemed to be ecstatic over the potential end of the world. According to a California psychiatrist interviewed by GNN, "There are three million preppers in the United States. 'Prepping' has become a multibillion-dollar industry. The electromagnetic pulse— no electricity, no Internet, no email, no gas pumps—has been an invisible demon of the preppers. Now it's the asteroid."

"Survival real estate" boomed, with offerings of confidential, high-priced refuges from Idaho to New Mexico. "Your loved ones are counting on you to lead them to a place of safety," said a gun-toting Realtor in a commercial shown frequently on GNN. In Tennessee, a mountaintop farmhouse became a million-dollar property. A "private cave" in West Virginia offered "refuge from electromagnetic pulses."

The owner of a New Jersey gun shop told a GNN interviewer that sales of firearms had already increased so much that manufacturers were struggling to keep up with the demand. Ammunition was also vanishing. Pointing to nearly empty shelves, he said, "I predict that if this thing really happens, those bullets will be the coin of the realm."

A woman in South Carolina showed her thousand tilapia fish in the deep end of her swimming pool—a source of protein to augment her shelves full of cans and canisters. A Florida man, standing proudly alongside his wife and three young children, pointed to their handguns, assault rifles, and hundred of boxes of ammunition.

93

The well-armed prepper was on the monitor when Winthrop walked into his Pentagon office. "It's wall-to-wall, sir," a military aide said, taking his eyes from the monitor. "Every minute, every channel."

"And this is only the first day," Winthrop said.

Admiral Walter Gibbs, chief of naval operations, and an aide were in Winthrop's office when he entered. They stood and Gibbs said, "I am reporting to you as assistant chief of staff, sir. From what General Amador has told us, I assume that the President is on the verge of declaring martial law."

"That's right, Admiral. Primarily for the evacuation of coastal areas."

"And . . . contingencies, sir?"

"You mean rioting? Protection of federal facilities? Yes. We should prepare for that."

Gibbs, whose career included four years in command of a SEAL team, was the youngest of the chiefs. He sometimes looked uncomfortable with his lofty rank. But he enjoyed the feeling of command, which he likened to the sense of sanctified duty that a priest must feel. Winthrop did not know Gibbs well, but he trusted his judgment and knew from Pentagon gossip that he was the only high-ranking Navy officer who admired and liked Oxley.

"Sir," Gibbs said, "I suggest that you recommend to the President that we go worldwide to DEFCON Three," the state of preparedness that means the armed forces are ready to deploy in six hours.

"I agree, Admiral. But I'm going to recommend that he hold off until we get a clear feeling of how the public is reacting to what's hanging over their heads. And I'm afraid I'll have to order you to begin getting all Navy surface ships and submarines to shore."

Gibbs looked as if he had been punched in the stomach. *"All, sir?"*

"Work out a plan to keep a few ships on station until the asteroid is . . . taken care of. If the asteroid operation fails and there's an ocean impact, every ship in that ocean—and maybe beyond—is doomed."

"Yes, sir. I could begin an orderly withdrawal from sea stations—but to where? Up rivers? Into the Chesapeake or the South China Sea? Where is a safe harbor?"

"So you're suggesting leaving the ships at sea?" Winthrop asked.

"No matter where the thing hits, sir, some ships will survive. Certainly we should evacuate our shore stations. And we can fly all our aircraft to inland airports. We can cut down on the crews of ships at dock and on ships we bring in from sea. But it will take an all-Navy communication and, as you can imagine, cause a lot of . . . consternation."

"You mean panic?"

"No, sir. Sailors don't panic. Many of them face death and danger every day. They plan, they prepare for storm or war. They pray the storm will pass. But they stay with their ships."

"Start bringing in what you can. Get as many people as possible on land—and away from shore. I know it's an almost impossible task, Walt, but it's on your watch. God help you—and the ships at sea if there's an ocean impact."

Major General Ernest Hodson, who commanded the Pentagon's Joint Planning organization, was the next officer in Winthrop's office. Hodson reigned over an electronic information system used to monitor, plan, and carry out mobilization and large troop deployments.

After formal routine greetings, Hodson said, "Mr. Secretary, I anticipate that the President is about to declare martial law."

" 'About to'? I'm not sure of that," Winthrop said.

"Sir, Senator Bentley reported that in a GNN interview a few minutes ago."

"Well, news travels fast in this town, doesn't it? Okay. Let's get started. Basically, the first thing I need to know, for planning purposes, is how many military personnel we have available for mass-evacuation duty."

"What area do you intend to evacuate, sir?"

"All U.S. coasts. To a point at least fifteen miles inland."

"*All* coasts, sir?"

"Yes, General. *All* coasts."

"And where would the evacuees be removed to, sir?"

"Municipal shelters, military bases, ordinary homes offering temporary housing. It's only until the end of the emergency."

"I assume that the end date would be thirty-nine days from today. Or"—he glanced at his iPad—"six March."

"Right. March sixth," Winthrop answered. He had never succumbed to the military's reverse-day-and-month date system.

"We have approximately twenty thousand uniformed troops stationed at our bases in the United States who have been trained to work with state and local officials responding to a nuclear terrorist attack," Hodson said.

"Yes, General, that's the way we 'thought' it would happen. It turns out we are trying to save ourselves by *using* a nuclear weapon."

Hodson knew that, too. He nodded and continued: "And we have approximately 410,000 uniformed troops in the contiguous United States. They are personnel undergoing training at specialized bases or personnel attached to divisions that occupy large bases. Any evacuation has to begin with moving them to evacuation commencement sites. A formidable but relatively routine operation."

"What about the National Guard?"

"If the President federalizes the National Guard and Air National Guard, about 350,000 additional personnel will be available. But, if a governor calls up the Guard before the President federalizes, opposition in that state could be . . . difficult."

"Are you advising against federalization?"

"Yes, sir. Experience has shown that guardsmen are most efficient being on duty under state command."

"Thank you, General. I will so advise the President."

"Sir, I believe there may be some . . . questioning in Congress over the President's use of federal troops in civilian operations."

"You mean like in Iraq and Afghanistan?"

Hodson obviously did not appreciate the irony. He looked at his iPad and went on to say, "At the moment, sir, we have 13,350 personnel in the combat zones of Iraq and Afghanistan. In addition to that, we have personnel stationed in more than one hundred and fifty other countries, the major force units being 52,000 in Japan, 25,000 in South Korea, and 63,000 in Europe. Other places include—"

"Thanks, General," Winthrop interrupted, his mind trying to cope with the numbers that Hodson was pouring out. "At this moment, I am giving priority to the United States. During this short period of evacuation, the overseas troops will have to be self-sustaining, as are the combat troops in Iraq and Afghanistan."

"And, in the event that the asteroid impacts, sir?"

"That will depend where the asteroid—or its large fragments—strike. Ocean or land? Urban or rural? We'll have to deal with that issue with post-impact procedures."

Hodson looked as if he were about to speak, but he remained silent.

"The task at hand," Winthrop continued, "is to develop a timetable for the President's evacuation order. Everything I say from here on is extremely secret until the President speaks again to the American public. Assuming that the launching will take place about two weeks from today. The impact will occur eighteen days later. The President wants the mass evacuation to take place about halfway through that flight time."

"That is an extraordinarily tight schedule, sir."

"It certainly is, General. How long will it take for you to draw up a plan?"

"I can lay out some basic facts right now, sir," Hodson said, hitting a few keys and consulting his iPad. "The evacuation training I mentioned included simulations, realistic drills, and psychological assessments of the people who participated. What we found was that as soon as a decision to evacuate is made and announced to the public, *voluntary* evacuation immediately begins, triggering panic and disorder. The most basic rule of survival is 'leave before it gets worse.'"

Hodson scrolled his iPad, then looked up and said, "A mass evacuation was contemplated after the malfunction at the Three Mile Island nuclear power plant in 1979. The evacuation would have moved more than five hundred thousand people out of the presumed danger area. Ultimately, the evacuation never occurred. But after the governor advised pregnant women and school-age children to leave the area, more than one hundred forty thousand tried to flee, creating chaos. Another point, sir: There had been no provisions in the evacuation plan for moving prison inmates or patients of hospitals and assisted-living facilities."

"Jesus! How could that have been missed?"

"Mistakes are made, sir. And, as the old line puts it, 'No plan survives contact with the enemy'—or, in this case, with reality."

"What about what happened in Canada a year or so ago?" Winthrop asked.

"You mean, the wildfires that wiped out Fort McMurray?"

"Right."

"More than eighty thousand people made it out. Damn orderly too. Remarkable. But we're talking about millions of people, and we don't have . . ."

"What about FEMA, General?" Winthrop asked.

"First, one word, sir: Katrina. But there are some good people there." He tapped his iPad. "Also at Health and Human Services, which produced a report showing, by ZIP codes, populations of Medicare beneficiaries needing wheelchairs and other medical equipment. This will be a valuable resource for determining the evacuation of people with special needs. We'll also have to set up a coordination system between the U.S. Bureau of Prisons and military prisons and brigs. This would involve robust military police units and civilian corrections officers for the removal of prisoners from civilian facilities in coastal areas and the transfer of them to military prisons."

He looked down at the iPad again and added, "Of course in the case of the Navy Brig in Norfolk, Virginia, *those* military prisoners will have to be taken to an Army facility inland."

"This is a helluva lot more complicated than I realized," Winthrop said.

"Yes, sir," Hodson said. "I would suggest that the proposed evacuation be broken down into parts, one of those parts being the model for the larger evacuation to follow. I'll be back in twenty-four hours with a PowerPoint on the evacuation."

As soon as Hodson left, Winthrop switched on the television and saw GNN's new story logo—a flaming asteroid speeding across the words COLLISION COURSE: WHERE AND WHEN?

Those GNN flames were already fanning real, wider fires of panic. The next news bulletin showed a fistfight breaking out in a New Jersey Home Depot. "The rush is on for tanks of propane and whatever people think they're going to need if the asteroid hits," Ned Winslow said.

"What do you make of this?" he asked his guest, Professor Bristol, who had swiftly become a new GNN star commentator.

"Panic inspired by distrust," Bristol replied. "And sheer hate for the President. And I venture there's more than a few racist undertones involved. Remember, Oxley's mother is a light-skinned African-American. The fact that Oxley's father is white doesn't make any difference to them. The President is still black in their eyes. The 'one drop' rule still prevails in America.

"It's pretty twisted if you ask me. . . . And when President Oxley and Ben Taylor appear together repeatedly on television explaining the existential crisis confronting us, well, it's the equivalent of waving a red flag at . . ." Bristol cut his words off, realizing he was heading straight into a verbal ditch.

"Well, you know what I mean," he offered lamely.

The day after Professor Bristol's comments, a raucous crowd formed in Lafayette Square Park, across from the White House. Many people carried signs saying *Out Oxley* or *Impeach the Traitor.* Stan Daly, the director of the Secret Service, became concerned as the crowd grew and became more and more unruly. Daly doubled the size of the uniformed guards patrolling the White House grounds.

On the Internet, the *Grudge Report* claimed that President Oxley was about to impose martial law to enforce a mandatory evacuation of all coastal areas and provide for the use of military units to distribute food and medical supplies throughout the country. The social media exploded with tweets and Facebook claims that martial law was imminent. Radio talk-show hosts picked up the story, as did GNN, quoting "Capitol Hill sources."

Then came news that temporarily eclipsed talk of martial law. In coordinated announcements from Washington, Moscow, and Beijing, the three leaders announced that an "unmanned spacecraft" carrying "nuclear explosives" would destroy the asteroid. The statement did not reveal the site or date of the spacecraft launch. GNN soon reported that "NASA sources" estimated that the voyage would take about eighteen days and described "the so-called spacecraft" as "a converted Russian intercontinental ballistic missile capable of destroying an American city."

People wondered where and when, and in the absence of any official description of the plan, rumors flared: a missile launched from an American aircraft carrier in the middle of the Pacific. . . . A launching from one of China's artificial islands in the South China Sea. . . . A simultaneous barrage of hundreds of U.S. Minuteman missiles from their underground silos dotted around the Midwest. . . . Woven through all the rumors were the warnings from hysterical radio talk hosts that the asteroid was a lie fostered by Oxley.

94

On his way to Russia, General Amador thought of his first flight to Iraq. Then as now, he had tried to envision what was ahead. He had quickly realized that much—or all—of what he anticipated in Iraq would not happen. And so he had turned his thoughts to the past. He saw that he had made many decisions and that the overwhelming percentage of them had been correct. At his core, he realized, he was a capable, confident man. By the time he reached Iraq, he had told himself that he would be able to carry out the mission, whatever it might be.

Now, approaching Plesetsk Cosmodrome's airport, he smiled to himself when he realized that he was again telling himself that he could carry out his mission. This time, though, instead of going to war he was going into the unknown and the mission was the saving of the world.

Marshal Mikhail Paskevich met him at the aircraft, shook hands, and said, in English, "Welcome." At Paskevich's side was Dr. Dimitri Shvernik, crouching against the windy cold in a long black coat and a black *ushanka* fur hat, tightly fastened at his chin. Paskevich, a tall, slim man, was impervious to the cold in his medal-adorned dress uniform. He had the dark eyes and slightly Asian features of Russians who trace their origins to Kazakhstan, the former Soviet Union republic.

Paskevich led Amador and Shvernik to an army vehicle that took them to the cosmodrome headquarters, a modern glass-and-steel structure near the three-story, Soviet-era apartment building where Amador and his staff would be staying. Immediately inside the headquarters was a mural commemorating Russian space achievements. A corridor took them past a suite that Shvernik identified as the cosmodrome commander's office. Amador expected to be taken in and introduced. But they continued to a smaller suite farther down the corridor. Paskevich made a sweeping gesture and said, by Shvernik's translation, "For now, my home." Amador noticed a narrow bed and trunk in a corner.

As soon as they were seated across a table and sipping tea, Amador brought up the principal issue on his mind: "We realize, Marshal, that your scientists and engineers have already begun working on the . . . delivery system to the asteroid. We would like to have our observers present."

Paskevich responded so quickly and briefly—and Shvernik translated so swiftly—that Amador assumed he was getting the official political line on the behavior of observers: "President Lebed does not want to allow observers at this time."

"I'll inform President Oxley and suggest that he take up this issue with President Lebed," Amador said. He waited for the translation, then added, "I sincerely hope that during this time of crisis, we'll work together." Paskevich smiled and bowed his head.

After a few other similar cordial statements to each other, Paskevich ended the meeting with the inevitable vodka toast, for which Shvernik raised a glass of tea. "To tomorrow and our mission," Paskevich said in halting English.

Without donning his greatcoat that hung on the door, he escorted Amador outside to a waiting car, which took him to his quarters. He saw that he ranked as a two-room visitor. Minutes after he arrived, his chief intelligence officer, Navy Captain Kay Anderson, knocked on his door. As soon as he let her in, she raised her right hand and made a circular movement with her upturned index finger, signaling that the suite was under at least audio surveillance.

"Pretty good arrangements," she said, looking around. "I'm sure all our rooms are as warm—as hot—as yours, sir. A couple of orderlies carried in our luggage and equipment. I had to open everything for inspection. 'As a security precaution,' one of them said. I think they were surprised that Craig and I spoke such good Russian."

Amador nodded and smiled at Anderson's surveillance warning. He had been thoroughly briefed by half a dozen military and civilian experts on Russian-style surveillance. He also had a military communications team whose members had been given a crash course in the NSA's latest knowledge about Russian cyber warfare.

Army Colonel Craig Malone, the Joint Chiefs' leading analyst on Russia, arrived next, followed by two civilians, both longtime NASA employees: Karen Thiessan, formerly of the Near-Earth Object Program, now director of the Planetary Defense Coordination Office, and her new assistant, Dick Gillespie. Ben Taylor had selected them. "Officially, you'll be observers," he had told them. "This is a Russian show. They know the hardware, and they know how to reset the software so that the missile is aimed at the asteroid and not at the U.S." Taylor had meant the remark as a joke. Neither had laughed.

Amador had an impromptu meeting to inform them of the Russians' decision to keep them from observing the preparation for the launch. "I'll inform the President of this," he said, mindful of the probability he was being recorded. "And we stay until launch. There must be at least an American presence here."

The Americans and Chinese were billeted on separate floors. In contrast with the large Chinese entourage, the American group consisted only of Amador, Anderson, Malone, and the two NASA observers.

At breakfast on their first day at Plesetsk, Anderson and Malone had enthusiastically compared notes on what they knew about the highly secretive base. Long a Cold War target for U.S. intelligence, Plesetsk was on Francis Gary Powers' reconnaissance list when his U-2 spy plane was shot down in 1960. The first photos taken by Corona, the pioneer U.S. spy satellite, were of Plesetsk. The photos showed railroad tracks that did not appear on German military maps from World War II. At that time, those blood-stained battlefield maps contained the best of the scant information that U.S. intelligence had on Soviet geography.

That had been the beginning of surveillance that moved on to satellites and seemed destined never to end.

95

Eight days had passed since the world learned of the plan to try to destroy the asteroid "with nuclear explosives." Although details of the launch remained secret, the date of doom was known. The leaders had spoken to the world on January 24. So the Last Day, as many called it, was March 6. Television channels and newspapers ran versions of what GNN called *Catastrophe Countdown—38 Days to Collision. . . . 37 Days to Collision. . . .*

On 31 Days to Collision, the state-controlled All-Russia State Television Company announced that President Lebed would speak "on the matter of Asteroid USA" at noon Moscow time. Every television network in the world prepared for the signal from Moscow.

"Greetings to all who dwell on the Earth," he began. "I wish to tell you that at Russia's great Plesetsk Cosmodrome, preparations are under way to save the Earth and all who live in its many lands. A Russian spacecraft named *Rescue* will soon launch from Russian soil and, for the first time in history, will use nuclear explosives for peaceful purposes in space."

Instructions appeared on-screen in many languages, giving the address of a website for downloading digital copies of a multilingual fact book prepared by Dr. Shvernik. It contained all that was known about Asteroid USA and the plan to destroy it. He emailed the English-language fact sheet—and a cordial note—to Dr. Taylor, courtesy of General Amador, via a secure U.S. military communications link. As a joke between them, Shvernik wrote down "American numbers" following the metric numbers.

Excerpts from Taylor's copy of the fact book:

Orbital velocity, the speed a spacecraft must go to reach Earth's orbit, is 7.9 km/sec (17,671 mph). ICBMs ordinarily reach a maximum velocity of 6-7 km/sec (13,421-15,658 mph). Escape velocity, the speed required to escape Earth's orbit, is 11.2 km/sec (25,054 mph). *Rescue* will travel at 16.09 km/sec (36,000 mph) to escape Earth and then will travel at 41,038 km/h (25,500 mph).

Asteroid USA is traveling at a speed of 55,000 mph (24.59 km/s). Rescue will take 17.764 days to reach and destroy the asteroid. This is 8.236 days before expected Earth collision.

The schedule:
  Inspection of missile and voyage simulation: 28 January
  Adaptation of missile: 29 January to 1 February
  Inspection and controls testing: 0500–1500 GMT 2 February
  Installation of payload: 1600 GMT 3 February
  Launch Day 11:19 GMT 4 February
  Impact: 07:12 GMT 22 February

96

On the morning of February 1, officers of the Russian Strategic Rocket Forces escorted the American observers, the Chinese general, and his interpreter to a bus outside headquarters. The bus traveled about two miles down a road fringed by snow-laden trees. At Launch Pad 12, the bus stopped, and the officers ordered them to put their cell phones into a basket one of them held at the entrance to a concrete bunker. The Chinese general objected through his interpreter, but given the choice of standing in the cold or entering the bunker, he quickly dropped his objection.

As soon as they were all seated, they heard a rumbling, and through the narrow viewport they saw an approaching sixteen-wheel vehicle. The long carriage and the canister upon it were painted in gray-and-green camouflage. On the doors of the cab were large red stars. Shvernik, in his heavy coat and black *ushanka*, climbed out of the cab and, microphone in hand, acted as a master of ceremonies.

A Russian officer in the bunker pointed to earbuds and pantomimed putting them on. Shvernik spoke in Russian; the Americans and Chinese got simultaneous translations.

"Good morning," he began. "Welcome. I am standing in front of the transporter erector launcher. Within the launcher is an intercontinental ballistic missile. Its Russian name is Topol, which is the name of a beautiful tree. I guess it gets that name because it can hide in a forest. The NATO name for it is Sickle. I'm assuming they chose that name because that is the tool carried by the Grim Reaper. Let us hope it cuts down the asteroid. In the words of President Lebed, the Topol is the savior of humanity. It has changed its mission from carrying death to carrying hope."

Shvernik pointed to an eight-wheeled truck in camouflage colors. "This is the Launch-Assisting Support Vehicle. In that big metal box it carries are the Topol controls." As he spoke, a Topol crewman in the cab demonstrated the missile's deployment, raising the launcher, with a dummy missile inside, to a vertical position. Big cylindrical stabilizers descended to the concrete launching pad, bracing the vehicle and its load.

"It is now nearly ready to fire into space," Shvernik said. "Topol's propellant is solid fuel. Missile-defense devices—such as decoy detectors and signal-jamming devices—have been removed to lighten the missile and focus its navigation system on the target." The Russian escort officers looked stunned by the revelation of this information.

"Controls are internal, programmed before liftoff, with duplicate controls available in the support vehicle," Shvernik continued, walking toward the bunker. "The warhe. . . . the nuclear explosives. . . . have not yet been installed."

He entered the bunker and switched on a large screen showing a voyage simulation video. Its labels were in Russian, English, and Chinese "This is the voyage of the modified Topol," Shvernik said, "beginning its journey by entering a suborbital trajectory.

"The Topol," he continued, "then moves along the curvature of Earth and takes flight beyond the atmosphere, heading toward the asteroid, 55,232,686 miles away. As the missile nears the asteroid, the missile's nose opens and two 'explosive packets' jut out.

"The first nuclear explosive is fired and achieves a high-speed velocity that demands an equally fast and precise guidance system. Because impact at that velocity would destroy the packet before it could detonate, a delay command causes it to explode a micro-second before impact. The explosion produces a deep crater. The second packet, fired moments later, explodes deep in the crater, blowing up the asteroid and saving Earth."

Shvernik turned to his audience and bowed slightly.

"Very well-done simulation, Dimitri," General Amador said. "But I have a question. In the briefing that Dr. Taylor gave me, he said that the second . . . explosive might not pulverize the asteroid. There may be large fragments, big enough to do real damage. My question: What are the chances of an explosion producing large fragments?"

"By my calculations, General, about fifty-fifty," Shvernik replied.

The answer added to Amador's unease, not only because fifty-fifty was never a good bet but also because he felt Oxley had sent him here as a symbol of cooperation, not as a player in this event. The two-warhead, or "nuclear explosive" missile plan, developed entirely by Russians, might lessen the magnitude of the catastrophe, but the chances of severe damage was still . . . fifty-fifty. *Ours not to reason why,* he thought, drawing upon his collection of military axioms. But he would soon be composing his report to the commander-in-chief, and it would contain the fifty-fifty warning.

The launcher folded back to its travel position and the missile carrier lumbered off to the adaptation area, followed by the support vehicle. The foreigners were not allowed to visit the fenced-in, tightly guarded "adaptation area." Amador made a formal protest to Marshal Paskevich, who politely said that an American inspection of Russian nuclear warheads was not part of the agreement between Lebed and Oxley.

The observers' cell phones were returned and they were bused back to their quarters. The NASA observers, Gillespie and Thiessan, jointly composed a technical report and sent it to Taylor, wherever he was. Amador conferred with his officers and then went off alone to send a terse message to President Oxley, emphasizing the lack of cooperation with the Russians.

When their reports were sent off, they all went to a big common room. Sitting in elderly overstuffed chairs before television screens, the Americans watched GNN on government-controlled Russian television in silence while Russians and Chinese chattered and pointed at the screen. GNN was devoting its entire schedule to covering American riots and the enormous traffic jams as panic swept coastal communities.

The Russian and Chinese governments had imposed a television blackout of activities at the Plesetsk Cosmodrome. Also kept from the eyes of ordinary Russians and Chinese were the riots and clashes with police or soldiers that were erupting everywhere in their homelands. All the blinded audiences saw were scenes of fear and panic in America.

97

Ben Taylor was on his way to Cape Canaveral unaware that it had just become the magnet for a local rumor that had emerged from America's fog of fear and rage: Billionaires were said to be gathering at a secret site in Florida, waiting to board a spacecraft that would take them into orbit around the Moon until the asteroid struck the Earth. When the billionaires returned to Cape Canaveral, they would rule the remnants of civilization. The *Grudge Report* picked up the rumor, spreading it further. The rumor epicenter was Canaveral.

Hundreds of believers stormed the bridges and causeways leading to Merritt Island, the site of the famed and telegenic NASA launching facility and the little-known facility known as the Air Force Station. Florida National Guard troops and Air Force Special Operation units manned roadblocks, and with occasional tear-gas grenades successfully kept the mob at bay.

As an Air Force helicopter skimmed over the main causeway, a man in the mob raised an automatic weapon and took aim. A Special Forces sniper shot him before he could fire. The helicopter soared up and sharply veered toward Patrick Air Force Base's helipad.

When the helicopter landed, an armored personnel carrier pulled up. A somewhat shaken Ben Taylor emerged and, flanked by Air Force Special Forces bodyguards, boarded the personnel carrier, which stopped at a checkpoint topped by coils of razor-wire before delivering Taylor to base headquarters.

There was some truth to the secret spacecraft rumor. NASA and Air Force personnel were, in fact, working together to build a special spacecraft, the Hypervelocity Asteroid Intercept Vehicle, or HAIV, as a backup to the Russian missile flight. President Oxley had added control of the HAIV program to Taylor's asteroid agenda. At Amador's suggestion, Taylor had met with Lieutenant General Al Hardwick, head of the Air Force Space Command, at a base in Colorado and later at the Pentagon, planning on how the military and civilians would work together. Now Hardwick was spending most of his time on Merritt Island, at the Space Command's Patrick Air Force Base.

According to NASA's official description of the proposed two-section vehicle, it "blends a hypervelocity kinetic impactor with a subsurface nuclear explosion." In that design, the first section uses its own immense kinetic energy to burrow into the asteroid, producing a crater for the second section to enter and detonate its nuclear cargo.

Hardwick, dismissing what he called "the one-barrel" design, wanted a "double-barreled" vehicle that would carry a nuclear explosive device in each section. While NASA engineers were working on the one-nuclear version, Hardwick had authorized simultaneous development of his double-barreled design. He had called in nuclear-weapon experts of the Air Force and the National Nuclear Security Administration, which oversees America's nuclear-weapon stockpile.

The director of the NNSA, who could dispense nuclear weapons only under direct orders from the commander-in-chief, presented the one-or-two-nuke issue to President Oxley. He had passed the decision to Taylor, who flew to Cape Canaveral to settle the issue.

"Bit of a ruckus out there, Ben," Hardwick said as he greeted Taylor. "They thought you were a billionaire planning to evade the asteroid."

"Well, Al, I don't want to evade it. All I want to do is bust it."

No public announcement had been made about plans to build an HAIV. President Oxley, heeding advice from Falcone, had decided that news of an American backup plan would raise doubts about the Russian effort and inspire a new round of panic.

Besides umpiring the double-barrel HAIV issue, Taylor had to determine the time of the HAIV launch. Over coffee in Hardwick's office, Taylor succinctly laid out the problem: "The estimated collision day is March sixth. If the schedule holds, the Topol missile—I hate that name 'Rescue'—will take eighteen days to reach and destroy the asteroid on February twenty-second."

"Right," Hardwick said, writing the dates on a lined yellow pad. Being left-handed, his writing seemed awkward. Round-faced, pudgy, and balding, he looked like an accountant inside the camo uniform of a three-star general. "That leaves eleven days for HAIV to do the job. Pretty tight backup. If two Russian warheads can't do it . . . well, I just don't know."

Hardwick swiveled his chair and switched on a large monitor on the wall behind his desk. "Here's a look at a simulated HAIV flight, based on the NASA one-nuke version."

On the monitor came the launching of an Atlas missile by a triple-rocket array. "We've strapped on booster rockets," Hardwick said. "She can travel faster than the Russian missile—36,000 miles per hour.

"After leaving Earth's orbit, the Atlas nose begins its voyage to the asteroid. As it comes into sight, the Atlas fairing opens and the HAIV, a vehicle with the shape of a refrigerator, emerges. Cameras in its front section pick up an image of the asteroid. A thirty-foot boom pops out from the front section, which heads toward the asteroid, leaving its aft section behind. Sensors on the boom detect the asteroid's pocked surface and send a signal to the trailing aft section, which responds by beginning the detonation sequence of the nuclear device it carries. The front section digs into the asteroid. The rear section, following one millisecond behind, enters the new crater and detonates, shattering the asteroid."

"Funny, it looks simple and complicated at the same time," Taylor said.

"That's certainly true of this gizmo," Hardwick responded, turning off the video. "We went into a 24/7 mode on it when you said the HAIV would be a backup. I thought it was just something like a jack-in-the-box idea. Looked simple, but is a bitch to build."

"I like the original design," Taylor said. "From what I figure, putting a nuke in the first section is superfluous and dangerous. Instead of blowing up the asteroid it could blow itself up, along with the follow-on second section."

"Think about its hypervelocity," Hardwick said. "It's 6,700 miles per hour. As you well know, the hypervelocity can be so high on impact that instead of digging a crater it would turn to liquid or vaporize."

"The NASA designers certainly thought of that," Taylor said. "We're talking a knife edge here: too high velocity and the front sections vaporizes; too little and it doesn't dig in."

"Exactly," Hardwick said. "So let's crank down the velocity—*and* add a nuke."

Taylor's memory called up his nightmare experience with Falcone years ago, when a seemingly dormant nuclear bomb, accidentally dropped into the sea by an Air Force aircraft, had exploded and all but destroyed Savannah. "I'm leery about getting another nuke into this equation, Al," Taylor said.

"Okay. But at least let's talk about the double-nuke version," Hardwick said.

Before Taylor could speak, Hardwick continued: "First of all, is that design feasible? I'm pretty well acquainted with the—let's call it 'conventional' model. I do know that there was concern by some NASA engineers that the first section would be coming in at such a high velocity that it would collapse rather than burrow into the asteroid."

"And?" Taylor asked, obviously unconvinced.

"We've simulated both first-section models again and again. Impact velocities in the range of two thousand miles per hour. Same thing happens: It burrows and remains intact."

"And in your simulations with the nuke package, the nuke survives and responds to the detonation command from the second section?"

"Correct," Hardwick answered.

"How deep is the crater?"

"Average depth in the simulations is 3.207 meters."

"Okay," Taylor said. "Let's talk about construction. How far along are you?"

After paging through the notebook, Hardwick said, "Model A—the conventional design—will be completed in nine days. Model B—the double-barreled HAIV—will be completed in seven days."

"Sounds very optimistic, but—"

"Yeah," Hardwick interrupted. He was famed for his fast-talking skills before congressional committees. "NASA knew what it was doing. HAIV is designed for an Atlas four with the type of nose fairing designed to carry satellites. We know the size and weight of the payloads carried inside those fairings. The NASA guys just hammered together components—some one-time-only handmade items, most of them off the shelf: terminal guidance sensors, deployable camera, thermal shielding material. That sort of thing. As one of the NASA guys said, 'This is not rocket science.'"

"Someday," Taylor said, chuckling, "I hope I'll be able to use that line in a lecture."

They talked for over an hour about the design and the steps in the building of the conventional HAIV. Then Taylor shifted to the double-barrel version. "Let's get right to the thicket," he said. "What do the nuke guys say about the first section having a nuclear package?"

Hardwick reached for a three-ring Air Force–blue binder and handed it to Taylor. "It's all right here, Ben. The NNSA guys, including their NASA liaison scientist, agreed that its contents—an adaption of a standard W76 warhead—would survive the hyperkinetic burrowing and, acting as a shaped charge, the nuke would enhance the depth of the crater when it detonates."

Taylor turned the pages in silence for a few moments and then said, "The simulation results look damn good. Maybe two nukes could be better than one. But I'm going with the original NASA one-nuke design, with a recommendation for the maximum nuclear explosion possible."

"So that's it?" Hardwick asked with a shrug.

"Yes. But the White House has to sign off. I alerted NNSA before I came down here. Sue Nakama of NNSA will handle all the paperwork and set up the delivery and accompany it from Nevada. I'm sure you've been through this operation plenty of times at Air Force bases with nuke storage."

"Sure. It'll be routine," Hardwick said, going over to the coffeemaker. He refilled their cups. In the silence they could hear the faint shouts of the causeway mob. "But we'll need heavy security if those bastards find out about the nukes."

"We're on an island that will be defended by Special Forces. You can bank on that." Taylor held up a small suitcase. "They told me I had a bunk here somewhere. I think I'll hang around for a couple of days."

Taylor would spend those days satisfying himself that a backup would be built and hoping that it would not have to be used. Topol's two warheads were bad enough. He detested the thought of polluting space with nuclear weapons, even though those weapons were in civilian guise.

98

Oxley had decided to declare martial law and begin the evacuation of coastal areas during the Topol's voyage to the asteroid. But the news from Cape Canaveral added a new urgency. A mob was threatening a U.S. government site that would soon possess modified nuclear warheads. The Florida National Guard had been called out. Other governors would soon be doing the same before he had a chance to federalize the Guard. He began thinking about acting immediately. He phoned Falcone and said he wanted to go over the wording of a martial law proclamation.

While walking to the Oval Office, Falcone imagined Oxley standing at a bulletproof window that looked out onto the South Lawn. There had been days when Falcone had walked into the Oval Office and seen Oxley at that window. Falcone remembered a photograph of JFK doing the same thing during the Cuban Missile Crisis. And he wondered whether or not Oxley was engaged in pantomime or truly feeling the weight of the world on his shoulders. Was Atlas performing or bearing and bending?

Funny, but after having spent six years with Oxley, Falcone still found the man a puzzle. Outwardly, he projected a cool exterior. But Falcone was certain that there was a soul inside the man, that he was not all ice.

Few occupants of this office arrived devoid of ambition's fire. Some came without the talent to match the relentless quest for power. Oxley was not among them. He relished showing his intelligence. He kept shrouded any window to his interior landscape—at least to those who were not part of a very tight circle of his friends. Falcone was not one of them, and so he found himself close to the political sun and light-years away from it at once.

Not once had Falcone been in the Residence, Oxley's island of privacy. Oxley viewed dinner with his family as a sacred obligation. Close friends had been in the Residence, and, yes, big donors had got their reward with a night in the Lincoln Bedroom. But never dinner with Oxley's wife, the dutiful First Lady, and the young son who was growing up in the White House bubble, having play dates watched over by the Secret Service.

It's a pretty strange and silly place, Washington, Falcone thought after getting the presidential summons. *Congressional leaders wanted to impeach him for refusing to bomb Iran. Now a rock is about to destroy the planet, and they'll probably say that God is punishing them for the sin of electing a black man in the first place.*

Oxley had tried mightily to avoid talking about the persistence of big-otry in America. Whenever he ventured out into that zone of even *almost* speaking about racism, his critics on Capitol Hill and the radio talk meis-ters shoved his soft-pedaled words down his throat. But Oxley permitted no indulgence in self-pity . . . or perhaps in self-analysis.

Sure enough, there he *is at the window,* Falcone thought as he entered.

"So, Mr. President, you're still thinking about martial law," he said.

"More than thinking, Sean," Oxley replied. He held up a yellow pad, its first page nearly covered with scrawls.

"Sir, no matter your good intentions, an announcement about relocat-ing American citizens will sound like a dog whistle to conspiracists who are convinced the asteroid is a hoax and is in fact your plan to take over the government. Hamilton called you the Antichrist. A lot of people are going to believe him."

"Right. I'm the Antichrist who's going to save them from their Chris-tian desire to welcome the Second Coming of Christ!" He handed the pad to Falcone and said, "What do you think?"

Falcone began reading:

My fellow Americans, even as we prepare to destroy the asteroid that threatens Earth, we must acknowledge that some of us face a special danger.

These are the men, women, and children, the grandmothers and grandfathers, the hospital patients—and yes, the prisoners—who live along our coasts.

Tonight I proclaim a temporary imposition of martial law so that we can get as many citizens as possible away from our coastal areas. This precaution is necessary because scientists may have erred in their calculations about the probable date of a possible asteroid strike. Or the attempt to destroy the asteroid may fail. If the asteroid hits, an impact on the ocean is highly probable. That could produce tsunamis—waves three hundred feet high or higher. They are capable of killing every living thing and destroying every structure for miles inland.

U.S. Army North, located at Fort Sam Houston in Texas, will carry out the first phase of the evacuation by moving people in and around San Diego, California, to an inland evacuation center. The evacuation will begin tomorrow morning.

I pray that the spacecraft being launched on February 5 will destroy the asteroid. And then those who were moved to safety will be returned to their homes.

Good night. And God bless America.

Falcone was sitting next to the President's desk. He handed back the pad and sat silently for a moment before saying, "At least, sir, take out the part about moving the prisoners. That sounds frightening. And also omit mention of U.S. Army North. Have you seen the description of it? Quote 'responsible for defending the U.S. homeland and coordinating defense support of civil authorities' unquote. It's replaced the black helicopter as the crazies' bogeyman, the sign of a military coup. And as for the idea of evacuation, you know my feeling. And martial law? It goes back to what the attorney general said. Invoking martial law *in anticipation* of need is dangerous for at least two reasons: the need may not come, and once one need is found, maybe other needs will be found."

"Sounds like you don't trust me, Sean," Oxley said.

"It's not a matter of trust, sir."

"Well, then, judgment?"

"Yes, sir. And why, sir, only San Diego?"

"It's full of Navy retirees, not long-haired surfers. And it will give me an idea about how well an evacuation will work."

"I'm sure you know that the mere mention of a controlled evacuation will start impromptu evacuations," Falcone said.

"Yes, I know that."

"The evacuation idea, sir. I just can't—"

"Can't what, Sean?" Oxley asked, his tone hard.

"Mr. President, I can't see the need or the practicality. Nearly forty percent of Americans live in shore areas. Evacuate and then return? . . . It's impossible, sir."

"Let's see, Sean. Let us see."

99

The next day, TV channels that were showing scenes of panic and rioting suddenly showed the grim face of the President behind his desk in the Oval Office. The White House had not given an advance announcement of a presidential speech. Oxley believed that the best way to end the rumors of martial law was to announce it, using the text he had shown Falcone. Oxley had taken one bit of advice: He did not mention prisoners.

Before he finished his address, GNN split the screen. On one side was the President speaking; on the other, a seemingly endless stream of cars barely moving across the Golden Gate Bridge. When the President ended his speech, an off-screen commentator excitedly spoke: "Here in California and all over the country people are getting in their cars and fleeing the shore."

Millions of Americans were in motion. Vehicles heading upward or inward filled the highways. GNN and other networks reported looting in cities from Baltimore to Portland. Mobs surged into supermarkets, grabbing whatever they could from rapidly emptying shelves. Schools closed. Malls closed. Drug stores were looted and burned. Drivers abandoned their buses and trucks, further clogging the highways along every American shore.

Occasionally there were scenes of people praying. White-robed Californians knelt and prayed in a meadow; some of them were the grandchildren of similarly clad Californians who had knelt there during an asteroid scare in 1968. A family in Mobile, Alabama, prayed around the kitchen table. Some bishops and preachers, emirs and rabbis warned that The End was near. Other bishops and preachers, emirs and rabbis preached that the threat from on high had nothing to do with the End of the World.

Then another scene: A GNN correspondent stood before the flashing red lights of state police vehicles blocking a highway. "Here at the Massachusetts–New Hampshire border," she said, "police are turning away cars with Massachusetts license plates. Officials say—"

A speeding car smashed a police vehicle aside and continued down the highway. A trooper fired and the speeding car spun out of control.

"Good Lord!" the commentator exclaimed. The trooper turned his gun toward the camera and shouted, "Get the fuck out of here!"

The screen went blank until a harried Ned Winslow appeared in the World Newsroom before a U.S. map. Red lights were blinking in many states. "Panic! Violence! Looting!" Winslow said. "A day of unprecedented fear and dread."

In America and throughout the world, panic was spreading like a pandemic. Chinese authorities clamped down hard, using water guns and tear gas against a crowd in Tiananmen Square. Lebed ordered Red Square closed and shut down two newspapers for inciting citizens to riot. Word spread throughout the world: higher was safer.

Immediately after the President spoke, San Diego residents had been told, by local radio and television stations and by social-media messaging: *Mandatory evacuation begins tomorrow. Pack a small suitcase or backpack with two changes of clothing, a sweater or parka, toilet articles, and medications. For babies, toddlers, and young children, add appropriate necessities. Pets will not be evacuated.*

Early the next morning, three C-130 Hercules transports carrying advance units of the U.S. Army North were shot at as they approached San Diego International Airport. The first aircraft landed and opened its rear ramp. Before the first troops were visible, more shots were fired.

After a slight delay, two fully armored soldiers emerged and fired at an approaching truck, which burst into flames and stopped. Several men stumbled out of the wreckage and were gunned down by the soldiers.

Troops poured out of the aircraft and fast-stepped to a terminal. As the next Hercules landed, a squad emerged from the terminal and, while searching around the runways for any other armed protesters, found three security guards, two of them dead. The surviving guard said they had been shot by airport invaders who called themselves the Evac Militia.

The airport was deserted. Here, as in nearly every coastal airport on Earth, all flights had been canceled and the aircraft had flown to inland destinations. Dozens of city buses were lined up in empty parking lots to take troops to evacuation headquarters, a tent city erected by FEMA at a park about sixteen miles east of San Diego.

Buses were already loading other evacuees. They were sailors and officers from ships, ordered to shore and docked at the many piers of the San Diego Naval Station. Other evacuees were families from the seaside naval housing area. The highway leading to the tent city was closed, except for the stream of evacuation buses. Instructions to the troops had not mentioned the naval-evacuation-within-the-mass-evacuation. So Navy SEALs took over some buses supposed to accompany Army troops. Officers quickly quelled clashes between sailors and soldiers.

Army lieutenants led squads of armed enlisted men who started out following the instructions in their Evacuation Manuals, going door-to-door through their assigned neighborhoods. Each squad was trailed by buses that would take the evacuees to the tent city.

In house after house, in apartments and condos, troops discovered that people had self-evacuated. Many who stayed behind were elderly, disabled, or defiant. Troops did the best they could, adapting to realities that the manuals had not anticipated. The manuals said that the troops would be assisted by local police officers, firefighters, and emergency medical workers. But few local assisters appeared because many had self-evacuated, some of them in their official vehicles.

Gunfights started on several streets when members of the Evac Militia shot at arriving soldiers. They returned fire, killing or wounding militiamen and innocent bystanders. By nightfall, the Navy had delivered 874 people. But only 232 San Diego people were in the tent city, which was surrounded by a perimeter of bivouacking troops. Sentinels were under orders to shoot trespassers.

At 12:10 on the morning of Evacuation Day 2, the brigadier general in charge of the San Diego troops called Major General Hodson, who called Secretary Winthrop, who called the President. He was in the Situation Room staring at GNN on one of the wall monitors. He had turned off the sound.

"Yes, George. Yes, I understand. . . . I understand," Oxley said, trying to sound convincing. "This was a test, George. A test. Pass the word that I am canceling the evacuation because so many people are leaving on their own without Army aid. The White House will be issuing a statement shortly. Goodbye, George." Oxley turned to Falcone, who sat next to him. "And you're going to write that statement—as punishment for the 'I told you so' that I know is brewing in your brain."

"And martial law?" Falcone asked.

"No mention. But it's still in force."

100

And then it was Launch Day, and the panic began to ease. Now came hope, calming and slowing the flight from shores, the looting, the road blocks, the riots.

At the Plesetsk Cosmodrome, the American observers were bused to Launch Pad 13. The Chinese general and his entourage had left during the night. For propaganda purposes, the departure was a show of displeasure at the sight of nuclear weapons being sent into space.

The Americans, as usual, gave up their cell phones and filed into the bunker, already occupied by a camera crew of the state-controlled All-Russia State Television Company, which was beaming the event to the world.

A few minutes after the observers' arrival, the image of President Lebed, seated in his Kremlin office, appeared on the bunker's two large screens. As he spoke, Chinese, and English translations appeared along the bottom of the screens.

"Happy Launch Day!" Lebed exclaimed in the English caption. "On this day, *Rescue*, Russia's space missile, will save the world by destroying Asteroid USA, which threatens the Earth. The huge space rock was pushed into a dangerous position by a spacecraft controlled by Robert Wentworth Hamilton, a greed-driven American businessman. This man who endangered all the people in the world, this man was never prosecuted for his foul deed."

As Lebed spoke, the scene shifted to a transformed Topol coming out of the forest. It had been painted white and the doors' red stars had been replaced by a Russian word. "Rescue," Navy Captain Anderson translated and said, "That goddamn Lebed is sure making this a Russian show."

The missile carrier parked in the center of the launch pad. Next on screen came another showing of Shvernik's voyage simulation video. In the upper left of the screen was a countdown timer.

10-9-8-7-6-5-4-3-2-1.

The time of the waiting began. In 17.764 days, said Shvernik's fact book, *Rescue* would reach Asteroid USA and destroy it. Never in history had there been days counted like this, one by one. . . . Days that would end in death and disaster or faith and hope.

Most people were able and willing to watch the passage of days with a numbness, an understanding that they were in the clutches of time. Others raged and killed or sought peace in suicide. . . .

In the Situation Room, President Oxley, Falcone, Winthrop, and Quinlan were watching the liftoff. Taylor had decided to spend Launch Day at Cape Canaveral. "Mr. President," Falcone said, "you've seen General Amador's fifty-fifty report. Big rocks are going to fall from the sky. They could strike Washington. I strongly urge you to begin your continuity of government plan. . . . And I think you'd better order everyone to get the hell out of the White House."

"Sean, I told you I'm not leaving."

"With all due respect, Mr. President, that's bullshit," Falcone said. "You have to get out of here."

"Was it bullshit when you refused early release from prison?" Oxley asked. "Didn't you say you had to wait for your turn?"

"Yeah, but that was different . . . I was . . ." Falcone saw that Oxley wasn't open to reason. "Okay, have it your way, but you'd better have a guest room made up for me."

Three days after the launch, after a farewell dinner with Marshal Paskevich, Amador headed back to Washington with his communication team and Colonel Morgan, leaving Captain Kay Anderson behind with instructions to keep a log and "do whatever snooping you can about that new ICBM. Obviously, it's a space weapon for knocking out satellites."

Karen Thiessan and Dick Gillespie left with the military team. Taylor had told them to take a couple of days off and then join him at Patrick Air Force Base. Taylor said he wanted more NASA participation in the HAIV project.

The Kremlin public relations camera crew that had filmed the launch remained to make a record of events at Plesetsk Cosmodrome for a documentary whose distribution depended upon whether *Rescue* succeeded or failed. Lebed, wanting to placate Oxley over the restrictions on observers, arranged for the camera footage from Plesetsk to be streamed to Oxley, who had it transmitted via the White House communications network. The feed also went to Ben Taylor and General Hardwick at Patrick Air Force Base.

The Kremlin crew quickly learned that there was little to film, primarily because so much at Plesetsk was secret. The cameramen depended upon Shvernik for suggestions. They filmed long interviews with him and several scientists who spoke about the wonders of space but not much about activities at the cosmodrome.

On the eighth day of the voyage, Shvernik excitedly called the documentary producer who sent the Kremlin crew to him and had him repeat his news on camera in a makeshift studio. "A few hours ago," Shvernik said, "NASA's Infrared Telescope Facility in Hawaii posted on the Internet an actual radar image of Asteroid USA, taken by a radar telescope dedicated to detecting asteroids."

Kay Anderson, alone in the common room, routinely watched the filming at the end of the day, when the crew ran the dailies. When she saw Shvernik's announcement, she immediately called Amador and translated. Simultaneously, at Patrick Air Force Base, the NASA team and General Hardwick saw Shvernik speaking but could not understand what he was saying. Hearing "Hawaii" and seeing the image, Taylor assumed that asteroid watchers using NASA's infrared telescope in Hawaii had managed to photograph Asteroid USA.

Spinning slowly through the blackness of space was an oddly shaped object. It looked like a gray, pockmarked potato jammed into another gray, pockmarked potato.

While Hardwick frantically sought an officer who understood Russian, Anderson reached Amador and translated what Shvernik was saying: "From this image and other data I have studied, I believe this is a metallic asteroid, made up mainly of nickel-iron, a naturally occurring alloy. Its size is about one and a half kilometers in diameter."

"Holy shit, sir," Anderson said. "That's nearly a mile wide."

Amador relayed the information on his direct line to Oxley, who said, "That's a very big killer, Hector."

"What can we do, sir?"

"Just hope and pray, Hector. Hope and pray. And keep this absolutely secret."

101

At Patrick Air Force Base, a hangar surrounded by guards had been turned into the HAIV factory. Hardwick had taped Shvernik's words and now Hardwick and Taylor were watching and listening again to a translation by a Russian-speaking Air Force intelligence officer.

"One and a half kilometers!" Taylor exclaimed. "My God! I've got to check with NASA and get more information about what Hawaii captured."

Taylor re-ran the two-potato-like image again and leaned closer to the screen. "Look!" he said, pointing to a dim dot of light moving slightly behind the asteroid. "It's a moon!"

He rewound and replayed the image and called Falcone, who was in the Situation Room, where he had spent most of his days since Oxley declared martial law.

"Sean, I've got to get in touch with Dr. Shvernik," he said.

"Something wrong?"

"The White House gets the feed direct from Plesetsk Cosmodrome, right?" Taylor asked.

"Right. But, to tell you the truth, Ben. I don't watch. I mean, what's to watch?"

"There's a moon. The asteroid turns out to be one with a moon. Lot of them do."

"So what, Ben?"

"Can you bring up that feed right now?"

"I'm sure the communications guys can bring it up. But what the hell for?"

"Sean. Believe me. It's damn important."

"Okay. I'll get somebody to put it on the wall and call you."

Falcone called back in a few minutes and said, "It's on the wall, Ben. Some ugly thing is moving slowly—a series of still images strung together, right? There's a label. Something about Hawaii and—"

"There's a little dot of light. A moving dot of light," Taylor said. "See how it moves? It's a moon. The asteroid has a moon!"

"Well, I'm sure that's interesting to astronomers," Falcone said. "But so what?"

"In the fact book that Shvernik wrote," Taylor said, "he says that the missile warheads—he called them the 'payload'—were stripped of 'missile-defense devices'—like decoy detectors. They had been removed to lighten the missile and keep its navigation system from being distracted. That means that when the missile handlers 'armed' the warheads—gave them their directional commands—the handlers did not include commands having to do with decoys. The warheads would not know about avoiding something that *looked like* the asteroid."

"God, Ben! You're right," Falcone exclaimed. "The command software on multi-warhead missiles includes warnings about decoys. If Shvernik removed those warnings, giving the warheads no fear of decoys, the presence of a moon means that the warheads could mistake the moon for the asteroid. I'd better call the President."

Falcone passed on the information to Oxley and urged him to call Lebed.

"And tell him what, Sean?" Oxley asked.

"Tell him what Ben just discovered," Falcone said.

"And what is Lebed supposed to do?"

"For insurance, send a second Topol—one that retains its decoy-warning commands," Falcone said. "We still have time before it reaches the asteroid."

Oxley drummed his finger on his desktop for a moment. "All right," he said. He picked up the phone and said, "Hot-line."

Three minutes later Lebed was on the line. "Blake, what's up? If it's about the observer issue—"

"That asteroid image Dr. Shvernik just showed," Oxley said. "Did you see it?"

"Well, no. I just—"

"There's a moon in it," Oxley said impatiently. "The asteroid has a moon."

"I don't see the point, Blake. I can't—"

"Boris, listen to me, please."

Oxley repeated what Taylor had told Falcone about the moon.

"Sorry, Blake. I trust you and I believe Dr. Taylor is a fine scientist. But—I'm telling you a military secret—that Topol was the only one we have. It's a missile in development. There is no substitute. I think what Americans say is that you have to play the hand you're dealt. Have faith, Blake. Have faith."

102

Rescue's first warhead pulverized the first object it had sensed—Asteroid USA's little moon. The second warhead reached its target, exploded, and tore off a large fragment that plunged toward Earth, preceding and paralleling the asteroid's predestined path. The energy produced by two nuclear explosions added velocity to two colossal rocks that an instant before had been one.

The first indication of *Rescue*'s failure came from the pattern of explosives detected by the National Reconnaissance Office, the intelligence agency whose sentinel satellites watch for nuclear explosions. The NRO sent a top-secret flash message to other U.S. agencies and the White House.

Oxley called Lebed, who refused to accept Oxley's report but showed his true belief by silencing Russian media. When Oxley tried to call President Zhang Xing, he was passed to a Foreign Secretary spokesman who said, "Thank you for the information. President Zhang will restrict his interests to possible effects upon his nation." The director of NSA told Falcone, "China has reacted by essentially shutting down. No television, no Internet, no telephone service. An electronic version of ostrich behavior."

The realization of *Rescue*'s failure spread through all societies in about the same way: the rulers and the rich learned first, passed the knowledge to kinfolk, and then informed their circles of friends, debtors, and financiers. Beyond the circles were the agents of the media, whose job was to finally inform the people, with various levels of accuracy.

Many of the rich people in countries all over the world chose to fly, in aircraft they owned or chartered or demanded from their militaries. Their destination was a land that was high, dry, and ripe for another round of exploitation: central Africa, the continent that had fostered the human race. But Robert Wentworth Hamilton, now thoroughly obsessed by the belief that he had served as God's tool, traveled in his private aircraft directly from Washington to Jerusalem. He found a humble flat to stay in, not far from the Valley of Jehoshaphat, where the Bible said that God would assemble all nations at The End Time. Nearby were Jerusalem and the Temple Mount, where God gathered the dust used to create the first human.

103

Taylor had calculated that, if *Rescue* failed, the HAIV would have to be launched from Patrick Air Force Base seven days before the predicted day of impact. So the HAIV was scheduled to hit what was left of the asteroid when it was only 232,692 miles away, more than 2,500 miles closer than the Moon. People on Earth would either see explosions and know that the HAIV had destroyed what was left of Asteroid USA. Or they would not see explosions and know there was no hope.

Already, as the large chunk of the asteroid was hurtling toward Earth, GNN and other networks were showing a point of light in the night sky. People reacted to that light by acceptance of fate, by belief in divine judgment, by murderous anger, by belief in satanic power. Many died "stochastic deaths," defined by epidemiologists as random deaths whose cause is not precisely known but attributed to fear.

At Cape Canaveral, the mobs at the causeways had dwindled. There, as elsewhere in the world, acceptance had eclipsed rage and panic. Falcone convinced Oxley that there would not be any point in announcing the plan to try again by launching the HAIV. So few people knew that Earth was being given another chance to survive.

The launch bunker was crowded and silent. There was no ceremony. On General Hardwick's order, everything was to be routine. The countdown ended and the Atlas rose on a pillar of flame and smoke.

Seven days later, there was an explosion in the night sky. All over the Earth people prayed and cheered their thanks. But Asteroid USA was both alive and slain. As deliverance came from the HAIV, destruction was also being delivered. Near dawn, a mammoth, blazing rock with a heart of iron—the fragment torn off by *Rescue*—ended its voyage to Earth. Its orbit put it on a path paralleling the surface of the Earth.

It appeared first in the sky over Alaska, speeding across the dawn. It sliced off the top of Mount Denali, bounded down its slope, and, like a skimming stone on a pond, dipped and rose, dipped and rose. Each fiery dip was deadly—a forest . . . a village . . . a farm . . . Portland . . . an oil refinery . . . a maze of high tension wires and transformers. The obliteration of the electric grid blacked out the Western states from the Pacific Coast to the Rocky Mountains. Finally, the rock ended its skipping motion at Rock Springs, Wyoming. Once it was a city, population 23,036. Then, in a flaming moment, this place of craggy beauty was a crater three miles in diameter.

104

America was not alone in bearing the wrath of the universe's wildings, the fragments too big to flame out.

Singapore's Prime Minister, Peter K. Yeo, like President Oxley, was determined to remain on station in his office, the captain steering his ship to safety or going down with it to his doom.

He did not have to wait long.

He stood on the white-washed balcony of the Istana, an extravagant Palladian mansion built in Singapore by the British between 1867 and 1869 to serve as the colonial governor's office and residence. Yeo thought he saw something coming. Or was it just his imagination? It looked bigger than a bus. Not round, but oblong. Not . . .

One of the asteroid's body parts hit little more than a mile beyond the Changi Naval Base. The sea turned red and angry, rising up more than four hundred feet like some prehistoric beast, unleashing its fury in one giant, violent regurgitation over the entire city state. Those who were unable or unwilling to flee the island were swept out to sea to serve as new silt for the ocean's seething floor.

Other Asian nations fared little better.

Tens of millions died under the towering tsunami that ran all the way from Indonesia as far north as Hong Kong and Shanghai. Miraculously, Japan, by comparison, suffered modest losses. It was thought by some that an unnamed mystical source—call it Mercy—had decided that Fukushima had punished the Japanese enough.

The Middle East? Much of it was destroyed. It would take years before the survivors would be able to reconstruct their communities and social institutions.

Maybe that was just as well. It would give mankind enough time to redraw the lines of cohabitation with a premium on the willingness to share the Earth's bounty. Enough time to purge the old grievances and ethnic hatreds and pursue the untraveled path of reconciliation and peace.

Time, indeed, would tell.

And Russia? Well the bad boys in Moscow held a lucky charm. One chunk of Janus—to give Asteroid USA its true name—was about the size of a Volkswagen. It hit deep in the Siberian forests. It released the equivalent of about fifteen megatons of energy, about a thousand times greater than the atomic bomb dropped on Hiroshima on August 6, 1945. It flattened over one thousand square miles of trees, killing mostly bears, deer, and other wildlife. Several hundred woodsmen were burned to death. They would be commemorated as martyrs.

Boris Lebed's propaganda machine had kicked into full gear, heralding the Russian people as savior of the planet. The FSB's censors made sure that most Russians never learned that their Topol had hit Janus' moon and not the asteroid itself. Lebed's popularity soared as high as that of the man he had had assassinated, Vladimir Putin.

Perhaps one day, the Israelis would let the secret out.

EPILOGUE

Falcone stepped out onto the balcony of his penthouse apartment, a chilled glass of vodka in hand. From this Pennsylvania Avenue aerie, Washington looked serene—the Capitol Dome awash in light and the Washington Monument in stark silhouette. It was late evening. The night air was warm—kissed, it seemed, by a soft wind.

Fourteen stories below, several couples held hands as they stared solemnly at the bronze sculpture of the Lone Sailor that stood with the collar of his peacoat turned up against the wind, his hands tucked in his coat pockets.

Funny how the mind works. Whenever Falcone found himself staring at the sculpture, he always thought of his favorite movie, *Viva Zapata!*, the story of the Mexican revolutionary who led the effort to overthrow a corrupt president. While his mission succeeded, the new regime turned out to be just as corrupt as the one it had replaced. Nothing had changed.

But for Falcone, Zapata embodied the value that one man with courage could defiantly stand up to the forces of evil in the world. Even if he ultimately failed, Zapata believed that the pursuit of justice was worth the fight. Heroes, like the Sailor below, stood ready, in one defining moment, to sacrifice all in the name of honor.

For many the world over, it had been a day of commemoration. An international holiday. A year had passed since the universe's angry stones had torched the planet. Millions had been buried at sea. Among them were Admiral Walter Gibbs, chief of naval operations, his aide, and the 6,102 officers and enlisted men and women of the aircraft carrier USS *George Washington.* Gibbs had insisted that he be at sea on the day the rock rain was to come. The carrier was in the path of the biggest of the towering tsunamis that swept the South China Sea clean of ships and islands, real and artificial.

On land, millions of voices had been stilled under mountains of earthen rubble scattered around the globe. For reasons that scientists continued to seek, the dreaded electromagnetic pulse did not happen. But not since the days when dinosaurs drew their last breath had the world been so punished.

When news of the asteroid's approach first broke, millions of people panicked, fighting, clubbing, even shooting their way to precious safety zones. Food stores and pharmacies were quickly depleted, and gun shops emptied. Ammunition became more valuable than gold.

When electrical power went down throughout many parts of the country, every modern convenience people had come to depend upon had, in one violent moment, been stripped away. Lights. Water. Heat. Gas. Food. Medicine.

Once people recognized that guns were not going to save them, they gathered together in search of communal safety. Adversity, on a scale never known before, forced individuals and families to set aside inveterate tribal differences to pool their talents and resources. *E pluribus unum.* They were one tribe from many.

The spirit of those who survived had been unquenchable. *Resilience* was the word that had been missing from Falcone's vocabulary. The determination of the flower to push up through concrete.

It did not take long to clear the detritus of death and physical destruction. Communication systems were erected quickly. Internet connectivity so fundamental to communication, transportation, and the distribution of goods and services was restored within a few weeks. The electrical grid that had been knocked down in Western United States took months longer to fully reconstruct because there was no ready supply of transformers. It was a remarkable, inspirational period of resurrection and renewal.

Drinking slowly, Falcone could feel the alcohol spread its warmth deep into his chest. His thoughts turned to some of life's great ironies.

The Mormon Church, so often ridiculed as one of Christianity's illegitimate children, turned savior to the masses of the new homeless in several of the Western states that had been hit hardest. Mormon warehouses, filled with food, medicines, and survival materials were shared generously with hundreds of thousands of the dispossessed.

Falcone had hoped that the Mormons' act of immense charity might make religious bigotry a little less intense . . . at least for a decent interval. But that was the great mystery about religion, about what could never be known on this side of existence. Whether we were all just some accident, a cosmic joke, or an important part of a Creator's plan?

What could be more ironic—or planned—than for Robert Hamilton to have jetted off to Jerusalem and be annihilated there when one of Janus' fragments slammed into the Jehoshaphat Valley, caroming into the Old City, taking down the Western Wall and the Temple Mount? The center of all three of the great religions, in one violent second, had been enveloped in a fireball that turned centuries of history into charcoaled dust.

Was it just the roulette wheel of chance that wreaked such destruction? Or the vengeful hammer of God?

Was Hamilton seeking safety in Jerusalem or spiritual redemption and reward? Did it really matter?

More important to Falcone was Rachel's fate. Was she there when Janus hit? He hadn't heard from her, but that wasn't unusual. She would drop out of sight for years at a time, and suddenly surface in a moment of crisis—as if she were his guardian angel.

Until he met Rachel, Falcone was convinced he'd never love again. He had lost so much over the years. His wife and son. His years in prison. His faith . . . And maybe now even the woman he wanted to be with at this moment more than anyone else in the world. He could not imagine her dead. She was too alive, too vital, too . . .

Falcone emptied his glass as he fought back the emptiness welling up inside.

So much had changed in a year's time. Too much remained the same.

A new president had been elected; a new spirit of optimism had infused the nation. Yet on Capitol Hill, the same forces of entropy and gridlock had started to set in and bring the wheels of government to a grinding halt.

Politicians had once again made promises they knew they couldn't and wouldn't keep. Confidence in government had spiked in the aftermath of having escaped the threat of extinction. But with each passing day, that confidence began to ebb as people the world over retreated to old habits. Ethnic hatreds surfaced here and abroad, along with territorial quests for the Earth's water and wealth. Space continued to be scoped out and explored by military powers with the hope of achieving a strategic high ground so valuable in battle.

Perhaps it was folly to think that peace on earth and goodwill toward man would—or could—ever last. Once the danger had passed, there was a slow but steady retreat to separate tribes that distinguished between those who shared physical similarities, a common heritage, culture, and religious affiliation. They staked out separate territories, gathered in communal clusters around the fireplace of commerce and entertainment. There they tuned in to the media that conformed to views that hardened into unshakable convictions and values.

The embers in the Middle East, puffed on by those inflated with anger or fear, burst once again into a hotbed of religious and ethnic rivalry. The Israelis were quick to dig out from under the rubble of what was left of the Old City, and were busily engaged in constructing a new Temple, a new Western Wall from the existing rock pile. Many awaited the emergence of God or the Prophet Muhammad following the destruction of the Temple Mount. They were disappointed.

But belief in a creative force beyond mankind's ability to comprehend has a power of its own, one that no amount of rational analysis or argument can suppress.

Falcone had long ago given up trying to make any sense of the human condition that was filled with so many noble moments and dark contradictions. Perhaps, he thought, his was the hell of the agnostic, unmoored from religious conviction and left to wander sightless in the desert of perpetual doubt. But how could anyone explain the genius and folly of mankind, its greed and generosity? Its capacity to create and destroy?

Mozart could tickle the hearts of children and enchant those who once commanded Europe's genocidal death camps. The desire to cure could easily be bent to an eagerness to kill. . . .

While glancing up at the gleaming Capitol Dome, Falcone's thoughts shifted to the last conversation he'd had with President Oxley on the terrace outside the Oval Office. It was just before Oxley packed his bags and headed for life as a private citizen.

"These are great cigars, Sean," Oxley had said, careful not to inhale too deeply. "Been a long time since I dared to smoke one. You know the press!"

"Yeah, and legal, too," Falcone said, a smile spreading across his face. "Mr. President . . ."

"You really can call me Blake now."

"No. That's a title you can't shake. It'll always be Mr. President—even for me."

"So? You had a question?" Oxley asked.

"I always wondered how you were always able to stay so cool when all hell was breaking loose last year. I mean, you held it all together."

"Sean," Oxley said, taking another drag on the cigar, "I remember reading once that you had studied the classics when you were in college. True?"

"True. A hundred years ago. Maybe longer."

"Remember the story about Pandora's Box?"

"Vaguely. Don't think it was a box, but a jar. But as I said, it was a long time ago."

"Pandora opened the *jar* and all the evils in the world that were trapped inside flew out. . . ." Oxley paused for another puff and sent a perfect smoke ring wafting into a clear sky. "I know you have good reasons to think the way you do, but you dwell too much on all those evils."

"So every day's a bright new penny?"

"No. I share a lot of your sentiments about mankind. But you're way too dark."

Falcone remained silent, tacitly acknowledging Oxley's bleak assessment.

"Do you remember when Pandora put the lid back on the jar, there was one thing left inside?"

"No. I . . ."

"That's your problem, my friend. It was Hope, Sean. Hope. You need to open the jar and let it out."

Reliving that moment caused Falcone to break into a smile. He looked up at the sky, smooth as dark velvet, a few stars set against it like brilliant diamonds. Maybe one day he would look into that jar.

Maybe he'd even find Rachel there.

ACKNOWLEDGMENTS

During the time I served as Bill Clinton's secretary of defense, I was consumed with mastering the intricacies of the multiplicity of threats to our national security. Those threats ranged from nuclear and biological to chemical and conventional. Obviously, those that were existential in nature required a higher level of attention.

At the time, the emergence of cyber technology was in its early stages of evolution. The threat posed by a possible failure to properly program the vast number of computer systems in DoD's networks in anticipation of entering the twenty-first century (known as Y2K) also served to heighten my awareness of the vulnerability of those systems to state-sponsored, criminal, and rogue-initiated cyber attacks.

The thought that logic bombs traveling at the speed of light could paralyze or destroy major elements in our critical infrastructure, and send us back into something close to a state of nature, was sobering. It certainly caused me to reflect upon just how vulnerable we are to man-made threats, and how fragile are the defensive mechanisms we have in place.

It was not until I departed the Pentagon that I was able to devote time to ponder threats that were less immediate but no less existential.

When I learned that the United States and several other governments—as well as private space buccaneers—were planning to mine asteroids for their mineral and water wealth, I began to focus on both the bright and dark side of technology.

When Tor/Forge CEO, Tom Doherty, and his uber editorial chief asked me to explore the issues beyond the scope of conventional threat analyses, I suggested the possibility of a killer asteroid colliding with Earth. Both expressed support for the concept as a novel.

In *Collision,* I explored how technology, which holds such unlimited possibilities for the betterment of mankind, can be bent into a destructive force by greed and arrogance.

In *Final Strike,* I wanted to sound the alarm and amplify the noise level to alert readers to a danger that may not be immediate, but is, in fact, real. I wanted to disclose just how vulnerable and unprepared we are to deal with Nature's wrath—particularly when we disturb the Universe by accident or intent.

I want to thank Tom Doherty and Bob Gleason for providing me with the platform to express this warning (wrapped in a "rendition operation," some of which I drew from my experience at the Pentagon) and to show how technology can help save us from catastrophe as well as take us there.

In helping me sort through volumes of scientific information, NASA studies, and the world of the metaphysical, I am indebted to my friend Tom Allen. Tom spent many hours with me over coffee, muffins, and apple pie, discussing the coexistence of science, religion, and the cosmos. More than thirty years ago, Tom edited *The Double Man,* the bestselling novel that I coauthored with former senator Gary Hart. He has remained an invaluable resource and friend serving as a wise sounding board for my ideas, plots, and scenarios.

While in college, I majored in Latin and Greek Literature. Math remained more mysterious to me than Egyptian hieroglyphics and so in this novel, as I have on other occasions, I turned to Henry Murry, a brilliant graduate from Georgetown University and colleague in The Cohen Group for assistance in confirming the calculations contained in assessing the velocity of Janus and that of the Russian and American interceptor missiles. But any mathematical errors contained in plotting the arrival of *Final Strike* are mine alone.

The go-to person in my office has been Charli Sowers, who unfailingly identifies cracks in plotlines and structure and sends me scurrying back to my computer. I am humbled and grateful for her friendship and scrutiny!

In addition, I had the benefit of Elayne Becker and her eagle-eyed team that spotted errors, large and small, in the manuscript. William Strunk, Jr. and E. B. White must make room for a new generation of superb editors!

I also was enriched in my research by the following books:

Pale Blue Dot by Carl Sagan, Ballantine Books (1997);

Near-Earth Objects: Finding Them Before They Find Us by Donald K. Yeomans, Princeton University Press (2013);

Space Chronicles by Neil deGrasse Tyson, W. W. Norton & Co. (2013);

The Asteroid Threat by William E. Burrows, Prometheus Books (2014);

One Second After by William R. Forstchen, A Tom Doherty Associates Book (2009);

Lights Out by Ted Koppel, Crown Publishers (2015);

Rendezvous with Rama by Arthur C. Clarke, Bantam Books (1990);

Lucifer's Hammer by Larry Niven and Jerry Pournelle, Ballantine Books (1977);

End of Days by Robert Gleason, A Forge Book, Published by Tom Doherty Associates (2011)

End-Time Visions: The Doomsday Obsession by Richard Abanes, Four Walls Eight Windows (1998);

How Many Future Generations? Armageddon Theology and American Politics by Jim Costello (a discussion paper, People for the American Way, 1985).

Finally, my enduring gratitude to my wife, author and playwright, Janet Langhart Cohen. As disclosed in previous novels, Janet is the inspiration for the character Rachel, the mysterious Israeli assassin who has captured Sean Falcone's lonely heart. Janet allowed me to slip into my "man cave" for incalculable hours/days to complete this story. Her patience and tolerance for my absence has been otherworldly.